Critical acclaim for Michael Connelly

'*The Closers* is more than just a terrific mystery that slowly builds into a breathless race against time, twisting and turning to the very last page. It is a fascinating portrait of a city that teems with people "hiding from others and hiding from themselves"' *Evening Standard*

'Connelly comes as close as anyone to being today's Dostoyevsky of crime literature, and this is one of his finest works to date, a likely candidate not only for book award nominations but for major bestsellerdom'
Publishers Weekly

'Excellent . . . Michael Connelly is always reliable and *The Closers* is as dark and thrilling as ever' *Daily Mail*

'A scrupulously plotted procedural . . . all the excitements of a terrific thriller well paced by a cool and fast-running narrative' *Literary Review*

'A cracking return to form by Connelly, and we can only hope Harry Bosch doesn't apply for retirement again'
Irish Independent

'There's a mountain of American detective fiction. At the summit are Connelly's Harry Bosch books' *Sunday Sport*

A former police reporter for the *Los Angeles Times*, Michael Connelly is the author of sixteen acclaimed and best-selling novels. His novels have won an Edgar Award, the Nero Wolfe prize and the Anthony Award. He lives in Florida with his wife and daughter. Visit his website at www.MichaelConnelly.com.

By Michael Connelly

The Black Echo
The Black Ice
The Concrete Blonde
The Last Coyote
The Poet
Trunk Music
Blood Work
Angels Flight
Void Moon
A Darkness More Than Night
City of Bones
Chasing the Dime
Lost Light
The Narrows
The Closers
The Lincoln Lawyer

MICHAEL CONNELLY

THE CLOSERS

ORION

An Orion paperback

First published in Great Britain in 2005
by Orion
This paperback edition published in 2005
by Orion Books Ltd,
Orion House, 5 Upper St Martin's Lane,
London WC2H 9EA

Published by arrangement with
Little, Brown and Company (Inc.), New York, NY, USA

3 5 7 9 10 8 6 4 2

A CIP catalogue record for this book is available
from the British Library.

ISBN 0 75286 464 5
EAN 9 780752 864648

Printed and bound at Mackays of Chatham plc

www.orionbooks.co.uk

To the detectives
who have to look into the abyss

PART ONE
BLUE RELIGION

1

Within the practice and protocol of the Los Angeles Police Department a two-six call is the one that draws the most immediate response while striking the most fear behind the bulletproof vest. For it is a call that often has a career riding on it. The designation is derived from the combination of the Code 2 radio call out, meaning "respond as soon as possible," and the sixth floor of Parker Center, from which the chief of police commands the department. A two-six is a forthwith from the chief's office, and any officer who knows and enjoys his position in the department will not delay.

Detective Harry Bosch spent over twenty-five years with the department in his first tour and never once received a forthwith from the chief of police. In fact, other than receiving his badge at the academy in 1972, he never shook hands or spoke personally with a chief again. He had outlasted several of them — and, of course, seen them at police functions and funerals — but simply never met them along the way. On the morning of his return to duty after a three-year retirement he received his first two-six while knotting his tie in the bathroom mirror. It was an adjutant to the chief calling Bosch's private cell phone. Bosch didn't bother asking how they had come up with the number. It was simply understood that the chief's office had the power to reach out in such a way. Bosch just said he would be there within the hour, to which the adjutant replied that he would be expected sooner. Harry finished knotting his tie in his car while driving as fast as traffic allowed on the 101 Freeway toward downtown.

It took Bosch exactly twenty-four minutes from the moment he closed the phone on the adjutant until he walked through the double doors of the chief's suite on the sixth floor at Parker Center. He thought it had to have been some kind of record, notwithstanding the fact that he had illegally parked on Los Angeles Street in front of the police headquarters. If they knew his private cell number, then surely they knew what a feat it had been to make it from the Hollywood Hills to the chief's office in under a half hour.

But the adjutant, a lieutenant named Hohman, stared him down with disinterested eyes and pointed to a plastic-sealed couch that already had two other people waiting on it.

"You're late," he said. "Take a seat."

Bosch decided not to protest, not to make matters possibly worse. He stepped over to the couch and sat between the two men in uniform, who had staked out the armrests. They sat bolt upright and did not small-talk. He figured they had been two-sixed as well.

Ten minutes went by. The men on either side of him were called in ahead of Bosch, each dispensed with by the chief in five minutes flat. While the second man was in with the chief, Bosch thought he heard loud voices from the inner sanctum, and when the officer came out his face was ashen. He had somehow fucked up in the eyes of the chief and the word — which had even filtered to Bosch in retirement — was that this new man did not suffer fuckups lightly. Bosch had read a story in the *Times* about a command staffer who was demoted for failing to inform the chief that the son of a city councilman usually allied against the department had been picked up on a deuce.

The chief only found out about it when the councilman called to complain about harassment, as if the department had forced his son to drink six vodka martinis at Bar Marmount and drive home via the trunk of a tree on Mulholland.

Finally Hohman put down the phone and pointed his finger at Bosch. He was up. He was quickly shuttled into a corner office with a view of Union Station and the surrounding train yards. It was a decent view but not a great one. It didn't matter because the place was coming down soon. The department would move into temporary offices while a new and modern police headquarters was rebuilt on the same spot. The current headquarters was known as the Glass House by the rank and file, supposedly because there were no secrets kept inside. Bosch wondered what the next place would become known as.

The chief of police was behind a large desk signing papers. Without looking up from this work he told Bosch to have a seat in front of the desk. Within thirty seconds the chief signed his last document and looked up at Bosch. He smiled.

"I wanted to meet you and welcome you back to the department."

His voice was marked by an eastern accent. *De-paht-ment.* This was fine with Bosch. In L.A. everybody was from somewhere else. Or so it seemed. It was both the strength and the weakness of the city.

"It is good to be back," Bosch said.

"You understand that you are here at my pleasure."

It wasn't a question.

"Yes sir, I do."

"Obviously, I checked you out extensively before approving your return. I had concerns about your ... shall we say *style*, but ultimately your talent won the day. You can also thank your partner, Kizmin Rider, for her lobbying effort. She's a good officer and I trust her. She trusts you."

"I have already thanked her but I will do it again."

"I know it has been less than three years since you retired but let me assure you, Detective Bosch, that the department you have rejoined is not the department you left."

"I understand that."

"I hope so. You know about the consent decree?"

Just after Bosch had left the department the previous chief had been forced to agree to a series of reforms in order to head off a federal takeover of the LAPD following an FBI investigation into wholesale corruption, violence and civil rights violations within the ranks. The current chief had to carry out the agreement or he would end up taking orders from the FBI. From the chief down to the lowliest boot, nobody wanted that.

"Yes," Bosch said. "I've read about it."

"Good. I'm glad you have kept yourself informed. And I am happy to report that despite what you may read in the *Times*, we are making great strides and we want to keep that momentum. We are also trying to update the department in terms of technology. We are pushing forward in community policing. We are doing a lot of good things, Detective Bosch, much of which can be undone in the eyes of the community if we resort to old ways. Do you understand what I am telling you?"

"I think so."

"Your return here is not guaranteed. You are on probation for a year. So consider yourself a rookie again. A boot — the oldest living boot at that. I approved your return — I can also wash you out without so much as a reason anytime in the course of the year. Don't give me a reason."

Bosch didn't answer. He didn't think he was supposed to.

"On Friday we graduate a new class of cadets at the academy. I would like you to be there."

"Sir?"

"I want you to be there. I want you to see the dedication in our young people's faces. I want to reacquaint you with the traditions of this department. I think it could help you, help you rededicate yourself."

"If you want me to be there I will be there."

"Good. I will see you there. You will sit under the VIP tent as my guest."

He made a note about the invite on a pad of paper next to the blotter. He then put the pen down and raised his hand to point a finger at Bosch. His eyes took on a fierceness.

"Listen to me, Bosch. Don't ever break the law to enforce the law. At all times you do your job constitutionally and compassionately. I will accept it no other way. This *city* will accept it no other way. Are we okay on that?"

"We are okay."

"Then we are good to go."

Bosch took his cue and stood up. The chief surprised him by also standing and extending his hand. Bosch thought he wanted to shake hands and extended his own. The chief put something in his hand and Bosch looked down to see the gold detective's shield. He had his old number back. It had not been given away. He almost smiled.

"Wear it well," the police chief said. "And proudly."

"I will."

Now they shook hands, but as they did so the chief didn't smile.

"The chorus of forgotten voices," he said.

7

"Excuse me, Chief?"

"That's what I think about when I think of the cases down there in Open-Unsolved. It's a house of horrors. Our greatest shame. All those cases. All those voices. Every one of them is like a stone thrown into a lake. The ripples move out through time and people. Families, friends, neighbors. How can we call ourselves a city when there are so many ripples, when so many voices have been forgotten by this department?"

Bosch let go of his hand and didn't say anything. There was no answer for the chief's question.

"I changed the name of the unit when I came into the department. Those aren't cold cases, Detective. They never go cold. Not for some people."

"I understand that."

"Then go down there and clear cases. That's what your art is. That's why we need you and why you are here. That's why I am taking a chance with you. Show them we do not forget. Show them that in Los Angeles cases don't go cold."

"I will."

Bosch left him there, still standing and maybe a little haunted by the voices. Like himself. Bosch thought that maybe for the first time he had actually connected on some level with the man at the top. In the military it is said that you go into battle and fight and are willing to die for the men who sent you. Bosch never felt that when he was moving through the darkness of the tunnels in Vietnam. He had felt alone and that he was fighting for himself, fighting to stay alive. That had carried with him into the department and he had at times adopted the view that he was fighting *in spite* of the men at the top. Now maybe things would be different.

In the hallway he punched the elevator button harder than he needed to. He had too much excitement and energy and he understood this. The chorus of forgotten voices. The chief seemed to know the song they were singing. And Bosch certainly did, too. Most of his life had been spent listening to that song.

2

Bosch rode the elevator just one flight down to five. This, too, was new territory for him. Five had always been a civilian floor. It primarily housed many of the department's mid- and low-level administrative offices, most of them filled with nonsworn employees, budgeters, analysts, pencil pushers. Civilians. Before now there had been no reason to come to the fifth.

There were no placards in the elevator lobby that pointed the way to specific offices. It was the kind of floor where you knew where you were going before you stepped off the elevator. But not Bosch. The hallways on the floor formed the letter H and he went the wrong way twice before finally finding the door marked 503. There was nothing else on the door. He paused before opening it and thought about what he was doing and what he was starting. He knew it was the right thing. It was almost as if he could hear the voices coming through the door. All eight thousand of them.

Kiz Rider was sitting on a desk just inside, sipping a cup of steaming coffee. The desk looked like a place for a receptionist but Bosch knew from his frequent calls in the prior weeks that there was no receptionist in this squad. There was no money for such a luxury. Rider raised her wrist and shook her head as she checked her watch.

"I thought we agreed on eight o'clock," she said. "Is that

how it's going to be, partner? You waltzing in every morning whenever you feel like it?"

Bosch looked at his watch. It was five minutes after eight. He looked back at her and smiled. Rider smiled and said, "We're over here."

Rider was a short woman who carried a few extra pounds. Her hair was short and now had some gray in it. She was very dark complected, which made her smile all the more brilliant. She slipped off the desk, and from behind where she had perched she raised a second cup of coffee to him.

"See if I remembered that right."

He checked and nodded.

"Black, just like I like my partners."

"Funny. I'll have to write you up for that."

She led the way. The office seemed to be empty. It was large, even for a squad room serving nine investigators — four teams and an OIC. The walls were painted a light shade of blue, like Bosch often saw on the screens of computers. It was carpeted in gray. There were no windows. At the positions on the walls where there should have been windows there were bulletin boards or nicely framed crime scene photos from many years back. Bosch could tell that in these black and whites the photographers had often put their artistic skills ahead of their clinical duties. The shots were heavy on mood and shadows. Not many of the crime scene details were apparent.

Rider must have known he was looking at the photos.

"They told me that writer James Ellroy picked these out and had them framed for the office," she said.

She led him around a partial wall that broke the room in two and into an alcove where two gray steel desks were pushed together so the detectives who sat at them would face each other. Rider put her coffee down on one. There were already files stacked on it and personal things like a coffee mug full of pens and a picture frame at an angle that hid the photo it held. A laptop computer was open and humming on the desk. She had moved into the squad the week before while Bosch was still clearing customs — customs being the medical exam and final paperwork that brought him back onto the job.

The other desk was clean, empty and waiting for him. He moved behind it and put his coffee down. He suppressed a smile as well as he could.

"Welcome back, Roy," Rider said.

That made the smile break through. It made Bosch feel good to be called Roy again. It was a tradition carried by many of the city's homicide detectives. There was a legendary homicide man named Russell Kuster who had worked out of Hollywood Division many years back. He was the ultimate professional, and many of the detectives working murders in the city today had come under his tutelage at one point or another. He was killed in an off-duty shootout in 1990. But his habit of calling people Roy — no matter their real name — was carried on. Its origin had become obscure. Some said it was because Kuster once had a partner who loved Roy Acuff and it had started with him. Others said it was because Kuster liked the idea of the homicide cop being the Roy Rogers type, wearing the white hat and riding to the rescue, making things right. It didn't matter anymore. Bosch knew it was an honor just to be called Roy again.

He sat down. The chair was old and lumpy, guaranteed to give him a backache if he spent too much time in it. But he hoped that would not be the case. In his first run as a homicide detective he had lived by the adage *Get off your ass and knock on doors*. He didn't see any reason that should change this time around.

"Where is everybody?" he asked.

"Having breakfast. I forgot. They told me last week that the routine is that on Monday mornings everybody meets early for breakfast. They usually go over to the Pacific. I didn't remember until I got in here this morning and found the place dead, but they should be back here soon."

Bosch knew the Pacific Dining Car was a longtime favorite with LAPD brass and the Robbery-Homicide Division. He also knew something else.

"Twelve bucks for a plate of eggs. I guess that means this is an overtime-approved squad."

Rider smiled in confirmation.

"You got that right. But you wouldn't have been able to finish your fancy eggs anyway, once you got the forthwith from the chief."

"You heard about that, huh?"

"I still have an ear out on six. Did you get your badge?"

"Yeah, he gave it to me."

"I told him what number you'd want. Did you get it?"

"Yeah, Kiz, thanks. Thanks for everything."

"You already told me that, partner. You don't need to keep saying that."

He nodded and looked around their space. He noticed that on the wall behind Rider was a photo of two detectives huddled beside a body lying in the dry concrete bed of the Los Angeles River. It looked like a shot from the early fifties, judging by the hats the detectives wore.

"So, where do we start?" he asked.

"The squad breaks the cases up in three-year increments. It provides some continuity. They say you get to know the era and some of the players in the department. It overlaps. It also helps with identifying serials. In two years they've already come up with four serials nobody ever knew about."

Bosch nodded. He was impressed.

"What years did we get?" he asked.

"Each team has four or five blocks. Since we're the new team we got four."

She opened the middle drawer of her desk, took out a piece of paper and handed it across to him.

Bosch/Rider — Case Assignments

1966	1972	1987	1996
1967	1973	1988	1997
1968	1974	1989	1998

Bosch studied the listing of years for which they would be responsible. He had been out of the city and in Vietnam for most of the first block.

"The summer of love," he said. "I missed it. Maybe that's what's wrong with me."

He said it just to be saying something. He noticed that the second block included 1972, the year he had come onto the force. He remembered a call out to a house off of Vermont on his second day on the job in patrol. A woman back east asked police to check on her mother, who was not answering the phone. Bosch found her drowned in a bathtub, her hands and feet bound with dog leashes. Her dead dog was in the tub with her. Bosch wondered if the old woman's murder was one of the open cases he would now be charged with solving.

"How was this arrived at? I mean, why did we get these years?"

"They came from the other teams. We lightened their caseload. In fact, they already started the ball rolling on cases from a lot of those years. And I heard on Friday that a cold hit came in from 'eighty-eight. We're supposed to run with it starting today. I guess you could say it's your welcome-back present."

"What's a cold hit?"

"When a DNA stamp or a latent we send through the

computers or the DOJ makes a blind match."

"What's ours?"

"I think it's a DNA match. We'll find out this morning."

"They didn't tell you anything last week? I could have come in over the weekend, you know."

"I know that, Harry. But this is an old case. There was no need to start running the minute a piece of paper came in the mail. Working Open-Unsolved is different."

"Yeah? How come?"

Rider looked exasperated, but before she could answer they heard the door open and the squad room started filling with voices. Rider stepped out of the alcove and Bosch followed. She introduced Bosch to the other members of the squad. Two of the detectives, Tim Marcia and Rick Jackson, Bosch knew well from previous cases. The other two pairs of partners were Robert Renner and Victor Robleto, and Kevin Robinson and Jean Nord. Bosch knew them, as well as Abel Pratt, the officer in charge of the unit, by reputation. Every one of them was a top-notch homicide investigator.

The greeting was cordial and subdued, a bit overly formal. Bosch knew that his posting in the unit was probably viewed with suspicion. An assignment on the squad would have been highly coveted by detectives throughout the department. The fact that he had gotten the posting after nearly three years in retirement raised questions. Bosch knew, as the chief of police had reminded him, that he had Rider to thank for the job. Her last posting had been in the chief's office as a policy analyst. She had cashed in whatever markers she had accrued with the chief in order to get Bosch back inside the department and working open-unsolved cases with her.

After all the handshakes, Pratt invited Bosch and Rider back into his office for a private welcome-aboard speech. He sat behind his desk and they took the side-by-side chairs in front of it. There was no room in the closet-sized space for other furnishings.

Pratt was a few years younger than Bosch, on the south side of fifty. He kept himself in shape and carried the esprit de corps of the vaunted Robbery-Homicide Division, of which the Open-Unsolved Unit was just one branch. Pratt appeared confident in his skills and his command of the unit. He had to be. The RHD took on the city's most difficult cases. Bosch knew that if you did not believe you were smarter, tougher and more cunning than the people you were after then you didn't belong.

"What I really should do is split you two up," he began. "Make you work with guys already established here in the unit because this is different from what you've done in the past. But I got the word from six and I don't mess with that. Besides, I understand you two have a prior chemistry that worked. So forget what I should do and let me tell you a little bit about working open-unsolveds. Kiz, I know you already got this speech last week but you'll just have to suffer along, okay?"

"Of course," Rider said.

"First of all, forget closure. Closure is bullshit. Closure is a media term, something they put in newspaper articles about cold cases. Closure is a joke. It's a fucking lie. All we do here is provide answers. Answers have to be enough. So don't mislead yourself about what you are doing here. Don't mislead the family members you deal with on these cases and don't be misled by them."

He paused for reaction, got none and moved on. Bosch noticed that the crime scene photo framed on the wall was of a man collapsed in a bullet-riddled phone booth. It was the kind of phone booth you only saw in old movies and at the Farmers Market or over at Phillippe's.

"Without a doubt," Pratt said, "this squad is the most noble place in the building. A city that forgets its murder

16

victims is a city lost. This is where we don't forget. We're like the guys they bring in in the bottom of the ninth inning to win or lose the game. The closers. If we can't do it, nobody can. If we blow it, the game is over because we're the last resort. Yes, we're outnumbered. We've got eight thousand open-unsolveds since nineteen sixty. But we are undaunted. Even if this whole unit clears only one case a month — just twelve a year — we are doing something. We're the closers, baby. If you're in homicide, this is the place to be."

Bosch was impressed by his fervor. He could see sincerity and even pain in his eyes. He nodded. He immediately knew that he wanted to work for this man, a rarity in his experience in the department.

"Just don't forget that closure isn't the same as being a closer," Pratt added.

"Got it," Bosch said.

"Now, I know you both have long experience working homicides. What you are going to find different here is your relationship with the cases."

"Relationship?" Bosch asked.

"Yes, relationship. What I mean is that working fresh kills is a completely different animal. You have the body, you have the autopsy, you carry the news to the family. Here you are dealing with victims long dead. There are no autopsies, no physical crime scenes. You deal with the murder books — if you can find them — and the records. When you go to the family — and believe me you don't go until you are good and ready — you find people who have already suffered the shock and found or not found ways to get past it. It wears on you. I hope you are prepared for that."

"Thanks for the warning," Bosch said.

"With fresh kills it is clinical because things move fast. With old cases it is emotional. You are going to see the toll of violence over time. Be prepared for it."

Pratt pulled a thick blue binder from the side of his desk to the center of his calendar blotter. He started to push it across to them then stopped.

"Another thing to be prepared for is the department. Count on files being incomplete or even missing. Count on physical evidence being destroyed or disappeared. Count on starting from scratch with some of these. This unit was put together two years ago. We spent the first eight months just going through the case logs and pulling out open-unsolveds. We fed what we could into the forensics pipelines, but even when we've gotten a hit we have been handicapped by the lack of case integrity. It has been abysmal. It has been frustrating. Even though there is no statute of limitations on murder we are finding that evidence and even files were routinely disposed of during at least one administration.

"What I am saying is that you are going to find that your biggest obstacle on some of these cases may very well be the department itself."

"Somebody said we have a cold hit that came out of one of our time blocks," Bosch said.

He'd heard enough. He just wanted to get moving on something.

"Yes, you do," Pratt said. "We'll get to that in a second. Let me just finish up with my little speech. After all, I don't get to make it that often. In a nutshell, what we try to do here is apply new technology and techniques to old cases. The technology is essentially threefold. You have DNA, fingerprints, and ballistics. In all three areas the advancements in comparative analysis have been phenomenal in the last ten years. The problem with this department is that it never took any of these advances and looked backward at old cases. Consequently, we have an estimated two thousand cases in which there is DNA evidence that has never been typed and compared. Since nineteen sixty we have four thousand cases with fingerprints that have never been run through a computer. Ours, the FBI's, DOJ's, anybody's computer. It's almost laughable but it's too fucking sad to laugh about. Same with ballistics. We are finding the evidence is still there in most of these cases but it has been ignored."

Bosch shook his head, already feeling the frustration of all the families of the victims, the cases swept away by time, indifference and incompetence.

"You will also find that techniques are different. Today's homicide copper is just plain better than one from, say, nineteen sixty or seventy. Even nineteen eighty. So even before you get to the physical evidence and you review these cases you are going to see things that seem obvious to you now, but that weren't obvious to anyone back at the time of the kill."

Pratt nodded. His speech was finished.

"Now, the cold hit," he said, pushing the faded blue murder book across the desk. "Run with that baby. It's all yours. Close it down and put somebody in jail."

3

After leaving Pratt's office they decided that Bosch would go get the next round of coffee while Rider started in on the murder book. They knew from prior experience that she was the faster reader and it didn't make sense to split the book up. They both needed to read it front to back, to have the investigation presented to them in the linear fashion in which it occurred and was documented.

Bosch said he would give her a good head start. He told her he might drink a cup in the cafeteria just because he missed the place. The place, not the coffee.

"Then I guess that gives me a few minutes to go down the hall," she said.

After she left the office for the restroom Bosch took the page listing the years that were assigned to them and put it into the inside pocket of his jacket. He left 503 and took the elevator down to the third floor. He then walked through the main RHD squad room to the captain's office.

The captain's office suite was broken into two rooms. One room was his actual office and the other was called the murder room. It was furnished with a long meeting table where murder investigations were discussed, and its walls on two sides were lined with shelves containing legal books and the city's murder logs. Every homicide that had occurred in Los Angeles, going back more than one hundred years, had a listing in these leather-bound journals. The routine over the decades was to update the journals every time one of the murders was cleared. It was the easy reference in the department for determining what cases were still open or had been closed.

Bosch ran his finger along the cracked spines of the books. Each one simply said HOMICIDES followed by the listing of the years the book recorded. Several years fit into each of the early books. But by the 1980s there were so many murders committed in the city that each book contained the accounts of only one year. He then noted that the year 1988 was reported in two books, and he suddenly had a very good idea why that year had been assigned to him and Rider as the new members of the Open-Unsolved Unit. The high point for murders in the city would certainly also mean the high point for unsolved cases.

When his finger found the book containing cases from 1972 he pulled the tome out and sat down with it at the table. He leafed through it, skimming the stories, hearing the voices. He found the old lady who was drowned in her bathtub. It was never solved. He moved on, through 1973 and 1974, then he went through the book containing 1966, '67 and '68. He read about Charles Manson and Robert Kennedy. He read about people whose names he had never heard or known. Names that were taken away from them along with everything else they'd had or would ever have.

As he read through the catalogs of the city's horrors, Bosch felt a familiar power begin to take hold of him and move in his veins again. Only an hour back on the job and he was already chasing a killer. It didn't matter how long ago the blood had fallen. There was a killer in the wind and Bosch was coming. Like the prodigal son returning, he knew he was back in his place now. He was baptized again in the waters of the one true church. The church of the blue religion. And he knew that he would find his salvation in those who were long lost, that he would find it in these musty bibles where the dead lined up in columns and there were ghosts on every page.

"Harry Bosch!"

Jarred by the intrusion, Bosch slammed the book closed and looked up. Captain Gabe Norona was standing in the doorway of the inner office.

"Captain."

"Welcome back!"

He came forward and vigorously shook Bosch's hand.

"Good to be back."

"I see they already have you doin' your homework."

Bosch nodded.

"Just sort of getting acquainted with it."

"New hope for the dead. Harry Bosch is on the case again."

Bosch didn't say anything. He didn't know if the captain was being sarcastic or not.

"It's the name of a book I read once," Norona said.

"Oh."

"Well, good luck to you. Get out there and lock 'em up."

"That's the plan."

The captain shook his hand again and then disappeared back into his office and closed the door.

His sacred moment ruined by the intrusion, Bosch stood up. He started returning the heavy murder catalogs to their places on the shelves. When he was finished, he left the office for the cafeteria.

4

Kiz Rider was almost halfway through the murder book when Bosch got back with the fresh round of coffees. She took her cup directly out of his hand.

"Thanks. I need something to keep me awake."

"What, you're going to sit there and tell me that this is boring compared to pushing paper in the chief's office?"

"No, it's not that. It's just all the catching up, the reading. We've got to know this book inside and out. We've got to be alert for the possibilities."

Bosch noticed she had a legal tablet next to the murder book and the top page was almost full of notes. He couldn't read the notes but could see that most of the lines were followed by question marks.

"Besides," she added, "I'm using different muscles now. Muscles I didn't use on the sixth floor."

"I get it," he said. "All right if I start in behind you now?"

"Be my guest."

She popped open the rings of the binder and pulled out the two-inch-thick sheaf of documents she had already read through. She handed them across to Bosch, who had sat down at his desk.

"You got an extra pad like that?" he asked. "I just have a little notebook."

She sighed in an exaggerated way. Bosch knew it was all an act and that she was happy they were working together again. She had spent most of the last two years evaluating policy and troubleshooting for the new chief. It wasn't the real cop work that she was best at. This was.

She slid a pad across the desk to him.

"You need a pen, too?"

"No, I think I can handle that."

He put the documents down in front of him and started reading. He was ready to go and he didn't need the coffee to stay charged.

The first page of the murder book was a color photograph in a plastic three-hole sleeve. The photo was a yearbook portrait of an exotically attractive young girl with almond-shaped eyes that were startling green against her mocha skin. She had tightly curled brown hair with what looked like natural blonde highlights that caught the flash of the camera. Her eyes were bright and her smile genuine. It was a grin that said she knew things nobody else did. Bosch didn't think she was beautiful. Not yet. Her features seemed to compete with one another in an uncoordinated way. But he knew that teenage awkwardness often smoothed over and became beauty later.

But for sixteen-year-old Rebecca Verloren there would be no later. Nineteen eighty-eight would be her last year. The cold hit had come from her murder.

Becky, as she was known by family and friends, was the only child of Robert and Muriel Verloren. Muriel was a homemaker. Robert was the chef and owner of a popular Malibu restaurant called the Island House Grill. They lived on Red Mesa Way off of Santa Susana Pass Road in Chatsworth, at the northwest corner of the sprawl that made up Los Angeles. The backyard of their house was the wooded incline of Oat Mountain, which rose above Chatsworth and served as the northwest border of the city. That summer Becky was between her sophomore and junior years at Hillside Preparatory School. It was a private school in nearby Porter Ranch, where she was on the honor roll and her mother volunteered in the cafeteria and often brought jerk chicken and other specialties from her husband's restaurant for the faculty lunchroom.

On the morning of July 6, 1988, the Verlorens discovered their daughter missing from their home. They found the back door unlocked, though they were sure it had been secured the night before. Thinking the girl might have gone for a walk they waited worriedly for two hours but she did not return. That day she was scheduled to go to the restaurant with her father to work the lunch shift as an assistant hostess and it was well past the time to leave for Malibu. While her mother called her friends hoping to locate her, her father went up the hillside behind the house looking for her. When he came back down the hill without finding a sign of her they decided it was time to call the police.

Patrol officers from the Devonshire Division were called to the home. They found no evidence of a break-in at the house. Citing this and the fact that the girl was in an age group with one of the highest runaway rates, the disappearance was viewed as a possible runaway situation and handled as a routine missing-persons case. This was against the protests of the missing girl's parents, who did not believe she had run away or left their home of her own volition.

The parents were proved horribly correct two days later when the decomposing body of Becky Verloren was found hidden beside the fallen trunk of an oak tree about ten yards off an equestrian trail on Oat Mountain. A woman riding her Appaloosa had gone off the path to investigate a bad smell and came across the body. The rider might have ignored the odor but had earlier seen signs posted on telephone poles about the missing girl from the area.

Becky Verloren had died less than a quarter mile from her house. It was likely that her father had passed within yards or even feet of her body when he was hiking the hillside and calling out her name. But on that morning there had been no odor yet to draw his attention.

Bosch was the father of a young girl. Though she lived far away from him with her mother, she was never far from his thoughts. He thought now of a father climbing a steep hillside, calling for a daughter who would never come home.

He tried to concentrate on the murder book.

The victim had been shot once in the chest by a high-powered pistol. The weapon, a .45 caliber Colt semi-automatic, was lying in the leaves by her left ankle. As Bosch studied the crime scene photos he saw what appeared to be a burn from a contact shot on the fabric of her light blue nightgown. The bullet hole was located directly above the heart, and Bosch knew by the size of the gun and the entry wound that death was likely immediate. Her heart would have been shattered by the round as it blasted through her body.

For a long time Bosch studied the photographs of the body as it had been found. The victim's hands were not bound. She was not gagged. Her face was turned in toward the trunk of the fallen tree. There were no indications of defensive wounds of any nature. There was no indication of sexual molestation or any other assault.

The police misinterpretation of the girl's disappearance was initially compounded by the misinterpretation of the death scene. The assessment at the scene resulted in the death being viewed as a probable suicide. As such the case was kept by the local division's homicide squad and the two detectives who rolled on the body call, Ron Green and Arturo Garcia. Devonshire Division was at that time and still is the LAPD's quietest station. Representing a large bedroom community with high property values and mostly upper-middle-class residents, Devonshire always had crime tables that were among the lowest in the city. Inside the department the station was known as Club Dev. It was a highly sought-after posting by officers and detectives who had put in many years and were tired or had simply seen enough action. Devonshire Division also represented the part of the city closest to Simi Valley, a quiet, relatively crime-free community in Ventura County where hundreds of LAPD officers chose to live. A posting at Devonshire made the commute a breeze and the workload the lightest in the department.

The Club Dev pedigree played in the back of Bosch's mind as he read the reports. He knew part of his task here was to make a judgment on Green and Garcia's work, to determine if they had been up to the task. He did not know them and had no experience with them. He had no idea what level of skills and dedication they had brought to the case. There was the initial misinterpretation of the death as a suicide. But by the appearance of the records, the two investigators seemed to recover quickly and move on with the case. Their reports seemed to be well written, thorough and complete. They seemed to have taken the extra step wherever possible.

Still, Bosch knew that a murder book could be manipulated to give this impression. The truth would be revealed as he delved deeper and continued his own investigation. He knew there could be a vast difference between what was recorded and what was not.

According to the murder book, Green and Garcia quickly reversed investigative directions when suicide was dismissed after the autopsy was completed and the gun found with the body was analyzed. The case was reclassified as a homicide that had been disguised as a suicide.

Bosch first came to the autopsy findings in the murder book. He had read a thousand autopsy protocols and had attended several hundred of the procedures as well. He knew to skip all the weights and measurements and descriptions of the actual procedure and go right to the summary section and the attendant photographs. Unsurprisingly, he found the cause of death listed as a gunshot wound to the chest. The estimated time of death was between midnight and 2 a.m. on July 6. The summary noted that no witness reported hearing the shot, so the time of death estimate was based solely on measuring loss of body temperature.

The surprises were in the other findings. Rebecca Verloren had long, thick hair. At the right side of the base of her neck, beneath the fall of her hair, the medical examiner found a small circular burn mark that was about the size of a button off an oxford shirt. Two inches from this mark was another burn mark, much smaller than the first. High white cell counts in the blood surrounding these wounds indicated that both had been sustained close to but not at the time of death.

The report concluded that the burns were caused by a stun gun, a handheld device that emits a powerful electric charge and renders its victims unconscious or incapacitated for several minutes or longer, depending on the charge. Normally, a charge from a stun gun would leave two small and almost unnoticeable marks on the skin indicating the location of the twin contacts. But if the contact points of the device were held unevenly against the skin, the electric charge would arc and often burn the skin in the manner seen on Becky Verloren's neck.

The autopsy summary also noted that an examination of the victim's bare feet found no soil deposits or cuts or bruises, which would be evident had the girl walked barefoot up the mountainside in the dark.

Bosch drummed his pen on the report and thought about this. He knew this was a mistake made by Green and Garcia. The victim's feet should have been examined at the scene and they should have made the jump right then to the idea that the suicide was a setup. Instead they missed it and they lost two days waiting for the autopsy on a weekend. Those days plus the two days lost when patrol wrote the parents' call off as a runaway case added up to a bad number in a murder investigation. There was no doubt that the case was slow out of the blocks. Bosch was beginning to see how badly the department had let Rebecca Verloren down.

The autopsy report also contained the results of a gunshot residue test conducted on the victim's hands. While GSR was found on Becky Verloren's right hand, there was no indication of it on her left. Even though Verloren was right-handed Bosch knew that the GSR test was an indicator that she had not actually fired the gun that killed her. Experience — no matter how limited — and common sense would have told the investigators that the girl would have needed to use both hands to properly hold the heavy gun pointed against her own chest and to pull the trigger. The result would have been GSR on both her hands.

There was one more notable point in the autopsy summary. The examination of the body determined that the victim had been sexually active, and scarring on the walls of the uterus was indicative of a recent gynecological dilation and curettage procedure to eliminate a pregnancy. The deputy coroner who conducted the autopsy estimated that this had occurred four to six weeks prior to her death.

Bosch read the first Investigator's Summary report, which was written and added to the book after the autopsy. Green and Garcia had now classified the death as a murder and established the theory that someone had entered the girl's bedroom while she was sleeping, incapacitated her with a stun gun and then carried her from the room and the house. She was carried up the mountainside to the location by the fallen oak tree, where the murder was committed and clumsily disguised as a suicide in what was possibly a spur-of-the-moment decision by her killer. The report was filed Monday, July 11 — five days after Rebecca Verloren had been left dead on the hillside.

Bosch moved on to the firearm analysis report. Though the autopsy had produced more than convincing evidence of staged suicide, the study of the gun and the attendant ballistics further confirmed the investigative theory.

The gun was found to be devoid of fingerprints except for those from Becky Verloren's right hand. The fact that there were no prints from her left hand or smudges of any kind on the pistol indicated to the investigators that the weapon had been carefully wiped clean of prints before being placed and held in Becky's hand, then turned toward her chest and fired. It was likely that the victim was unconscious — from the stun gun assault — at the time this manipulation occurred.

The bullet casing ejected from the pistol when the fatal shot was fired was recovered six feet from the body. There were no fingerprints or smudges on it, an indication that the weapon had been loaded with gloved hands.

The investigation's single most important piece of evidence was recovered during the analysis of the gun itself. It was actually found *inside* the gun. The weapon was the Mark IV Series 80 model manufactured by Colt in 1986, two years before the murder. It featured a long hammer spur, which was notable because the gun had a reputation for leaving a "tattoo" injury on the shooter if the weapon was not handled properly while firing. This usually occurred when a two-handed grip on the weapon pushed the primary shooting hand up high on the grip and too close to the hammer spur. The primary hand could then receive a painful stamp when the trigger was pulled, the weapon fired and the slide automatically came backward to eject the bullet casing. As the slide returned to firing position, it would pinch the skin of the shooter's hand — usually the webbing between the thumb and forefinger, often taking a piece of skin back with it inside the gun. All of this occurred in a fraction of a second, the novice shooter often not even knowing what had "bitten" him.

That was exactly what had happened with the gun used to kill Becky Verloren. When a firearms expert broke open the weapon he found a small piece of skin tissue and dried blood on the underside of the slide. It would not have been noticeable to someone examining the exterior of the gun or wiping it clean of blood and fingerprints.

Green and Garcia added this to their investigative theory. In the second Investigator's Summary report they wrote that evidence indicated that the killer wrapped Becky Verloren's hand around the gun and then pressed the muzzle to her chest. The killer used one or both of his own hands to steady the weapon and push or pull her finger over the trigger. The gun fired and the slide "tattooed" the killer, taking a piece of his skin with it inside the gun.

Bosch noted to himself that Green and Garcia made no mention of another possibility in their investigative theory. That being that the tissue and the blood found inside the weapon was already there on the night of the murder, that the weapon had tattooed someone other than the killer when it was fired at some point before the killing.

Regardless of that potential oversight, the blood and tissue was collected from the weapon and, while it was already known from the autopsy that Becky Verloren had no wounds on her hands, a routine blood comparison test was conducted. The blood collected from the gun was type O. Becky Verloren's blood was type AB positive. The investigators concluded they had the killer's blood on the weapon. The killer was blood type O.

But in 1988 the use of DNA comparison in criminal investigation was still years away from common and, more important, court-accepted practice in California. Databases containing the DNA profiles of criminal offenders were only on the verge of being funded and created. During the course of the 1988 investigation the detectives were left to compare blood type only to potential suspects as they arose. And no one emerged as a primary suspect in the Verloren killing. The case was worked hard and long but ultimately without an arrest ever being made. And it went cold.

"Until now," Bosch said out loud without realizing it.

"What?" Rider asked.

"Nothing. Just thinking out loud."

"You want to start talking about it?"

"Not yet. I want to finish reading first. You're done?"

"Just about."

"You know who we have to thank for this, don't you?" Bosch asked.

She looked at him quizzically.

"I give up."

"Mel Gibson."

"What are you talking about?"

"When did *Lethal Weapon* come out? Right around this time, right?"

"I guess. But what are you talking about? Those movies were so far-fetched."

"That's my point. That's the movie that started all of this holding the gun sideways and with two hands, one over the other. We got blood on this gun because the shooter was a *Lethal Weapon* fan."

Rider shook her head dismissively.

"You watch," Bosch said. "I'm going to ask the guy when we bring him in."

"Okay, Harry, you ask him."

"Mel Gibson saved a lot of lives. All those sideways shooters, they couldn't hit shit. We ought to make him like an honorary cop or something."

"Okay, Harry, I'm going to go back to reading, okay? I want to get through this."

"Yeah, okay. Me too."

5

Shortly after the LAPD's Open-Unsolved Unit began operation the DNA evidence from the Verloren case was forwarded to the California Department of Justice. It was delivered to the DNA lab along with evidence from dozens of other cases drawn from the unit's initial survey of the department's unsolved murders. The DOJ operated the state's primary DNA database. The backlog of comparison requests to the underfunded and undermanned lab was running more than a year at the time. But thanks to the tide of requests from the new LAPD unit it took almost eighteen months before the Verloren evidence was re-typed by DOJ analysts and compared to thousands of DNA profiles in the state data bank. It produced a single match, a "cold hit" in the parlance of DNA work.

Bosch looked at the single-page DOJ report unfolded in front of him. It stated that twelve of a possible fourteen markers matched the DNA from the weapon used to murder Rebecca Verloren to a now thirty-five-year-old man named Roland Mackey. He was a native of Los Angeles whose last known address was in Panorama City. Bosch felt his blood start moving a little faster as he read the cold hit report. Panorama City was in the San Fernando Valley, not more than fifteen minutes from Chatsworth, even in bad traffic. It added a level of credibility to the match. It was not that Bosch didn't believe the science. He did. But he also believed you needed more than the science to convince a jury beyond a doubt. You needed to bolster the scientific fact with connections of circumstantial evidence and common sense. This was one of those connections.

Bosch noticed the date on the cover letter of the DOJ report.

"You said we just got this?" he asked Rider.

"Yeah. I think it came in Friday. Why?"

"The date on it is from two Fridays ago. Ten days."

Rider shrugged.

"Bureaucracy," she said. "I guess it took its time getting down here from Sacramento."

"I know the case is old but you'd think they'd move a little faster than that."

Rider didn't respond. Bosch dropped it and read on. Mackey's DNA was in the DOJ computer base because all offenders convicted of any sex-related crime in California were forced under state law to submit blood and oral swabs for typing and inclusion in the DNA data bank. The offense that resulted in Mackey's DNA going into the bank was on the far margin of the state mandate. Two years earlier Mackey was convicted of lewd behavior in Los Angeles. The DOJ report did not offer details of the crime but stated Mackey was placed on twelve months probation, an indication that his was a minor offense.

Bosch was about to write a note on his pad when he looked up and saw Rider closing the murder book on the second half of the documents.

"Done?"

"Done."

"Now what?"

"I figured that while you were finishing the book I'd go over to the ESB and pick up the box."

Bosch had no trouble remembering the meaning of

what she said. He had slipped easily back into the world of acronyms and copspeak. The ESB was the Evidence Storage Building over at the Piper Tech compound. She would go there to pick up the physical evidence that would have been stored from the case. Items like the murder weapon, the victim's clothing and anything else accumulated while the case was initially worked. It was usually stored in a taped cardboard box and put on a shelf. The exception to this was storage of perishable and biological evidence — such as the blood and tissue recovered from the Verloren murder weapon — which was stored in lab vaults in the Scientific Investigation Division.

"Sounds like a good idea," Bosch said. "But first why don't you run this guy through DMV and NCIC and see if we can get a location?"

"Already did that."

She turned her laptop around on her desk so Bosch could see the screen. He recognized the National Crime Index Computer template on the screen. He reached across and started scrolling down the screen, his eyes scanning the information.

Rider had run Roland Mackey through NCIC and gotten his criminal record. His conviction two years earlier for lewd behavior was only the latest in a string of recorded arrests dating back to when he was eighteen — the same year as Rebecca Verloren's murder. Anything prior would not be listed because juvenile protection laws shielded that part of his record. Most of the crimes listed were property and drug-related crimes, beginning with car theft and a burglary at eighteen and leading to two drug-possession raps, two driving under the influence arrests, another burglary charge and a receiving stolen property hit. There was also an early solicitation of prostitution arrest. Overall it was the pedigree of a small-time criminal and drug user. It appeared that Mackey never went to state prison for any of his crimes. He was often given second chances and then, through plea agreements, was sentenced to probation or to short stints in county jail. It appeared that the longest he ever stayed in stir was six months served after pleading guilty to receiving stolen property when he was twenty-eight years old. He served his time at the county-run Wayside Honor Rancho.

Bosch leaned back after he was finished scrolling through the computer records. He felt uneasy about what he had just read. Mackey had the kind of record that might be seen as a pathway to murder. But in this case the murder came first — when Mackey was only eighteen years old — and the petty crimes came after. It didn't seem to quite fit.

"What?" Rider asked, sensing his mood.

"I don't know. I thought there'd be more, I guess. It's backwards. This guy goes from murder to petty crime? Doesn't seem to hold."

"Well, this is all he's ever gotten popped for. Doesn't mean it's all he ever did."

He nodded.

"Juvenile?" he asked.

"Maybe. Probably. But we'll never get those records now. They're probably long gone."

It was true. The state went out of its way to protect the privacy of juvenile offenders. Crimes rarely tailed offenders into the adult justice system. Nevertheless, Bosch thought that there had to be childhood crimes that would fit better with the seemingly cold-blooded murder of a sixteen-year-old girl who had been incapacitated with a stun gun and abducted from her home. Bosch began to have an uneasy feeling about the cold hit they were working. He was beginning to sense that Mackey was not the target. He was a means to the target.

"Did you run him through DMV for an address?" he asked.

"Harry, that's old-school. You only have to update your driver's license every four years. You want to find somebody you go to AutoTrack."

She opened the murder book and slid a loose piece of paper across to him. It was a computer printout that said AutoTrack at the top. Rider said it was a private company the police department contracted with. It provided computer searches of all public records, including DMV, public utility and cable service databases, as well as private databases such as credit reporting services, to determine an individual's past and current addresses. Bosch saw that the printout contained a listing of Roland Mackey's various addresses dating back to when he was eighteen. His current listing on all current data, including driver's license and car registration, was the address in Panorama City. But on the page, Rider had circled the address ascribed to Mackey when he was eighteen through twenty years old — the years 1988 through 1990. It was an apartment on Topanga Canyon Boulevard in Chatsworth. This meant that at the time of the murder Mackey was living very close to Rebecca Verloren's home. This made Bosch feel a little better about things. Proximity was a key piece to the puzzle. Bosch's misgivings over Mackey's criminal pedigree aside, knowing that he was in the immediate vicinity in 1988 and therefore could have seen or even known Rebecca Verloren was a large check mark in the positive column.

"Make you feel any better, Harry?"

"A little bit."

"Good. I'm going, then."

"I'll be here."

After Rider left, Bosch jumped back into his review of the murder book. The third Investigator's Summary focused on how the intruder got into the house. The door and window locks showed no signs of having been compromised and all known keys to the home were accounted for among family members and a housekeeper who was cleared of any suspicion. The investigators theorized that the killer came in through the garage, which had been left open, and then entered the house through the connecting door, which was usually not locked until after Robert Verloren came home from work at night.

According to Robert Verloren the garage was open when he came home from his restaurant about ten-thirty on the night of July fifth. The connecting door from the garage into the house was unlocked. He entered his home, closed the garage and locked the connecting door. The investigators theorized that by then the killer was already in the house.

The Verlorens' explanation for the open garage was that their daughter had recently received her driver's license and was on occasion allowed to use her mother's car. However, she had not yet acquired the habit of remembering to close the garage door upon leaving or coming home, and had been chastised by her parents on more than one occasion for this. Late in the afternoon before her abduction Rebecca was sent on an errand by her mother to pick up dry cleaning. She used her mother's car. The investigators confirmed that she picked up the clothing at 5:15 p.m. and then returned home. It was believed by the investigators that she once again forgot to close the garage or lock the connecting door after returning. Her mother said she never checked the garage that night, assuming wrongly that it was closed.

Two residents in the neighborhood canvassed after the murder reported seeing the garage door open that evening. This left the house easily accessible until Robert Verloren came home.

Bosch thought about how many times over the years he

had seen someone's seemingly innocent mistake turn into one of the keys to their own doom. A routine chore to pick up clothes may have led to the opportunity for a killer to get inside the house. Becky Verloren may have unwittingly engineered her own death.

Bosch pushed his chair back and stood up. He had finished the review of the first half of the murder book. He decided to get another cup of coffee before taking on the second half. He asked around in the office if anybody needed anything from the cafeteria and got one order for coffee from Jean Nord. He took the stairs down to the cafeteria and filled two cups from the urn, then paid for them and went over to the condiments counter to get Nord's cream and sugar. While he was pouring a shot of cream into one of the cups he felt a presence next to him at the counter. He made room at the station but no one reached for any condiments. He turned toward the presence and found himself looking at the smiling face of Deputy Chief Irvin S. Irving.

There had never been any love lost between Bosch and Deputy Chief Irving. The chief had at various times been his adversary and unwitting savior in the department. But Bosch had heard from Rider that Irving was on the outs now. He had been unceremoniously pushed out of power by the new chief and given a virtually meaningless posting and assignment outside of Parker Center.

"I thought that was you, Detective Bosch. I'd buy you a cup of coffee but I see you already have more than enough. Would you like to sit down for a minute anyway?"

Bosch held up both cups of coffee.

"I'm kind of in the middle of something, Chief. And somebody's waiting for one of these."

"One minute, Detective," Irving said, a stern tone entering his voice. "The coffee will still be hot when you get to where you have to go. I promise."

Without waiting for an answer he turned and walked to a nearby table. Bosch followed. Irving still had a shaved and gleaming skull. His muscular jaw was his most prominent feature. He took a seat and held his posture ramrod straight. He didn't look comfortable. He didn't speak until Bosch sat down. The pleasant tone was back in his voice.

"All I wanted to do was welcome you back to the department," he said.

He smiled like a shark. Bosch hesitated like a man stepping across a trapdoor before answering.

"It's good to be back, Chief."

"The Open-Unsolved Unit. I think that is the appropriate place for someone of your skills."

Bosch took a sip from his scalding cup of coffee. He didn't know if Irving had just complimented or insulted him. He wanted to leave.

"Well, we'll see," he said. "I hope so. I think I better —"

Irving held his hands out wide, as if to show he wasn't hiding anything.

"That's it," he said. "You can go. I just wanted to say welcome back. And to thank you."

Bosch hesitated, but then bit.

"Thank me for what, Chief?"

"For resurrecting me in this department."

Bosch shook his head and smiled as if he didn't understand.

"I don't get it, Chief," he said. "How am I supposed to do that? I mean, you're across the street in the City Hall Annex now, right? What is it, the Office of Strategic Planning or something? From what I hear, you get to leave your gun at home."

Irving folded his arms on the table and leaned in close to Bosch. All pretense of humor, false or otherwise, evaporated. He spoke strongly but quietly.

"Yes, that is where I am. But I guarantee you that it will not be for long. Not with the likes of you being welcomed back into the department."

He then leaned back and just as quickly adopted a casual manner for what he delivered as casual conversation.

"You know what you are, Bosch? You are a retread. This new chief likes putting retreads on the car. But you know what happens with a retread? It comes apart at the seams. The friction and the heat — they're too much for it. It comes apart and what happens? A blowout. And then the car goes off the road."

He nodded silently as he let Bosch think about that.

"You see, Bosch, you are my ticket. You will fuck up — if you will excuse my language. It is in your history. It is in your nature. It is guaranteed. And when you fuck up, our illustrious new chief fucks up for being the one who put a cheap retread on our car."

He smiled. Bosch thought that all he needed was a gold earring to complete the picture. Mr. Clean all the way.

"And when he goes down my stock goes right back up. I'm a patient man. I've waited for over forty years in this department. I can wait longer."

Bosch expected more but that was it. Irving nodded once and stood up. He quickly turned and headed out of the cafeteria. Bosch felt the anger rise in his throat. He looked down at the two cups of coffee in his hands and felt like an idiot for having sat there like a defenseless errand boy while Irving had verbally punched him out. He got up and threw both cups into a trash can. He decided that when he got back to room 503 he would tell Jean Nord to get her own damn coffee.

6

With the unease of the Irving confrontation still lingering, Bosch took the second half of the murder book over to his desk and sat down. He thought the best way to forget about the threat that Irving posed was to immerse himself in the case again. What he found left in the file was a thick sheaf of ancillary reports and updates, the things investigators always lumped into the back of the book, the reports that Bosch called the tumblers because they often seemed disparate but nevertheless could unlock a case when seen from the right angle or put together in the right pattern.

First was a lab report stating that testing was unable to determine exactly how long the blood and tissue sample taken from the murder weapon could have been in the gun. The report said that while most of the sample was preserved for comparison purposes, an examination of selected blood cells indicated decomposition was not extensive. The criminalist who wrote the report could not say the blood was deposited on the gun at the time of the killing — no one could. But he would be prepared to testify that the blood was deposited on the gun "close to or at the time of the killing."

Bosch knew this was a key report in terms of mounting a prosecution of Roland Mackey. It might also give Mackey the opportunity to build a defense around having had possession of the gun before the murder but not at the time of the murder. It would be a risky move to admit being in possession of the murder weapon, but the DNA match dictated that it was a move he would likely have to make. With the science unable to pinpoint exactly when the deposit of blood and tissue on the gun occurred, Bosch saw a gaping hole in the prosecution's case. The defense could clearly jump through it. Again, he felt the certainty of the cold hit DNA match slipping away. Science gives and takes at the same time. They needed more.

Next in the murder book was a report from the Firearms Unit, which had been assigned the ownership trace of the murder weapon. The serial number on the Colt had been filed down, but the number was raised in the lab with the application of an acid which accentuated the compressions in the metal where the number had been stamped during manufacture. The number was traced to a gun purchased from the manufacturer in 1987 by a Northridge gun shop. It was then traced through its sale that year to a man who lived in Chatsworth on Winnetka Avenue. The gun had then been reported stolen by the owner when his home was burglarized June 2, 1988, just a month before it was used in the murder of Rebecca Verloren.

This report helped their case somewhat because unless Mackey had a relationship with the gun's original owner, the burglary compressed the time period during which Mackey would have had possession of the gun. It made it more likely that he had the gun on the night Becky Verloren was taken from her home and murdered.

The original burglary report was contained in the file. The victim was named Sam Weiss. He lived alone and worked as a sound technician at Warner Bros. in Burbank. Bosch scanned the report and found only one other note of interest. In the investigating officer's comments section it was stated that the burglary victim had recently purchased the gun for protection after being harassed by anonymous phone calls in which the caller threatened him because he was Jewish. The victim reported that he did not know how his unlisted number fell into the hands of his harasser and he did not know what had brought on the threats.

Bosch quickly read through the next report from the Firearms Unit, which identified the stun gun used in the abduction. The report said the $2\frac{1}{4}$-inch span between contact points — as exhibited by the burn marks on the victim's flesh — was unique to the Professional 100 model manufactured by a company called SafetyCharge in Downey. The model was sold over the counter and through mail order and there were more than twelve thousand Professional 100 models distributed at the time of the murder. Bosch knew that without the actual device in hand there was no way to connect the marks on Becky Verloren's body with an ownership trail. That was a dead end.

He moved on, leafing through a series of 8 x 10 photos taken in the Verloren house after the body was found up on the hillside behind it. Bosch knew these were cover-your-ass photos. The case had been handled — or mishandled — as a runaway situation. The department did not go full field with it until after the body was found and an autopsy concluded the death was a homicide. Five days after the girl was reported missing, the police came back and turned the house into a crime scene. The question was what was lost in those five days.

The photos included interior and exterior shots of all three doors to the house — front, back, garage — and several close-ups of window locks. There was also a series of shots taken in Becky Verloren's bedroom. The first thing Bosch noticed was that the bed was made. He wondered if the abductor had made it, thereby further selling the suicide, or Becky's mother had simply made the bed at some point during the days she hoped and waited for her daughter to come home.

The bed was a four-poster with a white-and-pink spread with cats on it and a matching pink ruffle. The bedspread reminded Bosch of the one that had covered his own daughter's bed. It seemed to be something that a child much younger than sixteen would like and he wondered if Becky Verloren had kept it for nostalgic reasons or as some sort of psychological security blanket. The bed's ruffle did not uniformly skirt the floor. It was a couple inches too long, and so it bunched on the floor and alternately fluffed out or tucked under the bed too far.

There were photos of her bureau and bed tables. The room was festooned with stuffed animals from her younger years. There were posters on the walls from music groups that had come and gone. There was a poster of a John Travolta movie three comebacks old. The room was very neat and orderly, and again Bosch wondered if this was how it had been on the morning Rebecca Verloren was discovered missing or if her mother had straightened the room while awaiting her daughter's return.

Bosch knew the photos had to have been taken as the first step of the crime scene investigation. Nowhere did he see any fingerprint powder or any other indication of the upset that would come with the intrusion of the criminalists.

The photos were followed in the murder book by a packet of summaries from interviews the detectives conducted with numerous students at Hillside Prep. A checklist on the top page indicated that the investigators had talked to every student in Becky Verloren's class and every boy who attended the upper grades of the school. There were also summaries from interviews of several of the victim's teachers and school administrators.

Included in this section was a summary of a phone interview conducted with a former boyfriend of Becky Verloren's who had moved with his family to Hawaii the year before her murder. Attached to the summary was an alibi confirmation report stating that the teenager's supervisor had confirmed that the boy had worked in the car wash and detail facility at a Maui rent-a-car franchise on the days of and after the murder, making it unlikely that he could have been in Los Angeles to kill her.

There was a separate packet of summaries of interviews with employees of the Island House Grill, the restaurant owned by Robert Verloren. His daughter had just started a part-time summer job at the restaurant. She was an assistant hostess during lunch. Her job was to lead customers to their tables and to put down the menus. Though Bosch knew restaurants often drew a variety of drifters to the low-level kitchen jobs, Robert Verloren avoided hiring men with criminal records, instead drawing on the population of surfers and other free spirits who flocked to the beaches of Malibu. These people would have had limited contact with Rebecca, who worked in the dining room, but they were interviewed just the same and seemingly dismissed by the investigators.

There was also a victim's chronology in which the investigators outlined Rebecca Verloren's movements in the days leading up to her murder. In 1988 July Fourth fell on a Monday. Rebecca spent most of the holiday weekend at home, except for a Sunday-night sleepover with three girlfriends at one of their houses. The attached summaries of interviews with these three girls were long but contained no information of investigative value.

On Monday, the holiday, she stayed home until she and her parents went to Balboa Park to watch a fireworks display. It was a rare night off for Robert Verloren and he insisted that the family stay together, much to Becky's reported upset at missing out on a friend's party in the Porter Ranch area.

On Tuesday the summer routine began again with Rebecca going to the restaurant with her father to work the lunch shift as a hostess. At three o'clock her father drove her home. He stayed at home through the afternoon and then headed back to the restaurant for the dinner shift at about the same time Rebecca used her mother's car to run the errand of collecting the dry cleaning.

Bosch saw nothing in the schedule that raised suspicions, nothing that was missed by the original investigators.

He next came to a transcript of a formal interview with the parents. It was taken at Devonshire Division on July 14, more than a week after their daughter was discovered missing. By this point the detectives had accumulated a lot of case knowledge and were specific with their questions. Bosch carefully read this transcript, as much for the answers as for the insight it would give to the investigators' view of the case at that point.

Case No. 88-641, Verloren, Rebecca (DOD 7-6-88),
   I/O A. Garcia, #993
7/14/88 – 2:15 p.m., Devonshire Homicide

GARCIA: Thank you for coming in. I hope you don't mind but we are recording this so we will have a record. How are you managing?

ROBT. VERLOREN: About as well as expected. We're devastated. We don't know what to do.

MURIEL VERLOREN: We keep thinking, what could we have done to prevent this from happening to our little girl?

GREEN: We're truly sorry, ma'am. But you can't blame yourself for this. As far as we can tell it was nothing

48

you did or didn't do. It just happened. Don't blame yourself. Blame the person who did this.

GARCIA: And we are going to get him. You don't have to worry about that. Now, we have some questions we need to ask. Some of these might be painful but we need the answers if we are going to get this guy.

ROBT. VERLOREN: You keep saying "guy." Is there a suspect? Do you know it was a man?

GARCIA: We don't know anything for sure, sir. We're mostly going with the percentages there. But also you have that steep hill behind your house. Becky was definitely carried up that hill. She wasn't a big girl but we definitely think it would have to be a man.

MURIEL VERLOREN: But you said she wasn't... that there was no sexual assault.

GARCIA: That is true, ma'am. But that does not preclude this from being a sexually motivated or related crime.

ROBT. VERLOREN: How do you mean?

GARCIA: We will get to that, sir. If you don't mind, let us ask our questions and then we will get to your questions if you would like.

ROBT. VERLOREN: Go ahead, please. I'm sorry. It's just that we cannot understand what has happened. It's like we are underwater all the time.

GARCIA: That is completely understandable. As I said, you have our deepest sympathy. From the department, too. We have the upper echelon of this department watching over this case very closely.

GREEN: We would like to start by going back before her disappearance. Maybe a month before. Did your daughter go away at all during that time?

ROBT. VERLOREN: What do you mean, away?

GARCIA: Was she away from you at any time?

ROBT. VERLOREN: No. She was sixteen. She was in school. She didn't go away on her own.

GREEN: What about a sleepover with her friends?

MURIEL VERLOREN: No, I don't think so.

ROBT. VERLOREN: What are you looking for?

GREEN: Was she sick at all in the month or two prior to the disappearance?

MURIEL VERLOREN: Yes, she had the flu the first week after school ended. It delayed her going to work for Bob.

GREEN: Was she in bed sick?

MURIEL VERLOREN: A lot of the time. I don't see what this has to —

GARCIA: Mrs. Verloren, did your daughter go to see a doctor at this time?

MURIEL VERLOREN: No, she just said she had to rest. To tell you the truth, we thought she just didn't want to go to work in the restaurant. She didn't have a fever or a cold. We just thought she was being lazy.

GREEN: She didn't confide in you at this time that she had been pregnant?

MURIEL VERLOREN: What? No!

ROBT. VERLOREN: Look, Detective, what are you telling us?

GREEN: The autopsy revealed that Becky had had a procedure called a dilation and curettage about a month before her death. An abortion. Our guess is that she was resting and recovering from this procedure when she told you she had the flu.

GARCIA: Would you two like to take a break here?

GREEN: Why don't we take a break? We'll step out and get all of us some water.

[Break]

GARCIA: Okay, we're back. I hope you understand and forgive us. We do not ask questions or attempt to shock you to hurt you. We need to follow procedure and employ methods that allow us to collect information that is unfettered by preconceived perceptions.

ROBT. VERLOREN: We understand what you are doing. It's part of our life now. What's left of it.

MURIEL VERLOREN: You are saying our daughter was pregnant and chose to get an abortion?

GARCIA: Yes, that's right. And we think there is a possibility that it could have a bearing on what happened to her a month later. Do you have any idea where she would have gone for this procedure?

MURIEL VERLOREN: No. I had no idea about this. Neither of us.

GREEN: And as you said before, she did not go away overnight during that time?

MURIEL VERLOREN: No, she was home every night.

GARCIA: Any idea who the relationship could have been with? In our earlier talks you said she had no current boyfriend.

MURIEL VERLOREN: Well, obviously I guess we were wrong about that. But, no, we don't know who she was seeing or who could have . . . done this.

GREEN: Have either of you ever read the journal that your daughter kept?

ROBT. VERLOREN: No, we didn't even know there was a journal until you found it in her room.

MURIEL VERLOREN: I would like to get that back. Will I get that back?

GREEN: We will need to keep it through the investigation but you will eventually get it back.

GARCIA: There are several references in the journal to an individual referred to as MTL. This is a person we would like to identify and talk to.

MURIEL VERLOREN: I don't know anyone with those initials offhand.

GREEN: We looked at the school's yearbook. There is one boy named Michael Lewis. But we checked and his middle name is Charles. We think the initials were a code or an abbreviation. It could stand for My True Love.

MURIEL VERLOREN: So there was obviously someone we didn't know about, that she kept from us.

ROBT. VERLOREN: I can't believe this. You two are telling us we didn't really know our little girl.

GARCIA: I'm sorry, Bob. Sometimes the damage from a case like this goes deep. But it's our job to follow it where it goes. This is the current we are in right now.

GREEN: Basically, we need to pursue this aspect of the investigation and find out who MTL is. Which means we need to ask questions of your daughter's friends and acquaintances. Word about this, it will get around, I'm afraid.

ROBT. VERLOREN: We understand this, Detective. We will deal with it. As we said on the day we met, do what you have to do. Find the person who did this.

GARCIA: Thank you, sir. We will.

[End of interview, 2:40 p.m.]

Bosch read the transcript a second time, this time writing down notes on his pad as he went. He then moved on to three more formal interview transcripts. These were conducted with Becky Verloren's three closest friends, Tara Wood, Bailey Koster and Grace Tanaka. But none of the girls — girls at the time — said they had knowledge of Becky's pregnancy or the secret relationship that produced it. All three said they did not see her the week after school got out because she was not answering her phone and when they called the house's main number Muriel Verloren told them her daughter was sick. Tara Wood, who was splitting a work schedule as a hostess at the Island House Grill with Becky, said that her friend was moody and incommunicative in the weeks prior to her murder, but the reason for this was unknown because she rebuffed Wood's efforts to find out what was wrong.

The last entry in the murder book was the media file. It was where Garcia and Green kept the newspaper stories that accumulated in the early stages of the case. The crime played bigger in the *Daily News* than in the *Times*. This was understandable because the *News* circulated primarily in the San Fernando Valley and the *Times* usually treated the Valley as an unwanted stepchild, relegating the news emanating from its environs to the inside pages.

There was no coverage of Becky Verloren's initial disappearance. The newspapers had obviously viewed it in the same way as the police had. But once the body was found there were several stories on the investigation, the funeral and the impact the young girl's death had at her school. There was even a mood piece set at the Island House Grill. This story had been in the *Times* and had apparently been a stab at making the case meaningful to the paper's Westside circulation base. A restaurant in Malibu was something the Westsiders could relate to.

Both newspapers linked the murder weapon to a burglary that occurred a month before the killing but neither had the anti-Semitic angle. Neither reported on the blood evidence recovered from the weapon either. Bosch guessed that the blood and tissue recovery was the investigators' ace in the hole, the one piece of evidence held close to the vest to give them the advantage if a prime suspect was ever identified.

Finally Bosch noticed that there were no media

interviews with the grieving parents. The Verlorens apparently chose not to hold their loss out for public consumption. Bosch liked that about them. It seemed to him that increasingly the media forced the victims of tragedy to grieve in public, in front of cameras and in newspaper stories. Parents of murdered children became talking heads who appeared on the tube as experts the next time there was another child murdered and another set of parents grieving. It all didn't sit well with Bosch. It seemed to him that the best way to honor the dead was to keep them close to the heart, not to share them with the world across the electronic spectrum.

At the back of the murder book there was a pocket containing a manila envelope with the *Times*'s eagle insignia and address in the corner. Bosch pulled it out and opened it and found a series of 8 x 10 color photos taken at Rebecca Verloren's funeral one week after her murder. Apparently there had been a deal cut, the photos traded for access. Bosch remembered making such deals in the past when he was unable because of scheduling or budget to get a police photographer out to a funeral. He would promise the reporter working the story that he or she would be in line for an exclusive if the newspaper photographer wouldn't mind running off a complete set of crowd shots of the people attending the service. You never knew when the killer might show up to get a rise out of the anguish and grief he had caused. Reporters always went for the deal. Los Angeles was one of the most competitive media markets in the world and reporters lived and died by the access they had.

Bosch studied the photos but was handicapped in looking for Roland Mackey because he didn't know what he looked like in 1988. The photos Kiz Rider had pulled up on the computer were from his most recent arrest. They showed a balding man with a goatee and dark eyes. It was hard to trace that visage back to any of the teenaged faces that gathered to put one of their own in the ground.

For a while he studied Becky Verloren's parents in one of the photos. They were standing at the graveside, leaning against each other as if holding each other from falling. Tears lined their faces. Robert Verloren was black and Muriel Verloren was white. Bosch now understood where their daughter had gotten her growing beauty. The mix of races in a child often rose above the attendant social difficulties to achieve such grace.

Bosch put the photos down and thought for a moment. Nowhere in the murder book had there been mention of the possibility of race playing a part in the murder. But the murder weapon's coming from the burglary of a man being threatened because of his religion seemed to give rise to the possibility of at least a tenuous link to the murder of a girl of mixed races.

The fact that this was not mentioned in the murder book meant nothing. The aspect of race was always something held close to the vest in the LAPD. To commit something to the paperwork was to make it known within the department — investigative summaries were reviewed all the way up the line on hot cases. It could then be leaked and turned into something else, something political. So its absence was not seen by Bosch as a taint on the investigation. Not yet, at least.

He returned the photos to the envelope and closed the murder book. He guessed that there were more than three hundred pages of documents and photos in it, and nowhere on any of those pages had he seen the name Roland Mackey. Was it possible that he had escaped even peripheral notice in the investigation so many years before? If so, was it still possible he was indeed the killer?

These questions bothered Bosch. He always tried to keep faith in the murder book, meaning that he believed the answers usually lay within its plastic sides. But this time he was having difficulty believing the cold hit. Not the science. He had no doubt about Mackey being matched to the blood and tissue found inside the murder weapon. But he believed something was wrong. Something was missing.

He looked down at his pad. He had taken few notes. He had really only composed a list of people he wanted to talk to.

Green and Garcia
Mother/Father
school/friends/teachers
former boyfriend
probation agent
Mackey — school?

He knew that every note he had taken was obvious. He realized how little they had besides the DNA match, and once again he was uneasy about building a case without anything else.

Bosch was staring at his notes when Kiz Rider walked into the office. She was empty-handed and unsmiling.

"Well?" Bosch asked.

"Bad news. The murder weapon's gone. I don't know if you've read the whole book but there's mention of a journal in there. The girl kept a journal. That's gone, too. Everything's gone."

7

They decided that the best way to deal with and discuss bad news was to eat. Besides that, nothing made Bosch hungrier than sitting in an office all morning and reading through a murder book. They went over to Chinese Friends, a small place on Broadway at the end of Chinatown where they knew they could still get a table this early. It was a place where you could eat well and to capacity and barely go over five bucks. The trouble was that it filled up fast, mostly with headquarters staff from the Fire Department, the gold badges from Parker Center and the bureaucrats from City Hall. If you didn't get there by noon you ordered takeout and you had to sit and eat on the bus benches out front in the sun.

They left the murder book in the car so as not to disturb other patrons in the restaurant, where the tables were jammed as close as the desks in a public school. They did bring their notes, and discussed the case in an improvised shorthand designed to keep their conversation private. Rider explained that when she had said the gun and the journal were missing from the ESB what she meant was that no evidence carton from the case could be found during an hour-long search by two evidence clerks. This was not much of a surprise to Bosch. As Pratt had warned earlier, the department had taken haphazard care of evidence for decades. Evidence cartons were booked and filed on shelves in chronological order and without any sort of separation according to crime classification. Consequently, evidence from a murder might sit on a shelf next to evidence from a burglary. And when clerks came through periodically to clear out evidence from cases where the statute of limitations had expired, sometimes the wrong box got tossed. The security of the ESB was also a low priority for many years. It was not difficult for anyone with an LAPD badge to gain access to any piece of evidence in the facility. So the evidence cartons were subject to pilfering. It was not unusual for weapons to be missing, or other kinds of evidence from famous cases like the Black Dahlia, Charles Manson, and the Dollmaker crimes.

There was no indication in the Verloren case of evidence theft. It was probably more a case of carelessness, of trying to find a box that had been stored seventeen years ago in an acre-sized room crowded with matching boxes.

"They'll find it," Bosch said. "Maybe you can even get your buddy up on six to put the fear of God into them. Then they'll find it for sure."

"They better. The DNA is no good to us without that gun."

"I don't know about that."

"Harry, it's the chain of evidence. You can't go into trial with the DNA and not be able to show the jury the weapon it came from. We can't even go into the district attorney's office without it. They'll throw us right out on our asses."

"Look, all I'm saying is, right now we're the only ones who know we don't have the gun. We can fake it."

"What are you talking about?"

"Don't you think that this is all going to come down to Mackey and us in a little room? I mean, even if we had the gun in evidence we can't prove beyond a doubt that he left his blood in it during the shooting of Becky Verloren. All we can prove is that the blood is his. So if you ask me, it's going to come down to a confession. We're going to put him in the room, hit him with the DNA and see if he cops to it. That's it. So all I'm saying is, we put together a few props for the interview. We go to the armory and borrow a Colt forty-five and we pull that out of the box when we're in the room with him. We convince him we have the chain and he cops or he doesn't."

"I don't like tricks."

"Tricks are part of the trade. There's nothing illegal about that. The courts have even said so."

"I think we're going to need more than the DNA to turn him anyway."

"Me too. I was thinking we —"

Bosch stopped and waited while the waitress put down two steaming plates. Bosch had ordered shrimp fried rice. Rider ordered pork chops. Without a word he lifted his plate and pushed half of its contents onto her plate. He then used a fork to take three of her six pork chops. He almost smiled while he did this. He was back on the job with her less than a day and they had already dropped back into the easy rhythm of their prior partnership. He was happy.

"Hey, what's Jerry Edgar up to?" he asked.

"I don't know. I haven't talked to him in a while. We never really got over that thing."

Bosch nodded. When Bosch had worked at Hollywood Division with Rider the homicide table had been divided into teams of three. Jerry Edgar had been the third partner. Then Bosch retired and soon after Rider was promoted downtown. It left Edgar still in Hollywood, feeling isolated and passed over. And now that Bosch and Rider were working again and assigned to RHD, there had been only silence from Edgar.

"What were you going to say, Harry, when the food came?"

"Just that you're right. We'll need more. One thing I was

thinking was that I heard that since Nine-Eleven and the Patriot Act it's easier for us to get a wiretap."

She ate a piece of shrimp before responding.

"Yes, that's true. It's one of the things I was monitoring for the chief. Our request filings have gone up about three thousand percent. The approvals are way up, too. The word's sort of gotten around that this is a tool we can use now. How is it going to work here?"

"I was thinking we put a tap on Mackey and then we plant a story in the paper. You know, it says we're working the case again, mention the gun, maybe mention the DNA — you know, something new. Not that we have a match but that we *could* get a match. Then we sit back and watch him and listen to him and see what happens. We could follow up by paying him a visit, see if that stirs things up any."

Rider thought about this while eating a pork chop with her fingers. She seemed uneasy about something and it couldn't be the food.

"What?" Bosch asked.

"Who would he call?"

"I don't know. Whoever he did it with or did it for."

Rider nodded thoughtfully while chewing.

"I don't know, Harry. You're back on the job less than a day after three years in the fun and sun and already you are reading things into a case I don't see. I guess you are still the teacher."

"You're just rusty from sitting up there behind a big desk on six."

"I'm serious."

"So am I. Sort of. I think I've waited so long for this that I'm sort of on full alert, I guess."

"Just tell me how you see this, Harry. You don't have to make up excuses for your instincts."

"I actually don't see it yet and that's part of the problem.

Roland Mackey's name is nowhere in that book and that's a problem starting out the door. We know he was in the vicinity but we have nothing connecting him to the victim."

"What are you talking about? We have the gun with his DNA in it."

"The blood connects him to the gun, not the girl. You read the book. We can't prove his DNA was deposited at the time of the killing. That single report could blow this whole case out of the water. It's a big hole, Kiz. So big a jury could drive through it. All Mackey has to do at trial is get up there on the stand and say, 'Yeah, I stole the gun during a burglary on Winnetka. I then went up into the hills and shot it a few times, and I was making like Mel Gibson and the next thing I knew the damn thing bit me, took a chunk right out of my hand. I never saw that happen to Mel before. So I got so mad I threw that damn gun into the bushes and went home to get some Band-Aids.' The SID report — our *own* damn report — backs him up and that is the end of it."

Rider didn't smile during the story at all. He could tell she was seeing his point.

"That's all he has to say, Kiz, and he's got reasonable doubt and we can't prove otherwise. We've got no prints at the scene, we've got no hair, no fiber, we've got nothing. But added to this we do have his profile. And if you looked at his sheet before we were on this and knew about the DNA you would have never pegged this guy as a killer. Maybe spur-of-the-moment or heat of passion. But not something like this, something planned, and certainly not at age eighteen."

Rider shook her head in an almost wistful manner.

"A few hours ago this was given to us as a welcome-aboard present. It was supposed to be a slam dunk . . ."

"The DNA made everybody jump to a conclusion. It's

what's wrong with the world. People think technology is an easy ride. They're watching too much TV."

"Is that your weird way of saying you don't think he did this?"

"I don't know what I'm thinking yet."

"So we put a tail on him, tap his phone, spook him somehow and then see who he calls and how he acts."

Bosch nodded.

"That's what I'm thinking," he said.

"We'd need to clear it with Abel first."

"We follow the rules. Just like the chief told me today."

"Holy smoke — the new Harry Bosch."

"You're looking at him."

"Before we go for the tap we have to finish the due diligence. We have to make sure Roland Mackey was not known to any of the players. If that turns out to be the case then I say we go see Pratt about the tap."

"Sounds right to me. What else did you get on the read?"

He wanted to see if she picked up on the undercurrent of race before suggesting it.

"Just what was there," Rider responded. "Was there something I missed?"

"I don't know — nothing obvious."

"Then what?"

"I was thinking about the girl being biracial. Even in 'eighty-eight there would have been people that didn't like the idea of that. Then you add in the burglary the gun came from. The vic was Jewish. He said he was being harassed. That's why he bought the gun."

Rider nodded thoughtfully while she finished a mouthful of rice.

"It's something to look for," she said. "But I don't see enough there to hang a lantern on at the moment."

"There was nothing in the book . . ."

They ate in silence for a few minutes. Bosch always thought Chinese Friends had the softest and sweetest shrimp he had ever tasted in fried rice. The pork chops, as thin as the plastic plates they ate off of, were also perfect. And Kiz was right, they were best eaten by hand.

"What about Green and Garcia?" Rider finally asked.

"What about them?"

"How would you grade them on this?"

"I don't know. Maybe a C if I was being charitable. They made mistakes, slowed things down. After that they seemed to cover the bases. You?"

"Same thing. They wrote a good murder book but it's got CYA written all through it. Like they knew they were never going to break it but wanted the book to look like they turned over every stone."

Bosch nodded and looked down at his pad on the empty chair to the side. He looked at the list of people to interview.

"We've got to talk to the parents and Garcia and Green. We need to get a photo of Mackey, too. From when he was eighteen."

"I think we hold back on the parents until we talk to everybody else. They might be most important but they should be last. I want to know as much as possible before we hit them with this after seventeen years."

"Fine. Maybe we should start at probation. He only cleared a year ago. He probably was assigned to Van Nuys."

"Right. We could go there and then walk over to talk to Art Garcia."

"You found him? He's still around?"

"Didn't have to look. He's commander of Valley Bureau now."

Bosch nodded. He was not surprised. Garcia had done well. The rank of commander put him just below deputy chief. It meant he was second in command over the Valley's five police divisions, including Devonshire, where years earlier he had worked the Verloren case.

Rider continued.

"In addition to our regular projects in the chief's office, each of the special assistants was assigned as sort of a liaison to one of the four bureaus. My assignment was the Valley. So Commander Garcia and I spoke from time to time. Most often I dealt with his staff, or Deputy Chief Vartan, that sort of thing."

"I know what you're saying — I have a highly connected partner. You were probably telling Vartan and Garcia how to run the Valley."

She shook her head in false annoyance.

"Don't give me shit about all of that. Working on six gave me a good view of the department and how it works."

"Or doesn't. Speaking of which, there's something I should tell you."

"What is it?"

"I ran into Irving when I went down to get coffee. Right after you left."

Rider immediately looked concerned.

"What happened? What did he say?"

"Not a lot. He just called me a retread and mentioned that I was going to crash and burn and that when I did I would take the chief down with me for hiring me back. Then, of course, when the dust settles Mr. Clean would be there to step up."

"Jesus, Harry. One day on the job and you already have Irving biting you on the ass?"

Bosch spread his hands wide, almost hitting the shoulder of a man sitting at the next table.

"I went to get coffee. He was there. He approached me, Kiz. I was just minding my own business. I swear."

She bent her face down to look at her plate. She

continued eating without talking to him. She dropped her last pork chop half eaten on the plate.

"I can't eat any more, Harry. Let's get out of here."

"I'm ready."

Bosch left more than enough money on the table and Rider said she would get the next one. Outside they got into Bosch's car, a black Mercedes SUV, and drove back through Chinatown to the entrance of the northbound 101. They made it all the way to the freeway before Rider spoke again about Irving.

"Harry, don't take him lightly," she said. "Be very careful."

"I am always careful, Kiz, and I have never taken that man lightly."

"All I'm saying is, he's been passed over twice for the top spot. He may be getting desperate."

"Yeah, you know what I don't get? Why didn't your guy get rid of him when he came in here? I mean, just clean house. Pushing Irving across the street doesn't put an end to the threat. Anybody knows that."

"He couldn't push him. Irving's got forty-plus years on the job. He has a lot of connections that go outside the department and into City Hall. And he knows where a lot of the bodies are buried. The chief couldn't make a move against him unless he was sure there wouldn't be any blowback from it."

More silence followed. The early afternoon traffic out to the Valley was light. They had KFWB, the all news and traffic channel, on the radio and there were no reports of problems ahead. Bosch checked the gas and saw he had half a tank. That was plenty.

They had decided earlier to alternate use of their personal cars. A department car had been requisitioned and approved for them to share, but they both knew that getting the R&A was the easy part. It would most likely be months if not longer before they would actually get the wheels. The department had neither the spare car nor the money for a new one. Getting the R&A had simply been a paperwork approval needed before they could charge the department for gas and mileage on their personal cars. Bosch knew that over time he would probably put so many miles on his SUV that the expense payout would likely cost the department more than the approved car.

"Look," he finally said, "I know what you're thinking even if you're not saying it. It's not just me you're worried about. You stuck your neck out for me and you convinced the chief to take me back in. Believe me, Kiz, I know it's not just me riding on this — on this retread. You don't have to worry and you can tell the chief he doesn't have to worry. I get it. There won't be a blowout. There won't be any blowback from me."

"Good, Harry. I'm glad to hear that."

He tried to think of something that he could say to convince her further. He knew words were just words.

"You know, I don't know if I ever told you this, but after I quit I really sort of liked it at first. You know, being out of the squad and just sort of doing what I wanted. Then I started to miss it and then I started working cases again. On my own. Anyway, one thing that happened was I started walking with sort of a limp."

"A limp?"

"Just a little thing. Like one of my heels was lower than the other. Like I was uneven."

"Well, did you check your shoes?"

"I didn't need to check my shoes. It wasn't my shoes. It was my gun."

He looked over at her. She was staring straight ahead, her eyebrows set in that deep V she used so much with him. He looked back at the road ahead.

"I carried a gun for so long that when I no longer had it on me it threw off my balance. I was uneven."

"Harry, that's a strange story."

They were going through the Cahuenga Pass. Bosch looked out his window and up the hillside, searching for his house nestled in among the others in the folds of the mountain. He thought he saw a glimpse of the back deck sticking out over the brown brush.

"You want to call Garcia and see if we can drop in and see him after we go by probation?" he asked.

"Yeah, I will — as soon as you get to the point of that story."

He thought for a long moment before answering.

"The point is, I need the gun. I need the badge. Otherwise I'm out of balance. I need all of this. Okay?"

He looked over at Rider. She looked back at him but didn't answer.

"I know what I got with this chance. So fuck Irving and his calling me a retread. I won't fuck up."

8

Twenty minutes later they stepped into one of Bosch's least favorite places in the city: the probation and parole office of the state's Department of Corrections in Van Nuys. It was a single-story brick building crowded with people waiting to see probation and parole agents, to give urine samples, to make their court-ordered check-ins, to turn themselves in for incarceration or to plead for one more chance of freedom. It was a place where desperation, humiliation and rage were palpable in the air. It was a place where Bosch tried not to make eye contact with anyone.

Bosch and Rider had something none of the others had: badges. It helped them cut through the lines and get an immediate audience with the agent Roland Mackey had been assigned to after his arrest two years earlier for lewd and lascivious behavior. Thelma Kibble was recessed in a standard government-issue cubicle in a room crowded with many identical cubicles. Her desk and the one government-issue shelf that came with the cubicle were crowded with the files of the convicts she was charged with shepherding through probation or parole. She was of medium size and build. Her eyes were brightly set off against her dark brown skin. Bosch and Rider introduced themselves as detectives from RHD. There was only one chair in front of Kibble's desk so they remained standing.

"Is it robbery or homicide we are talking about here?" Kibble asked.

"Homicide," Rider said.

"Then why doesn't one of you grab the extra chair from that cubicle over there. She's still at lunch."

Bosch took the chair she pointed at and brought it back. Rider and Bosch sat down and told Kibble they wanted a look at the file belonging to Roland Mackey. Bosch could tell that Kibble recognized the name but not the case.

"It was a lewd and lash probation you caught two years ago," he said. "He cleared after twelve months."

"Oh, he's not current, then. Well, I need to go grab that one in archives. I don't remem — oh, yes I do, yes I do. Roland Mackey, yeah. I rather enjoyed that one."

"How so?" Rider asked.

Kibble smiled.

"Let's just say he had some difficulty reporting to a woman of color. Tell you what, though, let me go grab the file so we get the details right."

She double-checked the spelling of Mackey's name with them and left the cubicle.

"That might help," Bosch said.

"What?" Rider asked.

"If he had a problem with her he'll probably have a problem with you. We might be able to use it."

Rider nodded. Bosch saw she was looking at a newspaper article that was tacked to the fiberboard wall of the cubicle. It was yellowed with age. Bosch leaned closer to read it but he was too far away to read anything but the headline.

WOUNDED PAROLE OFFICER
GETS HERO'S WELCOME

"What is it?" he asked Rider.

"I know who this is," Rider said. "She got shot a few years ago. She went to some ex-con's house and somebody shot her. The convict called for help but then split. Something like that. We gave her an award at the BPO. God, she's lost a lot of weight."

Something about the story rang a bell with Bosch, too. He noticed there were two photographs accompanying the story. One was of Thelma Kibble standing in front of the DOC building, a banner welcoming her back hanging from the roof. Rider was right. Kibble looked like she'd dropped eighty pounds since the photo. Bosch suddenly remembered seeing that banner across the front of the building a few years back while one of his cases was in trial at the courthouse across the street. He nodded. Now he remembered.

Then something about the second photo caught his eye and memory. It was a mug shot of a white woman — the ex-convict who lived in the house where Kibble had been shot.

"That's not the shooter, right?" he asked.

"No, she's the one who called it in, who saved her. She disappeared."

Bosch suddenly stood up and leaned across the desk, putting his hands on stacks of files for support. He looked at the mug shot photo. It was a black-and-white shot that had darkened as the newspaper clipping had aged. But Bosch recognized the face in the photo. He was sure of it. The hair and eyes were different. The name underneath the photo was different, too. But he was sure he had encountered the woman in Las Vegas in the past year.

"Those are my files you're messing up."

Bosch immediately pulled himself back across the desk as Kibble came around it.

"Sorry about that. I was just trying to read the story."

"That's old news. Time I took that thing down. A lot of years and a lot of pounds ago."

"I was at the Black Peace Officers meeting when you were honored," Rider said.

"Oh, really?" Kibble said, her face breaking into a smile. "That was a really nice night for me."

"Whatever happened to the woman?" Bosch asked.

"Cassie Black? Oh, she's in the wind. Nobody's seen her since."

"She has charges?"

"The funny thing is, no. I mean, we violated her because she ran, but that's all she's got on her. Hell, she didn't shoot me. All she did was save my life. I wasn't going to have 'em charge her for it. But the parole violation I couldn't do anything about. She split. Far as I know, the guy who shot me might've got her and buried her out in the desert somewhere. I hope not, though. She did me a good turn."

Bosch was suddenly not so sure the woman he had temporarily lived next to in an airport motel while visiting his daughter in Las Vegas the year before had been Cassie Black. He sat down and didn't say anything.

"So you found the file?" Rider said.

"Right here," Kibble said. "You two can have at it. But if you want to ask me about the boy then do it now. My afternoon slate starts in five minutes. If I start late then I have a domino effect running through the whole damn day and I get outta here late. Can't do that tonight. I gotta date."

She was beaming at the prospect of her date.

"Okay, well, what do you remember about Mackey? Did you look at the file?"

"Yeah, I looked when I was coming back with it. Mackey was just a pissant weenie wagger. Small-time drug user who got racial religion somewhere along the way. He was no big thing. I rather enjoyed having him under my thumb. But that was about it."

Rider had opened the file and Bosch was leaning toward her to look into it.

"The lewd and lash was an exposure case?" he asked.

"Actually, I think you'll find in there that our boy got himself high on speed and alcohol — a lot of alcohol — and he decided to relieve himself in somebody's front yard. A thirteen-year-old girl happened to live there and she happened to be out front shooting baskets. Mr. Mackey decided upon seeing the girl that since he already had his little pud out and about in the wind that he might as well go ahead and ask the girl if she wanted to partake of it. Did I mention that the girl's father was LAPD Metro Division and happened to be off-duty and home at the time of this incident? He stepped outside and put Mr. Mackey on the ground. In fact, Mr. Mackey later complained that coincidentally or maybe not so coincidentally he had been put on the ground right on top of the puddle he had just made. He was rather unhappy about that."

Kibble smiled at the story. Bosch nodded. Her version was more colorful than the case summary in the file.

"And he just pleaded out."

"That's right. He got a probation deal and took it. He came to me."

"Any problems during his twelve months?"

"Nothing other than his problem with me. He asked for another agent and it got turned down and he got stuck with me. He kept it in check but it was there. Underneath, you know? Couldn't ever tell which bugged his ass more, me being black or me being a woman."

She looked at Rider as she said this last part and Rider nodded.

The file contained details of Mackey's past crimes and life. It had photos taken during earlier arrests. It would become the baseline resource on their target. There was too much in it to go through in front of Kibble.

"Can we get this copied?" Bosch asked. "We'd also like to borrow one of these early photos if we could."

Kibble's eyes narrowed for a moment.

"You two working an old case, huh?"

Rider nodded.

"From way back," she said.

"Like a cold case, huh?"

"We call it open-unsolved," Rider said.

Kibble nodded thoughtfully.

"Well, nothing surprises me in this place — I've seen people shoplift a frozen pizza and get popped two days before the end of a four-year tail. But from what I remember of this guy Mackey, he didn't seem to me to have the killer instinct. Not if you ask me. He's a follower, not a doer."

"That's a good read," Bosch said. "We're not sure he is the one. We just know he was involved."

He stood up, ready to go.

"What about the photo?" he asked. "A photocopy won't be clear enough to show."

"You can borrow that one as long as I get it back. I need to keep the file complete. People like Mackey have a tendency to come back to me, know what I mean?"

"Yes, and we'll get it back to you. Also, can I get a copy of your story there? I want to read it."

Kibble looked at the newspaper clip tacked to the cubicle's wall.

"Just don't look at the picture. That's the old me."

After clearing the DOC office Rider and Bosch crossed the street to the Van Nuys Civic Center and walked between the two courthouses to get to the plaza in the middle. They sat down on a bench by the library. Their next appointment was with Arturo Garcia in the LAPD's Van Nuys Division, which also was one of the buildings in the government center, but they were early and wanted to study the DOC file first.

The file contained detailed accounts of all the crimes Roland Mackey had been arrested for since his eighteenth birthday. It also contained biographical summaries used by probation and parole agents over the years in determining aspects of his supervision. Rider handed Bosch the arrest reports while she started going through the biographical details. She then immediately proceeded to interrupt his reading of a burglary case by calling out details of Mackey's bio that she thought might be pertinent to the Verloren case.

"He got a general education degree at Chatsworth High the summer of 'eighty-eight," she said. "So that puts him right in Chatsworth."

"If he got a GED, then he dropped out first. Does it say from where?"

"Nothing here. Says he grew up in Chatsworth. Dysfunctional family. Poor student. He lived with his father, a welder at the General Motors plant in Van Nuys. Doesn't sound like Hillside Prep material."

"We still need to check. Parents always want their kid to do better. If he went there and knew her and then dropped out, it would explain why he was never interviewed back in 'eighty-eight."

Rider just nodded. She was reading on.

"This guy never left the Valley," she said. "Every address is in the Valley."

"What's the last known?"

"Panorama City. Same as the AutoTrack hit. But if it's in here, then it's probably old."

Bosch nodded. Anybody who had been through the system as many times as Mackey would know to move house the day after clearing a probation tail. Don't leave an address with the man. Bosch and Rider would go to the Panorama City address to check it out but Bosch knew that Mackey would be gone. Wherever he had moved, he had not used his name on public utility applications and he had not updated his driver's license or vehicle registration. He was flying below radar.

"Says he was in the Wayside Whities," Rider said as she reviewed a report.

"No surprise."

The Wayside Whities was the name of a jail gang that had existed for years in the Wayside Honor Rancho in the northern county. Gangs usually formed along racial lines in the county jails as a means of protection rather than out of racial enmity. It was not unusual to find members of the Nazi-leaning Wayside Whities to secretly be Jewish. Protection was protection. It was a way of belonging to a group and staving off assault from other groups. It was a measure of jail survival. Mackey's membership was only a tenuous connection to Bosch's theory that race possibly played a part in the Verloren case.

"Anything else on that?" he asked.

"Not that I see."

"What about physical description? Any tattoos?"

Rider rifled through the paperwork and pulled out a jail intake form.

"Yeah, tattoos," she said, reading. "He's got his name on one bicep and I guess a girl's name on the other. RaHoWa."

She spelled the name and Bosch started to get the first tingling sense that his theory was coming strongly into play.

"It's not a name," he said. "It's code. Means 'racial holy war.' First two letters of each word. The guy's one of the believers. I think Garcia and Green missed this and it was right there."

He could feel the adrenaline picking up.

"Look at this," Rider said urgently. "He also has the number eighty-eight tattooed on his back. The guy's got a reminder of what he did in 'eighty-eight."

"Sort of," Bosch replied. "It's more code. I worked one of these white power cases once and I remember all the codes. To these guys eighty-eight stands for double H because H is the eighth letter of the alphabet. Eighty-eight equals H-H equals Heil Hitler. They also use one ninety-eight for Sieg Heil. They're pretty clever, aren't they?"

"I still think the year 'eighty-eight might have something to do with this."

"Maybe it does. You got anything in there about employment?"

"Looks like he drives a tow truck. He was driving a tow truck when he stopped to take the leak that got him the lewd and lash last time. This lists three different previous employers — all tow services."

"That's good. That's a start."

"We'll find him."

Bosch looked back down at the arrest report in front of him. It was a burglary from 1990. Mackey had been caught by a police dog in the concessions shop of the Pacific Drive-in Theater. He had broken in after hours, setting off a silent alarm. He had pilfered the cash drawer and filled a plastic bag with two hundred candy bars. His exit was slowed because he decided to turn on the cheese warmer and make himself some nachos. He was still inside the building when a responding officer with a dog sent the animal inside the shop. The report said Mackey was treated for dog bite injuries to the left arm and upper left thigh at County-USC Medical Center before being booked.

The record indicated that Mackey pleaded guilty to breaking and entering, a lesser charge, and was sentenced to time served — sixty-seven days in the Van Nuys jail — and two years probation.

The next report was a violation of that probation for

an assault arrest. Bosch was about to read the report when Rider took the sheaf of photocopies out of his hands.

"It's time to go see Garcia," she said. "His sergeant said if we're late we'll miss him."

She stood up and Bosch followed. They headed toward the Van Nuys Division. The Valley Bureau Command offices were on the third floor.

"In nineteen ninety Mackey was popped for a burglary at the old Pacific Drive-in," Bosch said as they walked.

"Okay."

"It was at Winnetka and Prairie. There's a multiplex there now. That puts it about five or six blocks from where the Verloren weapon was stolen a couple years before. The burglary."

"What do you think?"

"Two burglaries five blocks apart. I think maybe he liked working that area. I think he stole the gun. Or he was with the person who stole it."

Rider nodded and they went up the stairs to the police station lobby and then took the elevator the rest of the way up to Valley Bureau Command. They were on time but still were made to wait. While sitting on a couch Bosch said, "I remember that drive-in. I went there a couple times when I was a kid. The one in Van Nuys, too."

"We had our own on the south side," Rider said.

"They turn it into a multiplex, too?"

"No. It's just a parking lot. They don't put multiplex money down there."

"What about Magic Johnson?"

Bosch knew the former Laker basketball star had invested heavily in the community, including opening movie theaters.

"He's only one man."

"One man is a start, I guess."

A woman with P2 stripes on her uniform's sleeves came up to them.

"The commander will see you now."

9

Commander Arturo Garcia was standing behind his desk waiting as Bosch and Rider were led into his office by the uniformed assistant. Garcia was in uniform, too, and he wore it well and proudly. He had steel gray hair and a matching bottle-brush mustache. He exuded the confidence that the department used to carry and was fighting to recover.

"Detectives, come in, come in," he said. "Sit down here and tell an old homicide dick how it's hanging."

They took the chairs in front of the desk.

"Thank you for seeing us so quickly," Rider said.

Bosch and Rider had decided that she would take the lead with Garcia since she was more familiar with him through her liaison work in the chief's office. Bosch also wasn't sure he would be able to disguise his distaste for Garcia and the mistakes and missteps he and his partner had made on the Verloren investigation.

"Well, when Robbery-Homicide calls, you make the time, right?"

He smiled again.

"We actually work in the Open-Unsolved Unit," Rider said.

Garcia lost his smile and for a moment Bosch thought he saw a flash of pain enter his eyes. Rider had made the appointment through an assistant in the commander's office and had not revealed what case they were working.

"Becky Verloren," the commander said.

Rider nodded.

"How did you know?"

"How did I know? I was the one who called that guy down there, the OIC, and I told him there was DNA on that case and they ought to send it through."

"Detective Pratt?"

"Yeah, Pratt. As soon as that unit was up and operational I called him and said check out Becky Verloren, nineteen eighty-eight. What have you got? You got a match, right?"

Rider nodded.

"We got a very good match."

"Who? I've been waiting seventeen years for this. Somebody from the restaurant, right?"

This gave Bosch pause. In the murder book there were interview summaries from people who worked in Robert Verloren's restaurant but nothing that rose above the routine. Nothing that indicated suspicion or follow-up. Nothing in the investigative summaries that pointed the case toward the restaurant. To now hear one of the original investigators voice a long-held suspicion that the killer had come from that direction was incongruous with what they had spent the morning reading.

"Actually, no," Rider said. "The DNA matches a man named Roland Mackey. He was eighteen at the time of the murder. He was in Chatsworth at the time. We don't think he worked at the restaurant."

Garcia frowned as though he was puzzled or maybe disappointed.

"Does that name mean anything to you?" Rider asked. "We didn't come across it anywhere in the book."

Garcia shook his head.

"I don't place it, but it's been a long time. Who is he?"

"We don't know who he is yet. We're circling him. We're just starting."

"I'm sure I would have remembered the name. His blood was on the gun, right?"

"That's what we got. He's got a history. Burglaries, receiving, drugs. We're thinking he might be good for the burglary when the gun was taken."

"Absolutely," Garcia said, as if his excitement for the idea could make it so.

"We can connect him to the gun, no doubt," Rider said. "But we're looking for the connection to the girl. We thought maybe you'd remember something."

"Have you talked to the mother and father yet?"

"Not yet. You're our first stop."

"That poor family. That was it for them."

"You stayed in touch with the parents?"

"Initially, yeah. As long as I had the case. But once I made lieutenant and went back to patrol I had to give up the case. I kind of lost contact with them after that. It was Muriel mostly — the mother — who I had talked to. The father . . . there was something going on with him. He didn't do well. He left home, they divorced, the whole thing. Lost the restaurant. Last I heard, he was living on the street. He would show up at the house from time to time and ask Muriel for money."

"What made you guess it was somebody from the restaurant when we came in here?"

Garcia shook his head like he was frustrated by reaching for a memory he couldn't quite grasp.

"I don't know," he said. "I can't remember. It was more like a feeling. There was stuff wrong with the case. Something was hinky about it."

"How so?"

"Well, you read the book, I'm sure. She wasn't raped. She was carried up that hill and it was made to look like a suicide. It was done badly. It was really an execution. So we weren't talking about the random intruder. Somebody she

81

knew wanted her dead. And they either went in that house or sent somebody in that house."

"You think it was related to the pregnancy?" Rider asked.

Garcia nodded.

"We thought that was tied in but we could never nail it down."

"MTL — you never figured that one out."

Garcia looked at her, confusion on his face.

"Empty L?"

"No, M-T-L. The initials Rebecca used in her journal. You mentioned it in the formal interview with the parents. 'My true love,' remember?"

"Oh, yeah, the initials. It was like a code. We never knew for sure. We never found out who that was. Are you looking for the journal?"

Bosch nodded and Rider spoke.

"We're looking for everything. The journal, the gun, the whole evidence carton is lost somewhere in the ESB."

Garcia shook his head like a man who had spent a career dealing with the department's frustrations.

"That is not surprising. Par for the course, right?"

"Right."

"Tell you one thing, though. If they find the carton there won't be any journal in it."

"Why?"

"Because I gave it back."

"To the parents?"

"To the mother. Like I said, I made lieutenant and was shipping out, going to South Bureau. Ron Green had already retired. I was passing the case off and I knew that was going to be the end of it. Nobody was going to pay attention to it like we did. So I told Muriel I was leaving and I gave her the journal . . .

"That poor woman. It was like time stood still for her on

that day in July. She became frozen. Couldn't go forward, couldn't go back. I remember I went to see her before I left. This was a year or so after the murder. She had me look at Becky's bedroom. It was untouched. It was exactly the way it was on the night she was taken."

Rider nodded somberly. Garcia said nothing else. Bosch finally cleared his throat, leaned forward and spoke, hitting Garcia with the same question again.

"When we first came in and said we got a DNA match, you guessed it was somebody from the restaurant. Why?"

Bosch looked at Rider to see if she was annoyed that he was entering the questioning. She didn't appear to be.

"I don't know why," Garcia said. "Like I said, I always sort of thought that it might have come from that side of things, because I never felt we nailed everything down over there."

"You're talking about the father?"

Garcia nodded.

"The father was hinky. I don't know if you even say that anymore. But back then the word was hinky."

"How so?" Rider asked. "How was the father hinky?"

Before Garcia could answer the question one of the uniformed adjutants came into the office.

"Commander? They're all in the conference room and ready to start."

"Okay, Sergeant. I'll be there shortly."

After the sergeant left, Garcia looked back at Rider as if he had forgotten the question.

"There is nothing in the murder book that casts any suspicion on the father," Rider said. "Why did you think he was hinky?"

"Oh, I don't really know. Sort of a gut feeling. He never really acted like you would think a father would act, you know? He was too quiet. He never got mad, never yelled — I mean, somebody took his little girl. He never once took Ron or me aside and said, 'I want first shot at the guy when you find him.' I expected that."

As far as Bosch was concerned, everybody was still a suspect, even with the cold hit tying Mackey to the murder weapon. This certainly included Robert Verloren. But he immediately dismissed Garcia's gut instinct based on the father's emotional responses to his daughter's murder. He knew from working hundreds of murders that there was absolutely no way to judge such responses or to build suspicion on them. Bosch had seen every permutation of it and it all meant nothing. One of the biggest criers and screamers he had ever encountered on a case ended up being the killer.

In dismissing Garcia's instinct and suspicion Bosch was also dismissing Garcia. He and Green had made early mistakes but recovered to conduct a by-the-numbers investigation of the murder. The murder book bore this out. But Bosch now guessed that whatever was done well was probably done by Green. He knew he should have suspected as much when he heard that Garcia had given up homicide for management.

"How long did you work homicide?" Bosch asked.

"Three years."

"All in Devonshire Division?"

"That's right."

Bosch quickly did the math. Devonshire would have had a light caseload. He figured that Garcia had worked no more than a couple dozen murders at the most. It wasn't enough experience to do it well. He decided to move on.

"What about your former partner?" he asked. "Did he feel the same way about Robert Verloren?"

"He was willing to give the guy a little more slack than me."

"Are you still in touch with him?"

"Who, the father?"

"No. Green."

"No, he retired way back."

"I know, but are you still in touch?"

Garcia shook his head.

"No, he's dead. He retired up to Humboldt County. He should've left his gun down here. All that time and nothing to do up there."

"He killed himself?"

Garcia nodded.

Bosch looked down at the floor. It wasn't Ron Green's death that struck him. He didn't know Green. It was the loss of the connection to the case. He knew Garcia wasn't going to be much help.

"What about race?" Bosch asked, again stepping on Rider's lead.

"What about it?" Garcia asked. "In this case? I don't see it."

"Interracial couple, biracial kid, the gun came from a burglary where the victim was being harassed on religious lines."

"That's a stretch. You got something with this Mackey character?"

"There might be something."

"Well, we didn't have the luxury of a named suspect to work with. We didn't see any aspect of that with what we had back then."

Garcia said it forcefully and Bosch knew he had touched a nerve. He didn't like to be second-guessed. No detective did. Even an inexperienced one.

"I know it's Monday-morning quarterbacking to start with the guy and go backwards," Rider quickly said. "It's just something we're looking at."

Garcia seemed placated.

"I understand," he said. "Leave no stone unturned."

He stood up.

"Well, Detectives, I hate to rush this. I wish we could kick this around all day. I used to put people in jail. Now I go into meetings about budget and deployment."

That's what you deserve, Bosch thought. He glanced at Rider, wondering if she understood that he had saved her from a similar fate when he talked her into partnering with him in the Open-Unsolved Unit.

"Do me a favor," Garcia said. "When you hook up this guy Mackey, let me know. Maybe I'll come down and look through the window at him. I've been waiting for this one."

"No problem, sir," Rider said, breaking her stare away from Bosch. "We'll do that. If you think of anything else that might help us with this, give me a call. All my numbers are on this."

She stood up, placing a business card down on the table. "I'll do it."

Garcia started to go around his desk to head to his meeting.

"There's something we might need you to do," Bosch said.

Garcia stopped in his tracks and looked at him.

"What is it, Detective? I need to get in that meeting."

"We might try to flush the birds out of the bushes with a newspaper story. It might be good if it came from you. You know, former homicide guy, now a commander, haunted by the old case. He calls Open-Unsolved and gets them to run the DNA through the pipeline. What do you know, they get a cold hit."

Garcia nodded. Bosch could tell it played to his ego perfectly.

"Yeah, it might work. Whatever you want to do. Just call me and we'll set it up. The *Daily News*? I've got connections there. It's the Valley paper."

Bosch nodded.

"Yeah, that's what we were thinking," he said.

"Good. Let me know. I've got to go."

He quickly left the office. Rider and Bosch looked at each other and then followed. Out in the hallway, waiting for the elevator, Rider asked Bosch what he was doing when he asked him about planting the news story.

"He'd be perfect for the story because he doesn't know what he's talking about."

"So, we don't want that. We want to be careful."

"Don't worry. It'll work."

The elevator opened and they got on. No one else was in it. As soon as the door closed Rider was on him.

"Harry, let's get something straight right now. We're either partners or we're not. You should have told me you were going to hit him with that. We should've talked about it first."

Bosch nodded.

"You're right," he said. "We're partners. It won't happen again."

"Good."

The elevator door opened and she stepped out, leaving Bosch behind.

10

Hillside Preparatory School was a structure of Spanish design nestled against the hills of Porter Ranch. Its campus was marked by magnificent green lawns and the daunting rise of mountains behind it. The mountains almost seemed to cradle the school and protect it. Bosch thought it looked like a place that any parent would want their child to go. He thought about his own daughter, just a year away from starting school. He would want her to go to a school that looked like this — on the outside, at least.

He and Rider followed signs that led them to the administration offices. At a front counter Bosch showed his badge and explained that they wanted to see if a student named Roland Mackey had ever attended Hillside. The clerk disappeared into a back office and soon a man emerged. His most notable features were a basketball-sized paunch and thick glasses shaded by bushy eyebrows. Across his forehead his hair left the perfect line of a toupee.

"I'm Gordon Stoddard, principal here at Hillside. Mrs. Atkins told me you are detectives. I'm having her check that name for you. It didn't ring a bell with me and I've been here almost twenty-five years. Do you know exactly when he attended? It might help her with the search."

Bosch was surprised. Stoddard looked like he was in his mid-forties. He must have come to Hillside fresh from his own schooling and never left. Bosch didn't know if that was a testament to what they paid teachers here or Stoddard's own dedication to the place. But from what he knew about teachers private and public, he doubted it was the pay.

"We'd be talking about the eighties, if he went here. That's a long time ago for you to remember."

"Yes, but I have a memory for the students that have come through. Most of them. I haven't been principal for twenty-five years. I was a teacher first. I taught science and then I was dean of the science department."

"Do you remember Rebecca Verloren?" Rider asked.

Stoddard blanched.

"Yes, as a matter of fact I do. I taught her science. Is that what this is about? Have you arrested this boy, Mackey? I mean, I guess he'd be a man now. Is he the one?"

"We don't know that, sir," Bosch said quickly. "We're reviewing the case and his name came up and we need to check on it. That's all."

"Did you see the plaque?" Stoddard asked.

"Excuse me?"

"Outside on the wall in the main hallway. There is a plaque dedicated to Rebecca. The students in her class collected the funds for it and had it made. It is quite nice but of course it is also quite sad. But it does serve its purpose. People around here remember Rebecca Verloren."

"We missed it. We'll look at it on our way out."

"A lot of people still remember her. This school might not pay that well, and most of the faculty might have to work two jobs to make ends meet, but it has a very loyal faculty nonetheless. There are several teachers still here who taught Rebecca. We have one, Mrs. Sable, who was actually a student with her and then returned here to teach. In fact, Bailey was one of her good friends, I believe."

Bosch glanced at Rider, who raised her eyebrows. They

had a plan for approaching Becky Verloren's friends but here was an opportunity presenting itself. Bosch had recognized the name Bailey. One of the three friends Becky Verloren had spent the evening with two nights before her disappearance was named Bailey Koster.

Bosch knew that it was more than an opportunity to question a witness in the case. If they didn't get to Sable now she would likely hear about Roland Mackey from Stoddard. Bosch didn't want that. He wanted to control the flow of information on the case to the players involved in it.

"Is she here today?" Bosch asked. "Could we talk to her?"

Stoddard looked up at the clock on the wall next to the counter.

"Well, she is in class now but school lets out for the day in about twenty minutes. If you don't mind waiting I am sure you could talk to her then."

"That's no problem."

"Good, I will send a message to her classroom and have her come to the office after school."

Mrs. Atkins, the counter clerk, appeared behind Stoddard.

"Actually, if you don't mind," Rider said, "we'd rather go to her classroom to talk to her. We don't want to make her uncomfortable."

Bosch nodded. Rider was on the same frequency. They didn't want a message of any kind going to Mrs. Sable. They didn't want her thinking about Becky Verloren until they were right there watching and listening.

"Either way," Stoddard said. "Whatever you want to do."

He noticed Mrs. Atkins standing behind him and asked her to report her findings.

"We have no record of a Roland Mackey as a student here," she said.

"Did you come across anyone with that last name?" Rider asked.

"Yes, one Mackey, first name Gregory, attended for two years in nineteen ninety-six and -seven."

There was a long-shot possibility that it was a younger brother or a cousin. It might become necessary to check the name out.

"Can you see if there is a current address or contact number for him?" Rider asked.

Mrs. Atkins looked at Stoddard for approval and he nodded. She disappeared to go get the information. Bosch checked the wall clock. They had almost twenty minutes to kill.

"Mr. Stoddard, are there yearbooks from the late eighties that we could look at while we're waiting to see Mrs. Sable?" he asked.

"Yes, of course, I will take you to the library and get those for you."

On the way to the library Stoddard took them by the plaque Rebecca Verloren's classmates had put on the wall of the main hallway. It was a simple dedication with her name, the years of her birth and death and the youthful promise of WE WILL ALWAYS REMEMBER.

"She was a sweet kid," Stoddard said. "Always involved. Her family, too. What a tragedy."

Stoddard used the sleeve of his shirt to wipe the dust off the laminated photograph of the smiling Becky Verloren on the plaque.

The library was around the corner. There were few students at the tables or browsing the shelves as the end of the day drew near. In a whisper Stoddard told them to have a seat at a table and then he went off into the stacks. Less than a minute later he came back with three yearbooks and put them down on the table. Bosch saw that each book had the title *Veritas* and the year on the cover. Stoddard had brought yearbooks from 1986, 1987 and 1988.

"These are the last three years," Stoddard whispered. "I remember she went here from grade one, so if you want earlier books just let me know. They're on the shelf."

Bosch shook his head.

"That's okay. This will be fine for now. We'll come back by the office before we leave. We need to get that information from Mrs. Atkins anyway."

"Okay, then I will leave you to it."

"Oh, can you tell us where Mrs. Sable's classroom is?"

Stoddard gave them the room number and told them how to get there from the library. He then excused himself, saying he was returning to the office. Before leaving he whispered a few words to a table of boys near the door. The boys then reached down to the backpacks they had dropped on the floor and pulled them underneath the table so as to not impede foot traffic. Something about the way they had haphazardly dropped their packs reminded Bosch of the way the boys of Vietnam had done it — where they stood, not caring about anything but getting the weight off their shoulders.

After Stoddard had left, the boys made faces at the door he had passed through.

Rider took the 1988 yearbook ahead of Bosch and he took the 1986 edition. He wasn't expecting to find anything of value now that Mrs. Atkins had knocked down his theory that Roland Mackey had attended the school at one point but had dropped out before the murder. He was already resigned to the idea that the connection between Mackey and Becky Verloren — if it even existed — would be found somewhere else.

He did the math in his head and flipped through the book until he found the eighth grade photos. He quickly found Becky Verloren's picture. She wore pigtails and braces. She was smiling but looked like she was just beginning that period of prepubescent awkwardness. He doubted she had been happy with her appearance in the book. He checked the group photos showing the class's different clubs and organizations and was able to track her extracurricular activities. She played soccer and was seen in the photos for the science and art clubs and the homeroom representatives in student government. In all the photos she was always in the back row or off to the side. Bosch wondered if that was where she had been placed by a photographer or where she had felt comfortable.

Rider was taking her time with the 1988 edition. She was going through every page, at one point holding the book up to Bosch when she was going through the faculty section. She pointed to a photo of a young Gordon Stoddard, who had much longer hair back then and didn't wear glasses. He was leaner and looked stronger as well.

"Look at him," she said. "Nobody should grow old."

"And everybody should get the chance."

Bosch moved on to the 1987 yearbook and found that the photos of Becky Verloren showed a young girl who appeared to be blossoming. Her smile was fuller, more confident. If the braces were still there they were no longer noticeable. In the group photos she had moved to front and center. In the student government photos she was not a class officer yet, but she had her arms folded in a take-charge pose. Her posture and her unflinching stare at the camera told Bosch she was going places. Only somebody had stopped her.

Bosch flipped through a few more pages and then closed the book. He was waiting for the bell to ring so they could go interview Bailey Koster Sable.

"Nothing?" Rider asked.

"Of any value," he said. "It's good to look at her back then, though. In place. In her element."

"Yes. Look at this."

They were sitting across from each other. She turned the 1988 book around on the table so he could see it. She had finally gotten to the sophomore class photos. The top half of the page on the right showed a boy and four girls posing on a wall Bosch recognized as the entrance to the student parking lot. One of the girls was Becky Verloren. The caption above the photo said STUDENT LEADERS. Below the photo the students were identified and their positions listed. Becky Verloren was listed as student council representative. Bailey Koster was class president.

Rider tried to spin the book back toward herself but Bosch held it for a moment, studying the photograph. He could tell by her pose and her style that Becky Verloren had left her teen awkwardness behind. He would not describe the student in the photograph as a girl. She was on her way to becoming an attractive and confident young woman. He let the book go and Rider took it back.

"She was going to be a heartbreaker," he said.

"Maybe she already was. Maybe she picked the wrong one to break."

"Anything else in there?"

"Take a look."

She flipped the open book around again. The two pages were spread with photos from the Art Club's trip to France the summer before. There were photos of about twenty students, boys and girls, and several parents or teachers in front of Notre Dame, in the courtyard of the Louvre and on a tourist boat on the Seine. Rider pointed out Rebecca Verloren in one of the photos.

"She went to France," Bosch said. "What about it?"

"She could have met someone over there. Could be an international link to this thing. We might have to go over there and check it out."

She was trying to hold back a smile.

"Yeah," Bosch said. "You put the req in on that. Send it on up to six."

"Boy, Harry, I guess your sense of humor stayed retired."

"Yeah, I guess so."

The school bell rang, ending the discussion as well as classes for the day. Bosch and Rider got up, leaving the yearbooks on the table, and left the library. They followed Stoddard's directions to Bailey Sable's classroom, along the way dodging students hurrying to leave the school. The girls wore plaid skirts and white blouses, the boys khakis and white polo shirts.

They looked into the open door of room B-6 and saw a woman sitting at a desk at the front center of the classroom. She did not look up from the papers she was apparently grading. Bailey Sable bore almost no resemblance to the sophomore class president whose photo Bosch and Rider had just studied in the yearbook. The hair was darker and shorter now, the body wider and heavier. Like Stoddard, she wore glasses. Bosch knew she was only thirty-two or thirty-three but she looked older.

There was one last student in the room. She was a pretty blonde girl who was shoving books into a backpack. When she was finished she zipped the pack closed and headed to the door.

"See you tomorrow, Mrs. Sable."

"Good-bye, Kaitlyn."

The student gave Bosch and Rider a curious look as she went by them. The detectives stepped into the classroom and Bosch pulled the door closed. That made Bailey Sable look up from her papers.

"Can I help you?" she asked.

Bosch took the lead.

"You might be able to," he said. "Mr. Stoddard said it would be all right if we came to your classroom."

He approached the desk. The teacher looked up at him warily.

"Are you parents?"

"No, we're detectives, Mrs. Sable. My name is Harry Bosch and this is Kizmin Rider. We wanted to ask you a few questions about Becky Verloren."

She reacted as if she had just been punched in the gut. All these years and it was still that close to the surface.

"Oh my God, oh my God," she said.

"We're sorry to hit you with this out of the blue," Bosch said.

"Is something happening? Did you find who . . . ?"

She didn't finish.

"Well, we're working on it again," Bosch said. "And you might be able to help us."

"How?"

Bosch reached into his pocket and pulled out the mug shot taken from Roland Mackey's DOC probation file. It was a portrait of Mackey as an eighteen-year-old car thief. Bosch put it down on top of the paper she had been grading. She looked down at it.

"Do you recognize the person in that photo?" Bosch asked.

"It was taken seventeen years ago," Rider added. "About the time of Becky's death."

The teacher looked down at Mackey's defiant glare into the police camera. She didn't say anything for a long time. Bosch looked at Rider and nodded, a signal that maybe she should take over.

"Does it look like anyone you or Becky or any of your friends may have encountered back then?" Rider asked.

"Did he go to school here?" Sable asked.

"No, we don't think so. But we know he lived in this area."

"Is he the killer?"

"We don't know. We're just trying to see if there is a connection between Becky and him."

"What is his name?"

Rider looked at Bosch and he nodded again.

"His name is Roland Mackey. Does he look familiar?"

"Not really. It is hard for me to remember back then. Remember the faces of strangers, I mean."

"So he definitely is not someone you knew, right?"

"Definitely."

"Do you think Becky could have known him without you being aware of it?"

She thought for a long moment before answering.

"Well, it's possible. You know, it came out that she'd gotten pregnant. I didn't know about that, so I guess I might not have known about him. Was he the father?"

"We don't know."

Unbidden, she had jumped the interview forward to Bosch's next line of questioning.

"Mrs. Sable, you know, it's been a lot of years since then," he said. "If you were sort of sticking up for a friend back then, we understand that. But if there is more you know, you can tell us now. This is probably the last shot that anybody is going to take at solving this thing."

"You mean about her being pregnant? I really didn't know about it. I'm sorry. I was just as shocked as everybody else when the police started asking about that."

"If Becky were going to confide in someone about that, would it have been you?"

Again, she didn't answer right away. She gave it some thought.

"I don't know," she said. "We were very close but she was that way with a few other girls, too. There were four of us who had been together since first grade here. In first grade we called ourselves the Kitty Cat Club because we all had pet cats. At different times and different years one of us would be closer to one of the others. It changed all the time. But as a group we always stuck together."

Bosch nodded.

"That summer when Becky was taken, who would you say was closest to her?"

"It was probably Tara. She took it the hardest."

Bosch looked at Rider, trying to remember the names of the girls Becky had been with two nights before her death.

"Tara Wood?" Rider asked.

"Yes, that's Tara. They hung out together a lot that summer because Becky's dad owned a restaurant in Malibu and they were both working there. They were splitting a schedule there. It seemed that summer that all they did was talk about it."

"What would they say about it?" Rider asked.

"Oh, you know, like what stars came in there. People like Sean Penn and Charlie Sheen. And sometimes they talked about what guys worked there and who was cute. Nothing too interesting to me since I didn't work there."

"Was there any one guy in particular they talked about?"

She thought a moment before answering.

"Not really. Not that I remember. They just liked to talk about them because they were so different. They were surfers and would-be actors. Tara and Becky were Valley girls. It was like a culture clash for them."

"Was she dating anybody from the restaurant?" Bosch asked.

"Not that I knew of. But it's like I said, I didn't know about the pregnancy, so there was obviously somebody in her life I didn't know about. She kept it a secret."

"Were you jealous of them because they worked there?" Rider asked.

"Not at all. I didn't have to work and I was pretty happy about that."

Rider was going somewhere so Bosch let her continue.

"What did you guys do for fun when you got together?" she asked.

"I don't know, the usual," Sable said. "We went shopping and to movies, stuff like that."

"Who had cars?"

"Tara did and so did I. Tara had a convertible. We used to go up . . ."

She cut it off when she came to a memory.

"What?" Rider asked.

"I just remember driving up into Limekiln Canyon a lot after school. Tara had a cooler in the trunk and her dad never noticed if she'd taken some of his beers out of the refrigerator. One time we got pulled over up there by a police car. We hid the beers under our uniform skirts. They worked perfect for that. The policeman didn't notice."

She smiled at the memory.

"Of course, now that I teach here I'm on the watch for that sort of thing. We still have the same uniforms."

"What about before she started working at the restaurant?" Bosch said, drawing the interview back to Rebecca Verloren. "She was sick for a week, right after school let out. Did you visit her or talk to her then?"

"I'm sure I did. That is when they said she probably, you know, ended the pregnancy. So she wasn't really sick. She was just recovering. But I didn't know. I must have just thought she was sick, that's all. I can't really remember if we talked that week or not."

"Did the detectives back then ask you all of these questions?"

"Yes, I'm pretty sure they did."

"Where would a girl from Hillside Prep go if she got pregnant?" Rider asked. "Back then, I mean."

"You mean like a clinic or a doctor?"

"Yes."

Bailey Sable's neck flushed. She was embarrassed by the question. She shook her head.

"I don't know. That was as shocking really as Becky being, you know, killed. It made us all think we didn't really know our friend. It was really sad because I realized she hadn't trusted me enough to tell me these things. You know, I still think about that when I remember things back then."

"Did she have any boyfriends that you did know about?" Bosch asked.

"Not then. I mean, at the time. She had a boyfriend freshman year but he had moved away to Hawaii with his family. That was like the summer before. Then the whole school year I thought she was alone. You know, she didn't go to any of the dances or the games with anybody. But I was wrong, I guess."

"Because of the pregnancy," Rider said.

"Well, yeah. That's sort of obvious, isn't it?"

"Who was the father?" Bosch asked, hoping the direct question might elicit a response with something to pursue.

But Sable shrugged.

"I have no idea, and don't think I've ever stopped wondering."

Bosch nodded. He had gotten nothing.

"The breakup with the boy who moved to Hawaii — how was that with her?" he asked.

"Well, I thought it broke her heart. She took it really hard. It was like Romeo and Juliet."

"How so?"

"They were broken up by the parents."

"You mean they didn't want them going together?"

"No, his dad took a job or something in Hawaii. They had to move and it broke them up."

Bosch nodded again. He didn't know if any of the

information they were getting was useful but he knew it was important to cast as wide a net as possible.

"Do you know where Tara Wood is these days?" he asked.

Sable shook her head.

"We had a ten-year reunion and she didn't come. I lost touch with her. I still talk to Grace Tanaka from time to time. But she lives up in the Bay Area so I don't see her too much."

"Can you give us her number?"

"Sure, I have it here."

She reached down and opened a desk drawer and pulled out her purse. While she was getting out an address book Bosch took the photo of Mackey off the desk and put it back into his pocket. When Sable read off a phone number Rider wrote it down in a small notebook.

"Five ten," Rider said. "What is that, Oakland?"

"She lives in Hayward. She wants to live in San Francisco but it costs too much for what she makes."

"What does she do?"

"She's a metal sculptor."

"Her last name is still Tanaka?"

"Yes. She never married. She . . ."

"What?"

"She turned out to be gay."

"Turned out?"

"Well, what I mean is, we never knew. She never told us. She moved up there and once about eight years ago I went up to visit and then I knew."

"It was obvious?"

"Obvious."

"Did she come to the ten-year high school reunion?"

"Yes, she was there. We had fun, but it was sort of sad, too, because people talked about Becky and how it was never solved. I think that's probably why Tara didn't come.

She didn't want to be reminded of what happened to Becky."

"Well, maybe we'll change that by the twentieth reunion," Bosch said, immediately regretting the flippant remark. "Sorry, that wasn't a nice thing to say."

"Well, I hope you do change it. I think about her all the time. Always wondering who did it and why they have never been found. I look at her picture every day on the plaque when I come into school. It's weird. I helped raise the money for that plaque when I was class president."

"They?" Bosch asked.

"What?"

"You said they have never been found. Why did you say *they*?"

"I don't know. He, she, whatever."

Bosch nodded.

"Mrs. Sable, thanks for your time," he said. "Would you do us a favor and not talk about this with anyone? We don't want people being prepared for us, you know what I mean?"

"Like with me?"

"Exactly. And if you think of anything else, anything at all you want to talk about, my partner will give you a card with our numbers on it."

"Okay."

She seemed to be in a far-off reverie. The detectives said good-bye and left her there with the stack of papers to grade. Bosch thought she was probably remembering a time when four girls were the best of friends and the future sparkled in front of them like an ocean.

Before leaving the school they stopped by the office to see if the school had any current contact information for former student Tara Wood. Gordon Stoddard had Mrs. Atkins check but the answer was no. Bosch asked if they could borrow the 1988 yearbook to make copies of some of the photos and Stoddard gave his approval.

"I'm on my way out," he said. "I'll walk with you."

They small-talked on the way back to the library and Stoddard gave them the yearbook, which had already been returned to the shelves. On the way out to the parking lot Stoddard stopped with them once more in front of the memorial plaque. Bosch ran his fingers over the raised letters of Becky Verloren's name. He noticed that the edges had been worn smooth over the years by many students doing the same thing.

11

Rider worked the file and the phone while Bosch drove toward Panorama City, which was just on the east side of the 405 and across the Devonshire Division line.

Panorama City was a district carved off the north side of Van Nuys many years before when residents there decided they needed to distance themselves from negative connotations ascribed to Van Nuys. Nothing about the place was changed but the name and a few street signs. Still, Panorama City sounded clean and beautiful and crime free, and the residents felt better about themselves. But many years had passed and resident groups had petitioned to rename their neighborhoods again and to distance themselves, if not physically then image-wise, from negative connotations associated with Panorama City. Bosch guessed it was one of the ways Los Angeles kept reinventing itself. Like a writer or actor who keeps changing his name to leave past failings behind and start fresh, even with the same pen or face.

As expected, Roland Mackey was no longer at the auto towing company he had worked for while on his most recent stint of probation. But also as expected, the ex-con was not particularly smart when it came to covering his trail. The probation file contained his entire work history through a life that had largely been spent on probation or parole. He drove a tow truck for two other concerns during past periods of state monitoring. Posing as an acquaintance, Rider called each of them and easily located his current employer: Tampa Towing. She then called the tow service and asked if Mackey was working today. After a moment she closed the phone and looked at Bosch.

"Tampa Towing. He comes on at four."

Bosch checked his watch. Mackey reported for work in ten minutes.

"Let's go by and get a look at him. We'll check his address after. Tampa and what?"

"Tampa and Roscoe. Must be across from the hospital."

"The hospital is Roscoe and Reseda. I wonder why they didn't call it Roscoe Towing."

"Funny. Then what do we do after we get a look at him?"

"Well, we go up to him and ask him if he killed Becky Verloren seventeen years ago and then he says yes and we take him downtown."

"Come on, Bosch."

"I don't know. What do you want to do next?"

"We check his address like you said, and then I think we're ready for the parents. I'm thinking that we need to talk to them about this guy before we set up on him and make a play — especially in the newspaper. I say we go by the house and see the mother. We're already up here. Might as well."

"You mean if she's still there," he said. "Did you run an AutoTrack on her, too?"

"Didn't have to. She'll be there. You heard how Garcia was talking. Her baby's ghost is in that house. I doubt she'll ever leave it."

Bosch guessed that she was right about that but didn't respond. He drove east on Devonshire Boulevard to Tampa Avenue and then dropped down to Roscoe Boulevard. They got to the intersection a few minutes before four. Tampa Towing was actually a Chevron service station with two mechanics' bays. Bosch parked in the lot of a small strip shopping plaza across the street and killed the engine.

Bosch wasn't surprised when four o'clock came and went without any sign of Roland Mackey. He didn't strike Bosch as somebody who would be excited to come to work to tow cars.

At four-fifteen Rider said, "What do you think? You think my call could have —"

"There he is."

A thirty-year-old Camaro with gray primer on all four fenders pulled into the service station and parked near the air pump. Bosch had caught only a glimpse of the driver but it was enough for him to know. He reached over to the glove compartment and took out a pair of field glasses he had bought through an airline catalog he had read while on a flight to Las Vegas.

He slouched down in his seat and watched through the glasses. Mackey got out of the Camaro and walked toward the service station's open garage. He was wearing a uniform of dark blue pants and a lighter blue shirt. There was an oval-shaped patch over the left breast pocket that said *Ro.* He had work gloves sticking out of one of his back pockets.

There was an old Ford Taurus up on a hydraulic lift in the garage and a man working beneath it with an air wrench. When Mackey entered, the man with the wrench nonchalantly reached out and gave him a high five. Mackey stopped while the man told him something.

"I think he's telling him about the phone call," Bosch said. "Mackey doesn't look too concerned about it. He just pulled a cell out of his pocket. He's calling the person he probably thinks called him."

Reading Mackey's lips, Bosch said, "Hey, did you call me?"

Mackey quickly ended the conversation.

"I guess not," Bosch said.

Mackey put his phone back into his pocket.

"He tried one person," Rider said. "Must not have much of a social life."

"The name on the patch on his shirt is Ro," Bosch said. "If his buddy told him that the caller asked for Roland, then he may have narrowed it down to the one person who calls him that. Maybe it was dear old dad, the welder."

"So what's he doing?"

"Can't see him. He went into the back."

"Maybe we should get out of here before he starts looking around."

"Come on. One call and you think he's going to think somebody's onto him after seventeen years?"

"No, not for Becky. I'm worried about whatever else he's into now. We might be stumbling right into the middle of something and not even know it."

Bosch put down the binoculars. She was right about that. He started the car.

"Okay, we got our look," he said. "Let's get out of here. Let's go see Muriel Verloren."

"What about Panorama City?"

"PC can wait. We both know he doesn't live at that address anymore. Checking it is just a formality."

He started backing out of the space.

"Do you think we should call Muriel first?" Rider asked.

"No. Let's just go knock on the door."

"We're good at that."

12

In ten minutes they were in front of the Verloren house. The neighborhood where Becky Verloren had lived still seemed pleasant and safe. Red Mesa Way was wide, with sidewalks on both sides and no shortage of shade trees. Most of the homes were ranch houses that sprawled across the extra-large lots. In the sixties, the larger properties were what drew people to settle the northwest corner of the city. Forty years later the trees were mature and the neighborhood had a cohesive feel to it.

The Verlorens' house was one of the few that had a second floor. It was still the classic ranch-style home but the roof popped up over the double-slot garage. Bosch knew from the murder book that Becky's bedroom had been upstairs over the garage and in the back.

The garage door was closed. There was no apparent sign that anyone was home. They parked in the driveway and went to the front door. When Bosch pushed a doorbell button he could hear a chime echo inside, a single tone that seemed very distant and lonely to him.

The door was answered by a woman who wore a shapeless blue pullover dress that helped hide her own shapeless body. She wore flat sandals. Her hair was dyed a color red that had too much orange in it. It looked like a home job that didn't go as planned, but she either didn't notice or didn't care. As soon as she opened the door a gray cat shot out of the opening and into the front yard.

"Smoke, don't get hit!" she yelled first. Then she said, "Can I help you?"

"Mrs. Verloren?" Rider asked.

"Yes, what is it?"

"We're with the police. We'd like to talk to you about your daughter."

As soon as Rider said the word "police" and before she got to "daughter," Muriel Verloren brought both hands up to her mouth and reacted as though it was the moment she had learned her daughter was dead.

"Oh my God! Oh my God! Tell me you caught him. Tell me you caught the bastard who took my baby away from me."

Rider reached a comforting hand to the woman's shoulder.

"It's not quite that simple, ma'am," Rider said. "Can we come in and talk?"

She stepped back and let them in. She seemed to be whispering something and Bosch thought it might be a prayer. Once they were in she closed the door after yelling a warning one more time into the front yard to the escaped cat.

The home smelled as though the cat had not escaped often enough. The living room to which they were led was neatly kept but with furniture that was old and worn. There was the distinct odor of cat urine in the place. Bosch suddenly wished they had invited Muriel Verloren down to Parker Center for the interview, but knew that would have been a mistake. They needed to see this place.

They sat side by side on the couch and Muriel rushed to one of the chairs across the glass-topped coffee table from them. Bosch noticed paw prints on the glass.

"What is it?" she asked desperately. "Is there news?"

"Well, I guess the news is that we are looking into the

case again," Rider said. "I am Detective Rider and this is Detective Bosch. We work for the Open-Unsolved Unit out of Parker Center."

By agreement while driving to the house Bosch and Rider decided to be cautious with the information they gave members of the Verloren family. Until they knew the family situation it would be better to take rather than to give.

"Is there anything new?" Muriel asked urgently.

"Well, we are just starting out," Rider replied. "We're covering a lot of the old ground right now. Trying to get up to speed. We just wanted to come by and tell you we were working the case again."

She seemed a bit crestfallen. She had apparently thought that for the police to show up after so many years there would have to be something new. Bosch felt a twinge of guilt over withholding the fact that they had a rock-solid DNA lead — a cold hit — to work with, but at the moment he felt that it was for the best.

"There are a couple things," he said, speaking for the first time. "First, in looking through the files on the case, we came across this photo."

He took the photo of Roland Mackey as an eighteen-year-old out of his pocket and put it down on the coffee table in front of Muriel. She immediately leaned down to look at it.

"We're not sure what the connection is," he continued. "We thought maybe you might recognize this man and tell us if you knew him back then."

She continued to look without responding.

"This is a photo from nineteen eighty-eight," Bosch said as a means of prompting her.

"Who is he?" she finally asked.

"We're not sure. His name is Roland Mackey. He's got a small-time record for crimes committed after your daughter's death. We're not sure why his photo was in the file. Do you recognize him?"

"Did you ask Art or Ron about it?"

Bosch started to ask who Art and Ron were when he realized.

"Actually, Detective Green retired and passed away a long time ago. Detective Garcia is Commander Garcia now. We talked to him but he wasn't able to help us with Mackey. How about you? Could he have been one of your daughter's acquaintances? Do you recognize him?"

"He could have been. There is something about him that I recognize."

Bosch nodded.

"Do you know how you recognize him or from where?"

"No, I don't remember. Why don't you tell me and maybe that will help jog my memory."

Bosch made a quick side glance at Rider. This was not totally unexpected, but it always complicated things when the parent of a victim was so eager to help that he or she simply asked what it was the police wanted them to say. Muriel Verloren had waited seventeen years for her daughter's killer to be brought forward into the light of the justice system. It was very clear that she was going to carefully choose answers that would in no way hinder the possibility of that happening. At this point it might not even matter if it was a false light. The past years had been cruel to her and the memory of her daughter. Someone still needed to pay.

"We can't tell you that because we don't know, Mrs. Verloren," Bosch said. "Think about it and let us know if you remember him."

She nodded sadly, as if she thought it was yet another missed opportunity.

"Mrs. Verloren, what do you do for a living?" Rider asked.

It seemed to bring the woman in front of them back from her memories and desires.

"I sell things," she said matter-of-factly. "Online."

They waited for further explanation and didn't get any.

"Really?" Rider asked. "What things do you sell?"

"Whatever I can find. I go to yard sales. I find things. Books, toys, clothes. People will buy anything. And they'll pay anything. This morning I sold two napkin rings for fifty dollars. They were very old."

"We want to ask your husband about the photo," Bosch said then. "Do you know where we could find him?"

She shook her head.

"Somewhere down there in toyland. I haven't heard from him in a long, long time."

A somber moment of silence passed by. Most of the homeless missions in downtown Los Angeles were clustered at the edge of the Toy District, several blocks of toy manufacturers and wholesalers, even a few retailers. It wasn't unusual to find homeless people sleeping in the doorways of toy stores.

What Muriel Verloren was telling them was that her husband was lost in the world of floating human debris. He had descended from restaurateur to the stars to a homeless existence on the streets. But there was a contradiction there. He still had a home here. He just couldn't stay because of what had happened. Yet his wife would never leave.

"When were you divorced?" Rider asked.

"We never did get a divorce. I guess I always thought Robert would wake up and realize that no matter how far you run you can't get away from what happened to us. I thought he would realize that and come home. It hasn't happened yet."

"Do you think you knew all of your daughter's friends?" Bosch asked.

Muriel thought about this one for a long moment.

"Until the morning she disappeared I did. But then we learned things. She kept secrets. I think that is one of the things that bothers me most. Not that she kept secrets from us, but that she thought she had to. I think that maybe if she had come to us things would have been different."

"You mean the pregnancy?"

Muriel nodded.

"What makes you think that played into what happened to her?"

"Just a mother's instinct. I have no proof. I just think it started with that."

Bosch nodded. But he couldn't blame the daughter for her secrets. By the time he had been her age Bosch had been on his own, without real parents. He had no idea what that relationship would have been like.

"We spoke to Commander Garcia," Rider said. "He told us that several years ago he returned your daughter's journal to you. Do you still have that?"

Muriel looked alarmed.

"I read part of it every night. You're not going to take that away from me are you? It's my bible!"

"We need to borrow it and make a copy of it. Commander Garcia should have made a copy back then but he didn't."

"I don't want to lose it."

"You won't, Mrs. Verloren. I promise. We'll copy it and get it right back to you."

"Do you want it now? It's by my bed."

"Yes, if you could get it."

Muriel Verloren left them and disappeared down a hallway that led toward the left side of the house. Bosch looked at Rider and raised his eyebrows in a what-do-you-think sort of way. Rider shrugged, meaning that they would talk about it later.

"Once my daughter wanted to get another cat," Bosch whispered. "My ex said no, one was enough. Now I know why."

Rider was smiling inappropriately when Muriel came back in, carrying a small book with a flowery cover and the words *My Journal* embossed in gold on it. The gold was flaking off. The book had been handled a lot. She gave it to Rider, who went out of her way to handle it reverently.

"If you don't mind, Mrs. Verloren, we'd like to look around," Bosch said. "To sort of connect what we've seen and read in the book with the actual layout of the house."

"What book?"

"Oh, I'm sorry. That's copspeak. All the investigative records from the case are kept in a large binder. We call it a book."

"A murder book?"

"Yes, that's right. Is it all right if we look around? I would like to look at the back door and look around out back, too."

She signaled with a raised arm which way they should go. Bosch and Rider got up.

"It's changed," Muriel said. "It used to be there were no houses up there. You'd go out our door and walk straight up the mountain. But they terraced it. Now there are houses. Millions of dollars. They built a mansion on the spot where my baby was found. I hate it."

There was nothing to say to that. Bosch just nodded and followed her down a short hallway and into the kitchen. There was a door with a glass window in it. It led to the backyard. Muriel unlocked the door and they all stepped out. The yard was on a steep incline that led to a grove of eucalyptus trees. Through the trees Bosch could see the Spanish-tiled roofline of a large house.

"It used to be all open up there," Muriel said. "Just trees. Now there are houses. It's got a gate. They don't let me walk up there like I used to. They think I'm a bag lady or something because I liked to go up there sometimes and have a picnic at Becky's spot."

Bosch nodded and thought for a moment about a mother having a picnic at the spot where her daughter was murdered. He tried to drop the idea and instead study the terrain of the hillside. The autopsy had said Becky Verloren weighed ninety-six pounds. Even as light as that, it would have been a struggle taking her up that incline. He wondered about the possibility that there had been more than one killer. He thought of Bailey Sable saying *they*.

He looked at Muriel Verloren, who was standing still and silent, her eyes closed. She had canted her head so that the late afternoon sun warmed her face. Bosch wondered if this was some form of communion with her lost daughter. As if sensing that they were looking at her, she spoke, keeping her eyes closed.

"I love this place. I'll never leave."

"Can we look at your daughter's bedroom?" Bosch asked.

She opened her eyes.

"Just wipe your feet when we go back inside."

She led them back through the kitchen and into the hallway. The stairway up began next to the door that led to the garage. The door was open and Bosch caught a glimpse of a battered minivan surrounded by stacks of boxes and things Muriel Verloren had apparently collected on her rounds. He also noted how close the door to the garage was to the stairs. He didn't know whether this meant anything. But he recalled the summary report in the murder book that suggested the killer had hidden somewhere in the house and waited for the family to go to sleep. The garage was the likely place.

The stairway was narrow because there were boxes of

yard sale purchases lining one side all the way up. Rider went first. Muriel signaled for Bosch to go next and when he passed by her she whispered to him.

"Do you have children?"

He nodded, knowing his answer would hurt.

"A daughter."

She nodded back.

"Never let her out of your sight."

Bosch didn't tell her that she lived with her mother far out of his sight. He just nodded and started up the stairs.

On the second floor there was a landing and two bedrooms with a bathroom in between them. Becky Verloren's bedroom was to the rear, with windows that looked up the hillside.

The door was closed and Muriel opened it. When they stepped inside they stepped into a time warp. The room was unchanged from the seventeen-year-old photos Bosch had studied in the murder book. The rest of the house was crowded with junk and the detritus from a disintegrated life, but the room where Becky Verloren had slept and talked on the phone and written in her secret journal was unchanged. It had now been preserved longer than the girl had actually lived.

Bosch stepped further into the room and looked around silently. Even the cat didn't intrude here. The air smelled clean and fresh.

"This is just how it was on the morning she was gone," Muriel said. "Except I made the bed."

Bosch looked at the quilt with the cats on it. It flowed over the edges and draped down to the bed skirt, which flowed neatly to the floor.

"You and your husband were sleeping on the other side of the house, right?" Bosch asked.

"Yes. Rebecca was at that age where she wanted her privacy. There are two bedrooms downstairs, on the other side of the house. Her first bedroom was down there. But when she was fourteen she moved up here."

Bosch nodded and looked around before asking anything else.

"How often do you come up here, Mrs. Verloren?" Rider asked.

"Every single day. Sometimes when I can't sleep — which is a lot of the time — I come in here and lie down. I don't get under the covers, though. I want it to be her bed."

Bosch realized he was nodding again, as if what she had said made some sort of sense to him. He stepped over to the vanity. There were photos slid into the frame of the mirror. Bosch recognized a young Bailey Sable in one of them. There was also a photo of Becky by herself in front of the Eiffel Tower. She was wearing a black beret. None of the other kids from the Art Club trip were present.

Also on the mirror was a photo of a boy with Becky. It looked like they were on a ride at Disneyland, or maybe just down at the Santa Monica pier.

"Who is this?" he asked.

Muriel came over and looked.

"The boy? That's Danny Kotchof. Her first boyfriend."

Bosch nodded. The boy who had moved to Hawaii.

"When he moved away it just broke her heart," Muriel added.

"When exactly was that?"

"The summer before, in June. Right after her freshman year and his sophomore. He was a year older."

"Why did the family move, do you know?"

"Danny's dad worked for a rent-a-car company and he got transferred to a new franchise in Maui. It was a promotion."

Bosch glanced at Rider to see if she picked up on the significance of the information Muriel had just given them.

Rider subtly shook her head once. She didn't get it. But Bosch wanted to pursue it.

"Did Danny go to Hillside Prep?" he asked.

"Yes, that's where they met," Muriel said.

Bosch looked down at the vanity and noticed a cheap souvenir snow globe with the Eiffel Tower in it. Some of the water had evaporated, leaving a bubble in the top of the globe and the tip of the tower poking from the water into the air pocket.

"Was Danny in the Art Club?" he asked. "Did he make the trip to Paris with her?"

"No, they moved away before," Muriel said. "He left in June and the club went to Paris the last week of August."

"Did she ever see or hear from Danny again?" he asked.

"Oh, yes, they sent letters back and forth and there were phone calls. At first they phoned back and forth, but it got too expensive. And then Danny did all the calling. Every night before bedtime. That lasted almost right up until . . . until she was gone."

Bosch reached up and removed the photo from the mirror's border. He looked closely at Danny Kotchof.

"What happened when your daughter was taken? How did Danny find out? How did he react?"

"Well . . . we called there and told his father so that he could sit Danny down and tell him the bad news. We were told he did not take it well. Who would?"

"The father told Danny. Did either you or your husband talk directly to Danny?"

"No, but Danny wrote me a long letter about Becky and how much she meant to him. It was very sad and very sweet. Everything was."

"I'm sure it was. Did he come to the funeral?"

"No, no he didn't. His, uh, his parents thought it best for him if he stayed there in the islands. The trauma, you know? Mr. Kotchof called and said he wouldn't be coming."

Bosch nodded. He turned from the mirror, sliding the photo into his pocket. Muriel didn't notice.

"What about after?" he asked. "After the letter, I mean. Did he ever contact you? Maybe call and talk to you?"

"No, I don't think we ever heard from him. Not since the letter."

"Do you still have that letter?" Rider asked.

"Of course. I kept everything. I have a drawer full of letters we got about Rebecca. She was a well-loved girl."

"We need to borrow that letter from you, Mrs. Verloren," Bosch said. "We also might need to look through the whole drawer at some point."

"Why?"

"Because you never know," Bosch said.

"Because we want to leave no stone unturned," Rider added. "We know this is disruptive but please remember what we are doing. We want to find the person who did this to your daughter. It has been a long time but that doesn't mean anybody should get away with it."

Muriel Verloren nodded. She had absentmindedly picked up a small decorative pillow off the bed and was clutching it with both hands in front of her chest. It looked like it might have been made by her daughter many years ago. It was a small blue square with a red felt heart sewn across its middle. Holding it made Muriel Verloren look like a target.

13

While Bosch drove, Rider read the letter Danny Kotchof had sent to the Verlorens after Becky's murder. It was a single page, filled mostly with his fond memories of their lost daughter.

"'All I can tell you is that I am so sorry this had to happen. I will miss her always. Love, Danny.' And that's it."

"What's the postmark on it?"

She flipped over the envelope and looked at it.

"Maui, July twenty-ninth, nineteen eighty-eight."

"Sure took his time writing it."

"Maybe it was hard for him. Why are you keying on him, Harry?"

"I'm not. It's just that Garcia and Green relied on a phone call to clear him. You remember what it said in the book? It said the kid's supervisor said he was washing cars at the rent-a-car agency the day of and the day after. No time to fly to L.A., kill Becky, and get back home in time for work."

"Yeah, so?"

"Well, now we find out from Muriel that his old man ran a rent-a-car. There was nothing about that in the murder book. Did Garcia and Green know that? How much you want to bet that dad was running the place where the son washed cars? How much you want to bet that the supervisor who alibied the son was working for the father?"

"Man, I was kidding about going to Paris. Sounds like you're jonesing for a trip to Maui."

"I just don't like sloppy work. It leaves loose ends. We have to talk to Danny Kotchof and clear him ourselves. If that's even possible after so many years."

"AutoTrack, baby."

"That might find him for us. It won't clear him."

"Even if we knock down his alibi, what are you saying, that this sixteen-year-old kid snuck over here from Hawaii, knocked off his old girlfriend and then went back without anybody seeing him?"

"Maybe it wasn't planned like that. And he was seventeen — Muriel said he was a year older."

"Oh, seventeen," she said sarcastically, as if that made all the difference in the world.

"When I was eighteen I got a leave from Vietnam to Hawaii. You were not allowed to go stateside from there. Once I got there I changed clothes, bought a civilian-looking suitcase and walked right by the MPs to get on a plane to L.A. I think a seventeen-year-old could have done it."

"Okay, Harry."

"Look, all I'm saying is that it was sloppy work. According to the murder book, Green and Garcia cleared this guy with a phone call. There's nothing in there about checking airlines and now it's too late. It bugs me."

"I understand. But just remember. We have a logic triangle we have to complete. We can connect Danny to Becky easy enough, and the gun connects Becky to Mackey. But what connects Danny to Mackey?"

Bosch nodded. It was a good point. But it didn't make him feel any better about Danny Kotchof.

"Another thing is what he wrote in that letter," he said. "He said he was sorry that it had to happen. *Had* to happen — what does that mean?"

"It's just a figure of speech, Harry. You can't build a case on it."

"I'm not talking about building a case on it. I just wonder why he chose to say it that way."

"If he's still alive, we'll find him and you'll get to ask him."

They had crossed under the 405 and were in Panorama City. Bosch dropped the discussion of Danny Kotchof and Rider brought up Muriel Verloren.

"She's frozen solid," Rider said.

"Yeah."

"It's pitiful. There was no reason for them to take the daughter up the hill. They might as well have killed everybody in the house. They did anyway."

Bosch thought that was a harsh way of looking at it but didn't say anything.

"Them?" he asked instead.

"What?"

"You said there was no reason for *them* to take the daughter up the hill. You sound like Bailey Sable."

"I don't know. Looking at that hill. It would have been tough for one person. It's steep back there."

"Yeah. I was thinking the same thing. Two people."

"Your idea about spooking Mackey is getting better. If he was there, he could lead us to the other — whether it's Kotchof or somebody else."

Bosch turned south on Van Nuys Boulevard and stopped in front of an aging apartment complex that covered half the block. It was called the Panorama View Suites. There was a sign that said RENTAL OFFICE to the left of the glass doors of the lobby. It also announced that units were available on a monthly and weekly basis. Bosch put the transmission into park.

"Besides Kotchof, what else were you thinking, Harry?"

"I was thinking that I want to track down and talk to the

other two friends. Maybe you can take the lesbian. But the father is my priority — if we can find him."

"Okay, you take the father and I'll take the lesbian. Maybe I'll get to go up to San Francisco."

"It's Hayward. And if you need help I know an inspector up there who will track her down and save L.A. the cost of the trip."

"You are really no fun, Harry. I'd like to hang out with the northern sisters."

"Did the chief know about you?"

"Not at first. When he found out he didn't care."

Bosch nodded. He liked the chief for that.

"What else?" Rider asked.

"Sam Weiss."

"Who is that?"

"The burglary victim. The one whose gun was used to kill the girl."

"Why him?"

"They didn't have Roland Mackey back then. Might be worth running the name by him."

"Check."

"After that I think we'll be ready to make the play with Mackey, see how he reacts."

"Then let's get this over with and then go talk to Pratt."

They cracked the doors at the same time and got out. As Bosch came around the SUV he could feel her looking at him, studying him.

"What?" he asked.

"There's something else."

"What do you mean?"

"With you. When you get that little crease on your left eyebrow I know something's going on."

"My ex-wife always told me I'd make a bad poker player. Too many tells."

"Well, what is it?"

"I don't know yet. Something about that room."

"Back at the house? Her bedroom? You mean like it was creepy her keeping it like that?"

"No, actually, her keeping it was okay with me. I think I get that. It's something else. Something wrong, something different. I'll grind it out and let you know when I know."

"Okay, Harry, that's what you're good at."

They went through the glass doors into the Panorama View Suites. In ten minutes they confirmed what they knew going in; that Mackey had moved out soon after he had completed his probation.

As expected, he'd left no forwarding address.

14

Abel Pratt was behind his desk eating a concoction of yogurt and cornflakes out of a plastic tub. He made both a sucking and crackling sound as he ate and it was getting on Bosch's nerves. They had been sitting with him for twenty minutes, updating him on the day's progress on the cold hit.

"Shit, I'm still hungry," he said after finishing the last spoonful.

"What is that, the South Beach diet?" Rider asked.

"No, just my own thing. What I need, though, is the South Bureau diet."

"Really? And what is the South Bureau diet?"

Bosch could feel Rider tense. The South Bureau encompassed the majority of the city's black community. She had to wonder if what Pratt had just said was some sort of backhanded racial comment. Bosch had often seen in the department the elevation of the us versus them ethic to the point that white cops would make racially tinged comments in front of black or Latino cops simply because they believed that within the rank and file, the color blue superseded skin color. Rider was about to find out if Pratt was one of these cops.

"Put down your antenna," Pratt said. "All I'm saying is that I worked in South for ten years and I never had to worry about my weight. You're always on the run down there. Then I got to RHD and gained fifteen pounds in two years. It's sad."

Rider relaxed and so did Bosch.

"Get off your ass and knock on doors," Bosch said. "That was the rule in Hollywood."

"Good rule," Pratt said. "Except it's hard when they put you in charge. I have to sit in here and hear about how you guys get to knock on doors."

"But you get the big bucks," Rider said.

"Oh, yeah."

This was a joke because as a supervisor Pratt could not pull overtime. But those on his squad could, thereby setting up the possibility that some of his detectives would make more than him, even though he was the unit boss.

Pratt turned in his chair and opened a cooler on the floor beside him. He took out another tub of yogurt.

"Fuck it," he said as he straightened up and opened it.

He didn't add cornflakes this time. Bosch only had to put up with the slurping as he started spooning the white gunk into his mouth.

"Okay, back to this," Pratt said, his mouth full of it. "What you are telling me is that at the end of the day you can tie the gun to this mope Mackey. He fired this weapon. But you've got nobody who ties him to the victim yet and therefore you cannot tie him to the fatal shot."

"That and other things," Rider said.

"So if I was a defense lawyer," Pratt continued, "I would have Mackey cop to the burglary because the statute of limitations has long expired. He would say the gun bit him when he tried it out so he got rid of the damn thing — long before any murder. He'd say, 'No sir I didn't kill that little girl with it and you can't prove I did. You can't prove I ever laid eyes on her.'"

Rider and Bosch nodded.

"So you got nothing."

They nodded again.

"Not bad for a day's work. What do you want to do about it?"

"We want a wiretap," Bosch said. "Two, maybe three locations. One on his cell, one on the phone at the gas station. And then one on his home once we find it and if he's got a line there. We plant a story in the paper that says we're working the case again and make sure he sees it. Then we see if he talks about it with anybody."

"And what makes you think he would talk to someone else about a murder he may or may not have committed seventeen years ago?"

"Because, like we said, so far we can't connect this guy to the girl in any way. So we're thinking there is somebody in the middle in this thing. Mackey either did this for somebody or he got the gun for that somebody to do it himself."

"There is a third possibility," Rider added. "That he helped. That girl was carried up a steep hillside. It was either somebody big or somebody with help."

Pratt took two spoonfuls of yogurt, frowning as he looked down into the tub, before responding.

"Okay, what about the newspaper? You going to be able to make a plant?"

"We think so," Rider said. "We're going to use Commander Garcia of Valley Bureau. He was on the case originally. Haunted by the one that got away, that sort of pitch. He says he's got a connection at the *Daily News.*"

"Okay, sounds like a plan. Write up the warrants and give them to me. The captain has to approve them and then they go to the DA's office for approval before going to the judge. It's going to take some time. Once we get a judge to okay it we'll take the other teams off what they're doing and put them on the wire while you watch our guy."

Bosch and Rider stood up at the same time. Bosch felt a little charge of adrenaline drop into his blood.

"There's no chance this guy Mackey is into something right now, is there?" Pratt asked.

"What do you mean?" Bosch asked.

"It's just that if we could make a case that he was about to commit a crime we could probably expedite the warrants."

Bosch thought about this.

"We don't have that now," he said. "But we could work on it."

"Good. That would help."

15

Rider was the writer. She had an ease with the computer as well as the language of law. Bosch had seen her put these skills to use on several previous investigations. So their decision was unspoken. She would write the warrants seeking court authorization to trace and listen to calls made by or to Roland Mackey on his cell phone, the office phone at the service station where he worked, and his home if an additional phone existed there. It would be painstaking work; she had to lay out the case against Mackey, making sure the chain of logic and probable cause had no weak links. Her paper case had to first convince Pratt, then Captain Norona, then a deputy district attorney charged with making sure local law enforcement did not run roughshod over civil liberties, and finally a judge who had the same responsibilities but also answered to the electorate should he make a mistake that blew up in his face. They had one shot at this and they had to do it right. Rather, Rider had to do it right.

But all of that came after the initial hurdle of getting Mackey's various phone numbers without tipping the suspect to the investigation taking form around him.

They started with Tampa Towing, which ran a half-page ad in the yellow pages that carried two 24-hour phone numbers. Next, a call to directory assistance established that Mackey had no hardwired phone listing private or otherwise in his name. It meant he either had no phone at his home or he was living in a place where the phone was registered to someone else. That could be dealt with later once they established Mackey's residence.

Last and most difficult was Mackey's cell phone number. Directory assistance did not carry cell listings. To check every cellular service provider for a listing could take days if not weeks because most required a court-ordered search warrant before revealing a customer's private number. Instead, law enforcement investigators routinely planned ruses in order to get the numbers they needed. This often entailed leaving innocuous messages at workplaces so that the cell phone number could be captured upon callback. The most popular of these was the standard call-back-for-your-prize message, promising a television or DVD player to the first one hundred people who returned the call. However, this involved setting up a non-police line and could also result in long waiting periods with no guarantee of success if the target had masked his or her cell number. Rider and Bosch did not feel they had the luxury of time. They had put Mackey's name out into the public. They had to move quickly toward their goal.

"Don't worry," Bosch told Rider. "I've got a plan."

"Then I'll just sit back and watch the master."

Since he knew Mackey was on duty at the service station Bosch simply called the station and said he needed a tow. He was told to hold on and then a voice he believed belonged to Roland Mackey came onto the line.

"You need a tow?"

"Either a tow or a jump. I can't get it started."

"Where?"

"The Albertson's parking lot on Topanga near Devonshire."

"We're all the way over on Tampa. You can get somebody closer."

"I know but I live by you guys. Right off Roscoe and behind the hospital."

"Okay, then. What are you driving?"

Bosch thought of the car they had seen Mackey in earlier. He decided to use it to pull Mackey off the fence.

"Seventy-two Camaro."

"Restored?"

"I'm working on it."

"It should be about fifteen minutes before I'm there."

"Okay, great. What's your name?"

"Ro."

"Ro? Like row a boat?"

"Like in Roland, man. I'm on my way."

He hung up. Bosch and Rider waited five minutes, during which Bosch told her the rest of the plan and what part she would play in it. Her goal was to get two things: Mackey's cell number and his service provider so that a search warrant authorizing the wiretap could be delivered to the proper company.

Following Bosch's instructions, Rider called the Chevron station and started making a service appointment, going into great detail in describing the screeching her car's brakes made. While she was in the middle of it, Bosch called the station on the second line listed in the phone book. As expected Rider was put on hold. Bosch's call was answered and he said, "Do you have a number I can reach Ro on? He's coming here to give me a jump and I got it started already."

Mackey's harried co-worker said, "Try him on his cell."

He gave Bosch the number and Bosch flashed the thumbs-up across the desk to Rider. She finished her call without breaking the act and hung up.

"One down, one to go," Bosch said.

"You got the easy one," Rider said.

With Mackey's number in hand, Rider took over while

Bosch listened on an extension. Putting a disinterested bureaucratic glaze over her voice she called the number and when Mackey answered — presumably while looking for a stalled '72 Camaro in a shopping center parking lot — she announced that she was his AT&T Wireless provider and that she had some exciting news for savings over his current long-distance minutes plan.

"Bullshit," Mackey said, interrupting her in the middle of her spiel.

"Excuse me, sir?" Rider replied.

"I said bullshit. This is some sort of scam to make me switch."

"I don't understand, sir. I have you listed as an AT&T Wireless customer. Is that not the case?"

"Yeah, that's not the fucking case. I'm with Sprint and I like it and I don't even have or want long-distance service. So fuck off. Can you hear me now?"

He hung up and Rider started laughing.

"This is an angry guy we're dealing with," she said.

"Well, he just drove all the way across Chatsworth for nothing," Bosch said. "I'd be angry too."

"He's with Sprint," she said. "I'm ready to rock and roll on the paper. But maybe you should call him, so he won't be suspicious about you not calling when the guy in the shop tells him he gave out his number."

Bosch nodded and called Mackey's number. Thankfully it went to a message; Mackey was probably on the phone angrily telling the guy in the shop he could not find the car he was supposed to tow. Bosch left a message saying he was sorry but he was able to get his car started and was trying to get it home. He closed his phone and looked at Rider.

They talked some more about scheduling and decided that she would work exclusively on the warrant that night and the next day and then babysit it through the approval stages. She said she wanted Bosch with her when it got to the final approval. Having both members of the team in the judge's chambers would help cement the deal. Until then, Bosch would continue to work the field, tracking the remaining names on their list of people to be interviewed and putting the newspaper story in motion. Timing was going to be the issue. They didn't want a story about the case in the newspaper until they had taps in place on the phones Mackey used. Finessing all of this would be the key maneuver.

"I'm going home, Harry," Rider said. "I can get this started on my laptop."

"Have a good one."

"What will you do?"

"I've got a few things I want to get done tonight. Maybe go down to the Toy District, I think."

"By yourself?"

"They're only homeless people."

"Yeah, and eighty percent of them are homeless because they've got faulty wiring, faulty plumbing, the whole bit. You be careful. Maybe you ought to call Central Division and see if they'll send a car with you. Maybe they can spare the U-boat tonight."

The U-boat was a single-officer car primarily used as a gopher for the watch commander. But Bosch didn't think he needed a chaperone. He told Rider he would be all right and that she could go as soon as she showed him how to use the AutoTrack computer.

"Well, Harry, first you have to have a computer. I did it right from my laptop."

He came around to her side and watched as she went to the AutoTrack website, entered password information and arrived at a template for a name search.

"Who do you want to start with?" she asked.

"How about Robert Verloren?"

She typed in the name and set parameters for the search.

"How fast does this work?" Bosch asked.

"Fast."

In a few minutes she had located an address trail for Rebecca Verloren's father. But it stopped short at the house in Chatsworth. Robert Verloren had not updated his driver's license, bought property, registered to vote, applied for a credit card or had a utilities account in over ten years. He was a blank. He had disappeared — at least from the electronic grid.

"He must still be on the street," Rider said.

"If he's even still alive."

Rider put the names Tara Wood and Daniel Kotchof through the AutoTrack moves and came up with multiple name hits for both of them. But by using their approximate ages and focusing on Hawaii and California they narrowed the searches to two address trails they believed belonged to the correct Tara Wood and Daniel Kotchof. Wood may not have gone to her high school reunion but it wasn't because she had moved far away. She had only moved from the Valley over the hills to Santa Monica. Meanwhile, it appeared that Daniel Kotchof had returned from Hawaii many years earlier, lived in Venice for a few years and then returned to Maui, where his current address was located.

The last name Bosch gave Rider to run through the computer was Sam Weiss, the burglary victim whose gun was used to murder Rebecca Verloren. Though there were hundreds of hits on the name, it was easy to find the right Sam Weiss. He had never left the home where the burglary had taken place. He even had the same phone number. He had stood his ground.

Rider printed everything out for Bosch and also gave him the number for Grace Tanaka, which they had gotten earlier from Bailey Sable. She then gathered what she would need to work on the search warrant at home.

"If you need me give me a page," she said as she put her computer into a padded case.

After she was gone Bosch checked the clock over Pratt's door and saw it was just past six. He decided he would spend an hour or so chasing names before heading down to the Toy District to look for Robert Verloren. He knew he was just procrastinating over a search through the human throwaway zone that would be certain to leave him depressed. So he checked the clock again and promised himself he would spend no more than an hour working the phone.

He decided to go with the locals first but quickly struck out. Calls to both Tara Wood and Sam Weiss went unanswered and connected him with automated message systems. He left a message for Wood identifying himself, giving his cell phone number and mentioning that the call was in regard to Becky Verloren. He hoped that mentioning her friend's name would be enough to intrigue and draw a response from her. With Weiss he only left his name and number, not wanting to forewarn him that the call was about what might be a source of guilt for the man who had indirectly provided the weapon that killed a sixteen-year-old girl.

Next he called Grace Tanaka's number in Hayward and she answered after six rings. From the start she seemed put out by the call, as if it had interrupted something important, but her gruff manner and voice softened as soon as Bosch said he was calling about Rebecca Verloren.

"Oh my God, is something happening?" she asked.

"The department has taken an avid interest in reinvestigating the case," Bosch said. "A name has come up. This is an individual who may have been involved in the case in nineteen eighty-eight and we are trying to figure out if he fit in with Becky or her friends in any way."

"What's his name?" she asked quickly.

"Roland Mackey. He was a couple years older than Becky. Didn't go to Hillside but he lived right there in Chatsworth. Does the name mean anything to you?"

"Not really. I don't remember it. How was he connected? Was he the father?"

"The father?"

"The police said she was pregnant. I mean, that she had been pregnant."

"No, we don't know if he was connected that way or not. So you don't recognize the name?"

"No."

"He goes by Ro for short."

"Still don't."

"And you're saying you didn't know about the pregnancy, is that right?"

"I didn't. None of us did. I mean, her friends."

Bosch nodded even though he knew she couldn't see this. He didn't say anything, hoping that she might get uncomfortable with the silence and say something that might be of value.

"Um, do you have a picture of this man?" she finally asked.

It wasn't what Bosch was looking for.

"Yes," he said. "I'll have to figure out a way to get it up there for you to look at, see if it jogs anything loose."

"Can you just scan it and e-mail it?"

Bosch knew what she was asking him to do, and while he could not do it himself he guessed that Kiz Rider probably could.

"I think we could do that. My partner's the computer person and she's not here at the moment, though."

"I'll give you my e-mail address and she can send me the picture when she comes back."

Bosch wrote the address she recited in his small notebook. He told her she'd get the e-mail the following morning.

"Is there anything else, Detective?"

Bosch knew he could end the call and have Rider take a shot at bonding with Grace Tanaka after the photo was sent to her. But he decided not to miss the opportunity to start stirring emotions and memories. Maybe something would break loose.

"I have just a few more questions. Uh, that summer, how would you characterize your relationship with Becky?"

"What do you mean? We were friends. I'd known her since first grade."

"Right, well, were you the closest to her, do you think?"

"No, I think that would have been Tara."

Another confirmation that Tara Wood had been tightest with Becky at the end.

"So she didn't confide in you when she found out she was pregnant."

"No, I already told you, I didn't know about it until after she was dead."

"What about you? Did you confide in her?"

"Of course I did."

"Everything?"

"Detective, what are you getting at?"

"Did she know you were gay?"

"What did that have to do with anything?"

"I'm just trying to get a picture of the group. The Kitty Kat Club, I think the four of you called —"

"No," she said abruptly. "She didn't know. None of them knew. I don't think I even knew back then. Okay, Detective? Is that enough?"

"I'm sorry, Ms. Tanaka. I'm just trying to get as full a picture as I can. I appreciate your candor. One last question. If Becky was at a clinic after going through the procedure and she needed a ride home because she didn't think she could drive, who would she have called?"

There was a long silence before Grace Tanaka answered.

"I don't know, Detective. I would have hoped that it would have been me. That I was that kind of friend. But obviously it was somebody else."

"Tara Wood?"

"You'll have to ask her. Good night, Detective Bosch."

She hung up and Bosch pulled open the yearbook so he could look at her photo. She was a petite Asian and the photo — so many years old — didn't match the gruff demeanor of the voice he had just heard on the phone.

Bosch wrote a note for Rider that contained the e-mail address and instructions to scan and send the photo of Mackey. He also wrote a short warning about his encountering resistance from Tanaka when he brought up her sexuality. He slid the note over to her desk so she would see it first thing in the morning.

That left one last call, this one to Daniel Kotchof, who lived, according to AutoTrack, in Maui, where it was two hours earlier.

He called the number he had gotten from the Auto-Track search and a woman answered the line. She said she was Daniel Kotchof's wife and told Bosch that her husband was at work at the Four Seasons Hotel, where he was employed as the hospitality manager. Bosch called the work number she gave him and was put through to Daniel Kotchof. He said he could only talk for a few minutes and put Bosch on hold for five of them while he went to a more private spot in the hotel to talk. When he finally came back on the line the call started out unproductively. Like Grace Tanaka, he did not recognize the name Roland Mackey. He also seemed to treat the call as a nuisance or an intrusion. He explained that he was married and had three children and that he rarely thought about Becky Verloren anymore. He reminded Bosch that he and his family had moved from the mainland a year before her death.

"But I was led to believe that after you moved to Hawaii, you two continued to call each other quite often," Bosch said.

"I don't know who told you that," Kotchof said. "I mean, we talked. Especially at first. I would have to call her 'cause she said her parents told her it was too much money for her to call me. I thought that was kind of bogus. They just wanted me out of the picture is all. So I had to call, but it was like, what's the use? I was in Hawaii and she was in L.A. It was over, man. And pretty soon I got a girlfriend here — in fact, she's my wife now — and I stopped calling Beck. That was it until, you know, later, when I heard about what happened and the detective called me."

"Did you know about it before the detective called?"

"Yeah, I'd heard. Mrs. Verloren called my dad and he broke the news to me. I also got some calls on it from some of my friends out there. They knew I'd want to know about it. It was weird, man, this girl that I knew gets wiped out like that."

"Yeah."

Bosch thought about what else he could ask. Kotchof's story conflicted in small ways with Muriel Verloren's account. He knew he would need to square the stories at some point. Kotchof's alibi also continued to bother him.

"Hey, look, Detective, I should get going," Kotchof said. "I'm at work. Is there anything else?"

"Just a few more questions. Do you remember how long before Rebecca's death it was that you stopped calling her?"

"Um, I don't know. Somewhere around the end of that first summer. Something like that. It had been a while, almost a year."

Bosch decided to try to rattle Kotchof and see what came out. It was something he would rather have attempted in person but there was no time or money for a trip to Hawaii.

"So your relationship was definitely over by the time of her death?"

"Yes, definitely."

Bosch thought the chances of recovering phone records from back then were not very high.

"When you were still calling was it always at a certain time? You know, like an appointment."

"Sort of. I was two hours behind so I couldn't call too late. I usually called right after dinner and that was right before she was going to go to bed. But like I said, it didn't last too long."

"Okay. Now I have to ask you something pretty personal. Did you have sex with Rebecca Verloren?"

There was a pause.

"What's that got to do with this?"

"I can't explain that, Dan. But it is part of the investigation and it could have a bearing on the case. Do you mind answering?"

"No."

Bosch waited but Kotchof said nothing else.

"Is that your answer?" Bosch finally asked. "You two never had sex?"

"We never did. She said she wasn't ready and I didn't push it. Look, I have to go."

"Okay, Dan, just a few more. I'm sure you would like for us to catch the guy who did this, right?"

"Yes, right, it's just that I'm at work."

"Yes, you said that. Let me ask you, when was the last time you saw Rebecca?"

"I don't remember the exact date but it was like the day we left. When we said good-bye. That morning."

"So you never came back from Hawaii once your family moved?"

"No, not at first. I mean, I've been back since. I lived in Venice for a couple years after I finished school, but then I came back here."

"But not between the time your family moved and the time of Rebecca's murder. Is that what you are saying?"

"Yes, right."

"So if another witness I have spoken to said she saw you in town that weekend of July Fourth, right before Rebecca disappeared, then she would be wrong about that?"

"Yeah, she'd be wrong. Look, what is this? I told you. I never went back. I had a new girlfriend. I mean, I didn't even go back for the funeral. Who told you they saw me? Was it Grace? She never liked me — that dyke. She was always trying to get me in trouble with Beck."

"I can't tell you who it is, Dan. Just like if you want to tell me something in confidence then I will respect that."

"Whoever it is, she's a fucking liar," Kotchof said, his voice turning shrill. "That is a goddamn lie! Check your records, man! I had an alibi. I was working on the day she was taken, and I was working the next day, too. How could I have gotten there and back? Whoever told you that is totally fucking bogus!"

"It's your alibi that is bogus, Dan. Your old man could have put your supervisor up to it. That was easy."

A moment of silence passed before there was a response.

"I don't know what you are talking about. My father didn't put anybody up to anything and that's a goddamn fact. We had the time cards and my boss talked to the cops and that was it. Now you come along seventeen years later with this shit? Are you fucking kidding me?"

"Okay, Dan, take it easy. Sometimes people make

mistakes. Especially when you are going back all those years."

"This is all I need, to be dragged into this. Man, I've got a family over here."

"I said take it easy. You aren't being dragged into anything. This is just a phone call. Just a conversation, okay? Now, is there anything else you can tell me or want to tell me to help with this thing?"

"No. I told you all I know, which is nothing. And I have to go. I mean it this time."

"So were you upset when Rebecca told you she was pregnant and it was obvious to you that it was with another guy?"

There was no answer at first so Bosch tried to turn the screw a bit.

"Especially since she would never have relations with you when you two were together."

Bosch realized he had gone too far and tipped his hand. Kotchof realized that Bosch was playing good cop and bad cop with him all at once. When he responded, his voice was calm and modulated.

"She never told me that," he said. "I never knew until it came out after."

"Really? Who told you?"

"I can't remember. One of my friends, I guess."

"Really? Because Rebecca kept a journal. And you're all over it, man. And she says she told you and you weren't too happy about it."

Now Kotchof laughed and Bosch knew he had really blown it.

"Detective, you are full of shit. You're the one who's lying. This is really weak, man. I mean, I watch *Law and Order*, you know."

"Do you watch *CSI?*"

"Yeah, so?"

"Well, we got the killer's DNA. If we match it to somebody they're going to take a fall. DNA is the ultimate closer."

"Good. Check mine and maybe this can all be over for me."

Bosch knew he was the one backpedaling now. He had to end the call.

"Okay then, Dan, we'll let you know about that. Meantime, thank you for your help. One last question. What's a hospitality manager?"

"You mean here at the hotel? I take care of large parties and conferences and weddings and things like that. I make sure it all runs smoothly when these big groups come in here."

"Okay, well, I'll let you get back to it. Have a good day."

Bosch hung up and sat at the desk thinking about the call. He was embarrassed by how he had let the upper hand slip across the line to Kotchof. He knew his interviewing skills had largely been dormant for three years but that did not salve the burn. He knew he had to get better and it had to be soon.

Aside from that, there was a lot of content from the call to consider. He didn't read much into Kotchof's angry reaction to supposedly being seen in L.A. right before the murder. After all, Bosch had fabricated the witness and Kotchof's angry response would certainly be justified. But what was notable was how Kotchof's anger zeroed in on Grace Tanaka. Their relationship might be worth exploring further, maybe through Kiz Rider.

He also considered Kotchof's statement about not knowing about Rebecca Verloren's pregnancy. Bosch instinctively believed him. All in all it didn't drop Kotchof from the suspect list, but it at least pushed him to a back burner. He would discuss all of Kotchof's answers with Rider and see if she agreed.

The most interesting information gleaned from the call was in the conflicts between Kotchof's memories and those of Muriel Verloren, the victim's mother. Muriel Verloren had said Kotchof had called her daughter religiously, right up until the time of her death. Kotchof said he had done no such thing. Bosch didn't see any reason for Kotchof to lie about it. If he hadn't, then Muriel Verloren's memory was wrong. Or it was her daughter who had lied about who called her every night before bed. Since the girl was hiding a relationship and the pregnancy that came from it, it seemed likely that the phone calls did come in every night but they were not from Kotchof. They were from someone else, someone Bosch started thinking of as Mr. X.

After looking up Muriel Verloren's number in the murder book Bosch called the house. He apologized for intruding and said he had a few follow-up questions. Muriel said she was not bothered by the call.

"What are your questions?"

"I saw the phone on the table next to your daughter's bed. Was that an extension of the house phone or did she have her own phone number?"

"She had her own number. A private line."

"So when Daniel Kotchof called her at night she would be the one who answered the phone, right?"

"Yes, in her room. It was the only extension."

"So the only way you know that Danny was calling was because she told you."

"No, I heard the phone ring sometimes. He called."

"What I mean, Mrs. Verloren, is that you never answered those calls and you never talked to Danny Kotchof, right?"

"That's right. It was her private line."

"So when that phone rang and she talked to somebody, the only way you would know who it was on the line was if she told you. Is that correct?"

"Uh, yes, I guess that is right. Are you saying it wasn't Danny who called all of those times?"

"I'm not sure yet. But I talked to Danny in Hawaii and he said he stopped calling your daughter long before she was taken. He had a new girlfriend, you see. In Hawaii."

This information was treated with a long pause. Finally, Bosch spoke into the void.

"Do you have any idea who it could have been that she was talking to, Mrs. Verloren?"

After another pause Muriel Verloren weakly offered an answer.

"Maybe one of her girlfriends."

"It's possible," Bosch said. "Anybody else you can think of?"

"I don't like this," she responded quickly. "It's like I'm learning things all over again."

"I'm sorry, Mrs. Verloren. I will try not to hit you with these sorts of things unless it is necessary. But I am afraid this is necessary. Did you and your husband ever come to any conclusion about the pregnancy?"

"What do you mean? We didn't know about it until after."

"I understand that. What I mean is, did you think it came out of a hidden relationship or was it simply a mistake she made one day with, you know, someone she was not really in a relationship with?"

"You mean like a one-night stand? Is that what you are saying about my daughter?"

"No, ma'am, I am not saying anything about your daughter. I am simply asking questions. I do not want to upset you but I want to find the person who killed Rebecca. And I need to know all there is to know."

"We could never explain it, Detective," she responded coldly. "She was gone and we decided not to delve into it. We left everything to the police and we just tried to remember the daughter we knew and loved. You said you have a daughter. I hope you understand."

"I think I do. Thank you for your answers. One last question — and there is no pressure on this — but would you be willing to talk to a newspaper reporter about your daughter and the case?"

"Why would I do that? I didn't before. I don't believe in putting it out there for the public."

"I admire that. But this time I want you to do it because it might help us flush out the bird."

"You mean it might make the person who did this come out from cover?"

"Exactly."

"Then I'd do it in a heartbeat."

"Thank you, Mrs. Verloren. I will let you know."

16

Abel Pratt came out of his office with his suit jacket on. He noticed Bosch sitting at his desk in the alcove, using two fingers to type up a report on his telephone conversation with Muriel Verloren. The finished reports on the phone interviews with Grace Tanaka and Daniel Kotchof were on the desk.

"Where's Kiz?" Pratt asked.

"She's working on the warrant at home. She can think better there."

"I can't think when I get home. I can only react. I have twin boys."

"Good luck."

"Yeah, I need it. I'm going that way now. I'll see you tomorrow, Harry."

"Okay."

But Pratt didn't walk away. Bosch looked up from the typewriter at him. He thought maybe something was wrong. Maybe it was the typewriter.

"I found this on a desk on the other side," Bosch said. "It didn't look like it was being used by anybody."

"It wasn't. Most people use their computers now. You are definitely an old-school kind of guy, Harry."

"I guess. Kiz usually does the reports, but I have some time to kill."

"Working late?"

"I've got to go over to the Nickel."

147

"Fifth Street? What do you want over there?"

"Looking for our victim's father."

Pratt shook his head somberly.

"Another one of those. We've seen it before."

Bosch nodded.

"Ripples," he said.

"Yeah, ripples," Pratt agreed.

Bosch was thinking about offering to walk out with Pratt, maybe have a conversation and get to know him better, but his cell phone started to chirp. He pulled it off his belt and saw the name Sam Weiss in the caller ID screen.

"I better take this."

"All right, Harry. Be careful over there."

"Thanks, Boss."

He flipped open the phone.

"Detective Bosch," he said.

"Detective?"

Bosch remembered he had left no information on his message to Weiss.

"Mr. Weiss, my name is Harry Bosch. I am a detective with the LAPD. I'd like to ask you a few questions about an investigation I am conducting."

"I have all the time you need, Detective. Is this about my gun?"

The question caught Bosch off guard.

"Why would you ask that, sir?"

"Well, because I know it was used in a murder that was never solved. And that's the only thing I can think of that the LAPD would want to ask me about."

"Well, yes, sir, it's about the gun. Can I talk to you about it?"

"If it means you are trying to find who killed that girl, then you can ask me anything you want."

"Thank you. I guess the first thing I'd like is for you to

tell me how and when you knew or were told that the weapon stolen from you was used in a homicide."

"It was in the papers — the murder was — and I put two and two together. I called the detective assigned to my burglary and asked and got the answer I wish I hadn't."

"Why is that, Mr. Weiss?"

"Because I've had to live with it."

"But you didn't do anything wrong, sir."

"I know that, but it doesn't make a person feel any better. I bought that gun because I was having trouble with a bunch of punks. I wanted protection. Then the gun I bought ended up being the instrument of death for that young girl. Don't think I haven't thought about changing history. I mean, what if I wasn't so stubborn? What if I just pulled up stakes and moved instead of going and buying that damn thing? You see what I mean?"

"Yes, I see."

"Now, that said, what else can I tell you, Detective?"

"I have just a few questions. Calling you was sort of a shot in the dark. I thought it might be easier than trying to find my way back through seventeen years of paperwork and department history. I have the initial report on the burglary and the investigator is listed as John McClellan. Do you remember him?"

"Sure, I remember him."

"Did he ever clear the case?"

"Not as far as I know. At first John thought it might have been connected to the punks who had threatened me."

"And was it?"

"John told me no. But I was never sure. The burglars really tore the place apart. It wasn't like they were really looking for stuff to steal. They were just destroying things — my belongings. I walked in this place and, man, I could feel a lot of anger."

"Why do you say burglars? Did the police think it was more than one?"

"John figured it had to be at least two or three. I was only gone an hour — went to the store. One guy couldn't have done all that damage in that time."

"The report lists the gun, a coin collection and some cash that was taken. Anything else come up missing after?"

"No, that was it. That was enough. At least I got the coins back, and that was the most valuable thing. It was my father's collection from when he was a boy."

"How did you get it back?"

"John McClellan. He brought them back to me a couple weeks later."

"Did he say where he recovered them from?"

"He said a pawnshop in West Hollywood. And then, of course, we know what became of the gun. But that was not given back to me. I wouldn't have taken it anyway."

"I understand, sir. Did Detective McClellan ever tell you who he thought burglarized your home? Did he have any theories?"

"He thought it was just another set of punks, you know. Not the Chatsworth Eights."

The mention of the Chatsworth Eights stirred something in Bosch, but he couldn't place it.

"Mr. Weiss, act like I don't know anything. Who were the Chatsworth Eights?"

"It was a gang out here in the Valley. They were all white kids. Skinheads. And back in nineteen eighty-eight they committed a number of crimes out here. They were hate crimes. That's what they called them in the papers. Back then it was the new term for crimes motivated by race or religion."

"And you were the target of this gang?"

"Yeah, I started getting calls. The typical kill-the-Jew stuff."

"But then the police told you the Eights did not commit the burglary."

"That's right."

"Strange, isn't it? They didn't see any connection."

"That's what I thought at the time but he was the detective, not me."

"What made the Eights target you, Mr. Weiss? I know you are Jewish but what made them pick you out?"

"Simple. One of the little shits was a kid who lived in my neighborhood. Billy Burkhart was four houses away. I put a menorah in my window during Chanukah and that's when it all started."

"What happened to Burkhart?"

"He went to jail. Not for what he did to me, but to others. They got him and the others on other crimes. They burned a cross a few blocks from me. In the front lawn of a black family. And they did other things. Mean things, vandalism. They tried to burn a temple, too."

"But not the burglary at your house."

"That's right. That's what the police told me. You see, there was no graffiti or indication of religious motivation. The place was just torn apart. So they didn't classify the burglary as a hate crime."

Bosch hesitated, wondering if there was anything else to ask. He decided he didn't know enough to ask smart questions.

"Okay, Mr. Weiss, I appreciate your time. And I am sorry to reawaken bad memories."

"Don't worry about it, Detective. Believe me, they weren't asleep."

Bosch closed the phone. He tried to think of whom he could call about all of this. He didn't know John McClellan and the chances of his still being in Devonshire Division seventeen years later were slim. Then it hit him: Jerry

Edgar. His old partner at Hollywood Division had previously been assigned to Devonshire detectives. He would have been there in 1988.

Bosch called the Hollywood homicide table but got the machine. Everybody had cut out early. He called the main detective bureau number and asked if Edgar was around. Bosch knew that there was a sign-out chart at the front counter. The clerk who answered the phone said Edgar had signed out for the day.

The third call was to Edgar's cell phone. His old partner answered it promptly.

"You guys go home early in Hollywood," Bosch said.

"Who the hell is — Harry, that you?"

"That me. How's it hanging, Jerry?"

"I was wondering when I'd hear from you. You start again today?"

"The world's oldest boot. And I already got a hot shot. Kiz and I are working a breaking case."

Edgar didn't respond and Bosch knew mentioning Rider had been a mistake. The gulf between them not only still existed but was apparently frozen over.

"Anyway, I need to tap into that big brain of yours. This is going back to Club Dev days."

"Yeah, which day?"

"Nineteen eighty-eight. The Chatsworth Eights. You remember them?"

There was silence while Edgar thought for a moment.

"Yeah, I remember the Eights. They were a bunch of peckerwoods that thought shaved heads and tattoos made them men. They did a lot of shit, then they got stepped on. They didn't last long."

"You remember a guy named Roland Mackey? Would've been about eighteen back then."

After a pause Edgar said he didn't remember the name.

"Who was working the Eights?" Bosch asked.

"Not Club Dev, man. Everything with them went straight down the rabbit hole."

"PDU?"

"You got it."

The Public Disorder Unit. A shadowy downtown squad that gathered data and intelligence on conspiracies but made few cases. Back in 1988 the PDU would have been under the aegis of then commander Irvin Irving. The unit was not in existence anymore. When Irving rose to the level of deputy chief he promptly disbanded the PDU, with many in the department believing it was a measure taken to cover up and distance himself from its activities.

"That's not going to help," Bosch said.

"Sorry about that. What are you working?"

"The murder of a girl up on Oat Mountain."

"The one taken out of her house?"

"Yeah."

"I remember that one, too. I didn't work it — I had just gotten to the homicide table. But I remember that one. You're saying the Eights were in on that one?"

"No. Just that a name came up that might have a connection to the Eights. Might. So does Eights mean what I think?"

"Yeah, man, eight for H. Eighty-eight for H-H. And H-H for Heil —"

"— Hitler. Yeah, I thought so."

Then it struck Bosch that Kiz Rider had been right when she thought the year of the crime might be significant. The murder and the rest of the crimes committed by the Chatsworth Eights had occurred in 1988. It was all part of a confluence of seemingly small things coming together. And now Irvin Irving and the PDU were mixed into the soup as well. A cold hit match of DNA to a loser who drove a tow truck for a living was blossoming into something bigger.

"Jerry, you remember a guy who worked at Devonshire named John McClellan?"

"John McClellan? No, I don't remember. What did he work?"

"I got his name here on a burglary report."

"No, definitely not the burglary table. I worked burglary before going over to homicide. There was no John McClellan on burglary. Who is he?"

"Like I said, just a name on a report. I'll figure it out."

Bosch knew that this meant McClellan was likely in the PDU at the time and the investigation of the burglary of Sam Weiss's home was folded into the investigation of the Chatsworth Eights. He didn't care to discuss all of this with Edgar.

"Jerry, so you were new on the homicide table back then?"

"That's right."

"Did you know Green and Garcia very well?"

"Not really. I just got to the table and they weren't there that long after. Green pulled the pin and about a year after that Garcia made lieutenant."

"From what you saw, what was your take on them?"

"How so?"

"As homicide men."

"Well, Harry, I was pretty fresh back then. I mean, what did I know? I was still learning. But the take on them was that Green was the power. Garcia was just the housekeeper. What some people said about Garcia was that he couldn't find shit in his own mustache with a mirror and comb."

Bosch didn't respond. By labeling Garcia a housekeeper Edgar was saying that Garcia rode his partner's coattails. Green was the real homicide cop and Garcia was the guy who backed him up and kept the murder books tidy and up to date. A lot of partnerships got sanded down into such relationships. An alpha dog and his assistant.

"I guess he didn't need to," Edgar said.

"Didn't need to what?"

"Find shit in his mustache. He was going places, man. He made lieutenant and was out of there. You know he's currently second in command in the Valley, right?"

"Yeah, I know. In fact, if you see him you might not want to mention that mustache bit."

"Yeah, probably not."

Bosch thought some more about what this might have meant to the Verloren investigation. A small crack was moving under the surface of things.

"That it, Harry?"

"I heard Green ate his gun not too long after pulling the pin."

"Yeah, I heard that. I don't remember being surprised. He always looked like a guy carrying a full load of somethin'. You going to take a run at PDU, Harry? You know that was Irving's squad, don't you?"

"Yeah, Jerry, I know. I doubt I'm going that way."

"Be careful if you do, my man."

Bosch wanted to change the subject before hanging up. Edgar had always been a department gossip. Harry didn't want his old partner's loose lips to spread the word that Bosch was taking a run at Irving now that he was back with a badge.

"So how's things in Hollywood?" he asked.

"We just got back into the bureau after the earthquake retrofit. You missed all of that. We were stuck upstairs in roll call for like a year."

"How is it?"

"It's like an insurance office now. We have pods and sound filters between the desks. All done up in government gray. Nice but not the same."

"I know what you mean."

"Then they gave the D-threes double-wides — desks with two sides of drawers. The rest of us get one side."

Bosch smiled. Little slights like that got magnified in the department and the administrators who made such decisions never learned. Like when most of Internal Affairs moved out of Parker Center and into the old Bradbury Building and the word spread through the ranks that the captain over there had a fireplace in his office.

"So what are you gonna do, Jerry?"

"Same old same old, that's what I'm gonna do. Get off my ass and knock on doors."

"I hear you, man."

"Watch your six, Harry."

"Always."

After hanging up, Bosch sat motionless at his desk for a few moments as he thought through the conversation and the new meanings it brought to the case. If there was a connection between the case and PDU then they had a whole new ball game.

He looked down at the murder book, still open to the burglary report, and stared at the scrawled signature of John McClellan. He picked up the phone and called the Department of Operations in Parker Center and asked the duty officer for an assignment location for a detective named John McClellan. He read McClellan's badge number off the burglary report. He was put on hold and expected that he would be told that McClellan was long retired. It had been seventeen years.

But when the duty officer came back on the line he reported that an officer named John McClellan with the badge number Bosch provided was now a lieutenant assigned to the Office of Strategic Planning. The synapse connections in Bosch's brain started tripping. Seventeen years ago McClellan worked for Irving in the PDU. Now the assignment and rank were different but he was still working for him. And Irving just happened to run into Bosch in the Parker Center cafeteria on the day Bosch caught a case with ties to the PDU.

"High jingo," Bosch whispered to himself as he hung up.

Like a battleship going into a turn, the case was slowly, surely and unstoppably moving in a new direction. Bosch could feel something building inside his chest. He thought about the coincidence of Irving crossing his path. If it was a coincidence. Bosch wondered if the deputy chief already knew at that moment what case they had pulled the cold hit on and where it was going to lead.

The department buried secrets every day. It was a given. But who would have thought seventeen years ago that a chemical test run one day in a DOJ lab in Sacramento might put a shovel into the greasy dirt and turn over the past, bringing this secret to light.

17

Driving home Bosch thought about the many different tendrils of the investigation that were wrapping around the body of Rebecca Verloren. He knew he had to keep his eyes on the prize. The evidence was the key. The elements of departmental politics and possible corruption and cover-up all amounted to what was known as high jingo. It could be threatening and distracting from the intended goal. He had to avoid this at the same time that he had to be wary of it.

Eventually he was able to push thoughts of Irving's shadow over the investigation aside and concentrate on the case. His thoughts somehow led him to Rebecca's bedroom and how her mother had left it unchanged by time. He wondered if it was the loss of the daughter that did it or was it the circumstances of the loss? What if you lost a child by natural causes or accident or circumstances like divorce? Bosch had a daughter he rarely saw. It weighed on him. He knew that near or far his daughter left him completely vulnerable, that he could end up like the mother who preserved a daughter's bedroom like a museum, or the father who was long lost to the world.

More so than this question, something about the bedroom bothered him. He couldn't quite reach what it was but he knew it was there and it nagged at him. He looked from the elevated freeway out across Hollywood to his left. There was still some light in the sky but the evening was starting. Darkness had waited long enough. Searchlights that he knew could be traced down to the corner of Hollywood and Vine were crisscrossing the horizon. To him it looked nice. To him it looked like home.

When he got to his house on the hill he checked the mail and the phone for messages and then changed out of the suit he had bought for his return to the job. He carefully hung it in the closet, thinking he could wear it at least once more before having to take it in to the cleaners. He put on blue jeans, black sneakers and a black pullover shirt. He put on a sport coat that was fraying on the right shoulder from his cutting corners too close. He transferred his gun and badge and wallet. Then he got back into his car and headed downtown to the Toy District.

He decided to park in Japantown in the museum lot so he wouldn't have to worry about the car being broken into or vandalized. From there he walked over to Fifth Street, encountering an increasing density of homeless people as he progressed. The city's primary homeless encampments and the missions that catered to them lined a five-block stretch of Fifth Street south of Los Angeles Street. The sidewalks outside the missions and cheap residence hotels were lined with cardboard boxes and shopping carts filled with the dirty and meager belongings of lost people. It was as if some sort of social disintegration bomb had gone off and the shrapnel of damaged, disenfranchised lives had been hurled everywhere. Up and down the street there were men and women yelling, their shouts unintelligible or simply eerie non sequiturs in the night. It felt like a city with its own rule and reason, a hurt city with a wound so deep that the bandages the missions applied could not stop the bleeding.

As he walked, Bosch noted that he was not asked once for money or cigarettes or any kind of handout. The irony was not lost on him. It appeared that the place with the highest concentration of homeless people in the city was also the place where a citizen was safest from their entreaties, if nothing else.

The Los Angeles Mission and the Salvation Army had major help centers here. Bosch decided to start with them. He had a twelve-year-old driver's license photo of Robert Verloren and an even older photograph of him at his daughter's funeral. He showed these to the people operating the help centers and the kitchen workers who put free food on hundreds of plates every day. He got little response until a kitchen worker remembered Verloren as a "client" who came through the chow line pretty regularly a few years before.

"It's been a while," the man said. "Haven't seen him."

After spending an hour in each center Bosch started working his way down the street, stepping into the smaller missions and flop hotels and showing the photos. He got a few recognitions of Verloren but nothing fresh, nothing to lead him to the man who had completely dropped off the human radar screen so many years before. He worked it until ten-thirty and decided he would return the next day to finish canvassing the street. As he walked back toward Japantown he was depressed by what he had just immersed himself in and by the dwindling hopes of finding Robert Verloren. He walked with his head down, hands in his pockets, and therefore didn't see the two men until they had already seen him. They stepped out of the alcoves of two side-by-side toy stores as Bosch passed. One blocked his path. The other stepped out behind him. Bosch stopped.

"Hey, missionary man," said the one in front of him.

In the dim glow from a streetlight half a block away Bosch saw the glint of a blade down at the man's side. He turned slightly to check the man behind him. He was smaller. Bosch wasn't sure but it looked like he was simply holding a chunk of concrete in his hand. A piece of broken curb. Both men were dressed in layers, a common sight in this part of the city. One was black and one was white.

"The kitchens are all closed up and we're still hungry," said the one with the knife. "You got a few bucks for us? You know, like we could borrow."

Bosch shook his head.

"No, not really."

"Not really? You sure 'bout that, boy? You look like you got a nice fat wallet on you now. Don't be holding back on us."

A black rage grew in Bosch. In a moment of sharp focus he knew what he could and would do. He would draw his weapon and put bullets into both of these men. In that same instant he knew he would walk away from it after a cursory departmental investigation. The glint of the blade was Bosch's ticket and he knew it. The men on either side of him didn't know what they had just walked into. It was like being in the tunnels so many years before. Everything closed down to a tight space. Nothing but kill or be killed. There was something absolutely pure about it, no gray areas and no room for anything else.

Then suddenly the moment changed. Bosch saw the one with the knife staring intently at him, reading something in his eyes, one predator taking the measure of another. The knife man seemed to grow smaller by an almost imperceptible measure. He backed off without physically backing off.

Bosch knew there were people considered to be mind readers. The truth was they were face readers. Their skill was interpreting the myriad muscle constructions of the eyes, the mouth, the eyebrows. From this they decoded intent. Bosch had a level of skill in this. His ex-wife made a living playing poker because she had an even higher skill.

The man with the knife had a measure of this skill as well. It had surely saved his life this time.

"Nah, never mind," said the man.

He took a step back toward the store's alcove.

"Have a good night, missionary man," he said as he retreated into the darkness.

Bosch fully turned and looked at the other man. Without a word, he too stepped back into his crack to hide and wait for the next victim.

Bosch looked up and down the street. It seemed deserted now. He turned and headed on toward his ride. As he walked he took out his cell phone and called the Central Division patrol office. He told the watch sergeant about the two men he encountered and asked him to send a patrol car.

"That kind of stuff happens on every block down there in that hellhole," the sergeant said. "What do you want me to do about it?"

"I want you to send a car and roust them. They'll think twice about doing anything to anybody."

"Well, why didn't you do anything about it yourself?"

"Because I'm working a case, Sergeant, and I can't get off it to do your job or your paperwork."

"Look, buddy, don't be telling me how to do my job. You suits are all the same. You think —"

"Look, Sergeant, I'm going to check the crime reports in the morning. If I read that somebody got hurt down here and the suspects were a black and white team, then you're going to have more suits around you than at the Men's Warehouse. I guarantee it."

Bosch closed his phone, cutting off a last protest from the watch sergeant. He picked up his pace, got to his car and started back over to the 101 Freeway. He then headed back up to the Valley.

18

Finding cover with a visual line on Tampa Towing was difficult. Both strip shopping plazas located on the other corners were closed and their parking lots empty. Bosch would be obvious if he parked in either one. The competing service station on the third corner was still open and thus, unusable for surveillance. After considering the situation Bosch parked on Roscoe a block away and walked back to the intersection. Borrowing an idea from the would-be robbers of less than an hour before, he found a darkened alcove in one of the strip plazas from which he could watch the service station. He knew the problem with his choice of surveillance was getting back to his car fast enough to avoid losing Mackey when he went off shift.

The ad he had checked earlier in the phone book said Tampa Towing offered twenty-four-hour service. But it was coming up on midnight and Bosch was betting that Mackey, who had come on duty at 4 p.m., would be getting off soon. He would either be replaced by a midnight man or would be on call through the night.

It was at times like this that Bosch thought about smoking again. It always seemed to make the time go faster and it took the edge off the anxiety that always built through a surveillance. But it had been more than four years now and he didn't want to break stride. Learning two years earlier that he was a father had helped him get past the occasional weaknesses. He thought that if not for his daughter he'd probably be smoking again. At best he had controlled the addiction. By no means had he broken it.

He took out his cell phone and angled the light from its screen away from view of the service station while he punched in Kiz Rider's home number. She didn't answer. He tried her cell and got no answer again. He assumed she had shut down the phones so she could concentrate on writing the warrant. She had worked it that way in the past. He knew she would leave her pager on for emergencies but he didn't think the news he had gathered during the evening's phone calls rose to the level of emergency. He decided to wait until he saw her in the morning to tell her what he had learned.

He put his phone in his pocket and raised the binoculars to his eyes. Through the glass windows of the service station office he could see Mackey sitting behind a weathered gray desk. There was another man in a similar blue on blue uniform in the office. It must have been a slow night. Both of the men had their feet propped up on the desk and were looking up at something high on the wall over the front window. Bosch could not see what they were focused on but the changing light in the room told him it was a television.

Bosch's phone chirped and he pulled it from his pocket and answered without lowering the binoculars. He didn't check the display because he assumed it was Kiz Rider calling after noticing that she had missed his call.

"Hey."

"Detective Bosch?"

It wasn't Rider. Bosch lowered the field glasses.

"Yes, this is Bosch. How can I help you?"

"This is Tara Wood. I got your message."

"Oh, yeah, thanks for calling back."

"It sounds like this is your cell. I'm sorry to call so late.

I just got in. I thought I was just going to leave a message on your office line."

"No problem. I'm still working."

Bosch went through the same interview process he had employed with the others. As he mentioned the name Roland Mackey to her he checked on Mackey through the glasses. He was still at the desk, watching the tube. Like Rebecca Verloren's other friends, Tara Wood didn't recognize the tow truck driver's name. Bosch added a new question, asking if she remembered the Chatsworth Eights, and her memory was vague about that as well. Lastly he asked if the next day he could continue the interview and show her a photograph of Mackey. She agreed but told him he would have to come to the CBS television studios, where she worked as a publicist. Bosch knew that CBS was next to the Farmers Market, one of his favorite places in the city. He decided he could go to the market, maybe eat a bowl of gumbo for lunch, and then go see Tara Wood to show the photo of Mackey and ask about Rebecca Verloren's pregnancy. He made the appointment for 1 p.m. and she agreed to be in her office.

"This is such an old case," Wood said. "Are you like on a cold case squad?"

"We actually call it the Open-Unsolved Unit."

"You know, we have a show called *Cold Case*. It's on Sunday nights. It's one of the shows I work on. I'm thinking . . . maybe you could visit the set and meet some of your television counterparts. I am sure they would love to meet you."

Bosch realized she might be working up some sort of publicity angle. He looked through the glasses at Mackey staring up at the television and thought for a moment of trying to use her interest in the wiretap play they were going to put into motion. He then quickly shelved it, concluding that it would be easier to start the play with a newspaper plant.

"Yeah, maybe, but I think that would have to wait awhile. We're working this case pretty hard right now and I just need to talk to you tomorrow."

"No problem. I really hope you find who you are looking for. Ever since I was assigned to this show I've been thinking about Rebecca. You know, wondering if there was anything happening. Then out of the blue you called. It's weird, but in a good way. I'll see you tomorrow, Detective."

Bosch said good night and hung up.

A few minutes later, at midnight, the lights at the service station went out. Bosch knew that offering twenty-four-hour tow service didn't necessarily translate into being open twenty-four hours a day. Mackey or another driver was probably on call through the night.

Bosch slipped from his hiding spot and hustled down Roscoe to the SUV. Just as he got to it he heard the deep thrumming sound of Mackey's Camaro coming to life. He started his engine, pulled away from the curb, and headed back toward the intersection. As he got there and was stopping for the red light he saw the Camaro with the gray-painted fenders cross the intersection, heading south on Tampa. Bosch waited a few moments, checked all lanes of the intersection for other cars, and blew through the red light to follow.

Mackey's first stop was a bar called the Side Pocket. It was on Sepulveda Boulevard in Van Nuys near the railroad tracks. It was a small place with a blue neon sign and the barred windows painted black. Bosch had an idea what it would be like inside and what kind of men would be in there. Before leaving his car he took off his sport coat, wrapped his gun, handcuffs and extra clip in it and put it on the floor in front of the passenger seat. He got out and locked the door and headed toward the bar, pulling his shirt out of his jeans as he went.

The inside of the bar was as he expected. A couple of pool tables, a stand-up bar and a row of scarred wood booths. Even though smoking inside the place was illegal, blue smoke was heavy in the air and hanging like a ghost beneath each table light. Nobody was complaining.

Most of the men took their medicine straight up, meaning they were standing. Most had chains on their wallets and tattoos ringing their lower arms. Even with the changes to his appearance Bosch knew he would stand out, possibly even be advertising that he didn't belong. He saw an opening in the shadows where the bar curved under the television mounted in the corner. He slipped into the spot and leaned over the bar, hoping it helped hide his appearance.

The bartender, a worn woman wearing a black leather vest over a T-shirt, ignored Bosch for a while but that was all right. He wasn't there to drink. He watched Mackey put quarters on one of the tables and wait for his turn to play. He hadn't ordered a drink either.

Mackey spent ten minutes going through the assort-ment of pool cues on the wall racks until he found one he liked the feel of. He then stood by waiting and talking to some of the men standing around the pool table. It didn't appear to be anything more than casual conversation, as though he knew them but only from playing pool on previous nights.

While he waited and watched, nursing the beer and whisky shot the bartender had finally delivered to him, Bosch at first thought people were watching him as well, but then realized they were only staring at the television screen less than a foot above his head.

Finally Mackey got his game and he turned out to be good at it. He quickly won control of the table and defeated seven challengers, collecting money or beers from all of them. After a half hour he seemed to tire from the lack of competition and got sloppy. The eighth challenger beat him after Mackey missed a clean shot at the eight ball. Mackey took the loss well and slapped a five-dollar bill down on the green felt before stepping away. By Bosch's count he was at least twenty-five dollars and three beers ahead for the night.

Mackey took his Rolling Rock to a space at the bar and that was Bosch's cue to withdraw. He put a ten under his empty shot glass and turned away, never giving Mackey his face. He left the bar and went back to his car. The first thing he did was put the gun back on his right hip, grip forward. He started the engine and drove out onto Sepulveda and then a block south. He turned around and pulled to the curb in front of a hydrant. He had a good angle on the front door of the Side Pocket and was in position to follow Mackey's car north on Sepulveda toward Panorama City. Mackey may have changed apartments after completing probation but Bosch expected that he had not moved far.

The wait this time was not long. Mackey apparently only drank free beer. He left the bar ten minutes after Bosch had, got in the Camaro and headed south on Sepulveda.

Bosch had guessed wrong. Mackey was driving away from Panorama City and the north Valley. This meant Bosch had to pull a U-turn on a largely deserted Sepulveda Boulevard in order to follow him. The move would be highly noticeable in Mackey's rearview mirror. So he waited, watching the Camaro get smaller in his side-view mirror.

When he saw the turn signal on the Camaro start to blink he pinned the accelerator and took the SUV into a hard one-eighty. He almost lost it by overcompensating on the wheel but then righted the car and took off down Sepulveda. He turned right on Victory and caught up with the Camaro at the traffic signal at the 405 overpass. Mackey stayed off the freeway, however, and continued west on Victory.

With Bosch employing a variety of driving maneuvers to avoid detection, Mackey drove all the way into Woodland Hills. On Mariano Street, a wide street near the 101 Freeway, he finally pulled down a long driveway and parked beside a small house. Bosch drove by and parked further down, then got out and doubled back on foot. He heard the front door of the house closing and then saw the light over the porch go out.

Bosch looked around and realized it was a neighborhood of flag lots. When the neighborhood was first gridded decades before, the properties were cut into large pieces because they were meant to be horse ranches and small vegetable farms. Then the city grew out to the neighborhood and the horses and vegetables were crowded out. The lots were cut up, one property up front on the street and a narrow driveway running down the side of it to the property in the back — the flag-shaped lot.

It made observation difficult. Bosch crept down the long driveway, watching both the house on the front property and Mackey's house on the back piece. Mackey had parked his Camaro next to a beat-up Ford 150 pickup. It meant Mackey might have a roommate.

When he got closer Bosch stopped to write down the tag number on the F150. He noticed an old bumper sticker on the pickup that said WOULD THE LAST AMERICAN TO LEAVE L.A. PLEASE BRING THE FLAG. It was just one more small brushstroke on what Bosch felt was an emerging picture.

As quietly as he could, Bosch walked down a stone pathway that ran alongside the house. The house was built on knee-high footings which put the windows too far up for him to see in. When he got to the back of the house he heard voices and then realized it was television when he saw the undulating blue glow on the shades of the back room. He started to cross the backyard when suddenly his phone started to chirp. He quickly reached for it and cut off the sound. At the same time he moved quickly back down the pathway and to the driveway. He then ran up the driveway toward the street. He listened for any sound behind him but heard none. When he made it to the street he looked back at the house but saw nothing that gave him reason to believe the chirping from his phone had been heard inside the house above the sounds of the television.

Bosch knew it had been a close call. He was out of breath. He walked back to his car, trying to gather himself and recover from the near disaster. As with the badly handled interview with Daniel Kotchof, he knew he was showing signs of rust. He had forgotten to mute his phone before creeping the house. It was a mistake that could have blown everything and maybe put him into a confrontation with an investigative target. Three years ago, before he had left the job, it would never have happened. He started thinking about what Irving had said about his being a retread that would come apart at the seams, that would blow out.

Inside the car he checked the caller ID list on his phone and saw that the call had come from Kiz Rider. He called her back.

"Harry, I checked my call list and saw you had called me a little while ago. I had my phones off. What's up?"

"Nothing much. I was checking in to see how it was going."

"Well, it's going. I've got it all structured and most of the writing done. I'll finish tomorrow morning, then I'll start it through the channels."

"Good."

"Yeah, I'm about to call it a night. What about you? Did you find Robert Verloren?"

"Not yet. But I've got an address for you. I followed Mackey after he left work. He's got a little house by the freeway in Woodland Hills. There might be a phone line in there that you'll want to add to the tap."

"Good. Give me the address. That should be easy enough to check. But I'm not sure I want you following the suspect alone. That's not smart, Harry."

"We had to find his address."

He wasn't going to tell her about the near miss. He gave her the address and waited a moment while she wrote it down.

"I've got some other stuff, too," he said. "I made some calls."

"You've been busy for just a day back on the job. What've you got?"

He recounted the phone calls he made and received after she had left the office. Rider asked no questions and then was silent after he finished.

"That brings you up to date," Bosch said. "What do you think, Kiz?"

"I think there might be a picture coming together, Harry."

"Yeah, I was thinking the same thing. Plus, the year, nineteen eighty-eight. I think you were onto something about that. Maybe these assholes were trying to prove a point in 'eighty-eight. The problem is, it all went under the door at PDU. Who knows where all of that stuff ended up. Irving probably dumped it in the evidence incinerator at the ESB."

"Not all of it. When the new chief came in he wanted a full assessment of everything. He wanted to know where the bodies were buried. Anyway, I wasn't involved in that but I knew about it and I heard that a lot of the PDU files were kept after the unit was disbanded. A lot of it Irving put in Special Archives."

"Special Archives? What the hell is that?"

"It just means limited access. You need command approval. It's all in the basement at Parker Center. It's mostly in-house investigations. Political stuff. Dangerous stuff. This Chatsworth business doesn't really seem to qualify, unless it was connected to something else."

"Like what?"

"Like somebody in the department or somebody in the city."

The latter meant someone powerful in city politics.

"Can you get in there and see if any files on this still exist? What about your pal on six? Maybe he'd —"

"I can try."

"Then try."

"First thing. What about you? I thought you were going out to find Robert Verloren tonight, and now I hear you were following our suspect."

"I went down there. I didn't find him."

He proceeded to update her on his earlier swing through the Toy District, leaving out his encounter with the would-be robbers. That incident and the phone fiasco behind Mackey's house were not things he cared to share with her.

"I'll go back out there tomorrow morning," he said in conclusion.

"Okay, Harry. Sounds like a plan. I should have the warrant together by the time you get in. And I'll check on the PDU files."

Bosch hesitated but then decided not to hold back any warnings or concerns with his partner. He looked out the windshield at the dark street. He could hear the hiss from the nearby freeway.

"Kiz, be careful."

"How do you mean, Harry?"

"You know what it means when a case has high jingo?"

"Yeah, it means it's got command staff's fingers in the pie."

"That's right."

"And so?"

"So be careful. This thing has Irving all over it. It's not that obvious but it's there."

"You think his little visit with you at the coffee counter wasn't coincidence?"

"I don't believe in coincidences. Not like that."

There was silence for a bit before Rider answered.

"Okay, Harry, I'll watch myself. No holding back, though, right? We take it where it goes and let the chips fall. Everybody counts or nobody counts, remember?"

"Right. I remember. I'll see you tomorrow."

"Good night, Harry."

She hung up and Bosch sat in the car for a long time before turning the key.

19

Bosch started the engine, pulled a slow U-turn on Mariano and drove by the driveway that led to Mackey's house. It appeared to be all quiet down there. He saw no lights behind the windows.

He cut over to the freeway and took it east across the Valley and then down into the Cahuenga Pass. On the way he used his cell phone to call central dispatch and run the plate off the Ford pickup that Mackey had parked next to. It came back registered to a William Burkhart, who was thirty-seven years old and had a criminal record dating back to the late 1980s but nothing else in fifteen years. The dispatcher gave Bosch the California penal code numbers for his arrests because that's how they were listed on the computer.

Bosch immediately recognized aggravated assault and receiving stolen property charges. But there was one charge in 1988 with a code that he didn't recognize.

"Anybody there with a code book who can tell me what that is?" he asked, hoping things were quiet enough that the dispatcher would just do it herself. He knew that copies of the penal code were always in the dispatch center because officers often called in to get the proper citations when they were in the field.

"Hold on."

He waited. Meantime, he exited on Barham and took Woodrow Wilson up into the hills toward his home.

"Detective?"

"Still here."

"That was a hate crime violation."

"Okay. Thanks for looking it up."

"No problem."

Bosch pulled into his carport and killed the engine. Mackey's roommate or landlord was charged with a hate crime in 1988 — the same year as the murder of Rebecca Verloren. William Burkhart was likely the same Billy Burkhart whom Sam Weiss had identified as a neighbor and one of his tormentors. Bosch didn't know how all of this fit together but he knew it was part of the same picture. He now wished he had taken home the Department of Corrections file on Mackey. He was feeling too tired to go all the way back downtown to get it. He decided he would leave it be for the night and read it cover to cover when he got back to the office the next day. He would also get the file on William Burkhart's hate crime arrest.

The house was quiet when he got inside. He grabbed the phone and a beer out of the box and headed out onto the deck to check on the city. On the way he turned on the CD player. There was already a disc in the machine and he soon heard the voice of Boz Scaggs on the outside speakers. He was singing "For All We Know."

The song competed with the muted sound of the freeway down below. Bosch looked out and saw there were no searchlights cutting across the sky from Universal Studios. It was too late for that. Still, the view was captivating in the way it could only be at night. The city shimmered out there like a million dreams, not all of them good.

Bosch thought about calling Kiz Rider back and telling her about the William Burkhart connection but decided to let it wait until the morning. He looked out at the city and felt satisfied with the day's moves and accomplishments, but he was also out of sorts. High jingo did that to you.

The man with the knife had not been too far off in calling him a missionary man. He almost had it right. Bosch knew he had a mission in life and now, after three years, he was back on the beat. But he could not bring himself to believe it was all good. He felt that there was something out there beyond the shimmering lights and dreams, something he could not see. It was waiting for him.

He clicked on the phone and listened to an uninter-rupted dial tone. It meant he had no messages. He called the retrieval number anyway and replayed a message he had saved from the week before. It was his daughter's tiny voice, left the night she and her mother went traveling far away from him.

"Hello, Daddy," she said. "Good night, Daddy."

That was all she had said but that was enough. Bosch saved the message for the next time he needed it and then killed the line.

PART TWO
HIGH JINGO

20

At 7:50 a.m. the next day Bosch was back on the Nickel. He was watching the food line at the Metro Shelter and he had his eye on Robert Verloren back in the kitchen behind the steam tables. Bosch had gotten lucky. In the early morning, it was almost as if there had been a shift change among the homeless. The people who patrolled the street in darkness were sleeping off the night's failures. They were replaced by the first shift of homeless, the people who were smart enough to hide from the street at night. Bosch's intention had been to start at the big centers again and go from there. But as he had made his way into the homeless zone after parking again in Japantown, he started showing the photo of Verloren to the most lucid of the street people he encountered and almost immediately started getting responses. The day people recognized Verloren. Some said they had seen the man in the photo around but that he was much older now. Eventually Bosch came across one man who matter-of-factly said, "Yeah, that's Chef," and he pointed Bosch toward the Metro Shelter.

The Metro was one of the smaller satellite shelters that were clustered around the Salvation Army and the Los Angeles Mission and designed to handle the overflow of street people, particularly in the winter months when warmer weather in L.A. drew a migration from colder points north. These smaller centers didn't have the means to provide three squares a day and by agreement specialized in one service. At the Metro Shelter the service was a breakfast that started at 7 a.m. daily. By the time Bosch got there the line of wobbling, disheveled men and women was extending out the door of the chow center and the long rows of picnic-style tables inside were maxed out. The word on the street was that the Metro had the best breakfast on the Nickel.

Bosch had badged his way through the door and very quickly spotted Verloren in the kitchen beyond the serving tables. It didn't appear that Verloren was doing one particular job. Instead, he seemed to be checking on the preparation of several things. It appeared that he was in charge. He was neatly dressed in a white, double-breasted kitchen shirt over dark pants, a spotless white apron that went down past his knees and a tall white chef's hat.

The breakfast consisted of scrambled eggs with red and green peppers, hash browns, grits and disc sausages. It looked and smelled good to Bosch, who had left home without eating anything because he wanted to get moving. To the right of the serving line was a coffee station with two large serve-yourself urns. There were racks containing cups made of thick porcelain that had chipped and yellowed over time. Bosch took a cup and filled it with scalding black coffee and he sipped it and waited. When Verloren strode to the serving table, using the skirt of his apron to hold a hot and heavy replacement pan of eggs, Bosch made his move.

"Hey, Chef," he called above the clatter of serving spoons and voices.

Verloren looked over and Bosch saw him immediately determine that Bosch was not a "client." As with the night before, Bosch was dressed informally, but he thought Verloren might have even been able to guess he was a cop. He stepped away from the serving table and approached. But he didn't come all the way. There seemed to be an invisible line on the floor that was the demarcation between kitchen and eating space. Verloren didn't cross it. He stood there using his apron to hold the near-empty serving pan he had taken from the steam table.

"Can I help you?" he asked.

"Yes, do you have a minute? I would like to talk to you."

"No, I don't have a minute. I'm in the middle of breakfast."

"It's about your daughter."

Bosch saw the slight waver in Verloren's eyes. They dropped for a second and then came back up.

"You're the police?"

Bosch nodded.

"Can I just get through this rush? We're putting out the last trays now."

"No problem."

"You want to eat? You look like you're hungry."

"Uh . . ."

Bosch looked around the room at the crowded tables. He didn't know where he would sit. He knew that these sorts of chow halls had the same unspoken protocols as prisons. Add in the high degree of mental illness in the homeless population and you could be crossing some sort of line just by the seat you chose.

"Come back with me," Verloren said. "We have a table in the back."

Bosch turned back to Verloren but the breakfast chef was already heading back to the kitchen. Bosch followed and was led through the cooking and prep areas to a rear room where there was an empty stainless steel table with a full ashtray on it.

"Have a seat."

Verloren removed the ashtray and held it behind his back. It was not like he was hiding it. It was like he was a waiter or a maître d' and he wanted his table perfect for the customer. Bosch thanked him and sat down.

"I'll be right back."

It seemed that in less than a minute Verloren brought a plate back loaded with all the things Bosch had seen on the serving table. When he put down the silverware Bosch saw the shake in his hand.

"Thank you, but I was just thinking, will there be enough? You know, for the people coming through?"

"We're not turning anybody away today. Not as long as they're on time. How's your coffee?"

"It's fine, thanks. You know, it wasn't like I didn't want to sit out there with them. I just didn't know where to sit."

"I understand. You don't have to explain. Let me get those trays out and then we can talk. Is there an arrest?"

Bosch looked at him. There was a hopeful, maybe even pleading look in Verloren's eyes.

"Not yet," Bosch said. "But we're getting close to something."

"I'll be back as soon as I can. Eat. I call that Malibu scrambled."

Bosch looked down at his plate. Verloren went back to the kitchen.

The eggs were good. So was the whole breakfast. No toast, but that would have been asking too much. The break area where he sat was between the cooking area of the kitchen and the large room where two men loaded an industrial dishwasher. It was loud, the noise from both directions ricocheting off the gray tiled walls. There was a set of double doors leading to the back alley. One door was open and cool air came in and kept the steam from the dishwasher and the heat from the kitchen at bay.

After Bosch cleaned his plate and washed it down with the rest of his coffee he got up and stepped into the alley to make a phone call away from all the noise. He immediately saw the alley was an encampment. The rear walls of the missions on one side and the toy warehouses on the other were lined almost end to end with cardboard and canvas shanties. It was quiet. These were probably the self-made shelters of the night people. It wasn't that there was no room for them in the mission dormitories. It was that those beds came with basic rules attached and the people in the alley did not want to abide by such rules.

He called Kiz Rider's cell phone number and she answered right away. She was already in room 503 and had just finished distributing the wiretap application. Bosch spoke in a low voice.

"I found the father."

"Great work, Harry. You still got it. What did he say? Did he recognize Mackey?"

"I haven't talked to him yet."

He explained the situation and asked if there was anything new on her end.

"The warrant's on the captain's desk. Abel's going to push him on it if we don't hear back by ten, and then it goes up the chain."

"How early did you come in?"

"Early. I wanted to get this done."

"Did you ever get a chance to read the girl's journal last night?"

"Yeah, I read it in bed. It's not much help. It's high school confidential stuff. Unrequited love, weekly crushes, stuff like that. MTL is mentioned but no clue to identity. He might even be a fantasy figure, the way she writes about how special he is. I think Garcia was right to give it back to the mom. It's not going to help us."

"Is MTL referred to in the book as a *he*?"

"Hmm, Harry, that's clever. I didn't notice. I have it here and I'll check. You know something I don't know?"

"No, just covering all the bases. What about Danny Kotchof? Is he in there?"

"In the beginning. He's mentioned by name. Then he drops off and mysterious MTL takes his place."

"Mr. X . . ."

"Listen, I'm going up to six in a few minutes. I'm going to see about getting access to those old files we were talking about."

Bosch noticed that she hadn't mentioned that they were PDU files. He wondered if Pratt or someone else was nearby and she was taking precautions against being overheard.

"Is somebody there, Kiz?"

"That's right."

"Take all precautions, right?"

"You got it."

"Good. Good luck. By the way, did you find a phone on Mariano?"

"Yes," she said. "There's one phone and it's under the name William Burkhart. Must be a roommate. This guy is just a few years older than Mackey and has a record that includes a hate crime. Nothing in recent years but the hate crime was in 'eighty-eight."

"And guess what," Bosch said, "he was also Sam Weiss's neighbor. I must've left that out last night when we talked."

"Too much information coming in."

"Yeah. You know I was wondering about something. How come Mackey's cell didn't come up on the Auto-Track?"

"I'm ahead of you on that. I ran a check on the number and it's not his. It's held in the name of Belinda Messier. Her address is over on Melba, also in Woodland Hills. Her record's clean except for some traffic stuff. Maybe she's his girlfriend."

"Maybe."

"When I get time I will try to track her down. I'm sensing something here, Harry. It's all coming together. All of this eighty-eight stuff. I tried to pull the file on the hate crime but —"

"Public Disorder?"

"Exactly. And that's why I'm going up to six."

"Okay, anything else?"

"I checked with the ESB first thing. They still haven't found the evidence box. We still don't have the gun. I'm now wondering if it got misplaced or if it was taken."

"Yeah," Bosch said, thinking the same thing. If this case went inside the department, the evidence could have been purposely and permanently lost.

"All right," Bosch said. "Before I do this interview let's go back to the journal for a minute. Is there anything in it about the pregnancy?"

"No, she didn't write about it. The entries are dated and she stopped writing in the book in late April. Maybe it was when she found out. I think maybe she stopped writing in it in case her parents were secretly reading it."

"Does she mention any hangouts? You know, places she would go?"

"She does mention a lot of movies," Rider said. "Not who she went with but just that she saw specific movies and what she thought of them. What are you thinking, target acquisition?"

They needed to know where Mackey and Rebecca Verloren could have crossed paths. It was a hole in the case no matter what the motivation was. Where did Mackey come into contact with Verloren in order to target her?

"Movie theaters," he said. "It could have been where they intersected."

"Exactly. And I think all the theaters up there in the Valley are in malls. That makes the crossing zone even wider."

"It's something to think about."

Bosch said he would come into the office after talking with Robert Verloren, and they hung up. Bosch went back into the break room and the noise from the dishwashing room seemed louder. The meal service was almost over and the dishwashers were getting slammed. Bosch sat down at the table again and noticed that someone had cleared his empty plate. He tried to think about the conversation with Rider. He knew that a shopping mall would be a huge crossroads, a place where it would be easy to see someone like Mackey crossing paths with someone like Rebecca Verloren. He wondered if the crime could have all come down to a chance encounter — Mackey seeing a girl with the obvious mix of races in her face and hair and eyes. Could this have incensed him to the point that he followed her home and later came back alone or with others to abduct and kill her?

It seemed like a long shot but most theories began as long shots. He thought about the original investigation and the possibility of it having been tainted from within the department. There had been nothing in the murder book that played to the racial angle. But in 1988 the department would have gone out of its way not to play to it. The department and the city had a blind spot. An infection of racial animosities was festering beneath the surface in 1988 but the department and the city looked away. The skin over the seething wound finally broke a few years later and the city was torn apart by three days of rioting, the worst in the country in a quarter-century. Bosch had to consider that the investigation of Rebecca Verloren's murder might have been stunted in deference to keeping the sickness beneath the surface.

"You ready?"

Bosch looked up and saw Robert Verloren standing over him. His face was sweating from exertion. He now held the chef's hat in his hand. There was still a slight tremor in his arm.

"Yeah, sure. Do you want to sit down?"

Verloren took the seat across from Bosch.

"Is it always like this?" Bosch asked. "This crowded?"

"Every morning. Today we served a hundred sixty-two plates. A lot of people count on us. No, wait, make that a hundred sixty-three plates. I forgot about you. How was it?"

"It was damn good. Thank you, I needed the fuel."

"My specialty."

"A little different than cooking for Johnny Carson and the Malibu set, huh?"

"Yeah, but I don't miss that. Not at all. Just a stop-off on the road to finding the place where I belong. But I'm here now, thanks to the Lord Jesus, and this is where I want to be."

Bosch nodded. Whether intentionally or not, Verloren was communicating to Bosch that his new life had been achieved through the intervention of faith. Bosch had often found that those who talked about it the most had the weakest hold on it.

"How did you find me?" Verloren asked.

"My partner and I talked to your wife yesterday and she told us that the last time she had heard anything about you, you were down here. I started looking last night."

"I wouldn't go on these streets at night, if I were you."

There was a slight Caribbean lilt in his voice. But it was something that seemed to have receded over time.

"I thought I was going to find you standing in a line, not feeding the line."

"Well, not too long ago I was in the line. I had to stand there to stand where I am today."

Bosch nodded again. He had heard these one-day-at-a-time mantras before.

"How long have you been sober?"

Verloren smiled.

"This time? A little over three years."

"Look, I don't want to force you to relive the trauma of seventeen years ago, but we've reopened the case."

"It's okay, Detective. I reopen the case every night when I shut my eyes and every morning when I say my prayers to Jesus."

Bosch nodded again.

"Do you want to do this here or take a walk or go over to Parker Center where we can sit in a quiet room?"

"Here is good. I am comfortable here."

"Okay, then let me tell you a little bit about what is going on. I work for the Open-Unsolved Unit. We are currently looking into your daughter's murder again because we have some new information."

"What information?"

Bosch decided to take a different approach with him. Where he had held information back from the mother, he decided to give it all to the father.

"We have a match between blood found on the weapon used in the crime and an individual who we are pretty sure was living up there in Chatsworth at the time of the killing. It's a DNA match. Do you know what that is?"

Verloren nodded.

"I know. Like in O.J."

"This one's solid. It doesn't mean he is the one who killed Rebecca, but it means he was close to the crime, and that makes us closer."

"Who is it?"

"I'll get to that in a minute. But first, Mr. Verloren, I want to ask you some questions relating to yourself and the case."

"What about me?"

Bosch felt the tension rise. The skin around Verloren's eyes grew tighter. He realized that he could have been careless with this man, mistaking his position in the kitchen as a sign of health and forgetting the warning Rider had issued about the homeless population.

"Well," he said, "I'd like to know a little bit about what has happened to you in the years since Rebecca was taken."

"What's that got to do with anything?"

"Maybe nothing, but I want to know."

"What happened to me is that I tripped and fell into a black hole. Took me a long time to see the light and my way out. You got kids?"

"One. A girl."

"Then you know what I mean. You lose a kid the way I lost my girl and that's it, my friend. It's all over. You are like an empty bottle tossed out the window. The car keeps going but you are on the side of the road, broken."

Bosch nodded. He did know this. He lived a life of screaming vulnerability, knowing that what might happen in a city far away could cause him to live or die, or fall into the same black hole as Verloren.

"After your daughter's death you lost the restaurant?"

"That's right. It was the best thing that could have happened. I needed that to happen for me to find out who I really was. And to make my way here."

Bosch knew that such emotional defenses were fragile. Following Verloren's logic it could be said that his daughter's death was the best thing that could have happened because it led to the loss of the restaurant, which triggered all the wonderful personal discoveries he had made. It was bullshit and both men at the table knew it; one just couldn't admit it.

"Mr. Verloren, talk to me," Bosch said. "Leave all the self-help lessons for your meetings and the ragged people in line. Tell me how you tripped. Tell me how you fell into that black hole."

"I just did."

"Not everybody who loses a child falls so far into the hole. You're not the only one this has happened to, Mr. Verloren. Some people end up on TV, some run for Congress. What happened to you? Why are you different? And don't tell me it is because you loved your kid more. We all love our kids."

Verloren was quiet a moment. He pressed his lips tightly together as he composed. Bosch could tell he had made him angry. But that was okay. He needed to push things.

"All right," Verloren finally said. "All right."

But that was all. Bosch could see the muscles of his jaw working. The pain of the last seventeen years had set in his face. Bosch could read it like a menu. Appetizers, entrees, desserts. Frustration, anger, irredeemable loss.

"All right what, Mr. Verloren?"

Verloren nodded. He removed the final barricade.

"I could blame you people but I must blame myself. I abandoned my daughter in death, Detective. And then the only place I could hide from the betrayal was in the bottle. The bottle opens up the black hole. Do you understand?"

Bosch nodded.

"I am trying to. Tell me what you mean about blaming *you people*. Do you mean cops? Do you mean white people?"

"I mean all of it."

Verloren turned in his seat so that his back was against the tile wall next to the table. He looked toward the door to the alley. He wasn't looking at Bosch. Bosch wanted the eye contact, but he was willing to let things ride as long as Verloren kept talking.

"Let's start with the cops, then," Bosch said. "Why do

you blame the cops? What did the cops do?"

"You expect me to talk to you about what *you* people did?"

Bosch thought carefully before responding. He felt this was the make-or-break point of the interview and he sensed that this man had something important to give up.

"We start with the fact that you loved your daughter, right?" Bosch said.

"Of course."

"Well, Mr. Verloren, what happened to her should never have happened. I can't do anything about it. But I can try to speak for her. That's why I am here. What the cops did seventeen years ago is not what I am going to do. Most of them are dead now anyway. If you still love your daughter, if you love the memory of her, then you will tell me the story. You will help me speak for her. It's your only way of making up for what you did back then."

Verloren started nodding halfway through Bosch's plea. Bosch knew he had him, that he would open up. It was about redemption. It didn't matter how many years had gone by. Redemption was always the brass ring.

A single tear rolled down Verloren's left cheek, almost imperceptible against the dark skin. A man in dirty kitchen whites came into the break area with a clipboard in hand but Bosch quickly waved him away from Verloren. Bosch waited and finally Verloren spoke.

"I chose myself over her and in the end I lost myself anyway," he said.

"How did that happen?"

Verloren covered his mouth with his hand, as if to try to keep the secrets from being dispelled. Finally he dropped it and spoke.

"I read one day in the newspaper that my daughter had been killed with a gun that came from a burglary. Green and Garcia, they hadn't told me that. So I asked Detective

Green about it and he told me the man with the gun had it because he was afraid. He was a Jewish man and there had been threats against him. I thought..."

He stopped there and Bosch had to prompt him.

"You thought that maybe Rebecca had been targeted because of her mixed races? Because her father was black?"

Verloren nodded.

"I thought, yes, because from time to time there would be a comment or something. Not everybody saw the beauty in her. Not like we did. I wanted to live on the Westside, but Muriel, she was from up there. It was home to her."

"What did Green tell you?"

"He told me, no, that it wasn't there. They had looked at that and it wasn't a possibility. It wasn't... it didn't seem right to me. They were ignoring this, it seemed to me. I kept calling and asking. I was pushing it. Finally I went to a customer I had at the restaurant who was a member of the police commission. I told him about this thing and he said he would check into it for me."

Verloren nodded, more to himself than to Bosch. He was fortifying his faith in his actions as a father seeking justice for his daughter.

"And then what happened?" Bosch prompted.

"Then I got a visit from two police."

"Not Green and Garcia?"

"No, not them. Different police. They came to my restaurant."

"What were their names?"

Verloren shook his head.

"They never gave me their names. They just showed me their badges. They were detectives, I think. They told me I was wrong about what I was pushing Green about. They told me to back off it because I was just stirring the pot. That is what they called it, stirring the pot. Like it was about me and not my daughter."

He shook his head tightly, that anger still sharp after all the years. Bosch asked an obvious question, obvious because he knew so well how the LAPD worked back then.

"Did they threaten you?"

Verloren snorted.

"Yes, they threatened me," he said quietly. "They told me that they knew my daughter had been pregnant but they couldn't find the clinic she had gone to to get it taken care of. So there was no tissue they could use to identify the father. No way to tell who it was or wasn't. They said that all it would take was for them to ask a few questions about me and her, like with my customer on the police commission, and the rumors would start to run. They said just a few questions in the right places and pretty soon people would think it was me."

Bosch didn't interrupt. He felt his own anger tightening his throat.

"They said it would be hard for me to keep my business if everybody thought I had . . . I had done that to my daughter . . ."

Now more tears came down his dark face. He did nothing to stop their flow.

"And so I did what they wanted. I backed off and dropped it. Stopped stirring the pot. I told myself it didn't matter; it wouldn't bring Becky back to us. So I never called Detective Green again . . . and they never solved the case. After a while I started drinking to forget what I had lost and what I had done, that I had put myself and my pride and my reputation and my business ahead of my daughter. And pretty soon, before you knew it, I came to that black hole I was telling you about. I fell in and I'm still climbing out."

After a moment he turned and looked at Bosch.

"How's that for a story, Detective?"

"I'm sorry, Mr. Verloren. I'm sorry that happened. All of it."

"Is that the story you wanted to hear, Detective?"

"I just wanted to know the truth. Believe it or not, it is going to help me. It will help me speak for her. Can you describe these two men who came to you?"

Verloren shook his head.

"It's been a long time. I probably wouldn't recognize them if they stood in front of me. I just remember they were both white men. One of them I always thought of as Mr. Clean because his head was shaved and he stood with his arms folded like the guy on the bottle."

Bosch nodded and he felt his anger working into the muscles of his shoulders. He knew who Mr. Clean was.

"How much of all this did your wife know?" he asked in a calm tone.

Verloren shook his head.

"Muriel didn't know anything about this. I kept it from her. It was my water to carry."

Verloren wiped his cheeks and seemed to have earned some relief from finally telling the story.

Bosch reached into his back pocket and came up with the old photograph of Roland Mackey. He put it down on the table in front of Verloren.

"Do you recognize this kid?"

Verloren looked for a long moment before shaking his head in the negative.

"Should I? Who is he?"

"His name is Roland Mackey. He was a couple years older than your daughter in 'eighty-eight. He didn't go to school at Hillside but he lived in Chatsworth."

Bosch waited for a response but didn't get any. Verloren just stared at the photo on the table.

"That's a mug shot. What did he do?"

"Stole a car. But he has a record of associating with

white power extremists. In and outside of jail. Does the name mean anything to you?"

"No. Should it?"

"I don't know. I'm just asking. Can you remember if your daughter ever mentioned his name or maybe somebody named Ro?"

Verloren shook his head.

"What we are trying to do is figure out if they could have intersected anywhere. The Valley's a big place. They could've —"

"What school did he go to?"

"He went to Chatsworth High but never finished. He got a GED."

"Rebecca went to Chatsworth High for driver's ed the summer before she was taken."

"You mean 'eighty-seven?"

Verloren nodded.

"I'll check it out."

But Bosch didn't think it was a good lead. Mackey had dropped out before the summer of 1987 and didn't come back for his general education degree until 1988. Still, it was worth a thorough look.

"What about the movies? Did she like to go to movies and the mall?"

Verloren shrugged.

"She was a sixteen-year-old girl. Of course she liked movies. Most of her friends had cars. Once they hit sixteen and got mobile they were all over the place. My wife called it the three Ms — movies, malls, and Madonna."

"Which malls? Which theaters?"

"They went to the Northridge Mall because it was close, you know. They also liked to go to the drive-in over on Winnetka. That way they could sit in the car and talk during the movie. One of the girls had a convertible and they liked going in that."

Bosch zeroed in on the drive-in. He had forgotten about it when he had spoken about movie theaters with Rider earlier. But Roland Mackey had once been arrested burglarizing the same drive-in on Winnetka. That made it a key possibility as the point of intersection.

"How often did Rebecca and her friends go to the drive-in?"

"I think they liked to go on Friday nights, when the new movies were just out."

"Did they meet boys there?"

"I would assume so. You see, this is all just second-guessing. There was nothing wrong or unnatural about our daughter going to the movies with her friends and meeting up with boys and whatnot. It is only after the worst-case scenario happens that people ask, 'Why don't you know who she was with?' We thought everything was fine. We sent her to the best school we could find. Her friends were from nice families. We couldn't watch her every minute of the day. Friday nights — hell, most nights — I worked late at the restaurant."

"I understand. I am not judging you as a parent, Mr. Verloren. I see nothing wrong with that, okay? I am just dragging a net. I'm collecting as much information as I can because you never know what might become important."

"Yeah, well, that net got snagged and ripped on the rocks a long time ago."

"Maybe not."

"You think this Mackey fellow is the one, then?"

"He's connected somehow, that's all we know for sure. We'll know more soon enough. I promise you that."

Verloren turned and looked directly into Bosch's eyes for the first time during the interview.

"When you get to that point, you will speak for her, won't you, Detective?"

Bosch nodded slowly. He thought he knew what Verloren was asking.

"Yes sir, I will."

21

Kiz Rider sat at her desk with her arms folded, as if she had been waiting for Bosch all morning. She had a somber look on her face and Bosch knew something was up.

"You get the PDU file?" he asked.

"I got to look at it. I wasn't allowed to take it."

Bosch nodded. He slid into his seat across from her.

"Good stuff?" he asked.

"Depends on how you look at it."

"Well, I got some stuff, too."

He looked around. Abel Pratt's door was open and Bosch could see him in there, bending over to the little cooler he kept next to his desk. Pratt was in earshot. It wasn't that Bosch didn't trust Pratt. He did. But he didn't want to put him in a position of hearing something he didn't want to or was not ready to hear. Same as Rider when they had spoken on the phone earlier.

He looked back at his partner.

"You want to take a walk?"

"Yes, I do."

They got up and headed out. When Bosch went past the OIC's door he leaned in. Pratt was now on the phone. Bosch caught his attention and pantomimed drinking from a cup and then pointed to Pratt. Shaking his head no to the offer of coffee, Pratt held up a tub of yogurt as if to say he had what he needed. Bosch saw little chunks of green in the gunk. He tried to think of a green fruit and only came up with kiwi. He walked away thinking that the only possible way to make yogurt taste worse was to put kiwi into it.

They took the elevator down to the lobby and walked out front to where the memorial fountain was.

"So where do you want to go?" Kiz asked.

"Depends on how much there is to talk about."

"Probably a lot."

"Last time I worked in Parker Center I was a smoker. When I needed to walk and think I'd go over to Union Station and buy smokes in the shop over there. I liked that place. It's got those comfortable chairs in the main hall. Or it used to, at least."

"Sounds good to me."

They headed that way, taking Los Angeles Street to the north. The first building they passed was the federal office building, and Bosch noticed that the concrete barriers erected in 2001 to keep potential vehicle bombs away from the building were still in place. The threat of danger didn't seem to bother the people in the line stretching across the front of the building. They were waiting to get into the immigration offices, each clutching paperwork and ready to make a case for citizenship. They waited beneath the tile mosaics on the front façade that depicted people dressed like angels, their eyes skyward, waiting on heaven.

"Why don't you start, Harry," Rider said. "Tell me about Robert Verloren."

Bosch walked a little further before beginning.

"I liked the guy," he said. "He's digging himself out of the hole. He cooks a hundred or so breakfasts a day over there. I had a plate and it was pretty good stuff."

"And I'm sure it beats the hell out of the prices at Pacific Dining Car. What did he give you that's made you so angry?"

"What are you talking about?"

"You read me, I read you. I know he told you something that's got you going."

Bosch nodded. It sure didn't seem like three years since they had worked together.

"Irving. Or at least I think he gave me Irving."

"Tell it."

Bosch took her through the story Verloren had told him less than an hour before. He finished with Verloren's description, limited as it was, of the two men with badges who came to his restaurant and threatened him in order to make him back off the racial angle.

"Sounds like Irving to me, too," Rider said.

"And one of his poodles. Maybe it was McClellan."

"Maybe. So you think Verloren was straight? He's been on the Nickel a long time."

"I think so. He claims to have been sober for three years this time. But you know, grinding over something for seventeen years, pretty soon perceptions become facts. Still, everything he said just seems to fit into the underpinnings of this. I think they pushed this case, Kiz. It was going in one direction and they pushed it the other way. Maybe they knew what was coming, that the city was going to burn. Rodney King wasn't the gasoline. He was only the match. Things had been building and maybe the powers that be looked at this case and said for the public good, we have to go the other way. They sacrificed justice for Rebecca Verloren."

They were crossing over the 101 Freeway on the Los Angeles Street overpass. Eight lanes of crawling traffic smoked beneath them. The sun was bright, reflecting off windshields and buildings and concrete. Bosch put on his Ray-Bans.

The traffic was loud, too, and Rider had to raise her voice.

"That's not like you, Harry."

"What isn't?"

"Looking for a good reason for them to have done something so wrong. You usually look for the sinister angle."

"Are you telling me you found the sinister angle in that PDU file?"

She nodded glumly.

"I think so," she said.

"And they just let you waltz in there and get it?"

"I got in to see the man first thing this morning. I brought him a cup of coffee from Starbucks — he hates the cafeteria crap. That got me in. Then I told him what we had and what I wanted to do, and the bottom line is he trusts me. So he more or less let me have a look around in Special Archives."

"The Public Disorder Unit came and went long before he was here. Did he know about it?"

"I'm sure after he took the job he was briefed. Maybe even before he took it."

"Did you tell him specifically about Mackey and the Chatsworth Eights?"

"Not specifically. I just told him the case we caught was connected to an old PDU investigation and I needed to get into Special Archives to look for a file. He sent Lieutenant Hohman with me. We went in, found the file and I had to look through it while Hohman sat across a table from me. You know what, Harry? There are a hell of a lot of files in Special Archives."

"Where all the bodies are buried . . ."

Bosch wanted to say something more but wasn't sure how to say it. Rider looked at him and read him.

"What, Harry?"

He didn't say anything at first but she waited him out.

"Kiz, you said the man on six trusts you. Do you trust him?"

She looked him in the eye when she answered.

"Like I trust you, Harry. Okay?"

Bosch looked at her.

"That's good enough for me."

Rider made a move to turn down Arcadia but Bosch pointed toward the old pueblo, the place where the City of Angels was founded. He wanted to take the long way and walk through.

"I haven't been down here in a while. Let's check this out."

They cut through the circular courtyard where the padres blessed the animals every Easter and then past the Instituto Cultural Mexicano. They followed the curving arcade of cheap souvenir booths and churro stands. Recorded mariachi music came from unseen speakers, but in counterpoint was the sound of a live guitar.

They found the musician sitting on a bench in front of the Avila Adobe. They stopped and listened as the old man played a Mexican ballad Bosch thought he had heard before but could not identify.

Bosch studied the mud-walled structure behind the musician and wondered if Don Francisco Avila had any idea what he was helping to set in motion when he staked his claim to the spot in 1818. A city would grow tall and wide from this place. A city as great as any other. And just as mean. A destination city, a city of invention and reinvention. A place where the dream seemed as easy to reach as the sign they put up on the hill, but a place where the reality was always something different. The road to that sign on the hill had a locked gate across it.

It was a city full of haves and have-nots, movie stars and extras, drivers and the driven, predators and prey. The fat and the hungry and little room in between. A city that despite all of that still had them lining up and waiting every day behind the bomb barriers to get in and stay in.

Bosch pulled the fold of money from his pocket and dropped a five in the old musician's basket. He and Rider then cut through the old Cucamonga Winery, its cask rooms converted into galleries and artists' stalls, and out to Alameda. They crossed the street to the train station, its clock tower rising in front of them. In the front walkway they passed a sundial with an inscription cut into its granite pedestal.

Vision to See
Faith to Believe
Courage to Do

Union Station was designed to mirror the city it served and the way in which it was supposed to work. It was a melting pot of architectural styles — Spanish Colonial, Mission, Streamline Moderne, Art Deco, Southwestern and Moorish design flourishes among them. But unlike the rest of the city, where the pot more often than not boiled over, the styles at the train station blended smoothly into something unique, something beautiful. Bosch loved it for that.

Through the glass doors they came into the cavernous entry hall, and an archway three stories tall led to the immense waiting room beyond. As Bosch took it in he remembered that he used to walk over here not only for cigarettes, but also to renew himself a little bit. Going to Union Station was like paying a visit to church, a cathedral where the graceful lines of design and function and civic pride all intersected. In the central waiting room the voices of travelers rose into its high empty spaces and were transformed into a choir of languid whispers.

"I love this place," Rider said. "Did you ever see the movie *Blade Runner*?"

Bosch nodded. He had seen it.

"This was the police station, right?" he asked.

"Yeah."

"Did you ever see *True Confessions*?" he asked.

"No, was it good?"

"Yeah, you should see it. Another take on the Black Dahlia and LAPD conspiracy."

She groaned.

"Thanks, but I don't think that's what I need right now."

They got cups of coffee at Union Bagel and then walked into the waiting room, where rows of brown leather seats were lined up like luxurious pews. Bosch looked up as he was always drawn to do. Six huge chandeliers hung forty feet above them in two rows. Rider looked up, too.

Bosch then pointed to two side-by-side seats open near the newsstand. They sat down on the soft padded leather and put their cups on the wide wooden armrests.

"You ready to talk about this now?" Rider asked.

"If you are," he answered. "What was in the file you saw in Special Archives? What was so sinister?"

"For one thing, Mackey is in there."

"As a suspect in Verloren?"

"No, the file has nothing to do with Verloren. Verloren was not even a blip on the screen as far as the file goes. It's all about an investigation that went down and was buttoned up before Rebecca Verloren was even pregnant, let alone snatched from her bed in the night."

"All right, then what's it got to do with us?"

"Maybe nothing and maybe everything. You know the guy Mackey lives with, William Burkhart?"

"Yeah."

"He's in there, too. Only back then he was better known as Billy Blitzkrieg. That was his moniker in this gang, the Eights."

"Okay."

"In March of 'eighty-eight Billy Blitzkrieg went away

for a year for vandalizing a synagogue in North Hollywood. Property damage, graffiti, defecation, the whole thing."

"The hate crime. He was the only one they bagged?"

She nodded.

"They got a latent off a spray can they found in a gutter trap about a block from the synagogue. So he went down for it. Took a plea or they would have made an example of him and he knew it."

Bosch nodded. He didn't want to say anything that would interrupt her flow.

"In the reports and in the press Burkhart — or Blitzkrieg or whatever you want to call him — was portrayed as the leader of the Eights. They said he called for nineteen eighty-eight to be a year of racial and ethnic upheaval to honor their beloved Adolf Hitler. You know the crap. RaHoWa, revenge of the white trash and all that. They all ran around in Minnesota Vikings jerseys — the Vikings apparently were a pure race. They all wore number eighty-eight."

"I'm getting the picture."

"Anyway, they had a lot on Burkhart. They had him cold on the synagogue and they had the feds chomping at the bit to do a civil rights dance on his pointy little head. There were a lot of crimes, beginning right at the start of the year, when they toasted New Year's by burning a cross on a black family's lawn in Chatsworth. After that there were more cross burnings, threatening phone calls, bomb scares. The synagogue break-in. They even trashed a Jewish daycare center in Encino. This was all in early January. They also started going to street corners, picking up Mexican laborers and taking them out into the desert, where they assaulted or abandoned them or both, usually both. To use their terminology, they were fomenting disharmony, which they believed would help lead to a separation of the races."

"Yeah, I've heard the song."

"Okay, well, like I said, they were ready to make Burkhart the poster boy for all of this and, if they went with it to Justice, he could have ended up going away for a ten-year minimum in a federal pen."

"So it was a no-brainer. He took a deal."

Rider nodded.

"He took a year in Wayside and a five-year tail, and the rest of it went away. And the Eights went away with it. They were broken up and that was the end of the threat. All of this went down by the end of March, long before Verloren."

As he thought about all of this Bosch watched a woman in a hurry as she pulled a young girl by the hand toward the gateway to the Metroline tracks. The woman was also lugging a heavy suitcase and her focus was only on the gate ahead. The child was pulled along with her face turned upward as she looked at the ceiling. She was smiling at something. Bosch looked up and saw a child's balloon trapped in one of the ceiling's vaulted squares. One child's disaster was another's secret smile. The balloon was orange and white and shaped like a fish, and Bosch knew because of his daughter that it was an animated character named Nemo. He had a flash of his daughter but just as quickly pushed it away so he could concentrate. He looked at Rider.

"So where was Mackey in all of this?" he asked.

"He was sort of the runt of the litter," Rider answered. "One of the minions. He was thought to be the perfect recruit. High school dropout with no life and no prospects. He was on probation for burglary and his juvie jacket was full of pops for car theft, burglary and drugs. So he was just the kind of guy they were looking for. A loser they could mold into a white warrior. But once they jumped him in they found out he was — to use a quote from Burkhart —

dumber than a nigger off the boat. He apparently was so stupid that they had to take him off the graffiti runs because he couldn't even spell their basic racist vocabulary. In fact, his homey name in the group became Wej. Not like you wedge your way into a door. Wej like Jew spelled backwards because that was how he sprayed it once on a synagogue wall."

"Dyslexic?"

"I'd say."

Bosch shook his head.

"Even with the giveaways in the Verloren scene, I'm not seeing this guy."

"I agree. I think he had a part but not the main part. He doesn't have it between the ears."

Bosch decided to drop Mackey and double back to the beginning of her report.

"So if they had all of this intel on these guys, how come only Burkhart went down?"

"I'm getting to that."

"This is where the high jingo comes in?"

"You got it. You see, Burkhart was a leader of the Eights but he wasn't *the* leader."

"Ah."

"The leader was identified as a guy named Richard Ross. He was older than the others. A true believer. He was twenty-one and was the smooth talker who recruited Burkhart and then most of the other Eights and got the whole thing going."

Bosch nodded. Richard Ross was a common name but he thought he knew where this was going.

"This Richard Ross, was that as in Richard Ross Junior?"

"Exactly. The good Captain Ross's progeny."

Captain Richard Ross had been the longtime head of Internal Affairs Division during the early part of Bosch's career in the department. He was now retired.

For Bosch the rest of the story tumbled into place.

"So they kept Junior out of it and saved Senior and the department all the embarrassment," he said. "They laid it all on Burkhart, Ross's second in command. He went away to Wayside and the group was broken up. Chalk it all up to youthful misadventure."

"You got it."

"And let me guess: all the intel came from Richard Ross Junior."

"You're good. It was part of the deal. Richard Junior gave up everybody and it was all PDU needed to quietly splinter the group. Junior then got to walk away from it."

"All in a day's work for Irving."

"And you know what's funny? I think Irving is a Jewish name."

Bosch shook his head.

"Whether it is or isn't, it's not very funny," he said.

"Yeah, I know."

"Not if Irving saw an angle."

"Reading between the lines of the report, I would say he saw all the angles."

"This deal gave him control of IAD. I mean real, absolute control over who was investigated and how investigations were conducted. It put Ross deep in his pocket. It explains a lot about what was going on back then."

"It was mostly before my time."

"So they take care of the Eights and Irving gets a nice big prize in having Richard Ross Senior wearing a collar on the poodle squad," Bosch said, thinking out loud. "But then Rebecca Verloren ends up dead by a gun stolen from a guy the Eights had been harassing, a gun likely stolen by one of the little runts they let run free. Their whole deal could fall apart if the murder came back on the Eights and then on them."

"That's right. So they step in and push the investigation.

They steer it away and nobody ever goes down for it."

"Motherfuckers," Bosch whispered.

"Poor Harry. You still must have a lot of rust from your lay-off. You thought maybe they pushed the case because they were trying to save the city from burning. It was nothing so heroic."

"No, they were just trying to save their own asses and the position the deal with Ross had given them. Given Irving."

"This is all supposition," Rider cautioned.

"Yeah, just reading between the fucking lines."

Bosch felt the strongest craving for a cigarette he'd had in at least a year. He looked over at the newsstand and saw all of the packages in the racks behind the counter. He looked away. He looked up at the balloon trapped at the ceiling. He thought he knew how Nemo felt being stuck up there.

"When did Ross retire?" he asked.

"'Ninety-one. He rode it out until he hit twenty-five years — they allowed him that — and then he retired. I checked — he moved up to Idaho. I ran Junior on the box, too, and he'd already moved up there ahead of him. Probably one of those gated white enclaves where he felt right at home."

"And he was probably up there laughing his ass off when this place came apart after Rodney King in 'ninety-two."

"Probably, but not for long. He was killed in a DUI in 'ninety-three. He was coming back from an antigovernment rally out in the boonies. What goes around comes around, I guess."

A dull thud hit Bosch in the stomach. He had started liking Richard Ross Jr. for the Verloren killing. He could have used Mackey to procure the weapon and maybe help carry the victim up the hill. But now he was dead. Could their investigation be leading them to such a dead end? Would they end up going back to Rebecca Verloren's parents and telling them their long-dead daughter had been taken from them by someone who also was long dead? What kind of justice would that be?

"I know what you're thinking," Rider said. "He could have been our guy. But I don't think so. According to the box, he got his Idaho driver's license in May of 'eighty-eight. He was supposedly already up there when Verloren went down."

"Yeah, supposedly."

Bosch wasn't convinced by a simple DMV computer check. He pushed all of the information through the filters again to see if anything else jumped out at him.

"Okay, let's review for a minute, make sure I have it all straight. Back in 'eighty-eight we have a bunch of these Valley boys calling themselves the Eights and running around in their football jerseys trying to kick-start a racial holy war. The department takes a look and pretty soon finds out that the brains behind this group is the son of our own Captain Ross of IAD. Commander Irving puts his finger into the wind and thinks, 'Hmmm, I think I can use this to my advantage.' So he puts the kibosh on going after Richard Junior and they sacrifice William 'Billy Blitz' Burkhart to the Justice Gods instead. The Eights are splintered, score one for the good guys. And Richard Junior skates away, score one for Irving because now he has Richard Senior in his pocket. Everybody lives happily ever after. Am I missing anything?"

"Actually, it's Billy *Blitzkrieg*."

"Blitzkrieg, then. So all of this gets wrapped up by early spring, right?"

"By the end of March. And by early May Richard Ross Junior has moved to Idaho."

"Okay, so then in June somebody breaks into Sam

Weiss's house and steals his gun. Then in July — the day after our nation's birthday, no less — a girl of mixed race is taken out of her house and murdered. Not raped, but murdered — which is important to remember. The murder is made to look like a suicide. But it is done badly, by all appearances by someone who was new at this. Garcia and Green catch the case, eventually see through it and conduct an investigation that leads them nowhere because, whether knowingly or not, they are pushed in that direction. Now, seventeen years later, the murder weapon is incontrovertibly tied to someone who just a few months before the killing was running around with the Eights. What am I missing here?"

"I think you've got it all."

"So the question is, could it be that the Eights were not finished? That they continued to foment, only they tried to disguise their signature now? And that they raised the ante to include murder?"

Rider slowly shook her head.

"Anything is possible, but it doesn't make much sense. The Eights were about statements — public statements. Burning crosses and painting synagogues. But it's not much of a statement if you murder somebody and then try to disguise it as a suicide."

Bosch nodded. She was right. There was not a smooth flow to any of the logic.

"Then again, they knew they had the LAPD on their backs," he said. "Maybe some of them continued to operate but as sort of an underground movement."

"Like I said, anything is possible."

"Okay, so we have Ross Junior supposedly up in Idaho and we have Burkhart in Wayside. The two leaders. Who was left besides Mackey?"

"There are five other names in the file. None of the names jumped out at me."

"That's our suspect list for now. We need to run them and see where they went from — wait a minute, wait a minute. *Was* Burkhart still in Wayside? You said he got a year, right? That meant he'd be out in five or six months unless he got into trouble up there. When exactly did he go in?"

Rider shook her head.

"No, it would have been late March or early April when he checked into Wayside. He couldn't have —"

"Doesn't matter when he checked into Wayside. When was he popped? When was the synagogue thing?"

"It was January. Early January. I have the exact date back in the file."

"All right, early January. You said prints on a paint can tripped them to Burkhart. What did that take back in 'eighty-eight, when they were probably still doing it by hand — a week if it was a hot case like this? If they popped Burkhart by the end of January and he didn't make bail . . ."

He held his hands wide, allowing Rider to finish.

"February, March, April, May, June," she said excitedly. "Five months. With gain time he could easily have been out by July!"

Bosch nodded. The county jail system housed inmates awaiting trial or serving sentences of a year or less. For decades the system had been overcrowded and under court-ordered maximum population counts. This resulted in the routine early release of inmates through gain-time ratios that fluctuated according to individual jail population but sometimes were as high as three days earned for every one day served.

"This looks good, Harry."

"Maybe too good. We have to nail it down."

"When we get back I'll go on the computer and find out when he left Wayside. What's this do to the wiretap?"

Bosch thought for a moment about whether they should slow things down.

"I think we go ahead with the wiretap. If the Wayside date fits, then we watch Mackey *and* Burkhart. We still spook Mackey because he's the weak one. We do it when he's at work and away from Burkhart. If we're right, he'll call him."

He stood up.

"But we still have to run down the other names, the other members of the Eights," he added.

Rider didn't get up. She looked up at him.

"You think this is going to work?"

Bosch shrugged.

"It has to."

He looked around the cavernous train station. He checked faces and eyes, looking for any that might quickly turn away from his own. He half expected to see Irving in the crowd of travelers. Mr. Clean on the scene. That's what Bosch used to think when Irving would show up at a crime scene.

Rider stood up. They dropped their empty cups into a nearby trash can and walked toward the front doors of the station. When he got there Bosch looked behind them, again searching for a follower. He knew they now had to consider such possibilities. The place that had been so warm and inviting to him twenty minutes before was now suspicious and forbidding. The voices inside were no longer graceful whispers. There was a sharp edge to them. They sounded angry.

When they got outside he noticed that the sun had moved behind the clouds. He wouldn't need his sunglasses for the walk back.

"I'm sorry, Harry," Rider said.

"For what?"

"I just thought that it would be different, you coming back. Now here we are, your first case back and what do you get, a case with high jingo all over it."

Bosch nodded as they crossed to the front walkway. He saw the sundial and the words etched in granite beneath it. His eyes held on the last line.

Courage to Do

"I'm not worried," he said. "But they should be."

22

"Good to go," Commander Garcia replied when Bosch asked if he was ready.

Bosch nodded and went to the door to usher in the two women from the *Daily News*.

"Hi, I'm McKenzie Ward," said the one leading the way. She was obviously the reporter. The other woman was carrying a camera bag and a tripod.

"I'm Emmy Ward," said the photographer.

"Sisters?" Garcia asked, though the answer was obvious because of how much the two women, both in their twenties, looked alike: both attractive blondes with big smiles.

"I'm older," said McKenzie. "But not by much."

They all shook hands.

"How did two sisters get on the same paper together, then the same story together?" Garcia said.

"I was here a few years and then Emmy just applied. It's no big deal. We've worked together a lot. It's just a blind draw on who gets the photo assignments. Today we work together. Tomorrow maybe not."

"Do you mind if we take some photos first?" Emmy asked. "I have another assignment I need to get to right after this."

"Of course," Garcia said, ever accommodating. "Where do you want me?"

Emmy Ward set up a shot with Garcia seated at the

meeting table with the murder book open in front of him. Bosch had brought it with him to use as a prop. As the photo session proceeded, Bosch and McKenzie Ward stood off to the side and talked casually. Earlier, they had spoken at length on the phone. She had agreed to the deal. If she got the story into the paper the following day, she would be first in line for the exclusive when they took down the killer. She had not agreed easily. Garcia had initially been clumsy in his approach to her before turning the negotiation over to Bosch. Bosch was wise enough to know that no reporter would allow the police department to dictate when a story would be published and how it would be written. So Bosch concentrated on the when, not the how. He went with the assumption that McKenzie Ward would and could write a story that would serve his purposes. He just needed it in the paper sooner rather than later. Kiz Rider had an appointment with a judge that afternoon. If the wiretap application was approved, they would be in business by the next morning.

"Did you talk to Muriel Verloren?" the reporter asked Bosch.

"Yeah, she's there all afternoon and she's ready to talk."

"I pulled the clips and read everything from back then — like I was eight years old at the time — and there were several mentions of the father and his restaurant. Will he be there, too?"

"I don't think so. He's gone. It's more of a mother's story, anyway. She's the one who has kept her daughter's bedroom untouched for seventeen years. She said you could photograph in there, too, if you want."

"Really?"

"Really."

Bosch watched her looking at the shot being set up with Garcia. He knew what she was thinking. The mother in the bedroom frozen in time would be a lot better shot than an old cop at a table with a binder. She looked at Bosch while she started digging in her purse.

"Then I have to make a call to see if I can keep Emmy."

"Go ahead."

She left the office, probably because she didn't want Garcia to overhear her telling an editor that she needed Emmy to stay on the assignment because she had a better shot with the mother.

She was back in three minutes and nodded to Bosch, which he took to mean that Emmy was going to stay with her on the story.

"So this thing is a go for tomorrow?" he asked, just to make sure once again.

"It's slotted for the window — depending on the art. My editor wanted to hold it for Sunday, make a nice long feature, but I told him we were competitive on it. Anytime we can beat the *Times* on a story we do."

"Yeah, but what will he say when the *Times* doesn't run anything? He'll know you tricked him."

"No, he'll think that the *Times* killed their story because we beat them to the punch. Happens all the time."

Bosch nodded thoughtfully, then asked, "What did you mean about it being slotted for the window?"

"We run a news feature every day with a photo on the front page. We call it the window because it's in the center of the page. Also because you can see the art in the window of the newspaper boxes on the street. It's a prime spot."

"Good."

Bosch was excited by the play the story was going to get.

"If you guys screw me on this, I won't forget it," McKenzie said quietly.

There was a threat in her tone, the tough reporter coming to the surface. Bosch held his hands wide, as if he had nothing to hide.

"That's not going to happen. You've got the exclusive. As soon as we wrap somebody up, I'm calling you and you only."

"Thank you. Now, just to go over the rules again, I can quote you by name in the story but you don't want to be in any photos, right?"

"Right. I may have to do some undercover work on this. I don't want my face in the paper."

"Got it. What undercover?"

"You never know. I just want to keep the option open. Besides, the commander is better for the photo. He's lived with the case longer than I have."

"Well, I think I already have most of what I need from the clips and our call earlier but I still want to sit down with you two for a few minutes."

"Whatever you need."

"Done," Emmy said, a few minutes later. She started breaking down her equipment.

"Call the photo desk," her sister said. "I think there's been a change and you are staying with me."

"Oh," Emmy said, not seeming to mind.

"Why don't you make the call outside while we get going with the interview?" McKenzie said. "I want to get back to writing this as soon as we can."

The reporter and Bosch took seats at the table with Garcia while the photographer went out to check on her new assignment. McKenzie started by asking Garcia what stuck with him about the case for so long and what made him push it forward through the Open-Unsolved Unit. While Garcia gave a rambling response about the ones that haunt you, Bosch felt the waters of contempt rise in him. He knew what the reporter didn't know, that Garcia had knowingly or unknowingly allowed the investigation to be shunted aside seventeen years earlier. The fact that it appeared Garcia did not know that his investigation had been tampered with somehow seemed like the lesser sin to Bosch. Still, if it didn't show personal corruption or a giving way to pressure from the upper reaches of the department, at the very least it showed incompetence.

After a few more questions of Garcia the reporter turned her attention to Bosch and asked what was new in the case seventeen years later.

"The main thing is we have the DNA of the shooter," he said. "Tissue and blood from the murder weapon was preserved by our Scientific Investigation Division. We are hoping that analysis of it will allow us either to match it to a suspect whose DNA is already in the Department of Justice data bank, or to use it in comparisons to eliminate or identify suspects. We are in the process of going back to everybody in the case. Anybody who looks like a suspect will have their DNA checked against what we've got. That is something Commander Garcia couldn't do in 'eighty-eight. We're hoping it will change things this time."

Bosch further explained how the weapon extracted a DNA sample from the person who shot it. The reporter seemed very interested in the happenstance of this and took detailed notes.

Bosch was pleased. The gun and DNA story was what he wanted to get into the paper. He wanted Mackey to read the story and know that his DNA was in the pipeline. It was being analyzed and compared. He would know that a sample from him was already in the DOJ database. The hope was that this would make him panic. Maybe he would try to run, maybe he would make a mistake and make a call in which he discussed the crime. One mistake would be all it would take.

"How long before you get results from the DOJ?" McKenzie asked.

Bosch fidgeted. He was trying not to lie directly to the reporter.

"Uh, that's hard to say," he answered. "The DOJ prioritizes comparison requests and there is always a backup. We should have something any day now."

Bosch was pleased with his response but then the reporter threw another grenade into his foxhole.

"What about race?" she said. "I read all the clips and it seemed like nothing was ever brought up one way or the other about this girl being biracial. Do you think that played at all into the motivation of this murder?"

Bosch flicked a look at Garcia and hoped he would answer first.

"The case was fully explored in that regard in nineteen eighty-eight," Garcia said. "We found nothing to support the racial angle. That's probably why it wasn't in the clips."

The reporter turned her focus to Bosch, wanting the present take on the question as well.

"We've thoroughly reviewed the murder book and there is nothing there that would support a racial motivation in the case," Bosch said. "We obviously are in the process of reworking the case, front to back, and we'll be looking for anything that might have played a part in the motivation behind the crime."

He looked at her and braced himself for her not accepting his answer and pressing it further. He thought about floating the racial angle into the story. It might improve the chances of some kind of response from Mackey. But it might also tip Mackey to how close they were to him. He decided to leave his answer as is.

Instead of pursuing the question further, the reporter flipped her notebook closed.

"I think I have what I need for right now," she said. "I am going to go talk to Mrs. Verloren and then I have to hurry back and write this up to get it in tomorrow. Is there a number I can reach you at, Detective Bosch? Quickly, if I need to."

Bosch knew she had him. He reluctantly gave her his cell number, knowing it meant that in the future she would have a direct line to him and would use it in regard to any case or story. It was the last payment on the deal they had made.

Everyone got up from the table and Bosch noticed that Emmy Ward had quietly come back into the office and had been sitting by the door during the interview. He and Garcia thanked them both for coming in and said good-bye. Bosch remained in the office with Garcia.

"I think that went well," Garcia said after the door had closed.

"I hope so," Bosch said. "It cost me a cell phone number. I've had that number for three years. Now I'll have to change it and notify everybody about the new number. A big pain in the ass is what it's going to be."

Garcia ignored the complaint.

"How sure are you that this guy Mackey will even see the story?"

"We're not. In fact, we believe he's dyslexic. He might not read at all."

Garcia's jaw dropped.

"Then what are we doing?"

"Well, we have a plan for making sure he's aware of the story. Don't worry about that. We've got it covered. There's also another name that's come up since yesterday. An associate of Mackey then and now. His name is William Burkhart. Back when you were on the case he was known as Billy Blitzkrieg. That ring a bell?"

Garcia put on his best deep thinking look, like the one he had used for the camera, and moved around behind his desk. He then shook his head.

"Don't think it came up," he said.

"Yeah, you probably would have remembered."

Garcia remained standing but leaned over the desk to look at his schedule.

"Let's see. What have I got next?"

"You've got me, Commander," Bosch said.

Garcia looked at him.

"Excuse me?"

"I need a few more minutes to clear up some of this stuff that's come up."

"What stuff? You mean this new guy, Blitzkrieg?"

"Yes, and the stuff the reporter asked about and we lied about. The racial angle."

Bosch watched Garcia's face set sternly into stone.

"I didn't lie to her and I didn't lie to you yesterday. We didn't find it. We didn't see a racial angle to this."

"We?"

"My partner and I."

"Are you sure about that?"

The phone on his desk buzzed. Garcia grabbed it up angrily and said, "No calls, no intrusions," into it before dropping it back into its cradle.

"Detective, I want to remind you whom you are talking to," Garcia said evenly. "Now what the fuck do you mean, 'Are you sure?' What are you saying?"

"With all due respect to the rank, sir, the case was pushed away from the racial angle in 'eighty-eight. I believe you when you say you didn't see it. Otherwise, I can't see you calling Pratt down at Open-Unsolved and reminding him there was DNA in the case. But if you didn't know what was happening, then your partner certainly did. Did he ever talk about the pressure brought to bear on him from the command side on this case?"

"Ron Green was the finest detective I ever knew or worked with. I'm not going to let you besmirch his reputation."

They stood just a few feet apart, the desk between them, their eyes locked in battle.

"I'm not interested in reputations. I'm interested in the

truth. You said yesterday he ate his own gun a few years after this case. Why? Was there a note?"

"The burden, Detective. He couldn't carry it anymore. He was haunted by the ones who got away."

"What about the ones he *let* get away?"

Garcia pointed an angry finger at Bosch.

"How fucking dare you? You are on thin ice here, Bosch. I could make one call to the sixth floor and you'd be out on the street before sundown. You understand me? I know about you. You're just back from retirement and that makes you expendable with one phone call. You understand me?"

"Sure. I understand you."

Bosch sat down in one of the chairs in front of the desk, hoping it might defuse the tension in the room a little bit. Garcia hesitated and then he sat down as well.

"I find what you have just said to me completely insulting," he said, his voice juiced with anger.

"I'm sorry, Commander. I was trying to see what you knew."

"I don't understand."

"I am sorry, sir, but the case was definitely stonewalled by chain of command. I don't want to get into names with you at this point. Some of them are still active. But I think this case revolved on race — the connection to Mackey and now Burkhart proves it. And you didn't have Mackey or Burkhart back then, but you had the gun and there were other things. I needed to find out if you were part of it. I would say by your reaction that you weren't."

"But you are telling me my partner was, and that he kept it from me."

Bosch nodded.

"Impossible," Garcia protested. "Ron and I were close."

"All partners are close, Commander. But not that close. From what I understand, you took care of the book and Green pressed the case forward. If he encountered resistance from within the department, he might have chosen to keep it from you. I think he did. Maybe he was protecting you, maybe he was humiliated about being vulnerable to the push."

Garcia dropped his eyes from Bosch and looked down at his desk. Bosch could tell he was looking at a memory. Something in the stone wall of his face broke and gave way.

"I think maybe I knew something was wrong," he said quietly. "About halfway through."

"How so?"

"Early on we decided to split up the parents. Ron took the father and I took the mother. You know, to establish relationships. Ron was having trouble with the father. He was volatile. He had been passive and then all of a sudden he's on Ron's ass wanting results. But there was something more there and Ron kept it from me."

"Did you ask about it?"

"Yeah. I asked. He just told me the father was a handful. He said he was paranoid about race, that he thought his daughter was killed because of the race thing. And then he said something that I still remember. He said, 'We can't go there.' That's all he said, but it stuck with me because that didn't sound like the Ron Green I knew. We can't go there. The Ron Green I knew would go wherever it led. There were no can't-go-theres with him. Not until that case."

Garcia raised his eyes to Bosch and Bosch nodded, his way of thanking him for opening up.

"You think it had something to do with what happened later?" Bosch asked.

"You mean the suicide?"

"Yeah."

"Maybe. I don't know. Anything's possible. After this case we sort of went in different directions. The thing about partners is that once the work stops, there isn't a whole lot to talk about."

"True," Bosch said.

"I was in a command staff meeting at Seventy-seventh — I was assigned there after making lieutenant. That was when I found out he was dead. It came across in a staff notice. I guess that shows how far apart we had gotten. I found out he had killed himself a week after he did it."

Bosch just nodded. There was nothing he could say to that.

"I think I have a staff meeting now, Detective," Garcia said. "It's time for you to go."

"Yes, sir. But you know, I was thinking, in order for them to push Ron Green so hard, they must have already had something to push him with. You remember anything like that? Did he have an IAD beef running at the time?"

Garcia shook his head. He wasn't saying no to Bosch's question. He was saying something else.

"You know, this department has always had more cops assigned to investigating cops than it has to investigating murders. I always thought that if I reached the top, I would change that."

"Are you saying there was an investigation?"

"I'm saying it was rare in the department not to have something on your record. There was a file on Ron, sure. He had been accused of assaulting a suspect. It was bullshit. The kid bumped his head and needed stitches when Ron was putting him in the back of the car. Big deal, right? Turned out the kid had connections and the IAD wasn't letting it go away."

"So they could have used that to push this case."

"Could have, depending on how much a believer in conspiracy theories you are."

When it comes to the LAPD I am a believer, Bosch thought but didn't say.

"Okay, sir, I think I have the picture," he said instead. "I'll get out of here now."

Bosch stood up to leave.

"I understand your need to know all of this," Garcia said. "I just don't appreciate how you sandbagged me."

"I'm sorry, sir."

"No you're not, Detective Bosch. Not really."

Bosch said nothing. He moved to the door and opened it. He looked back at Garcia and tried to think of something to say. He came up blank. He turned and left, closing the door behind him.

23

Kiz Rider was still sitting in the waiting area outside Judge Anne Demchak's chambers when Bosch got there. He had been caught in mid-afternoon traffic coming back to downtown from Van Nuys and thought he might have missed the conference with the judge. Rider was reading a magazine, but Bosch's first thought was that at this point in the case he would be unable to leisurely start flipping through a magazine. At this point his focus could not be split. He was all about one thing. In a strange way, he likened it to surfing, a pursuit he had not followed since the summer of 1964, when he ran away from a foster home and lived on the beach. Many years had passed since then but he still remembered the water tunnel. The goal was to tuck yourself into the tube, the place where water swirled completely around you, where there was nothing but the water and the ride. Bosch was in the tube now. There was nothing but the case.

"How long you been here?" he asked.

Rider checked her watch.

"About forty minutes."

"Has she been in there with it the whole time?"

"Yup."

"You worried?"

"No. I've gone to her before. Once on a Hollywood case after you left. She's just thorough. She reads every page. It takes a while but she's one of the good ones."

"The story's running tomorrow. We need her to sign this today."

"I know, Harry. Relax. Sit down."

Bosch stayed standing. The judges rotated warrant duty. Getting Demchak was luck of the draw.

"I've never dealt with her before," he said. "Was she a DA?"

"No. Other side. Public defender."

Bosch groaned. His experience had been that criminal defense attorneys who became judges always brought at least the shadow of their allegiance to the defendant with them to the bench.

"We're in trouble," he said.

"No we're not. We'll be okay. Please sit down. You're making me nervous."

"Is Judy Champagne still on the bench? Maybe we can take it into her."

Judy Champagne was a former prosecutor married to a former cop. They used to say he hooked them and she cooked them. Once she became a judge she was Bosch's favorite for taking warrants to. Not because she leaned toward the cops. She didn't. She was down-the-line fair, and that's what Bosch could count on.

"She's still a judge but we can't shop search warrants around the building. You know that, Harry. Now would you please sit down? I've got something to show you."

Bosch sat down in a chair next to her.

"What?"

"I've got Burkhart's probation jacket."

She pulled a file from her bag, opened it and slid it in front of Bosch on the coffee table. She tapped a fingernail on a line on a release form. Bosch leaned down to read it.

"Released from Wayside July first, nineteen eighty-eight. Reported to probation and parole in Van Nuys on July fifth."

He straightened up and looked at her.

"So he's in play."

"Absolutely. They took him in on the synagogue vandalism on January twenty-sixth. Never made bail and, with time served credits, got out of Wayside five months later. He's totally in play on this, Harry."

Bosch felt a charge of excitement as things seemed to fall closer together.

"Okay, good. Did you amend the warrant to include him?"

"I put him in but not in too big a way. Mackey's still the direct link because of the gun."

Bosch nodded and looked across the room at the empty desk where the judge's clerk would normally sit. The name plate on the desk said KATHY CHRZANOWSKI and Bosch wondered how the name would be pronounced and where she was. He then decided to try not to think about what was happening inside the judge's chambers.

"You want to hear the latest from Commander Garcia?" he asked.

Rider was putting the probation file back in her bag.

"Sure."

Bosch spent the next ten minutes recounting his visit to Garcia's office, the newspaper interview, and the commander's revelations at the end.

"You think he told you everything?" she asked.

"You mean about how much he knew of what happened back then? No, but he told me as much as he was willing to."

"I think he had to have been part of the deal. I can't see one partner making a deal the other one doesn't know about. Not a deal like that."

"Then if he was in on it, why would he call up Pratt and tell him to send the DNA through the DOJ? Wouldn't he have just sat on it like he had been doing for seventeen years?"

"Not necessarily. A guilty conscience works in strange ways, Harry. Maybe this has been working on Garcia all these years and he decided to call Pratt to make himself feel better about it. Plus, say he was in on the deal back then with Irving. He might have felt safe to make that call once Irving was pushed to the side by the new chief."

Bosch thought about Garcia's reaction to his saying Green might have been haunted by the ones he let get away. Maybe Garcia got heated because it was he who was haunted.

"I don't know," Bosch said. "Maybe —"

Bosch's cell phone chirped. As he pulled it out of his pocket, Rider said, "You better turn that off before we go in. That's one thing Judge Demchak doesn't like going off in chambers. I heard about a DA whose phone she confiscated."

Bosch nodded and opened his phone and said hello.

"Detective Bosch?"

"Yes."

"It's Tara Wood. I thought we had an appointment."

It struck Bosch before she finished the sentence that he had forgotten the meeting at CBS and the bowl of gumbo he was planning for lunch beforehand. He hadn't even had time for lunch.

"Tara, I am really sorry. Something came up and we had to sort of run with it. I should have called you but it slipped my mind. I'm going to need to reschedule the interview, if you will still talk to me after this."

"Um, sure, no problem. I just had a couple of the writers from the show hanging around. They were going to try to talk to you."

"What show?"

"*Cold Case*. Remember, I told you we have a —"

"Oh, right, the show. Well, I'm sorry about that."

Now Bosch didn't feel so bad. She had been trying to use his interview appointment to work up a publicity angle of some kind. He wondered if there was any feeling left in her for Rebecca Verloren. As if knowing his thoughts, she asked about the case.

"Is something happening on the case? Is that why you weren't here?"

"Sort of. We're making progress but there is nothing I can tell you right — actually, there is something. Did you think at all about that name I mentioned last night? Roland Mackey? Ringing any bells?"

"No, still no."

"I've got another one. What about William Burkhart? Maybe Bill Burkhart?"

There was a long silence while Wood did a memory scan.

"No, I'm sorry. I don't think I know him."

"What about the name Billy Blitzkrieg?"

"Billy Blitzkrieg? You're kidding, right?"

"No, why, you recognize it?"

"No, not at all. It sounds like a heavy metal rock star or something."

"No, he's not. But you're sure none of the names do anything for you?"

"I'm sorry, Detective."

Bosch looked up and saw a woman beckoning to them from the open door of the chambers. Rider looked at him and drew a finger across her throat.

"Look, Tara, I need to go now. I will call you to set up the interview as soon as I can. I apologize again and I will call you soon. Thank you."

He closed the phone before she could respond and then he turned it off. He followed Rider through the door being held open by a woman Bosch assumed was Kathy Chrzanowski.

The shades were drawn over the floor-to-ceiling windows at the far end of the room. A single desk lamp lit the chambers. Behind the desk Bosch saw a woman who appeared to be in her late sixties. She looked small behind the large dark wood desk. She had a kind face, which gave Bosch hope that they would get out of the office with her approval for the phone taps.

"Detectives, come in and sit down," she said. "I am sorry to have held you out there waiting."

"No problem, Your Honor," Rider said. "We appreciate your taking a thorough look at this."

Bosch and Rider sat in chairs in front of the desk. The judge was not wearing her black robe. Bosch noticed it hanging on a hat rack in the corner. Next to it on the wall was a framed photograph of Demchak with a notoriously liberal state supreme court justice. Bosch felt his stomach tighten. Then on the desk he saw two framed photographs. One was of an older man and a young boy holding golf clubs. Her husband and a grandson maybe. The other photo showed a young girl of maybe nine or ten riding on a swing. But the colors were fading. It was an old photo. Maybe it was her daughter. Bosch started to think that the connection to children might make the difference.

"You seem to be in quite a hurry with this," the judge said. "Is there a reason for that?"

Bosch looked at Rider and she leaned forward to answer. This was her show. He was just there as a backup and to send the message to the judge that this one was important. Cops had to be lobbyists on occasion.

"Yes, Your Honor, a couple reasons," Rider began. "The main one is that we believe there is a newspaper article that will be in the *Daily News* tomorrow. It may cause our primary suspect, Roland Mackey, to contact other suspects — one of whom is listed in the warrant — and talk about the murder. As you can see from the warrant, we believe more than one individual was involved in this crime but we have only directly linked Mackey to it. If we are up and running our taps when the newspaper story hits, we might be able to identify the others involved through his calls and conversations."

The judge nodded but she wasn't looking at them. Her eyes were cast down on the application and authorization forms. She had a serious look on her face and Bosch began to get a bad feeling. After a few moments of silence, she said, "And the other reason for your hurry?"

"Oh, yes," Rider said, having apparently forgotten. "The other reason is we believe Roland Mackey still may be engaged in criminal activities. We don't know exactly what they are at this time, but we believe that the quicker we can start listening in on his conversations the sooner we will ascertain that and be able to stop someone from becoming a victim. As you can see from the application, we know he has been involved in at least one murder before. We didn't think we should waste time."

Bosch admired Rider's response. It was a carefully designed answer that would put a lot of pressure on the judge to sign the authorization. After all, she was an elected official. She had to consider the ramifications of her turning down the application. If Mackey committed a crime that could have been stopped had the police been listening to his phone calls, the judge could be held responsible by an electorate that wouldn't care much about whether she had been trying to safeguard Mackey's personal rights.

"I see," Demchak said coldly in response to Rider. "And what is your probable cause to believe he is engaged in current criminal activities since you cannot cite a specific crime."

"A variety of things, Judge. Mr. Mackey cleared

probation for a sex crime twelve months ago and immediately moved to a new address where his name is not listed on a deed or rental agreement. He left no forwarding address with his former landlord or the post office. He is living on the same property as an ex-convict with whom he has previously engaged in documented criminal activity. That is William Burkhart, also listed in the application. And, as you can see from the application, he is using a phone not registered in his name. He is clearly flying below radar, Your Honor. All of these things together paint a picture of someone taking precautions to hide involvement in criminal activity."

"Or maybe he just wants to avoid government intrusion," the judge said. "It is still very thin, Detective. Do you have anything else? I could use something else."

Rider glanced sideways at Bosch, her eyes wide. Her confidence in the waiting room was leaving her. Bosch knew she had put everything into the application and her comments in chambers. What was left? Bosch cleared his throat and leaned forward to speak for the first time.

"The previous criminal activity he took part in with the man he now lives with were hate crimes, Judge. These guys hurt and threatened a lot of people. A lot of people."

He settled back in his seat, hoping he had just ratcheted the pressure up at least another notch.

"And how long ago were these crimes?" the judge asked.

"They were prosecuted in the late eighties," Bosch said. "But who knows how long they have continued? The association of these two men has obviously continued."

The judge said nothing for another minute as she seemed to be reading and rereading the summation section of Rider's application. A small red light at the side of the desk went on. Bosch knew it meant that whatever was scheduled in her courtroom was ready to begin. All attorneys and parties were present.

Finally, Judge Demchak shook her head.

"I just don't think you have it here, Detectives. You have him with the gun but not at the murder scene. He could have handled the gun days or weeks before the killing."

She waved dismissively at the papers spread in front of her.

"This bit about him burglarizing a drive-in movie theater where the victim and her friends liked to go is tenuous at best. You really put me on the spot here by asking me to sign off on something that just isn't there."

"It is there," Bosch said. "We know it is there."

Rider put a hand on his arm, a warning not to lose it.

"I'm not seeing it, Detective," Demchak said. "You are asking me to bail you out here. You don't have enough probable cause and you are asking me to make up the difference. I can't do it. Not as it is."

"Your Honor," Rider said. "If we don't get this signed we will lose the opportunity with the newspaper story."

The judge smiled at her.

"That has nothing to do with me and what I must do here, Detective. You know that. I am not an arm of the police department. I am independent and I have to deal with the facts of the case as presented."

"The victim was biracial," Bosch said. "This guy is a documented hater. He stole that gun and it was used to kill a girl of mixed race. The connection is right there."

"Not a connection of evidence, Detective. A circumstantial connection of inference."

Bosch stared at the judge for a moment and the judge stared right back.

"Do you have children, Judge?" he asked.

The color immediately rose in the judge's cheeks.

"What does that have to do with this?"

"Your Honor," Rider broke in. "We'll come back to you with this."

"No," Bosch said. "No, we're not coming back. We need this now, Judge. This guy has been out there free for seventeen years. What if it had been your daughter? Could you look away then? Rebecca Verloren was an only child."

Judge Demchak's eyes grew darker. When she spoke it was with measures of both calm and anger.

"I am not looking away from anything, Detective. I happen to be the only one in this room that is looking closely at this. And I might add that if you continue to insult and question the court, then I will remand you to the lockup for contempt. I could have a bailiff in here in five seconds. Perhaps you could use the downtime to contemplate the deficiencies of your presentation."

Bosch pressed on undaunted.

"Her mother still lives in the house," Bosch said. "The bedroom she was taken from is still the same as the day she was killed. Same bedspread, same pillows, same everything. The room — and the mother — are frozen in time."

"But those facts are not germane to this."

"Her father became a drunk. He lost his business, then his wife and home. I visited with him on Fifth Street this morning. That's where he lives now. I know that's not germane either, but I thought you might want to know. I guess we don't have enough facts for you but we have a lot of the ripples, Your Honor."

The judge held his eyes and Bosch knew he was either about to go to jail or walk out with a signed warrant. No in-between. After a moment he saw the glimmer of pain in her eyes. Anybody who spends time in the trenches of the criminal justice system — either side — gets that look after a while.

"Very well, Detective," she finally said.

She looked down and scribbled a signature at the

bottom of the last page and started to fill in the spaces that dictated the length of the wiretaps.

"But I am still not convinced," she said sternly. "So I am giving you seventy-two hours."

"Your Honor," Bosch said.

But Rider put her hand on Bosch's arm again, trying to stop him from turning a yes into a no. Then she spoke.

"Your Honor, seventy-two hours is a very short time period for this. We were hoping that we would have at least a week."

"You said the newspaper article is coming out tomorrow," the judge responded.

"Yes, Judge, it is supposed to, but —"

"You will know something pretty quick then. If you feel you need to extend it then come back and see me on Friday and try to convince me. Seventy-two hours, and I want daily summaries delivered each morning. If I don't get them I am going to hold you both in contempt. I am not going to allow you to go fishing. If what is on the summaries is not on point then I will shut you down early. Is all of that clear?"

"Yes, Your Honor," Bosch and Rider said in unison.

"Good. Now, I have a status conference in my courtroom. It is time for you to go and for me to go back to work."

Rider collected the paperwork and they said their thanks. As they headed to the door, Judge Demchak called out to their backs.

"Detective Bosch?"

Bosch turned around and looked at her.

"Yes, Judge?"

"You saw the picture, didn't you?" she said. "Of my daughter. You guessed I have only one child."

Bosch looked at her for a moment and then nodded.

"I only have one myself," he said. "I know what it's like."

She held his eyes for a moment before speaking.

"You can go now," she said.

Bosch nodded and followed Rider through the door.

24

They didn't speak to each other as they left the court-house. It was as if they wanted to get out of there without putting the jinx on it, as if their saying one word about what had happened might echo back through the building and make the judge change her mind and recall them. Now that they had the judge's signature on the authorization forms, all they cared about was getting out.

Once on the sidewalk in front of the monolithic courthouse Bosch looked at Rider and smiled.

"That was close," he said.

She smiled and nodded her approval.

"Ripples, huh? You took it right up to the red line with her. I thought I was going to have to go downstairs and post a bond for you."

They started walking toward Parker Center. Bosch pulled his phone out and turned it back on.

"Yeah, it was close," he said. "But we got it. You want to tell Abel to set up the meeting with the others?"

"Yeah, I'll tell him. I was just going to wait until we got over there."

Bosch checked his phone and saw he had missed a call and had a message. He didn't recognize the number but it had an 818 area code — the Valley. He checked the message and heard a voice he didn't want to hear.

"Detective Bosch, it's McKenzie Ward at the *News*. I

need to talk to you about Roland Mackey as soon as possible. I need to hear from you or I may have to hold the story. Call me."

"Shit," Bosch said as he deleted the message.

"What?" Rider asked.

"It's the reporter. I told Muriel Verloren not to mention Mackey to her. But it sounds like she let it slip. Either that or the reporter is talking to somebody else."

"Shit."

"That's what I said."

They walked a little further without speaking. Bosch was thinking of a way to deal with the reporter. They had to keep Mackey out of the story or else he'd probably just cut and run without bothering to call anyone else.

"What are you going to do?" Rider finally asked.

"I don't know. Try to talk her out of it. Lie to her if I have to. She can't put his name in the story."

"But she has to run the story, Harry. We only have seventy-two hours."

"I know. Let me think."

He opened his phone and called Muriel Verloren. She answered and he asked her how the interview went. She said it was fine and she was glad it was over.

"Did they take photos?"

"Yes, they wanted pictures of the bedroom. I didn't feel good, opening it up like that to them. But I did."

"I understand. Thank you for doing that. Just remember, the story is going to help us. We're getting close, Muriel, and the newspaper story will push things. We appreciate your doing it."

"If it helps, then I am glad to do it."

"Good. Let me ask you something else. Did you mention the name Roland Mackey to the reporter?"

"No, you told me not to. So I didn't."

"Are you sure?"

"I'm more than sure. She asked me what you people were telling me but I didn't say anything about him. Why?"

"No reason. I just wanted to make sure, that's all. Thank you, Muriel. I'll call you as soon as I have some news."

He closed the phone. He didn't think Muriel Verloren would lie to him. The reporter had to have another source.

"What?" Rider asked.

"She didn't tell her."

"Then who did?"

"Good question."

The phone started to vibrate and chirp while he was still holding it. He looked at the screen and recognized the number.

"It's her — the reporter. I have to take this."

He answered the call.

"Detective Bosch, it's McKenzie Ward. I'm on deadline and we need to talk."

"Right. I just got your message. My phone was off because I was in court."

"Why didn't you tell me about Roland Mackey?"

"What are you talking about?"

"Roland Mackey. I was told you already have a suspect named Roland Mackey."

"Who told you that?"

"That doesn't matter. What matters is that you withheld a key piece of information from me. Is Roland Mackey your prime suspect? Let me guess. You are playing both sides and giving that to the *Times*."

Bosch had to think quickly. The reporter was sounding pressed and upset. A reporter who goes off angry could be a problem. He had to calm the situation and at the same time take Mackey out of the mix. The one thing he had going for him was that she had not mentioned a DNA link between Mackey and the gun. This made Bosch think that her source of information was outside the department. Someone with limited information.

"First of all, I'm not talking to the *Times* on this. As long as it runs tomorrow, you are the only one with this story. Secondly, it does matter where you got that name from because your information is wrong. I am trying to help you here, McKenzie. You would be making a big mistake if you put that name in the article. You might even get sued."

"Then who is he?"

"Who is your source?"

"You know I can't give you that."

"Why not?"

Bosch was stalling for time while he thought it out. While the reporter rattled off a standard response about shield laws and protecting sources, Bosch was ticking off the names of people outside the department whom he and Rider had talked to about Mackey. They included Rebecca Verloren's three friends — Tara Wood, Bailey Sable and Grace Tanaka. There was also Robert Verloren, Danny Kotchof, Thelma Kibble, the parole agent, and Gordon Stoddard, the school principal, as well as Mrs. Atkins, the secretary who looked for Mackey's name in the school's rolls.

There was also Judge Demchak but Bosch dismissed that as a long shot. Ward's message had been left on his line while he and Rider were with the judge. The idea that the judge would have picked up the phone and called the reporter while she had been alone in chambers studying the search warrant application seemed out of the question. She hadn't even known of the pending newspaper story let alone the reporter assigned to it.

Bosch guessed that because of time constraints, the reporter had simply gone back to the office and made a few phone calls to round out the story. She had gotten the name Roland Mackey from someone she had called.

Bosch doubted that she could have located or even contacted Robert Verloren in the few hours since the interview. He also scratched Grace Tanaka and Danny Kotchof because they weren't local. Without Mackey's name, there was no link to Kibble. That left Tara Wood and the school — either Stoddard, Sable or the secretary. The most obvious answer was the school because it would have been the easiest link for the reporter to make. He now felt better and thought he could contain the threat.

"Detective, are you still there?"

"Yes, sorry, I'm trying to dodge some traffic here."

"Then what is your answer? Who is Roland Mackey?"

"He's nobody. He's a loose end. Or was, actually. We've tied that up now."

"Explain that."

"Look, we inherited this case, right? Well, over the years the murder book got shelved, reshelved, moved around a bit. Things got mixed up. So part of what we had to do was some basic housekeeping. We had to put things in order. We found a picture of this Roland Mackey guy loose in the book and we weren't sure who he was and what his connection was. When we were out doing interviews, getting acquainted with the players in the case, we showed his picture to a few people to see if they knew who he was and where he fit. At no time, McKenzie, did we tell anyone he was a prime suspect. That is the truth. So either you are exaggerating or whoever mentioned this guy to you was exaggerating."

There was a silence and Bosch guessed she was revisiting the interview that gave her the name Mackey.

"Then who is he?" she finally asked.

"Just some guy with a juvie record who was living in Chatsworth back then. He hung out at the old drive-in on Winnetka, and that was apparently a hangout for Rebecca and her friends as well. But it turns out that back in 1988 he was cleared of any involvement. We didn't find out until after we showed the photo to a few people."

It was a mixture of truth and shadings of the truth. Again the reporter was silent while she considered his answer.

"Who told you about him, Gordon Stoddard or Bailey Sable?" Bosch asked. "We took the photo to the school to see if he fit in there, and it turns out he didn't even go to school there. We dropped it after that."

"You sure about this?"

"Look, do what you want but if you put that guy's name in the paper simply because we asked about him, you could be getting calls from him and his lawyer. We ask about a lot of people, McKenzie. That's our job."

More silence slipped by. Bosch thought the silence meant he had successfully defused the bomb.

"We went over to the school to look at the yearbook and copy photos," Ward finally said. "We found out you took the only one they had in the library from 'eighty-eight."

It was her way of confirming that Bosch had it right, but without giving up her source.

"Sorry about that," he said. "I have the yearbook on my desk. I don't know what kind of time you have but you can send somebody over to pick it up if you want."

"No, there's no time. We took a picture of the plaque that's on the wall at the school. That will work. Besides, I found a shot of the vic in our archives. We'll use that."

"I saw the plaque. It's nice."

"They're very proud of it."

"So we're all right on this, McKenzie?"

"Yes, we're fine. I just got a little excited there when I thought you were holding back something big."

"Don't have anything big to report. Yet."

"All right, then I better get back to finishing the story."

"It's still running in the window tomorrow?"

"If I get it finished. Call me tomorrow and tell me what you think."

"I will."

Bosch closed the phone and looked at Rider.

"I think we're okay," he said.

"Boy, Harry, you've really got it going today. The artful dodger. I think you could probably talk a zebra out of his white stripes if you had to."

Bosch smiled. He then looked up at the City Hall Annex on Spring Street. Banished from Parker Center, Irvin Irving now operated from the Annex. Bosch wondered if Mr. Clean was looking down on them right now from behind one of the mirrored windows of the Office of Strategic Planning. He thought of something.

"Kiz?"

"What?"

"Do you know McClellan?"

"No, not really."

"But you know what he looks like?"

"Sure. I saw him at command staff meetings. Irving stopped going once he was moved out to the Annex. He sent McClellan most of the time as his representative."

"So you could pick him out, then?"

"Sure. But what are you talking about, Harry?"

"Maybe we should go talk to him, maybe spook him and send a message back down the pipe to Irving."

"You mean right now?"

"Why not? We're here."

He gestured toward the Annex building.

"We don't have the time, Harry. Besides, why pick a fight you can avoid? Let's not deal with Irving until we have to."

"All right, Kiz. But we will have to deal with him. I know we will."

They didn't speak again, each focused on thoughts on the case, until they reached the Glass House and went inside.

25

Abel Pratt convened all members of the Open-Unsolved Unit in the squad room as well as four other RHD detectives loaned to the unit for the surveillance. The meeting was turned over to Bosch and Rider, who took a verbal walk through the case that lasted a half hour. On a bulletin board behind them they pinned blowups of the most recent driver's license photos of Roland Mackey and William Burkhart. The other detectives asked few questions. Bosch and Rider then turned the show back over to Pratt.

"All right, we're going to need all hands on deck with this," he said. "We'll be working the sixes. Two pairs working the sound room, two pairs working Mackey and two pairs working Burkhart. I want the OU teams on Mackey and the surveillance room. The four loaners from RHD will watch Burkhart. Kiz and Harry have dibs and they want the second shift on Mackey. The rest of you can work out how you want to cover the remaining shifts. We start tomorrow morning at six, just about the time the paper will be hitting the streets."

The plan translated into six pairs of detectives working twelve-hour shifts. The shifts changed at 6 a.m. and 6 p.m. Since it was their case, Bosch and Rider got first choice of shifts and had elected to cover Mackey beginning each day at 6 p.m. This meant working through the night, but it was Bosch's hunch that if Mackey made a move or a call it would occur in the evening. And Bosch wanted to be there when it happened.

They would alternate with one of the other teams. The remaining two OU teams would alternate their time in the City of Industry, where a private contractor called Listen-Tech had what amounted to a wiretap center which was used by all law enforcement agencies in Los Angeles County. Sitting in a van next to the telephone pole carrying the line you were listening to was a thing of the past. ListenTech provided a quiet, air-conditioned center where electronic consoles were set up for monitoring and recording conversations placed or received on any phone numbers in the county, including cell phones. There was even a cafeteria with fresh coffee and vending machines. Pizza could be delivered if needed.

ListenTech could service as many as ninety taps at a time. Rider had told Bosch that the company was spawned in 2001 when law enforcement agencies began taking increasing advantage of the widening laws governing wire-taps. A private company that saw the growing need stepped in with regional wiretap centers, also known as sound rooms. They made the work easier. But there were still rules to follow.

"We're going to hit a bit of a snag in the sound room," Pratt said. "The law still requires that each line be monitored by a single individual — no listening to two lines at once. But we need to monitor three lines with two cops because that's all we got. So how do we do this and still stay within the law? We alternate. One line is Roland Mackey's cell. We monitor that full-time. But the other two lines are secondary. That's where we alternate. They come from the property where he lives and the place where he works. So what we do is we stay with the first line when he is home and then from four to midnight, when he is at work, we switch to the work line. No matter what lines we are actually listening to, we will still get twenty-four-hour pen registers on all three."

"Can't we get one more loaner from RHD to cover the third line?" Rider asked.

Pratt shook his head.

"Captain Norona gave us four bodies and that's it," Pratt said. "We won't miss much. Like I said, we have the pen registers."

Pen registers were part of the telephone monitoring process. While the investigators were allowed to listen in on phone calls on the monitored lines, the equipment also registered all incoming and outgoing calls on all the lines listed in the warrant, even if they were not being monitored. This would provide the investigators with a listing by time and length of call, as well as the numbers dialed on outgoing calls and the originating numbers for incoming calls.

"Any questions?" Pratt asked.

Bosch didn't think there would be any questions. The plan was simple enough. But then an OU detective named Renner raised his hand and Pratt nodded at him.

"Is this thing OT authorized?"

"Yes, it is," Pratt replied. "But as was said before, as of now we only have seventy-two hours on the warrant."

"Well, let's hope it goes the whole seventy-two," Renner said. "I gotta pay for my kid's summer camp in Malibu."

The others laughed.

Tim Marcia and Rick Jackson volunteered to be the other street team working with Bosch and Rider. The other four got the sound-room detail, with Renner and Robleto taking the day shift and Robinson and Nord taking the same shift as Bosch and Rider. The ListenTech center was nice and comfortable, but some cops didn't want to be cooped up no matter what the circumstances. Some would always choose the street and, like Marcia and Jackson, Bosch knew he was one of them.

Pratt ended the meeting by handing out copies of a piece of paper with everyone's cell phone number on it as well as the radio channel they would use during the surveillance.

"For you teams in the field, I've got rovers on hold down in the equipment shed," Pratt said. "Make sure you have the radio on. Harry, Kiz, did I miss anything?"

"I think you got it covered," Rider said.

"Since our time is short on this one," Bosch said, "Kiz and I are working something up to sort of push the action if we don't see any signs by tomorrow night. We have the newspaper article and we have to make sure he sees it."

"How's he going to read it if he's dyslexic?" Renner asked.

"He got a GED," Bosch said. "He should be able to read it. We just have to make sure it somehow gets in front of him."

Everybody nodded their agreement and then Pratt wrapped things up.

"Okay, gang, that's it," Pratt said. "I will be checking with everybody through the days and nights. Stay loose and be careful with these guys. We don't want anything turning back on us. You people taking the first shift might want to head home now and get a good night. Just remember, the clock's ticking on the warrant. We have till Friday night and then it's pumpkins. So let's get out there and get what's to be got. We're the closers. So let's close this one out."

Bosch and Rider stood and small-talked about the case with the others for a few minutes and then Bosch made his way back to their alcove. He pulled the copy of the probation file out of the stack of accumulated case files. He had not gotten a chance to read through it thoroughly and now was the time.

The file was an add-on file, meaning that as Mackey

repeatedly was arrested and continued a lifelong trek through the criminal justice system the reports and court transcripts were merely added to the front of the file. Therefore the reports ran in reverse chronological order. Bosch was most interested in Mackey's earlier years. He went to the back of the file with the idea of moving forward in time.

Mackey's first arrest as an adult came only a month after he turned eighteen. In August 1987 he was picked up for car theft in what the follow-up reports classified as a joyriding incident. Mackey had been living at home at the time and stole a neighbor's Corvette. He had jumped in the car and taken off after the neighbor had left it running in the driveway and gone back inside his house for a forgotten pair of sunglasses.

Mackey pleaded guilty and the presentencing report contained in the file cited his juvenile record but made no mention of the Chatsworth Eights. In September 1987 the young car thief was placed on one year probation by a superior court judge, who tried to talk Mackey out of a life of crime.

The transcript of the sentencing hearing was in the file. Bosch read the judge's two-page lecture, in which he told Mackey he had seen young men like him a hundred times before. He told Mackey he was standing at the same precipice as the others. One simple crime could be a life lesson, or it could be the first step down a spiral. He urged Mackey not to go down the wrong path. He told him to think hard and make the right decision on which way to go.

The words of warning had obviously fallen on deaf ears. Six weeks later Mackey was arrested for burglarizing a neighborhood home while the husband and wife who lived there were at work. Mackey had cut an alarm, but the break in current had registered with the alarm company and a patrol car was dispatched. When Mackey came out the back door carrying a video camera and assorted other electronics and jewelry, two officers were waiting with guns drawn.

Because Mackey had been on probation for the car theft he was held in the county jail while awaiting disposition of the case. After thirty-six days in stir he stood before the same judge again and, according to the transcript, begged forgiveness and for one more chance. This time the presentencing report noted that drug testing indicated that Mackey was a marijuana user and that he had begun hanging around an unsavory group of young men from the Chatsworth area.

Bosch knew that these men were likely the Chatsworth Eights. It was early December and their plan of terror and symbolic homage to Adolf Hitler was just a few weeks away. But none of this was in the PSR. The report simply stated that Mackey was hanging with the wrong crowd. As he sentenced Mackey, the judge would not have known how wrong that crowd was.

Mackey was sentenced to three years of prison reduced to time served. He was also placed on two years probation. The judge, knowing that prison would be just a finishing school for a young criminal like Mackey, was giving him a break and attempting to break him at the same time. Mackey walked out of court free, but the judge had placed a series of heavy restrictions on his probation. They included weekly drug tests, maintaining gainful employment and a requirement that the high school dropout get his general education degree within nine months. The judge told Mackey that if he failed in any part of the probation order he would be sent to a state prison to complete his three-year sentence.

"You may consider this harsh, Mr. Mackey," the judge said in the transcript. "But I consider it quite kind. I am giving you a last chance here. If you fail me on this, you will without a doubt be going to prison. Society will be through with trying to help you at that point. It will simply throw you away. Do you understand this?"

"Yes, Your Honor," Mackey said.

The file came with copies of the court-requested completion reports from Chatsworth High. Mackey got his GED in August 1988, a little more than a month after Rebecca Verloren was taken from her bed and murdered.

Despite the judge's admirable efforts to steer Mackey from a life of crime, Bosch had to wonder if those efforts had cost Rebecca Verloren her life. Whether Mackey was the actual triggerman or not, he'd had possession of the gun that killed her. Was it reasonable to think that the chain of events leading to the murder would have been broken if Mackey had been behind bars? Bosch wasn't sure. It was possible that Mackey simply filled a role as weapon delivery man. If it wasn't him it could have been someone else. Bosch knew there was no sense in breaking down the chain into what could or could not have happened.

"Anything?"

Bosch looked up from his thoughts. Rider was standing at her desk. He flipped the file closed.

"Nah, not really. I was reading the probation file. The early stuff. A judge took an interest at first but then sort of let him go. The best he could do was make him get the GED."

"And that served him so well, didn't it?"

"Yeah."

Bosch said nothing else. He only had a GED himself. He'd also stood before a judge once as a car thief. The car he had gone joyriding in had also been a Corvette. Except it had not been a neighbor's. It had been his foster father's. Bosch had taken it as a way to say fuck you. But it was the foster father who sent the ultimate fuck you. Bosch was sent back to the youth hall to fend for himself.

"My mother died when I was eleven," Bosch suddenly said.

Rider looked at him, doing her eyebrow thing.

"I know. Why'd you bring that up?"

"I don't know. I spent a lot of time in the youth hall after that. I mean, I had some stays with foster families but it never lasted long. I always went back."

Rider waited but Bosch didn't continue.

"And?" she prompted.

"Well, we didn't have gangs in the hall," he said. "But there was sort of a natural segregation. You know, the whites stuck together. The blacks. The Hispanics. There weren't any Asians back then."

"What are you saying, that you feel sorry for this asshole Mackey?"

"No."

"He killed a girl or at least helped kill her, Harry."

"I know that, Kiz. That's not my point."

"What is your point?"

"I don't know. I'm just sort of wondering, you know, what makes people go down different paths. How come this guy became a hater? How come I didn't?"

"Harry, you're overthinking. Go home tonight and get a good night's sleep. You'll need it because there won't be any tomorrow night."

Bosch nodded but didn't move.

"You going to take off?" Rider asked.

"Yeah, in a few. You heading out?"

"Yeah, unless you want me to go with you over to Hollywood Vice."

"Nah, I'll be all right. Let's talk in the morning after we get the paper."

"Yeah, I'm not sure where I can get the *Daily News* in the south end. I might have to call you up and let you read it to me."

The *Daily News* was circulated widely in the Valley but sometimes hard to locate elsewhere in the city. Rider lived down near Inglewood, in the same neighborhood where she had grown up.

"That's cool. Give me a call and I'll have it. There's a box down at the bottom of the hill from my place."

Rider opened one of her desk drawers and pulled out her purse. She looked at Bosch and did her eyebrow thing once again.

"You sure about doing this, marking yourself like that?"

She was talking about their plan for pushing Mackey the next day. Bosch nodded.

"I have to be able to sell it," he said. "Besides, I can wear long sleeves for a while. It isn't summer yet."

"But what if it's not necessary? What if he sees the story in the paper and gets on the phone and starts talking a blue streak?"

"Something tells me that isn't going to happen. Anyway, it isn't permanent. Vicki Landreth told me it lasts a couple weeks at the most, depending on how often you shower. It's not like those henna tattoos kids get on the Santa Monica pier. They last longer."

She nodded her agreement.

"Okay, Harry. I'll catch you in the a.m., then."

"See ya, Kiz. Have a good one."

She started walking out of the alcove.

"Hey, Kiz?" Bosch called after her.

"What?" she said, stopping and looking back at him.

"What do you think? You happy to be back on it?"

She knew what he was talking about. Being back in homicide.

"Oh yeah, Harry, I'm happy. I'll be downright giddy once we take this pale rider down and solve the mystery."

"Yeah," Bosch said.

After she left, Bosch thought for a few moments about

what she meant by calling Mackey a pale rider. He thought it might be some sort of biblical reference but he couldn't place it. Maybe in the south end it was what some people called racists. He decided to ask her about it the next day. He started to look through the probation file again but soon gave up. He knew it was time to focus on the here and now. Not the past. Not the choices made and the paths not taken. He got up and stacked the file and the murder book under his arm. If things were slow on the surveillance the next day, they might make for good reading. He stuck his head in Abel Pratt's office to say good-bye.

"Good luck, Harry," Pratt said. "Close it out."

"We're going to."

26

Bosch parked in the rear lot and walked in through the back doors of Hollywood Division. It had been a long time since he had been in the place and he immediately found it different. The earthquake renovation that Edgar had spoken of had seemingly touched every space in the building. He found the watch office in the place where a holding tank had been located. He found a report writing room for patrol officers, whereas before they'd had to steal space in the detective bureau.

Before going upstairs to the vice unit he had to go by the detective bureau to see if he could pull a file. He went down the rear hallway, passing a patrol sergeant named McDonald whose first name he couldn't remember.

"Hey, Harry, you back? Long time no see, man."

"I'm back, Six."

"Good deal."

Six was the radio designation for Hollywood Division. Calling the patrol sergeant Six was like calling a homicide detective Roy. It worked and it got Bosch past his awkward memory loss. By the time he got to the end of the hallway he remembered that the sergeant's name was Bob.

The homicide unit was at the back end of the vast detective squad room. Edgar had been right. It didn't look like any detective bureau Bosch had ever seen. It was gray and sterile. It looked like a warehouse where yaks made cold calls and ripped off businesses and old ladies for overpriced pens or time-share units. He recognized the top of Edgar's head just cresting above one of the sound partitions between the cubicles. It looked like he was the only one left in the whole bureau. It was late in the day but not that late.

He walked over and looked over the partition and down on Edgar. He had his head down and was working on the *Times* crossword puzzle. It had always been a ritual with Edgar. He'd work the puzzle throughout each day, taking it with him to the restroom and to lunch and out on surveillances. He never liked to go home without finishing it.

Edgar hadn't noticed Bosch's presence. Bosch quietly stepped back and ducked into the cubicle next to Edgar's. He carefully lifted the steel trash can out of the desk's foot well and duck-walked out of the cubicle to a position right behind Edgar. He stood up and let the trash can fall to the new gray linoleum from about four feet. The resulting sound was loud and sharp, almost like a shot. Edgar leaped out of his seat, his crossword pencil flying toward the ceiling. He was about to yell something when he saw it was Bosch.

"Goddamn it, Bosch!"

"How you doin', Jerry?" Bosch said, barely getting it out while laughing.

"Goddamn it, Bosch!"

"Yeah, you said that. I take it things are pretty slow in Hollywood tonight."

"What the fuck you doing here? I mean, besides scaring the shit out of me."

"I'm working, man. I've got an appointment with the vice artist upstairs. What are you doing?"

"I'm finishing up. I was about to get out of here."

Bosch leaned forward and saw that the grid of the crossword was almost entirely filled out with words. There were several erasure marks. Edgar never worked a crossword in ink. Bosch noticed his old red dictionary was off the shelf and on the desk.

"Cheating again, Jerry? You know you aren't supposed to be using the dictionary like that."

Edgar dropped back into his seat. He looked exasperated by the scare and now the questions.

"Bullshit. I can do whatever I want. There aren't any rules, Harry. Why don't you get on upstairs and leave me alone? Have her put some eyeliner on you and put you out on the stroll."

"Yeah, you wish. You'd be my first customer."

"All right, all right. Is there something you need here or did you just drop by to bust my chops?"

Edgar finally smiled and Bosch knew everything was all right between them.

"A little of both," Bosch said. "I need to pull an old file. Where do they keep them now in this palace?"

"How old is it? They started shipping stuff downtown to be microfilmed."

"Would've been in two thousand. You remember Michael Allen Smith?"

Edgar nodded.

"Of course I do. Someone like me isn't going to forget Smith. What do you want with him?"

"I just want his picture. That file still here?"

"Yeah, anything that fresh is still around. Follow me."

He led Bosch to a locked door. Edgar had a key and soon they were in a small room lined with shelves crowded with blue binders. Edgar located the Michael Allen Smith murder book and pulled it off a shelf. He dropped it into Bosch's hands. It was heavy. It had been a tough case.

Bosch took the murder book to the cubicle next to Edgar's and started flipping through it until he came to a section of photographs that showed Smith's upper torso and several close-ups of his tattoos. His markings had been used to identify and charge him with the murders of three prostitutes five years earlier. Bosch, Edgar and Rider had worked the case. Smith was an avowed white supremacist who secretly hired black transvestite prostitutes he picked up on Santa Monica Boulevard. Then out of guilt for crossing both racial and sexual lines, he would kill them. It somehow made him feel better about his transgressions. The key break in the case came when Rider found a prostitute who had seen one of the victims get into a van with a customer. He was able to describe a distinctive tattoo on the john's hand. That eventually led them to Smith, who had collected a variety of tattoos while in various prisons around the country. He was tried, convicted and sent to death row, where he was still dodging the needle with a barrage of legal appeals.

Bosch removed the photos that showed Smith's neck, hands and upper left arm, all of which were festooned with prison ink.

"I need these while I'm upstairs. If you're leaving and need to lock the file room I can just leave these on your desk."

Edgar nodded.

"That'll be fine. So what are you getting into, man? You're going to put that shit on yourself?"

"That's right. I want to be like Mike."

Edgar narrowed his eyes.

"This connected to that Chatsworth Eights stuff we were talking about yesterday?"

Bosch smiled.

"You know, Jerry, you ought to be a detective. You're good at it."

Edgar nodded like he was merely putting up with another sarcastic assault.

"You going to get the haircut, too?" he asked.

"Nah, I wasn't planning on going that far," Bosch said. "I'm going to be sort of a reformed skinhead, I think."

"I get it."

"So, listen, are you busy tonight? This shouldn't take too long up there. If you want to wait and finish your puzzle, we could go grab a steak over at Musso's."

Just saying it made Bosch hungry for it. That and a vodka martini.

"Nah, Harry, I gotta go over the hill to the Sportsmen's Lodge for Sheree Riley's retirement gig. That's why I was killing time here. I was just waiting out the traffic."

Sheree Riley was a sex crimes investigator. Bosch had worked with her on occasion but they had never been close. When sex and murder entwined, the cases were usually so brutal and difficult there wasn't much room for anything but the work. Bosch didn't know she was retiring.

"Maybe we can get that steak some other time," Edgar said. "That cool?"

"Everything's cool, Jerry. Have a good time up there and tell her I said hello and good luck. And thanks for the pictures. They'll be on your desk."

Bosch headed back toward the hallway but heard Edgar curse. He turned around and saw his old partner standing and looking into his cubicle with his arms wide.

"Where'd my damn pencil go?"

Bosch scanned the floor and didn't see it. Eventually his eyes rose and he saw the pencil stuck into the sound-absorption tiles in the ceiling above Edgar's head.

"Jerry, sometimes what goes up doesn't come down."

Edgar looked up and saw his pencil. It took him two jumps to grab it.

The door to the vice unit on the second floor was locked but this was not unusual. Bosch knocked and it was quickly answered by an undercover officer Bosch didn't recognize.

"Is Vicki here? She's expecting me."

"Then come on in."

The officer stepped back and let Bosch enter. He saw that this room had not been changed dramatically during the retrofitting. It was a long room with work counters running down both sides. Above each vice officer's space was a framed movie poster. In Hollywood Division, only posters from movies actually filmed in the division were allowed to grace the walls. He found Vicki Landreth at a workspace under a poster from *Blue Neon Night,* a film Bosch had not seen. She and the other officer were the only ones in the office. Bosch guessed everybody else was already out on the streets for the night shift.

"Hey, Bosch," Landreth said.

"Hey, Vic. You still have time to do this?"

"For you, honey, I will always make time."

Landreth was a former Hollywood makeup artist. One day twenty years earlier she was talked into taking a ride-along with one of the off-duty officers working security on the set. The guy was just trying to make time with her, hoping maybe she'd catch a thrill on the ride-along and it would lead to something else. What it led to was Landreth's enrollment in the police academy and her becoming a reserve officer, working two shifts a month on patrol, filling in where needed. Then someone in vice found out about her daytime job and asked her to work her two shifts in vice, where she could be used to make undercover officers look more like prostitutes and pimps and drug users and street people. Soon Vicki found the cop work more interesting than the movie work. She quit the industry and became a full-time cop. Her makeup skills were highly coveted and her niche in Hollywood Division was secure.

Bosch showed her the photos of Michael Allen Smith's tattoos and she studied them for a few moments.

"Nice guy, huh?" she finally said.

"One of the best."

"And you want all of this done tonight?"

"No. I was thinking about the lightning bolts on the neck. And maybe the bicep, if you could do it."

"It's all jailhouse. No real art to it. One color. I can do it. Sit down over here and take off your shirt."

She led him to a makeup station, where he sat on a stool next to a rack of various body paints and powders. On an upper shelf there were mannequin heads with wigs and beards on them. Below these someone had taped the names of various supervisors in the division.

Bosch took off his shirt and tie. He was wearing a T-shirt underneath.

"I want these to be seen but I don't want to be too obvious about it," he said. "I was thinking that you could work it so if I had on a T-shirt like this you would sort of see parts of the tats sticking out. Enough to know what they are and what they mean."

"Not a problem. Hold still."

She used a piece of chalk to mark the lines on his skin where the shirt's sleeve and neck reached.

"These will be the visibility lines," she explained. "You just tell me how much you want to go above and below them."

"Got it."

"Now take it all off, Harry."

She said it with undisguised sensuality in her voice. Bosch pulled his shirt over his head and tossed it over a chair with his other shirt and the tie. He turned back to her and Landreth was studying his chest and shoulders. She reached over and touched the scar on his left shoulder.

"That's new," she said.

"That's old."

"Well, it has been a long time since I saw you naked, Harry."

"Yeah, I guess so."

"Back when you were a boy in blue and could talk me into anything, even joining the cops."

"I talked you into my car, not the department. Blame yourself for that."

Bosch felt embarrassed and felt his skin blush. Their liaison twenty years earlier had flickered out for no reason other than that neither was looking for any sort of commitment to or from anybody. They went their separate ways but always remained easy friends, especially when Bosch was transferred to the Hollywood Division homicide squad and they were working out of the same building.

"Look at you blushing," Landreth said. "After all these years."

"Well, you know . . ."

He said nothing further. Landreth rolled her stool closer to Bosch. She reached up and rubbed her thumb over the tunnel rat tattoo at the top of his right arm.

"I do remember this one," she said. "It's not holding up so well, is it?"

She was right. That tattoo he had gotten in Vietnam had lost its lines over time and the colors had blurred. The character of the rat with a gun emerging from a tunnel was not recognizable. That tattoo looked like a painful bruise.

"I'm not holding up so well myself, Vicki," Bosch said.

She ignored his complaint and got down to work. She first used an eyeliner pencil to sketch out the tattoos on his body. Michael Allen Smith had what he had called a Gestapo collar tattooed on his neck. On each side of his neck was the twin lightning bolt insignia of the SS. This symbolized the emblems attached to the collar points of the uniforms worn by Hitler's elite force. Landreth etched these onto Bosch's skin easily and quickly. It tickled and he had a hard time holding still. Then it was time for the bicep piece.

"Which arm?" she asked.

"I think the left."

He was thinking of the play with Mackey. He thought the chances were better that he would end up sitting on Mackey's right as opposed to his left. That meant his left arm would be in Mackey's line of sight.

Landreth asked him to hold the photo of Smith's arm up next to his own so she could copy it. Tattooed on Smith's bicep was a skull with a swastika inside a circle on the crown. While Smith had never admitted to the murders he was charged with, he had always been quite open about his racist beliefs and the origins of his many body markings. The bicep skull, he said, had been copied from a World War II propaganda poster.

Shifting the sketch work from his neck to his arm allowed Bosch to breathe easier and Landreth to engage him in conversation.

"So what's new with you?" she asked.

"Not a lot."

"Retirement was boring?"

"You could say that."

"What did you do with yourself, Harry?"

"I worked a couple old cases, but mostly I spent time in Las Vegas trying to get to know my daughter."

She leaned back away from her work and looked up at Bosch with surprise in her eyes.

"Yeah, I was surprised too when I found out," he said.

"How old?"

"Almost six."

"You still going to be able to see her now that you're on the job?"

"Doesn't matter, she's not there."

"Well, where is she?"

"Her mother took her to Hong Kong for a year."

"Hong Kong? What's in Hong Kong?"

"A job. She signed a year contract."

"She didn't consult you about it?"

"I don't know if 'consulted' is the right word. She told me she was going. I talked to a lawyer about it and there wasn't much I could do."

"That's not fair, Harry."

"I'm all right. I talk to her once a week. As soon as I earn up some vacation I'll go over there."

"I'm not talking about it being unfair to you. I'm talking about her. A girl should be close to her father."

Bosch nodded because that was all he could do. A few minutes later Landreth finished the sketch work, opened a case and took out a jar of Hollywood tattoo ink along with a penlike applicator.

"This is Bic blue," she said. "It's what most of them use in the jails. I won't be perforating the skin so it should come off in a couple weeks."

"Should?"

"Most times. There was one actor I worked with, though. I put an ace of spades on his arm. And the funny thing was that it wouldn't come off. Not all the way. So he just ended up having a real tattoo put over my piece. He wasn't too happy about it."

"Just like I'm not going to be happy if I have lightning bolts on my neck for the rest of my life. Before you start putting that stuff on me, Vicki, is there —"

He stopped when he realized she was laughing at him.

"Just kidding, Bosch. It's Hollywood magic. It comes off with a couple of good scrubs, okay?"

"Okay, then."

"Then hold still and let's get this done."

She went to work applying the dark blue ink to the pencil drawing on his skin. She blotted it regularly with a

266

cloth and repeatedly told him to stop breathing, which he told her he couldn't do. She was finished in under a half hour. She gave him a hand mirror and he studied his neck. It looked good in that it looked real to him. It also looked strange to see such displays of hate on his own skin.

"Can I put my shirt on now?"

"Give it a few more minutes."

She touched the scar on his shoulder once again.

"Is that from when you got shot in that tunnel downtown?"

"Yes."

"Poor Harry."

"More like Lucky Harry."

She started packing up her equipment while he sat there with his shirt off and feeling awkward about it.

"So what's the assignment tonight?" he asked, just to be saying something.

"For me? Nothing. I'm out of here."

"You're done?"

"Yeah, we worked a day shift today. Working girls invading the hotel by the Kodak Center. Can't have that in the new Hollywood, can we? So we bagged four of them."

"I'm sorry, Vicki. I didn't know I was holding you up. I would've come in sooner. Hell, I was downstairs shooting the shit with Edgar before coming up. You should've told me you'd be waiting on me."

"It's all right. It was good to see you. And I wanted to tell you I'm glad you're back on the job."

Bosch suddenly thought of something.

"Hey, you want to hit Musso's for dinner or are you going up to the Sportsmen's Lodge?"

"Forget the Sportsmen's Lodge. Those things remind me too much of wrap parties. I didn't like them either."

"Then what do you think?"

"I don't know if I want to be seen in that place with such an obvious racist pig."

This time Bosch knew she was kidding. He smiled and she smiled and she said dinner was a go.

"I'll go on one condition," she said.

"What's that?"

"You put your shirt back on."

27

Without need of an alarm, Bosch awoke at five-thirty the next morning. This was not unusual for him. He knew that this was what happened when you surfed into the tube on a case. Waking hours overpowered the sleeping hours. You did all you could to stay up on that board and in the pipeline. Though not scheduled to begin work for more than twelve hours, he knew this would be the pivotal day in the case. He could not sleep anymore.

In darkness and unfamiliar surroundings he got dressed and made his way to the kitchen, where he found a pad for writing down needed grocery items. He wrote a note and left it in front of the automatic coffeemaker, which he had watched Vicki Landreth set the night before to begin brewing at 7 a.m. The note said very little other than thank you for the evening and good-bye. There were no promises or see-you-laters. Bosch knew she would not be expecting any. They both knew that little had changed in the twenty years between their liaisons. They liked each other fine but that wasn't enough to build a house on.

The streets between Vicki Landreth's Los Feliz home and the Cahuenga Pass were misted and gray. People drove with their lights on, either because they had been driving through the night or because they thought it might help wake up the world. Bosch knew the dawn had nothing on the dusk. Dawn always came up ugly, as if the sun was clumsy and in a hurry. The dusk was smoother, the moon more graceful. Maybe it was because the moon was more patient. In life and nature, Bosch thought, darkness always waits.

He tried to push thoughts of the night before out of his mind so that he could focus only on the case. He knew the others would be moving into position now on Mariano Street in Woodland Hills and in the ListenTech sound room in the City of Industry. While Roland Mackey slept, the forces of justice were quietly closing in on him. That's how Bosch looked at it. That was what put the wire in his blood. He still believed it was unlikely that Mackey had been the one to pull the trigger on Rebecca Verloren. But Bosch felt no doubt that Mackey provided the gun and would lead them on this day to the triggerman, whether it would be William Burkhart or someone else.

Bosch pulled into the parking lot in front of the Poquito Mas at the bottom of the hill from his house. He left the Mercedes running and got out and went to the row of newspaper boxes. He saw the face of Rebecca Verloren staring out at him through the smeared plastic window of the box. He felt a little catch in his rhythm. It didn't matter what the story said, they were now in play.

He dropped the coins into the box and took a paper out. He repeated the process, taking a second paper. One for the files and one for Mackey. He didn't bother reading the story until he had driven up the hill to his house. He put a pot of coffee on and read the story while standing in the kitchen. The window photo was a shot of Muriel Verloren sitting on her daughter's bed. The room was neat and the bed perfectly made, right down to the ruffle skirting the floor. There was an inset photograph of Rebecca in the top corner. It turned out that the *Daily News* archives had held the same shot as the yearbook. A headline above the photo said A MOTHER'S LONG VIGIL.

The bedroom photograph was credited to Emerson

Ward, the photographer apparently using her given name. Below it was a caption that read: "Muriel Verloren sits in her daughter's bedroom. The room, like Mrs. Verloren's grief, has been untouched by time."

Beneath the photo and above the body of the story was what a reporter had once told Bosch was a deck headline — a fuller description of the story. It read: "HAUNTED: Muriel Verloren has waited 17 years to learn who took her daughter's life. In a renewed effort the LAPD may be close to finding out."

Bosch thought the deck was perfect. If and when Mackey saw it, he would feel the cold finger of fear poke him in the chest. Bosch anxiously read the story.

By McKenzie Ward, Staff Writer

Seventeen years ago this summer, a young and beautiful high-school girl named Rebecca Verloren was stolen away from her Chatsworth home and brutally murdered on Oat Mountain. The case was never solved, leaving in its wake a splintered family, haunted police officers and a community with no sense of closure from the crime.

But in a measure of hope for the victim's mother, the Los Angeles Police Department has launched a new investigation of the case that may see results and closure for Muriel Verloren. This time out the detectives have something they didn't in 1988: the killer's DNA.

The LAPD's Open-Unsolved Unit began the intense refocus on the Verloren case after one of the original detectives — now a Valley area commander — urged that it be reopened two years ago when the squad was formed to investigate cold cases.

"As soon as I heard we were going to start looking at cold cases I was on the phone to them," Cmdr. Arturo

Garcia said yesterday from his office in the Valley Bureau command center. "This was the case that always stuck with me. That beautiful young girl taken from her home like that. No murder in our society is acceptable, but this one hurt more than most. It haunted me all these years."

So, too, Muriel Verloren. Rebecca's mother has continued to live in the house on Red Mesa Way from which her 16-year-old daughter was taken. Rebecca's bedroom remains unaltered from the night she was carried out a back door, never to return.

"I don't want to change anything," the tearful mother said yesterday while smoothing the spread on her daughter's bed. "It's my way of remaining close to her. I will never change this room and I will never leave this house."

Det. Harry Bosch, who is assigned to the renewed investigation, told the News that there are several promising leads in the case now. The greatest aid in the case has been the technological advances made since 1988. Blood that did not belong to Rebecca Verloren was actually found inside the murder weapon. Bosch explained that the pistol's hammer "bit" the shooter on the hand, taking a sample of blood and tissue. In 1988 it could only be analyzed, typed and preserved. Now it can be directly matched to a suspect. The challenge is finding that suspect.

"The case was thoroughly investigated previously," Bosch said. "Hundreds of people were questioned and hundreds of leads were followed. We are backtracking on all of that but our real hope lies in the DNA. It will be the case breaker, I think."

The detective explained that while the victim was not sexually assaulted, there were elements to the crime of a psychosexual nature. Ten years ago the state

Department of Justice started a database containing DNA samples from every person convicted of a sexually related crime. The DNA from the Verloren case is in the process of being compared to those samples. Bosch believes it is likely that Rebecca Verloren's killing was not an isolated crime.

"I think it is unlikely that this killer only committed this one crime and then led a law-abiding existence. The nature of this offense indicates to us that this person likely committed other crimes. If he was ever caught and his DNA put into a data bank, then it's only a matter of time before we identify him."

Rebecca was carried from her home in the dead of night on July 5, 1988. For three days police and community members searched for her. A woman riding a horse on Oat Mountain found the body secreted by a fallen tree. While the investigation revealed many things, including that Rebecca had terminated a pregnancy about six weeks before her death, the police were unable to determine who her killer was and how he got into the house.

In the years since, the crime has echoed through many lives. The victim's parents have split up and Muriel Verloren could not say where her husband, Robert Verloren, a former Malibu restaurateur, is now located. She said the disintegration of their marriage was directly attributed to the strain and grief brought on by their daughter's murder.

One of the original investigators on the case, Ronald Green, retired early from the department and later committed suicide. Garcia said he believes the unsolved Verloren case played a part in his former partner's decision to end his life.

"Ronnie took things to heart, and I think this one always bothered him," Garcia said.

And at Hillside Preparatory School, where Rebecca Verloren was a popular student, there is a daily reminder of her life and death. A plaque erected by her classmates remains affixed to the wall in the exclusive school's main hallway.

"We don't ever want to forget someone like Rebecca," said Principal Gordon Stoddard, who was a teacher when Verloren was a student at the school.

One of Rebecca's friends and classmates is now a teacher at Hillside. Bailey Koster Sable spent an evening with Rebecca just two days before she was murdered. The loss has haunted her, and she says she thinks about her friend all the time.

"I think about it because it feels like it could have happened to anybody," Sable said after classes yesterday. "So it leads me to always ask the same thing: why her?"

That is a question the Los Angeles police hope to finally answer soon.

Bosch looked at the photo on the inside page where the story jumped to. It showed Bailey Sable and Gordon Stoddard standing on either side of the plaque on the wall at Hillside Prep. Emerson Ward was credited with this photo as well. The caption read: "FRIEND AND TEACHER: Bailey Sable went to school with Rebecca Verloren, and Gordon Stoddard taught her science class. Now school principal, Stoddard said, 'Becky was a good kid. This shouldn't have happened.'"

Bosch poured coffee into a mug and then read the story again while sipping his breakfast. He then excitedly grabbed the phone off the counter and called Kizmin Rider's home number. She answered with a blurry voice.

"Kiz, the story is perfect. She put in everything we wanted."

"Harry? What time is it, Harry?"

"Almost seven. We're in business."

"Harry, we have to work all night. What are you doing awake? What are you doing calling me at seven o'clock?"

Bosch realized his mistake.

"I'm sorry. I'm just excited about it."

"Call me back in two hours."

She hung up. There had not been a pleasant tone in her voice.

Undaunted, Bosch pulled a folded sheet of paper from his jacket pocket. It was the sheet of numbers Pratt had passed out during the staff meeting. He called Tim Marcia's cell number.

"It's Bosch," he said. "You guys in position?"

"Yeah, we're here."

"Anything shaking?"

"It's a sleepy hollow right now. We figure if this guy worked till midnight last night, then he's going to be sleeping late."

"His car is there? The Camaro?"

"Yes, Harry, it's here."

"Okay. Did you read the story in the paper?"

"Not yet. But we've got two teams sitting on this house for Mackey and Burkhart. We're about to break off to get coffee and pick up the paper."

"It's good. It's going to work."

"Let's hope so."

After Bosch hung up he realized that until Mackey or Burkhart left the house on Mariano there would be double surveillance on the place. It was a waste of time and money but he didn't see any way around it. There was no telling when one of the surveillance subjects might take off from the house. They knew very little about Burkhart. They didn't even know if he had a job.

He next called Renner in the sound room at Listen-

Tech. He was the oldest detective on the squad and had used seniority to get him and his partner the day shift in the sound room.

"Anything yet?" Bosch asked him.

"Not yet, but you'll be the first to know."

Bosch thanked him and hung up. He checked his watch. It wasn't even seven-thirty and he knew it was going to be a long day waiting for his surveillance shift to begin. He refilled his coffee mug and looked at the paper again. The photo of the dead girl's bedroom bothered him in a way he could not pinpoint. There was something there but he could not pull it out. He closed his eyes for a five count and then brought them open, hoping the trick would jar something loose. But the photo did not reveal the secret. A sense of frustration started to rise in him but then the phone rang.

It was Rider.

"Great, now I can't go back to sleep. You better be bright-eyed tonight, Harry, because I won't be."

"Sorry, Kiz. I will."

"Read me the story."

He did, and when he was finished she seemed to have caught some of his excitement. They both knew that the story would play perfectly into provoking a response from Mackey. The key would be to make sure that he saw it and read it, and they thought they had that covered.

"Okay, Harry, I'm going to get going. I have some things to do today."

"All right, Kiz, see you up there. How 'bout we meet at quarter to six on Tampa about a block south of the service station?"

"I'll be there unless something happens before."

"Yeah, me too."

After hanging up, Bosch went into his bedroom and changed into fresh clothes that would be comfortable during an all-night surveillance and useful as well for the play he intended for Mackey. He chose a white T-shirt that had been washed many times and had shrunk so that its sleeves were tight and short on his biceps. Before putting on a shirt over it he checked his look in the mirror. A full half of the skull was exposed and the SS bolts pointed up above the cotton on his neck.

The tattoos looked more authentic than they had the night before. He had taken a shower at Vicki Landreth's and she told him that the water would slightly blur the ink on his skin as was the case with most prison-applied tattoos. She warned him that the ink would start to wash away after two or three showers and, if needed, she could maintain his look with further applications. He told her he wasn't planning on needing the tattoos more than one day. They would work or not work when he made his play.

He put on a long-sleeved button-down shirt over the T-shirt. He checked this in the mirror and thought he could see details of the skull tattoo showing through the cotton. The thick black swastika on the crown was coming through.

Ready to go but with hours before he was needed, Bosch paced nervously around his living room for a few moments, wondering what to do. He decided to call his daughter, hoping that her sweet voice and cheerfulness would give him an added charge for the day.

He got the number for the Intercontinental Hotel in Kowloon off the Post-it on his refrigerator and punched it into his phone. It would be almost 8 p.m. there. His daughter should still be awake. But when his call was connected to Eleanor Wish's room there was no answer. He wondered if he had the time change wrong. Maybe he was calling too early or too late.

After six rings an answering service picked up, giving Bosch instructions in English and Cantonese in how to leave a message. He left a short message for both Eleanor and his daughter and hung up the phone.

Now not wanting to dwell on his daughter or thoughts about where she was, Bosch opened the murder book and began reviewing its contents again, always looking for details of the case he had possibly missed. Despite everything he had learned about the case and how it was pushed off track by the powers that be, he still believed in the book. He believed the answers to the mysteries were always found in the details.

He finished a read-through and was going to take up the copy of Mackey's probation file when he thought of something and called Muriel Verloren. She was at home.

"Did you see the story in the paper?" he asked.

"Yes, it makes me feel so sad to see that."

"Why is that?"

"Because it makes it all real to me. I had pushed it away."

"I'm sorry but it is going to help us. I promise. I'm glad you did it. Thank you."

"Whatever will help I want to do."

"Thank you, Muriel. Listen, I wanted to tell you that I located your husband. I spoke to him yesterday morning."

There was a long silence before she spoke.

"Really? Where is he?"

"Down on Fifth Street. He runs a soup kitchen for the homeless. He serves breakfast to them. It's called the Metro Shelter. I thought you might want to know."

Again a silence. Bosch guessed she wanted to ask him questions and he was willing to wait.

"You mean he works there?"

"Yes. He's sober now. He said it's been three years. I guess he first went there for a meal and he's sort of worked his way up. He runs the kitchen now. And it's good food. I ate there yesterday."

"I see."

"Um, I have a number that he gave me. It's not a direct line. He doesn't have a phone in his room. But it's in the kitchen and he's there in the mornings. He said it slows down after about nine."

"Okay."

"Do you want the number, Muriel?"

This question was followed by the longest silence of all. Bosch finally answered the question himself.

"I'll tell you what, Muriel. I've got the number, and if you ever want it you can just call me. Is that okay?"

"That would be fine, Detective. Thank you."

"No problem. I'm going to go now. We're hoping something breaks on the case today."

"Please call me."

"It will be the first call I make."

After hanging up, Bosch realized that talking about breakfast had made him hungry. It was now almost noon and he hadn't eaten anything since the steak at Musso's the night before. He decided that he would go into the bedroom and rest for a while and then have a late lunch before reporting for the surveillance. He would go over to Dupar's in Studio City. It was on the way out to Northridge. Pancakes were the perfect surveillance food. He would order a full stack of buttered pancakes and they would sit in his stomach like clay and keep him full all night if necessary.

In the bedroom he lay on his back and shut his eyes. He tried to think of the case but his mind wandered to the drunken time he got the tattoo put on his arm in a dirty studio in Saigon. As he drifted off to sleep he remembered the man with the needle and his smile and his body odor. He remembered the man had said, "Are you sure? Remember, you'll be marked forever with this."

Bosch had smiled back and said, "I already am."

Then in his dream the man's smiling face turned into Vicki Landreth's face. She had red lipstick smeared across her mouth. She held up a buzzing tattoo needle.

She said, "Are you ready, Michael?"

He said, "I'm not Michael."

She said, "It's all right. It doesn't matter who you are. Everybody's dodging the needle. But nobody gets away."

28

Kiz Rider was already at the meeting spot when Bosch got there. He got out of his car and brought the murder book and the other files to her car, a nondescript white Taurus.

"You have any room in your trunk?" he asked before getting in.

"It's empty. Why?"

"Pop it. I forgot to leave my spare tire at home."

He went back to his car, a Mercedes-Benz SUV, and took the spare tire out of the back and transferred it to Rider's trunk. Using a screwdriver from the tool kit he removed the license plates from his car and put them in the trunk as well. He then got in with her and they drove up Tampa to the plaza shopping center across from the service station where Mackey worked. The day team, Marcia and Jackson, were waiting in their car in the lot.

The space next to them was open and Rider pulled in. Everybody put down their windows so they could talk and transfer the two rovers without having to get out of their cars. Bosch took the radios but knew he and Rider wouldn't use them.

"Well?" Bosch asked.

"Well, nothing," Jackson said. "Seems like we're pumping a dry hole here, Harry."

"Nothing at all?" Rider asked.

"There has been absolutely no indication at all that

he's seen the paper or that anybody he knows has seen it. We checked with the sound room twenty minutes ago and this guy hasn't even gotten a phone call, let alone one about this. He hasn't even had a tow call since he came on."

Bosch nodded. He wasn't concerned yet. Sometimes things needed a little push and that was what he was ready to do.

"I hope you've got a good plan, Harry," Marcia called over. He was in the driver's side of their car and Bosch was furthest away on the passenger side of Rider's car.

"You want to stick around?" Bosch replied. "No use waiting on it if there hasn't been any action. I'm ready to go."

Jackson nodded.

"I don't mind," he said. "You going to need backup?"

"I doubt it. I'm just going to plant a seed. But you never know. It couldn't hurt."

"All right. We'll watch anyway. Just in case, what's your flare going to be?"

Bosch hadn't thought about how he would send up a flare if things went wrong and he had to call in backup.

"I guess I'll hit the horn," he said. "Or you'll hear the shots."

He smiled and everybody nodded and then Rider backed out of the space and they headed back down Tampa to his car.

"You sure about this?" Rider asked as she pulled in next to the Mercedes.

"I'm sure."

He had noticed on the way over that she had brought an accordion file with her. It was on the armrest between the seats.

"What's this?"

"Since you woke me up early I decided to go to work. I

traced down the other five members of the Chatsworth Eights."

"Great work. Any of them still local?"

"Two of them are still around. But it looks like they have grown out of their so-called youthful indiscretions. No records. They've got pretty decent jobs."

"What about the others?"

"The only one that still seems like he's a believer in the cause is a guy named Frank Simmons. Moved down here from Oregon when he was in high school. A couple years later he joins the Eights. He now lives in Fresno. But he did a two-year bit in Obispo for selling machine guns."

"I might be able to use that. When was he there?"

"Hold on a second."

She opened her file and dug through it until she came up with a slim manila folder with the name Frank Simmons on it. She opened it and showed Bosch a prison mug shot of Simmons.

"Six years ago," she said. "He got out six years ago."

Bosch studied the photo, committing the details of Simmons's look to memory. He had dark short hair and dark eyes. His skin was very pale and his face was tracked with acne scars. He tried to cover these with a goatee that would also make him look tougher.

"Where was the case, here?" he asked.

"No, actually, it was from Fresno. He apparently moved up there after the troubles down here."

"Who was he selling the machine guns to?"

"I called the FBI office up there, talked to the agent. He didn't want to cooperate with me until he checked me out. I'm still waiting for the callback."

"Great."

"I got the feeling that Mr. Simmons is still of active interest to the bureau up there and the agent wasn't into sharing."

Bosch nodded.

"Where was Simmons living at the time of the Verloren thing?"

"Can't tell. He was one of the younger ones, so he was probably living with his parents. AutoTrack doesn't trace him back further than 'ninety. By then he was in Fresno."

"So unless his parents moved out after this thing, he was probably right there in the Valley."

"It's possible."

"Okay, this is good, Kiz. I might be able to use some of this. Follow me over to the top of Balboa Park by Woodley. I think that's a good spot. There's a golf course there with a parking lot. There will be a lot of cars. You guys will be able to park there and it will be good cover. Okay?"

"Okay."

"Tell the other guys."

He took out his badge wallet, his cuffs and his service pistol and put them all down on the floor of the car.

"Harry, you got a backup?"

"I've got you, right?"

"I mean it."

"Yes, Kiz, I've got a little popper on my ankle. I'll be all right."

He got out and got into his own car. On the drive over to the park he rehearsed the play in his mind. He got ready and got excited.

Ten minutes later he pulled over onto the shoulder of the park road, killed the engine and got out. He went to the right front side of the car and let the air out of the tire through the valve. Because he knew some tow trucks come equipped with compressed air, he opened his pocket knife and slashed open the stem of the tire's valve. The tire would have to be repaired, not refilled.

Ready to go, he opened his cell phone and called the service station where Mackey worked. He said he needed a tow and was put on hold. A whole minute went by before another voice came on the line. Roland Mackey.

"What do you need?"

"I need a tow. I got a flat and the valve looks like it's fucked up."

"What kind of car is it?"

"Black Mercedes SUV."

"What about the spare?"

"It got stolen by some ni — it was stolen when I was in South-Central last week."

"That's too bad. Shouldn't go down there."

"I had no choice. Can you tow me or not?"

"Okay, okay. Where are you?"

Bosch told him. It was close enough that this time Mackey didn't try to talk him into calling someone else.

"All right, ten minutes," Mackey said. "Be there with your car when I get there."

"I've got nowhere else to go."

Bosch closed the phone and opened the back of the SUV. He pulled his outer shirt out of his pants and then took it off. He put it in the back. His new tattoos were now partially displayed. He sat down on the tailgate and waited. Two minutes later his cell phone chirped. It was Rider.

"Harry, they were able to pipe the call over to me from ListenTech. You sounded legit."

"Good."

"I just talked to the guys. Mackey's moving. They're with him."

"Okay, I'm ready."

"I kind of wish now we had gotten you a body wire. You never know what this guy is going to say to you."

"Too risky in just a T-shirt. Besides, the chances of the guy telling a stranger he was the one who killed the girl in the newspaper story are probably longer than me winning the lotto without buying a ticket."

"I guess."

"I gotta go, Kiz."

"Good luck, Harry. Be careful."

"All the time."

He closed the phone.

29

The tow truck slowed as it approached the Mercedes. Bosch looked up from the rear hatch, where he was sitting below the shade of the overhead door and reading the Daily News. He waved the paper at the tow truck driver and stood up. The truck drove by and then onto the shoulder in front of the Mercedes. It then backed up to within five feet of it. Its driver got out. It was Roland Mackey.

Mackey was wearing leather gloves that were grease-stained dark in the palms. Rather than acknowledge Bosch, he walked around the front of the Mercedes and looked down at the flattened tire. As Bosch came around, still holding the paper, Mackey squatted down and looked at the tire's valve. He reached out and bent it back and forth, exposing the slice that had been cut into it.

"Almost looks like it was cut," Mackey said.

"Maybe glass in the road or something," Bosch offered.

"And no spare. Ain't that a bitch?"

He looked up at Bosch, squinting in the light from the sun that was beginning to go down behind Bosch.

"You're telling me," Bosch replied.

"Well, I can tow it in and then have my guy put a new valve on the tire. Take about fifteen minutes once we get it into the garage."

"Fine. Do it."

"This going to be on Triple A or insurance?"

"No, cash."

Mackey told him it would be eighty-five dollars for the tow plus three dollars for every mile his car was towed. The charge for the valve replacement would be another twenty-five plus the cost of the valve.

"Fine, do it," Bosch said again.

Mackey stood up and looked at Bosch. He appeared to glance directly at Bosch's neck and then away. He said nothing about the tattoos.

"You should close the back," he said instead. "Unless you want to dump everything out on the way."

He smiled. A little tow truck humor.

"I'll grab my shirt out of there and close it," Bosch said. "All right if I ride with you?"

"Unless you want to call a cab and ride in style."

"I'd rather ride with somebody who speaks English."

Mackey laughed loudly while Bosch went to the back of his car. Bosch then stood off to the side while Mackey went through the procedures for hooking the vehicle to the truck. It took him no more than ten minutes before he was standing at the side of his truck, holding down a lever that raised the front end of the SUV into the air. After it was high enough for Mackey, he checked all the chains and harnesses and said he was ready to go. When Bosch got into the tow truck he had his shirt over his arm and the folded newspaper in his hand. It was folded so the photo of Rebecca Verloren was noticeable.

"Does this thing have air-conditioning?" Bosch said as he pulled the door closed. "I was sweating my ass off out there."

"You and me both. You should've stayed in the vehicle with your own AC blowing while you waited. This piece of shit doesn't have air in the summer or heat in the winter. Kind of like my ex-wife."

More tow truck humor, Bosch guessed. Mackey handed him a clipboard with an information page and a pen attached.

"Fill that out," he said. "Then we're set."

"Okay."

Bosch started to fill the form in with the false name and address he had come up with earlier. Mackey pulled a microphone off the dashboard and spoke into it.

"Hey, Kenny?"

A few moments later there was a response.

"Go ahead."

"Tell Spider not to leave yet," Mackey said. "I'm bringing in a tire that needs a valve."

"He's not going to like that. He's already washed up."

"Just tell him. Out."

Mackey returned the microphone to its dash holder.

"Think he'll stay?" Bosch asked.

"You better hope so. Or you're going to be waiting till tomorrow for your tire to get done."

"I can't do that. I have to get back on the road."

"Yeah? Where to?"

"Barstow."

Mackey started the tow truck and turned his body to the left so he could look out the side window and make sure it was okay to pull off the shoulder onto the road. He could not see Bosch from this position. Bosch quickly hiked the left sleeve on his T-shirt up so that more than half of the skull tattoo was visible.

The tow truck pulled into the street and they started off. Bosch glanced out his window and saw the cars belonging to both Rider and the other surveillance team in the parking lot of the golf course. Bosch put his elbow on the sill of the open window and his hand on the top frame. Out of Mackey's view, he was able to give the thumbs-up sign to the watchers.

"What's out in Barstow?" Mackey asked.

"Home, that's all. I want to get home tonight."

"What have you been doing down here?"

"This and that."

"What about South-Central? What were you doing down there with those people last week?"

Bosch understood the reference to *those people* as meaning the predominant minority population of South L.A. He turned and looked pointedly at Mackey, as if telling him he was asking too many questions.

"This and that," he said evenly.

"That's cool," Mackey responded, taking his hands off the wheel in a backing off gesture.

"Tell you what, though, it doesn't matter what I was doing, you can just fucking keep this city, man."

Mackey smiled.

"I know what you mean," he said.

Bosch thought they were close to sharing more than small talk. He believed Mackey had gotten a glimpse of the tattoos and was trying to draw from Bosch a signal as to what kind of person he was. He thought the moment was right for another subtle move toward the newspaper article.

Bosch put the newspaper down on the seat between them, making sure the photo of Rebecca Verloren was still noticeable. He then started putting his shirt back on. He leaned forward and extended his arms to do it. He didn't look at Mackey but knew the skull on his left arm would be very noticeable as he did this. He put his right arm into the shirt first and then brought the shirt behind his back and put his left arm into its sleeve. He leaned back and started buttoning the shirt.

"Just a little too third world around here for me," Bosch said.

"I'm with you on that."

"Yeah? Is this where you're from?"

"My whole life."

"Well, pal, you ought to take your family — if you have a family — and the flag with you and leave. Just fucking leave this place."

Mackey laughed and nodded.

"I got a friend says the same thing. All the time."

"Yeah, well, it's not an original idea."

"Got that right."

Then the radio interrupted the momentum of the conversation.

"Hey, Ro?"

Mackey grabbed the mike.

"Yeah, Ken?"

"I'm gonna run over to KFC while Spider's waiting on you. You want something?"

"Nah, I'll go out later. Out."

He hung the mike up. They drove in silence for a few moments while Bosch tried to think of a way to naturally get the conversation going again and in the right direction. Mackey had driven down to Burbank Boulevard and gone right. They were coming up on Tampa. He would turn right again and then it would be a straight shot to the station. In less than ten minutes the ride would be over.

But it was Mackey who got it going again.

"So where'd you do your time?" he suddenly asked.

Bosch waited a moment so that his excitement wouldn't show.

"What are you talking about?" he asked.

"I saw your markings, man. It's no big deal. But they're either homemade or prison-made. That's obvious."

Bosch nodded.

"Obispo. I spent a nickel up there."

"Yeah? For what?"

Bosch turned and looked at him again.

"This and that."

Mackey nodded, apparently not put off by his passenger's reluctance to open up.

"That's cool, man. I have a friend that was there for a while. Late nineties. He said it wasn't so bad. It's kind of a white-collar place. Not as many niggers there as other places, at least."

Bosch was silent for a long moment. He knew Mackey's use of the racial slur was like a password. If Bosch responded in the proper way, then he would be accepted. It was code work.

"Yeah," Bosch said, nodding his head. "That made the conditions a little more livable. I probably missed your friend, though. I got out in early 'ninety-eight."

"Frank Simmons. That's his name. He was only there for like eighteen months or something. He was from Fresno."

"Frank Simmons from Fresno," Bosch said as if trying to recall the name. "I don't think I knew him."

"He's good people."

Bosch nodded.

"There was one guy who came in like a few weeks before I walked out of that place," he said. "I heard he was from Fresno. But, man, I was on short time and I wasn't into meeting new people, you know what I mean?"

"Yeah, that's cool. I was just wondering, you know."

"Did your guy have dark hair and his face had a lot a scars like from zits and stuff?"

Mackey started smiling and nodding.

"That's him! That's Frank. We used to call him Crater Face from Crater Lake."

"And I'm sure he was happy about that."

The tow truck turned onto Tampa and headed north. Bosch knew he might have more time with Mackey in the service station while the tire was being fixed but he couldn't count on it. There could be another tow call or myriad other distractions. He had to finish the play and plant the seed now, while he was alone with the target. He picked up the newspaper and held it in his lap, glancing down as if he was reading the headlines. He had to figure out a way to naturally steer the conversation directly toward the Verloren article.

Mackey took his right hand off the wheel and pulled off his glove by biting one of the fingers. It reminded Bosch of the way a child would do it. Mackey then extended his hand to Bosch.

"I'm Ro, by the way."

Bosch shook his hand.

"Ro?"

"Short for Roland. Roland Mackey. Pleased to meet you."

"George Reichert," Bosch said, giving the name he had made up after careful thought earlier in the day.

"Reichert?" Mackey said. "German, right?"

"Means 'heart of the Reich.'"

"That's cool. And I guess that explains the Mercedes. You know, I deal with cars all fucking day. You can tell a lot about people by the cars they drive and how they take care of them."

"I suppose."

Bosch nodded. He now saw the direct way to his goal. Once again Mackey had unwittingly helped.

"German engineering," Bosch said. "The best fucking carmakers in the world. What do you drive when you're not in this rig?"

"I'm restoring a 'seventy-two Camaro. It's going to be a sweet ride when I'm finished."

"Good year," Bosch offered.

"Yeah, but I wouldn't buy anything out of Detroit nowadays. You know who's making our cars now, don't you? All the fucking mud people. I wouldn't drive one, let alone put my family in one."

"In Germany," Bosch responded, "you go into a factory and everybody's got blue eyes, you know what I mean? I've seen pictures."

Mackey nodded thoughtfully. Bosch thought it was time to make the direct move. He unfolded the newspaper on his lap. He held it up so that the full front page, and the full Verloren story, could be seen.

"Talk about mud people," he said. "Did you read this story?"

"No, what's it say?"

"It's about this mother sittin' on a bed boohooing about her mud child who got killed seventeen years ago. And the police are still on the case. But I mean, who cares, man?"

Mackey glanced over at the paper and saw the photo with the inset shot of Rebecca Verloren's face. But he didn't say anything and his own face did not betray any recognition. Bosch lowered the paper so as not to be too obvious about it. He refolded it and discarded it on the seat between them. He pushed things one more time.

"I mean, you mix the races like that and what are you going to get?" he asked.

"Exactly," Mackey said.

It wasn't a strong reply. It was almost hesitant, as if Mackey was thinking about something else. Bosch took this as a good sign. Maybe Mackey had just felt that cold finger go down his spine. Maybe it was the first time in seventeen years.

Bosch decided he had given it his best shot. If he tried to do anything more he might cross the line into obviousness and give himself away. He decided to ride the rest of the way silently, and Mackey seemed to make the same choice.

But a few blocks later Mackey swerved the truck into the second lane to get around a slow-moving Pinto.

"You believe there is still one of those on the street?" he said.

As they passed the little car Bosch saw a man of Asian descent huddled behind the wheel. Bosch thought he might be Cambodian.

"Figures," Mackey said, as he saw the driver. "Watch this."

Mackey then steered back into the original lane, squeezing the Pinto between the towed Mercedes and a row of cars parked against the curb. The Pinto driver had no choice but to pull to a screeching stop. Mackey's laughter drowned out the weak horn blast from the Pinto.

"Fuck you!" Mackey yelled. "Get back on your fucking boat!"

He looked to Bosch for affirmation and Bosch smiled, the hardest thing he'd had to do in a long while.

"Hey, man, that was my car you almost hit that guy with," he said in mock protest.

"Hey, were you in Vietnam?" Mackey asked.

"Why?"

"Because, man. You were there, weren't you?"

"So?"

"So, man, I had a friend who was there. He said they dusted mooks like that guy back there like it was nothing. A dozen for breakfast and another dozen for lunch. I wish I'd been there, is all I'm saying."

Bosch looked away from him and out the side window. Mackey's statement had left an opening for him to ask about guns and killing people. But Bosch couldn't bring himself to go there. All at once he just wanted to get away from Mackey.

But Mackey kept talking.

"I tried to sign up for the Gulf — the first one — but they wouldn't take me."

Bosch recovered some and got back into it.

"Why not?" he asked.

"I don't know. They needed the slot for a nigger, I guess."

"Or maybe you had a criminal record."

Bosch had turned to look at him as he said this. He immediately thought he had sounded too accusatory about it. Mackey turned and held his stare for as long as he could before having to return his eyes to the road.

"I've got a record, man, big fucking deal. They still could've used me over there."

The conversation died there, and in a few blocks they were pulling into the service station.

"I don't think we'll need to put it in the garage," Mackey said. "Spider can just take the wheel off while I have it on the hook. We'll do it quick."

"Whatever you want to do," Bosch said. "You're sure he didn't leave yet?"

"No, that's him right there."

As the tow truck went by the double bays of the garage a man emerged from the shadows and headed toward the back of the truck. He was holding a pneumatic drill with one hand and pulling the air line with the other. Bosch saw the webwork tattooed on his neck. Prison blue. Something about the man's face immediately struck Bosch as familiar. In a rushed moment of dread he thought he knew the man because he'd had dealings with him as a cop. He had arrested him or questioned him before, maybe even sent him to the prison where he had gotten the webwork done.

Bosch suddenly knew he had to stay clear of the man called Spider. He pulled his phone off his belt.

"All right if I sit here and make a call?" he asked Mackey, who was getting out of the truck.

"Yeah, go ahead. This won't take long."

Mackey closed the door, leaving Bosch alone. As he heard the drill start taking the lugs off the wheel of his SUV, Bosch rolled the window up and called Rider's cell phone.

"How's it going?" she said by way of a greeting.

"It was going good till we got back to the station," Bosch said in a low voice. "I think I know the mechanic. If he knows me, this could be a problem."

"You mean he might know you're a cop?"

"Exactly."

"Shit."

"Exactly."

"What do you want us to do? Tim and Rick are still floating around."

"Call them and tell them what's happening. Tell them to stay loose until I get clear. I'm going to stay in the truck as long as I can. If I hold the phone up like I am talking I can keep him from seeing my face."

"Okay."

"I just hope Mackey doesn't want to introduce me. I think I made an impression on him. He might want to show me off."

"Okay, Harry, just stay cool and we'll move in if we have —"

"I'm not worried about me. I'm worried about the play with —"

"Hey, he's coming over."

Just as she said the warning there was a sharp rap on the window. Bosch lowered the phone and turned to see Mackey staring at him. He rolled the window down.

"It's done," he said.

"Already?"

"Yup. You can come into the office and pay while he puts the wheel back on. You'll make it home in a couple hours."

"Great."

Holding the phone up to his right ear, Bosch got out of the truck and walked to the office, never allowing Spider a decent look at his face. He spoke to Rider while he walked.

"It looks like I'm getting out of here," he said.

"Good," she said. "The man in question is putting on your wheel. Watch yourself when you leave."

"Will do."

Once he was in the little office Bosch closed the phone. Mackey had gone behind a greasy, cluttered desk. He took several seconds to use a calculator to do the simple arithmetic of the tow and repair charges.

"Comes to one twenty-five even," he said. "Four miles towing and the valve was three bucks."

Bosch sat down in a chair in front of the desk and pulled out his fold of money.

"Can I get a receipt for it?"

As he counted out six twenties and a five he heard the drill outside. The tire was being put back on. He held the money out, but Mackey was preoccupied by looking at a Post-it note he had found on the desk. He held it at an angle that allowed Bosch to read it.

Ro — FYI. Visa called to confirm employment on your app.

Bosch read it in a few seconds, but Mackey looked at it for a long time before finally dropping the note back on the desk and taking the money from Bosch. Mackey put the money in a cash drawer and then started fishing around on the desk for a receipt pad. He was taking a long time.

"Kenny usually writes up the receipts," he said. "And he went to get some chicken."

Bosch was about to say never mind about the receipt when he heard the scrape of a step behind him and knew that someone had entered the office. He didn't turn in case it was Spider.

"All right, Ro, it's done. You just need to let her down."

Bosch knew this was the tight moment. Mackey would either introduce him or not.

"All right, Spider," Mackey said.

"Then I'm outta here."

"Okay, man, thanks for sticking. Catch you tomorrow."

Spider left the office without Bosch ever turning around. Mackey found what he was looking for in the center drawer and scribbled something on it. He gave it to Bosch. It was a blank receipt. He had written $125 in a childlike scrawl at the bottom.

"You can just fill that out," Mackey said as he got up. "I'll go drop your machine and you can get out of here."

Bosch followed him out, realizing he had left the newspaper on the seat of the truck. He wondered if he should leave it there or come up with an excuse to go back into the truck so he could get it and maybe leave it in the office where he knew Mackey watched television during the slow parts of his shift.

He decided to leave it where it was. He had planted the seed as best he could. It was time now to just step back and see what grew from it.

The Mercedes was off the truck now. Bosch walked around to the driver's side. Mackey was stowing the harness in the back of the tow truck.

"Thanks, Roland," Bosch said.

"Just Ro, man," Mackey responded. "You take care, man. And do yourself a favor and stay out of South-Central."

"Don't worry about me," Bosch said. "I will."

Mackey smiled and winked as he pulled off his glove again and offered Bosch his hand. Bosch shook it and smiled back. He then looked down at their hands and saw a tiny white scar in the fleshy part between Mackey's right thumb and finger. The tattoo from a Colt .45.

"I'll catch you later," he said.

30

Bosch drove to the spot where he had met Rider at the start of the surveillance shift and she was there waiting. He parked and got into her Taurus.

"That was close," she said. "Turns out you probably did know that guy. Jerry Townsend. Ring a bell? We ran the plate on his pickup when he left work and got the ID."

"Jerry Townsend? No, not the name. I just recognized his face."

"He has a manslaughter conviction in 'ninety-six. Served five years. Sounds like it was a domestic abuse case, but that's all they could pull off the computer. I bet if we pulled the file your name would be on it. That's how you recognized him."

"You think he could be connected to this thing we're working?"

"I doubt it. What's probably going on is that whoever owns that station doesn't mind hiring ex-cons. They come cheap, you know? And if he's scamming on repairs, then who's going to complain?"

"Well, let's get back and see what happens."

She put the car into gear and pulled out on Tampa to head back up to the intersection where the service station was.

"How did it go with him?" Rider asked.

"Pretty good. I did all but read the story to him. He didn't show anything, no recognition, but the seed is definitely planted."

"Did he see the tattoos?"

"Yeah, they worked good. He started asking questions right after he saw them. Your file on Simmons paid off, too. He came up in the conversation. And for what it's worth, he had a scar on the webbing by his right thumb. From the bite."

"Harry, man, you covered everything. I guess all we do now is sit back and see what happens."

"Did the other guys take off?"

"As soon as we get back on post they're leaving."

When they got to the intersection of Tampa and Roscoe they saw Mackey's tow truck waiting to pull onto Roscoe to head west.

"He's on the move," Bosch said. "Why didn't anybody tell us?"

Just as he said it Rider's cell phone buzzed. She handed it to Bosch so she could concentrate on driving. She cut into the left turn lane so she would be able to follow Mackey onto Roscoe. Bosch opened her phone. It was Tim Marcia. He explained that Mackey went on the move without a call coming into the station for a tow. Jackson had checked with the sound room. There had been no call on the lines they were listening to.

"All right," Bosch said. "He said something when I was in the truck about going to grab dinner. Maybe this is it."

"Maybe."

"Okay, Tim, we got him now. Thanks for sticking around. Tell Rick the same."

"Good luck, Harry."

They followed the tow truck to a plaza shopping center and watched Mackey go into a Subway fast food restaurant. He did not take the newspaper Bosch had left in the truck with him, but after getting his food he sat down at one of the inside tables and started to eat.

"You going to get hungry, Harry?" Rider asked. "Now might be the time."

"I did Dupar's on the way in so I'll be fine. Unless we see a Cupid's around. I'd go for that."

"No way. That's one thing I got over after you left. I don't eat that fast food crap anymore."

"What do you mean? We ate good. Didn't we go to Musso's every Thursday?"

"If you call chicken pot pie a healthy meal, yeah, we ate good. Besides, I'm talking about stakeouts. Did you hear about Rice and Beans in Hollywood?"

Rice and Beans was the designation given to a pair of robbery detectives in Hollywood Division named Choi and Ortega. They were there when Bosch worked in the division.

"No, what happened?"

"They were on a surveillance gig on these guys that were taking down street prostitutes, and Ortega was sittin' in the car eating a hotdog. He suddenly started choking on it and he couldn't clear himself. He's turning purple and pointing to his throat and Choi's like, what the fuck? So finally Beans jumps out of the car and Choi finally gets what's going on. He comes running around to give him the Heimlich. He popped the hotdog onto the hood of the car. And they blew the surveillance."

Bosch laughed as he pictured it. He knew it was a story Rice and Beans would never live down in the division. Not with people like Edgar there to tell and retell it to anyone who transferred in.

"Well, see, they don't have a Cupid's down in Hollywood," he said. "If he'd been eating a nice soft dog from Cupid's there wouldn't have been a problem like that."

"I don't care, Harry. No hotdogs on stakeout. No crap.

That's my new rule. I don't want people talking about me like that the rest of my —"

Bosch's phone chirped. It was Robinson, who was working the late shift in the sound room with Nord.

"They just had a tow call come into the station. They then turned around and called Mackey. He must not be at the station."

Bosch explained the situation and apologized for not keeping the sound room in the loop.

"Where's the tow?" he asked.

"It's an accident on Reseda at Parthenia. I guess the car's DOA. He's got to tow it into a dealership."

"Okay, we're with him."

A few minutes later Mackey came out of the fast food restaurant carrying a large soda cup with a straw sticking out. They followed him to Reseda Boulevard and Parthenia Street, where a Toyota with the front end caved in had been pushed off the road. Another tow truck was just jacking up the other car, a large SUV that had its back end realigned by the accident. Mackey spoke briefly with the other tow truck driver — a professional courtesy — and went to work on the Toyota. An LAPD patrol car was sitting in the parking lot of the corner plaza and the officer inside was writing up a report. Bosch saw no drivers. He thought this meant that they might have all been transported to an emergency room because of injuries.

Mackey towed the Toyota to a dealership all the way over on Van Nuys Boulevard. While he was there, letting the wreck down in the service drive, Bosch got another call. Robinson told him that Mackey had been summoned again. This time to the Northridge Fashion Center, where an employee of the Borders bookstore needed a battery jump.

"This guy isn't going to have time to read the paper if

he stays busy like this," Rider said after Bosch reported on the phone call.

"I don't know," Bosch said. "I'm wondering if he can even read."

"You mean the dyslexia?"

"Yeah, but not just that. I haven't seen him do any reading or writing. He told me to fill in the forms for the tow. Then he either didn't want to or couldn't fill out a receipt at the end. And then there was this note on the desk for him."

"What note?"

"He picked it up and stared at it for a long time but I wasn't really sure he knew what it said."

"Could you read it? What did it say?"

"It was a note from the dayshift people. Visa had called to confirm his employment on an application he had made, I guess."

Rider wrinkled her brow.

"What?" Bosch asked.

"Just seems weird, him applying for a credit card. That would make him findable, which I thought he was trying to avoid."

"Maybe he's starting to feel safe."

Mackey went from the Toyota dealership straight to the shopping mall, where he jump-started a woman's car. He then turned his truck toward the home base. It was almost ten o'clock by the time he pulled back into the station. Bosch's sagging hopes were buoyed when he looked through the binoculars from the plaza across the street and saw Mackey walking from the truck to the office.

"We might still be in play," he said to Rider. "He's carrying the paper with him."

It was hard to keep track of Mackey inside the station. The front office was glass on two sides and that was not a problem. But the garage doors were now closed and oftentimes it seemed that Mackey would disappear into these areas, where Bosch could not see him.

"You want me to be the eyes for a while?" Rider asked.

Bosch lowered the binoculars and looked at her. He could barely read her face in the darkness of the car.

"Nah, I'm okay. You're doing all the driving anyway. Why don't you rest? I woke you up early today."

He raised the binoculars back up.

"I'm fine," Rider said. "But anytime you need a break . . ."

"Besides," Bosch said, "I sort of feel responsible for this guy."

"What do you mean?"

"You know. This whole thing. I mean, we could've just pulled Mackey in and sweated him in the box, tried to break him. Instead we went this way, and it's my plan. I'm responsible."

"We can still sweat him. If this doesn't work, then that's probably what we'll need to do."

Bosch's phone began to chirp.

"Maybe this is what we're waiting for," he said as he answered.

It was Nord.

"I thought you told us this guy got his general education degree, Harry."

"He did. What's going on?"

"He just had to call someone to read the story to him out of the paper."

Bosch sat up a little straighter. They were in play. It didn't matter how the story was communicated to Mackey, the important thing was that he wanted to know what it said.

"Who did he call?"

"A woman named Michelle Murphy. Sounded like an old girlfriend. He asked if she still got the paper every day, like he wasn't sure anymore. She said yeah and he asked her to read the story to him."

"Did they talk about it after she read it?"

"Yeah. She asked him if he knew the girl the story was about. He said no, but then he said, 'I knew the gun.' Just like that. Then she said she didn't want to know anything else and that was it. They hung up."

Bosch thought about all of this. The play earlier in the day had worked. It had kicked over a rock that had not been moved in seventeen years. He was excited, and he could feel the charge building in his blood.

"Can you pipe the recording over the line to us here?" he asked. "I want to hear it."

"I think we can," Nord said. "Let me get one of the techs who are floating around here to — hey, Harry, I gotta call you back. Mackey's making a call."

"Call me back."

Bosch quickly closed the phone so Nord could get back to her monitor. He excitedly recounted for Rider the report on Mackey's phone call to Michelle Murphy. He could tell Rider caught the charge as well.

"We might be in business, Harry."

Bosch was looking through the binoculars at Mackey. He was sitting behind the desk in the office and talking on his cell phone.

"Come on, Mackey," Bosch whispered. "Spill it. Tell us the story."

But then Mackey closed the phone. Bosch knew the call was too short.

Ten seconds later Nord called Bosch back.

"He just called Billy Blitzkrieg."

"What did he say?"

"He said, 'I might be in trouble' and 'I might need to make a move,' and then Burkhart cut him off and said, 'I don't care what it is, don't talk about it on the phone.' So they agreed to meet after Mackey gets off work."

"Where?"

"Sounded like at the house. Mackey said, 'You'll be up?' and Burkhart said he would be. Mackey then said, 'What about Belinda, she still there?' and Burkhart said she'd be asleep and not to worry about her. They ended it like that."

Bosch immediately felt a crushing blow to his hopes of breaking the case that night. If Mackey met Burkhart inside the house, they would not hear what transpired inside. They'd be locked out of the confession they had set up the surveillance to get.

"Call me if he makes any other calls," he said quickly and then hung up.

He looked at Rider, who was waiting expectantly in the dark.

"Not good?" she asked. She had obviously read something in his tone to Nord.

"Not good."

He told her about the calls and the obstacle they would face if Mackey met with Burkhart to discuss his "trouble" behind closed doors.

"It's not all bad, Harry," she said after hearing everything. "He made a solid admission to the Murphy woman and a lesser admission to Burkhart. But we're getting close so don't get depressed. Let's figure this out. What can we do to make them meet outside of the house? Like at a Starbucks or something."

"Yeah, right. Mackey ordering a latte."

"You know what I mean."

"Even if we roust them out of the house, how are we going to get close? We can't. We need this to be a phone call. It's the blind spot — my blind spot — to this whole thing."

"We just need to sit tight and see what happens. It's all we can do right now. Look, it would be good to have an ear on this but maybe it's not the end of the world. We already have Mackey on the phone saying he might have to make a move. If he does, if he runs, then that could be seen by a jury as a shading of guilt. And if you take that and what we already have on tape it might be enough to squeeze more out of him when we finally bring him in. So all is not lost here, okay?"

"Okay."

"You want me to call it in to Abel? He'd want to know."

"Yeah. Fine, call it in. There's nothing to call in, but go ahead."

"Just cool down, Harry."

Bosch shut her out by raising the binoculars and looking at Mackey. He was still behind the desk and appeared deep in thought. The other night man, the one Bosch assumed was Kenny, was sitting on another chair and his face was angled up for viewing the television. He was laughing at something he was watching.

Mackey was not laughing or watching. His face was cast down. He was looking at something in memory.

The wait until midnight was the longest ninety minutes of surveillance Bosch had ever spent. As they waited for the station to close and Mackey to head to his rendezvous with Burkhart, nothing happened. The phones were silent, Mackey did not move from his spot at the desk and Bosch came up with no plan to either avert the rendezvous or infiltrate it in some way. It was as though they were all frozen until the clock struck twelve.

Finally, the exterior lights of the station went off and the two men closed the business for the night. When Mackey walked out, he was carrying the newspaper he could not read. Bosch knew he was going to show it to Burkhart and most likely discuss the murder.

"And we won't be there," Bosch mumbled as he tracked Mackey through the binoculars.

Mackey got into his Camaro and revved the engine loudly after firing it up. He then pulled out onto Tampa and headed south toward his home, the intended meeting place. Rider waited an appropriate amount of time and then pulled out of the plaza lot, cut across the northbound lanes of Tampa and headed south as well. Bosch called Nord in the sound room and told her Mackey had left the station and they should switch their monitoring to the house line.

The lights of Mackey's car were three blocks ahead. Traffic was sparse and Rider kept a safe distance back. As they passed the lot where Bosch had left his car he checked on the Mercedes just to make sure it was still there.

"Uh oh," Rider said.

Bosch turned back to the street ahead in time to see Mackey's car complete a fast U-turn. He was now heading back toward Bosch and Rider.

"Harry, what do I do?" Rider asked.

"Nothing. Don't do anything obvious."

"He's coming right back at us. He must have seen the tail!"

"Sit tight. Maybe he saw my car parked back there."

The deep-throated engine of the Camaro could be heard long before the car got to them. It sounded menacing and evil, like a monster roaring and coming for them.

31

The old Camaro went screaming by Bosch and Rider without hesitation. It blew the light at Saticoy and kept going. Bosch watched its lights disappearing to the north.

"What was that?" Rider said. "You think he knows there's a tail?"

"I don't —"

Bosch's cell phone sounded and he quickly answered it. It was Robinson.

"He just got called back by the Triple A answering service. He seemed pretty upset but they have to take it, I guess."

"What do you mean, he's got a tow?"

"Yeah. It was Triple A dispatch. I guess if he didn't take it they would go to another company and that could mean trouble. Like losing the Triple A business."

"Where's the tow?"

"It's a breakdown on the Reagan. On the westbound side near the Tampa Avenue overpass. So it's close. He said he was on the way."

"Okay. We got him."

Bosch closed the phone and told Rider to turn around, that their cover was still intact, that Mackey was simply hurrying back to get the tow truck.

By the time they were back to the intersection of Tampa and Roscoe, the tow truck was pulling out of the darkened station. Mackey wasn't wasting any time.

Since they knew Mackey's destination Rider could afford to hang back and not risk being noticed in the tow truck's rearview mirror. They headed north on Tampa toward the freeway. The Reagan was the 118 Freeway, which ran east-west across the northern stretch of the Valley. It was one of the few freeways that was not crowded with traffic twenty-four hours a day. Named after the late governor and president, it led to Simi Valley, where Reagan's presidential library was located. Still, it had been jarring to Bosch to hear Robinson call it the Reagan. To Bosch it was always simply the 118.

The westbound entrance to the 118 ramped down from Tampa Avenue to the ten lanes of freeway. Rider slowed and hung back and they watched the tow truck turn left and head down the ramp out of sight. She then pulled up and made the same turn. As they came on the ramp and started down they immediately realized their problem. The disabled car was not on the freeway as Nord had said but actually on the entrance ramp. They were quickly coming up on the tow truck. It was pulled onto the ramp's shoulder about fifty yards ahead. Its rear spreader lights were on and it was backing toward a small red car that was parked on the shoulder with its emergency lights blinking.

"What do we do, Harry?" Rider said. "If we pull over it's going to be obvious."

She was right. They would blow their cover.

"Just go on by," he replied.

He had to think quickly. He knew that once they were on the freeway they could pull onto the shoulder and wait until Mackey's tow truck came by with the disabled car on its hook. But that was risky. Mackey might recognize Rider's car, or even stop to see if they needed assistance. If he saw Bosch then the surveillance would be blown.

"You got a Thomas Guide?"

"Under the seat."

Rider drove by the disabled car and the tow truck as Bosch reached under the seat for the map book. Once they were clear of the tow truck he put on the overhead light and quickly flipped through the map pages. A Thomas map book was the driving bible of Los Angeles. Bosch had years of experience with them and quickly found the page depicting the section of the city they were in. He made a quick study of their situation and gave Rider directions.

"The next exit is Porter Ranch Drive," he said. "Less than a mile. We get off and go right and then another right on Rinaldi. It takes us back to Tampa. We either wait up on top of the overpass and watch or we just keep circling."

"I think we wait up on top," Rider said. "If we keep going down that ramp in the same car he might notice."

"Sounds like a plan."

"I don't like it but I don't know what choice we have."

They covered the distance to the Porter Ranch exit quickly.

"Did you check out the tow car?" Bosch asked. "I was looking for the map book."

"Small foreign job," Rider responded. "It looked like one person behind the wheel and that was it. The lights from the truck were too bright to see anything else."

Rider kept her speed up until they pulled into the exit lane for Porter Ranch Drive. As instructed, she took a right and then another right and they were quickly heading back toward Tampa. They got stopped at the light at Corbin but then Rider drove through it after checking to make sure it was clear. Less than three minutes after passing the tow truck they were back on Tampa. Rider pulled to the side of the road in the middle of the overpass. Bosch cracked his door.

"I'll check it out," he said.

He stepped out of the car. At this angle he couldn't see

the tow truck but the spreader lights on the top of the cab cast a glow above the entrance ramp.

"Harry, take this," Rider called.

Bosch ducked back into the car and took the rover Rider was holding out to him.

He walked back along the overpass. The freeway wasn't crowded, but it was still loud with the cars passing beneath him. When he got to the top of the ramp and looked down, it took him a few moments to adjust his vision because the lights from the back of the tow truck were still slashing through the darkness.

But soon he realized that the blinking lights of the disabled car were not there. He looked closer and saw that the car was no longer on the shoulder. His eyes traveled down the ramp to the freeway and he saw the red taillights of dozens of cars moving westbound into the distance.

He looked back at the tow truck. Everything was still. There was no sign of Mackey.

Bosch raised the radio to his mouth and keyed the mike. "Kiz?"

"Yeah, Harry?"

"You better get over here."

Bosch started walking down the ramp. As he did so he drew his weapon and carried it down by his side. In thirty seconds lights flashed behind him and Rider pulled her car onto the shoulder. She got out with a flashlight and they continued down the ramp.

"What's going on?" she asked.

"I don't know."

There was still no sign of Mackey in or around the tow truck. Bosch felt his chest tighten. He instinctively knew something was wrong. The closer they got the more he knew it.

"What do we say if he's here and everything's okay?" Rider whispered.

"It isn't," Bosch said.

The light from the back of the truck was almost blinding and Bosch knew they were in a vulnerable position. He could not see anyone on the front side of the tow truck. He moved to his right so that he and Rider would be spread apart. Rider could not move to the left or she would be walking into the entrance lane.

A semi-truck roared by on the ramp, wafting petroleum-tinged wind and sound over them and making the ground shake like an earthquake. Bosch was now walking in the weeds that were on the upward slope off the shoulder. He still didn't see anyone up ahead.

Bosch and Rider did not communicate. The noise from passing traffic on the freeway just below was echoing from beneath the overpass. They would have to shout now and that would detract from their concentration.

They came back together when they got to the tow truck. Bosch checked the cab and there was no sign of Mackey. The truck was still running. He stepped back to the rear and looked at the ground illuminated by the spreader lights. There were curving black tire marks leading right up to the truck's rear gate. And on the gravel was one of the leather gloves, grease-stained in the palm, that he had seen Mackey wearing earlier in the day.

"Let me borrow this," he said, taking the flashlight from Rider. He noticed that it was one of the short rubber models approved by the police chief after an officer was videotaped beating a suspect with one of the heavy steel lights.

Bosch pointed the beam at the truck's rear gate, running it over the underside that had been cast in shadows by the bright glare from the spreader above.

Blood reflected brightly on the dark steel. It could not be mistaken for oil. It was as red and real as life. Bosch squatted down and pointed the light beneath the truck. It had been dark here, too, made all the more impervious to vision by the bright lights above.

He saw Mackey's body crumpled against the rear axle differential. Fully one-half of his face was bathed in blood from a long and deep laceration that cut across the left side of his head. His blue uniform shirt was maroon down the front from blood from other unseen injuries. The crotch of his pants was stained with blood or urine or both. The one arm Bosch could see was bent oddly at the forearm and a jagged, ivory white bone protruded from the flesh. The arm was cradled against Mackey's chest, which heaved with non-rhythmic gasps. He was still alive.

"Oh God!" Rider called out from behind Bosch.

"Get an ambulance!" Bosch ordered as he started to crawl under the truck.

Hearing Rider's feet crunch on the gravel as she ran back to her car and the radio, Bosch moved as close to Mackey as he could get. He knew he might be destroying a crime scene but he had to get close.

"Ro, can you hear me? Ro, who did this? What happened?"

Mackey seemed to stir at the sound of his name. His mouth started moving and that was when Bosch could tell his jaw was broken or dislocated. Its movements were uncoordinated. It was like Mackey was trying it out for the first time.

"Take your time, Ro. Tell me who did this. Did you see him?"

Mackey whispered something but a car speeding by on the entrance ramp drowned it out.

"Tell me again, Ro. Say it again."

Bosch pushed forward and leaned his head down by Mackey's mouth. What he heard was half gasp, half whisper.

". . . sworth . . ."

He pulled back and looked at Mackey. He put the light into his face, hoping it might rouse him. He saw that the bone structure around Mackey's left eye was also crushed and hemorrhaging. He wasn't going to make it.

"Ro, if you have something to say, say it now. Did you kill Rebecca Verloren? Were you there that night?"

Bosch leaned forward. If Mackey said anything it was drowned in the noise of another car going by. When Bosch pulled back to look at him again he appeared to be dead. Bosch pushed two fingers into the bloodied side of Mackey's neck and could not find a pulse.

"Ro? Roland, are you still with me?"

The one undamaged eye was open but at half-mast. Bosch moved the light in close and saw no pupil movement. He was gone.

Bosch carefully crawled out from beneath the truck. Rider was standing there, her arms folded tightly in front of her.

"Ambulance on the way," she said.

"Call 'em off."

He handed her back her flashlight.

"Harry, if you think he's dead, the paramedics should confirm it."

"Don't worry, he's dead. They'll just get under there and ruin our crime scene. Call them off."

"Did he say anything?"

"It sounded like he said 'Chatsworth.' That was it. Anything else, I couldn't hear."

She seemed to be pacing now, in a small track, nervously moving back and forth.

"Oh God," she said. "I think I'm going to be sick."

"Then move back over there, away from the scene."

She walked off behind her car. Bosch felt sick to his stomach as well, but he knew he could keep it in. It wasn't seeing Mackey's torn and broken body that was causing the bile to rise in his throat. Bosch, like Rider, had seen far worse. It was the circumstances that were sickening. Instinctively he knew that this was no accident. This had been an assassination. And it was he who had put it all into motion.

He was sick because he had just gotten Roland Mackey killed. And with the death he might have lost the last, best link to Rebecca Verloren's killer.

PART THREE
DARKNESS WAITS

32

The Tampa Avenue entrance ramp to the Ronald Reagan Freeway was closed and traffic was routed down Rinaldi to the Porter Ranch Drive entrance. The entire freeway ramp was choked with official police vehicles. The LAPD's Scientific Investigation Division, California Highway Patrol and the Medical Examiner's Office were all represented, along with members of the Open-Unsolved Unit. Abel Pratt had made calls and had greased the takeover of the case by the unit. Because the murder of Roland Mackey had taken place on a state freeway entrance, the case technically belonged to the jurisdiction of the CHP. But the agency was more than happy to hand it off, especially since the death was seen as part of an ongoing LAPD investigation. In other words, the LAPD was going to be allowed to clean up its own mess.

The commander of the local CHP barracks did offer the use of his squad's best accident expert, and Pratt took him up on that. Added to this, Pratt had assembled some of the best forensics people the department could muster, all in the middle of the night.

Bosch and Rider spent much of the time during the crime scene investigation sitting in the back of Pratt's car, where they were interviewed at length by Pratt and then by Tim Marcia and Rick Jackson, who were called in from home to head up the investigation into Mackey's death. Since Bosch and Rider were part of some events and witnesses to others, it was determined that they would not investigate the case as leads. This was a technical formality. It was clear that Bosch and Rider would be continuing to pursue the Verloren case, and in doing so they would obviously be pursuing Roland Mackey's killer.

At about 3 a.m. the forensics investigators gathered with the homicide detectives to go over what they knew so far. Mackey's body had just been removed from beneath the truck and the scene had been thoroughly photographed, videoed and sketched. It was now considered an open scene and everyone could walk freely about.

Pratt asked the CHP investigator, a tall man named David Allmand, to go first. Allmand used a laser pointer to delineate the tire marks on the roadway and the gravel that he believed were involved in the incident with Mackey. He also pointed to the back of the tow truck, where chalk circles had been drawn around several scratches, dents and breaks in the heavy steel gate. He said he concluded the same thing Bosch and Rider had concluded within seconds of finding Mackey. He was murdered.

"The tire markings tell us that the victim pulled the tow truck onto the shoulder about thirty yards west of this point," Allmand said. "This was likely to avoid the disabled vehicle already on the shoulder. The tow truck was then backed down the shoulder to this position here. The driver put the transmission in park and set the parking brake before exiting the truck. If he was in a hurry, as some of the ancillary information indicates, he may have gone right to the tail here to lower the towing assembly. This is where he got it.

"The disabled car was obviously not disabled. The driver floored the accelerator and it lurched forward, striking the tow truck driver and pinning him against the back of the truck and the tow assembly. To get ready for the tow the vic would have bent over here to free the hook assembly. He was likely doing this when he was struck, and this would explain the head injuries. He went face first into the assembly. There's blood on the tow arm. "

Allmand ran the red eye of his laser over the tow truck's hook assembly to illustrate.

"The car then backed up," he continued. "And that's where you get the striated markings on the asphalt here. He then moved forward for another strike. The victim was probably already fatally injured from the first impact. But he wasn't dead yet. It is likely he fell to the ground after the first impact and with his last strength crawled under the truck to avoid the second impact. Either way, the vehicle did strike the tow truck a second time. And of course, the victim succumbed to his injuries while beneath the truck."

Allmand paused there for questions but he was met only with grim silence. Bosch could think of nothing to ask. Unchecked, Allmand finished up his report by pointing to two tire lines made in the gravel and asphalt.

"You've got a wheel base on the striking vehicle that is not very wide," he said. "That will cut it down some. It's probably going to be a little foreign job. I took measurements, and as soon as I consult my manufacturers' catalogs I will be able to come up with a list of cars those treads could have come from. I'll let you know."

When no one said anything Allmand used his laser to circle a small oil spot on the asphalt.

"Additionally, the striking vehicle was leaking oil. Not a big deal, but if it becomes important for a prosecutor to be able to say how long the killer sat here and waited for the victim, then we can time the leak once the vehicle is recovered and come up with a rough estimate of how long it would have taken to make this little spot here."

Pratt nodded.

"Good to know," he said.

Pratt thanked Allmand and asked the assistant medical examiner, Ravi Patel, to report on his preliminary examination of the body. Patel began by listing the numerous broken bones and injuries that were obvious from external examination of the body. He said the impact had likely fractured Mackey's skull, crushed the orbit of his left eye and dislocated his jaw. His hips were crushed along with the left side of his upper torso. His left arm and left thigh were broken as well.

"It is likely these injuries were sustained in one initial impact," he said. "The victim was likely standing and the impact came from the right rear side."

"Would he have been able to crawl under the truck?" Rick Jackson asked.

"It is possible," Patel answered. "We have seen the instinct for survival allow people to do amazing things. I won't know until I open him up, but what we often see in cases like this is that the compression perforates the lungs. The lungs fill with blood. This takes time. He could have crawled to what he thought was safety."

And then drowned on the side of the freeway, Bosch thought.

Next to report was the lead SID investigator, who happened to be Ravi Patel's brother, Raj. Bosch knew them both from previous cases and knew they were both among the best.

Raj Patel gave the basics of the crime scene investigation and reported that Mackey's efforts to save his life by crawling under the truck could ultimately allow the investigators to catch his killer.

"The second impact on the truck was without the body as a buffer, you see. It was metal on metal. We have both metal and paint transference and we have collected several samples. If you find the vehicle that did this, we can match it with one hundred percent accuracy."

That was one piece of light in all the darkness, Bosch thought.

After Patel finished his report the crime scene began to break up, with the investigators heading out to follow various assignments Pratt wanted completed before the entire unit was to meet at the Pacific Dining Car at 9 a.m. to discuss the case.

Marcia and Jackson were assigned to search Mackey's home. This would entail rousting a judge from sleep and getting a search warrant signed, because Mackey shared the home with William Burkhart and Burkhart was a possible suspect in the killing. The home — with Burkhart presumed to be in it — was under surveillance at the time Mackey was cut down on the freeway. Nevertheless, Burkhart could have directed someone else to carry out the killing and was viewed as a suspect until cleared of involvement.

One of the first calls Bosch and Rider had made after finding Mackey beneath the tow truck was to Kehoe and Bradshaw, the two RHD detectives watching the home on Mariano Street. They immediately went to the house and took Burkhart and a woman identified as Belinda Messier into custody.

They were now waiting to be interviewed at Parker Center and Bosch and Rider drew that assignment from Pratt.

But as they turned to walk up the slope of the freeway exit to Rider's car, Pratt asked them to hold up. He then huddled with them and spoke so no one else remaining at the scene could hear.

"I guess I don't have to tell you two that we're going to get some heat on this," he said.

"We know," Rider said.

"I don't know what form the review will take but I think you can count on a review," Pratt said.

"We'll be ready," Rider said.

"You might want to talk about that on the way down-town," Pratt suggested. "Make sure everybody's on the same page."

Bosch knew Pratt was telling them to get their story straight so that it could be presented in unison and in the light that served them best, even if they were interviewed separately.

"We'll be all right," Rider said.

Pratt glanced at Bosch and then looked away, back at the tow truck.

"I know," Bosch said. "I'm a boot. If somebody takes a fall for this it will be me. That's okay. The whole thing was my idea."

"Harry," Rider said. "That's not —"

"It was my plan," Bosch said, cutting her off. "I'm the one."

"Well, you might not have to be the one," Pratt said. "The sooner we get this thing put together the better off we'll be. Success makes a lot of bad shit go away. So let's close this fucker by breakfast."

"You got it, Boss," Rider said.

As Bosch and Rider headed up the slope they didn't speak.

33

Parker Center was deserted when they arrived. Though several investigative units operated from the headquarters building, it was primarily filled each day with command staff and support services. It didn't come alive until after sunup. In the elevator Bosch and Rider split up, Bosch going directly to the Robbery-Homicide Division on the third floor to relieve Kehoe and Bradshaw, while Rider made a stop by the Open-Unsolved office to pick up the file she had put together earlier on William Burkhart.

"See you in a few," she said to Bosch as he stepped off. "I hope Kehoe and Bradshaw made some coffee."

Bosch turned the corner out of the elevator alcove and headed down the hallway to the double doors of RHD. A voice from behind stopped him.

"What did I tell you about retreads?"

Bosch turned. It was Irving, coming from the opposite hallway. There was nothing down that way but computer services. Bosch guessed that he had been waiting in the hallway. He tried not to show surprise that Irving apparently already knew about what had happened on the freeway.

"What are you doing here?"

"Oh, I wanted to get an early start. It's going to be a big day."

"Is that right?"

"That's right. And I'll give you fair warning. In the

morning the media will be alerted to this middle-of-the-night fuckup of yours. The reporters will be told how you used this man Mackey as bait, only to let him be killed in a most horrible way. They will ask questions about how a retired detective could have been allowed back into the department to do this. But don't worry. These questions will most likely be addressed to the chief of police who set it all in motion."

Bosch laughed and shook his head, acting as though he didn't feel the threat.

"Is that all?" he asked.

"I will also be urging the commander of the Internal Affairs Division to open an investigation into how you conducted this investigation, Detective Bosch. I wouldn't get too used to being back."

Bosch took a step toward Irving, hoping to turn some of the threat back at him.

"Good, Chief, you do that. I hope you also prepare the commander for what I will be telling his investigators as well as the reporters about your own culpability in all of this."

There was a long pause before Irving bit.

"What nonsense are you talking about?"

"This man you're so worried about being used as bait was cut loose by you seventeen years ago, Chief. Cut loose so you could make your deal with Richard Ross. Mackey should've been in jail. Instead he used the gun from one of his little burglaries to kill an innocent sixteen-year-old girl."

Bosch waited but Irving didn't say anything.

"That's right," Bosch said. "I might have Roland Mackey's blood on my hands but you've got Rebecca Verloren's on yours. You want to go to the media and IAD with it? Fine, take your best shot and we'll see how it all comes out."

A pinched look formed in Irving's eyes. He took a step toward Bosch until their faces were only inches apart.

"You are wrong, Bosch. All of those kids back then, they were cleared of involvement in Verloren."

"Yeah, how? Who cleared them? Green and Garcia sure didn't. They were pushed away from them by you. Just like the girl's father. You and one of your dogs scared him away from it, too."

Bosch pointed a finger at his chest.

"You let murderers walk so you could keep your little deal intact."

An urgency entered Irving's voice when he responded.

"You are completely wrong on this," he said. "Do you really think that we would let murderers walk?"

Bosch shook his head, stepped back and almost laughed.

"As a matter of fact, I do."

"Listen to me, Bosch. We checked alibis on every last one of those boys. They were all clean. For some of them, *we* were the alibi because we were still watching them. But we made sure every member of that group was clean on this, *then* we told Green and Garcia to back off. The father was told, too, but he wouldn't stand down."

"So you pushed him down, right, Chief? Pushed him into a hole."

"Things had to be done. The city was very tense back then. We couldn't have her father running around saying things that weren't true."

"Don't give me that good-of-the-community bullshit, Chief. You had your deal, that's all you cared about. You had Ross and IAD in your pocket and you wanted to keep it that way. Only you were dead wrong. The DNA proves it. Mackey was good for Verloren and your investigation was for shit."

"No, wait just a minute. It only proves one thing. That he had the gun. I read the story you planted in the paper today, too. The DNA connects him to the gun, not to the murder."

Bosch waved him off. He knew there was no sense going back and forth with Irving. His only hope was that his own threat to go to the media and IAD would neutralize Irving's threat. He believed they were at a stalemate.

"Who checked the alibis?" he asked calmly.

Irving didn't answer.

"Let me guess. McClellan. He's got his prints all over this."

Again Irving didn't answer. It was like he had drifted off into the memory of seventeen years before.

"Chief, I want you to call your dog. I know he still works for you. Tell him I want to know about the alibis. I want details. I want reports. I want everything he's got by seven a.m. today or that's it. We do what we have to do and we see where the chips fall."

Bosch was about to turn away when Irving finally spoke.

"There are no alibi reports," he said. "There never would have been any."

Bosch heard the elevator open and Rider soon rounded the corner, carrying a file. She stopped dead when she saw the confrontation. She said nothing.

"No reports?" Bosch said to Irving. "Then you better hope he's got a good memory. Good night, Chief."

Bosch turned and started down the hall. Rider hurried to catch up to him. She looked back over her shoulder to make sure Irving was not following. After they turned in through the double doors to RHD, she spoke.

"Are we in trouble, Harry? Is he going to turn this against the man up on six?"

Bosch looked at her. The mix of dread and fear on her face told him how important his answer was going to be.

"Not if I can help it," he told her.

34

William Burkhart and Belinda Messier were being held in separate interview rooms. Bosch and Rider decided to take Messier first so that Burkhart would have to sit and wait and wonder. It would also give them time to let Marcia and Jackson get the warrant and get into the house on Mariano. What they found might be helpful during the interview with Burkhart.

Belinda Messier had come up in the investigation before. The number on the cell phone Mackey carried around was registered to her. In the briefing Kehoe and Bradshaw had given Bosch and Rider upon their arrival she was described as Burkhart's girlfriend. She had volunteered as much when the RHD detectives had taken both of them into custody. She told them little else after that.

Belinda Messier was a petite woman with mousy blonde hair that framed her face. Her look belied the hard case she turned out to be. She asked to see an attorney the moment Rider and Bosch entered the room.

"Why do you want to see an attorney?" Bosch asked. "Do you think you are under arrest?"

"Are you telling me I can leave?"

She stood up.

"Sit down," Bosch said. "Roland Mackey was killed tonight and you could be in danger, too. You're in protective custody. That means you're not getting out of here until we get some things straight."

"I don't know anything about it. I was with Billy all night until you people showed up."

Over the next forty-five minutes Messier gave up information only grudgingly. She explained that she knew Mackey through Burkhart and that she agreed to apply for cell phone service and turn the phone over to Mackey because he didn't have a viable credit report. She told the detectives that Burkhart did not work and lived off a damages award he had received after a car accident two years before. He bought the house on Mariano Street with the payout and charged Mackey rent. Messier said she didn't live in the house but spent many nights there visiting Burkhart. When asked about Burkhart and Mackey's past ties to white power groups, she feigned surprise. When asked about the tiny swastika tattooed on the webbing between her right thumb and forefinger, she said she thought it was a Navajo good luck symbol.

"Do you know who killed Roland Mackey?" Bosch asked after the long preamble of questions.

"No," she said. "He was a real nice guy. That's all I know."

"What did your boyfriend say after Mackey called him?"

"Nothin'. He just told me he was going to stay up and talk to Ro about something when he came home. He said they might go out for some privacy."

"That's all?"

"Yeah, that's what he said."

They went at her several times and from several different angles, with Bosch and Rider trading the lead back and forth, but the interview produced nothing of real value to the investigation.

Burkhart was next, but before going into the interview Bosch called Marcia and Jackson for an update.

"You guys in the house yet?" Bosch asked Marcia.

"Yeah, we're in. We haven't found anything yet."

"What about a cell phone?"

"No cell phone so far. Do you think Burkhart could have slipped out on Kehoe and Bradshaw?"

"Anything's possible but I doubt it. They weren't sleeping."

They were silent a moment as they thought about things and then Marcia spoke.

"How long was it between the time Mackey got it and you called Kehoe and Bradshaw and told them to take Burkhart in?"

Bosch reviewed his actions on the freeway before answering.

"It was pretty quick," he finally said. "Ten minutes max."

"Then there you go," Marcia said. "Getting from the one eighteen in Porter Ranch all the way to Mariano Street in Woodland Hills in ten minutes max? And without being seen by our guys? No way. It wasn't him. Kehoe and Bradshaw are his alibi."

"And no cell phone in the house . . ."

They all already knew that the landline in the house was not used to make a call because it would have registered on the monitoring equipment at ListenTech.

"Nope," Marcia said. "No cell phone and no call on the landline. I don't think this is our guy."

Bosch wasn't ready to agree yet. He thanked him and hung up, then gave the bad news to Rider.

"So what do we do with him?" she asked.

"Well, he might not be our guy on Mackey, but Mackey called him after the story was read to him. I still like him for Verloren."

"But that doesn't make sense. Whoever hit Mackey had to have been his partner on Verloren — unless you're saying what happened on the on-ramp is just coincidental to all of this."

Bosch shook his head.

"No, I'm not saying that. We're just missing something. Burkhart had to have gotten a message out of that house."

"You mean like dial-a-hitman or something? It's not working for me, Harry."

Now Bosch nodded. He knew she was right. It wasn't coming together.

"All right, then let's just go in there and see what he has to say for himself."

Rider agreed and they spent a few minutes working out an interview strategy before going back into the hallway behind the squad room and entering the interview room where Burkhart waited.

The room was stuffy with Burkhart's body odor and Bosch left the door open. Burkhart had his head down on his folded arms. When he didn't rouse from his feigned sleep Bosch kicked the leg of his chair and that brought his head up.

"Rise and shine, Billy Blitzkrieg," Bosch said.

Burkhart had scraggly dark hair that flopped around a face of pasty white skin. He looked like he didn't go out much except at night.

"I want a lawyer," Burkhart said.

"We all do. But let's start with first things first. My name is Bosch and this is Rider. You are William Burkhart and you are under arrest for suspicion of murder."

Rider started to read him his rights but he cut her off.

"Are you crazy? I never left my house. My girlfriend was there the whole time."

Bosch held a finger to his lips.

"Let her finish, Billy, and then you can lie to us as much as you like."

Rider finished reading the rights off the back of one of her business cards. Then Bosch took back over.

"Now, you were saying?"

"I'm saying you are fucked. I was home the whole time and I have a witness who can prove it. Besides, Ro was my friend. Why would I kill him? This is just a fucking joke, so why don't you go ahead and get me my lawyer now so he can laugh your asses out of here."

"You finished, Bill? 'Cause I have some news for you. We're not talking about Roland Mackey. We're taking you back seventeen years to Rebecca Verloren. You remember her? You and Mackey? The girl you took up into the hills? That's who we're talking about here."

Burkhart showed nothing. Bosch had been hoping for a tell, some sort of sign that he was on the right track.

"I don't know what you're talking about," Burkhart said, his face a stone.

"We've got you on tape. Mackey called last night. It's over, Burkhart. Seventeen years is a long run, but it's over."

"You got shit. If there is a tape then all you'll hear is me tellin' him to shut up. I don't have a cell phone and I don't trust 'em. That's standing operating procedure. If he was going to start telling me his problems I didn't want to do it on a goddamn cell phone. As far as Rebecca whatever-her-name-is, I don't know nothing about that. I guess you should've asked Ro while you had the chance."

He looked at Bosch and winked and Bosch felt like coming across the table at him. But he didn't.

They verbally sparred for another twenty minutes but neither Bosch nor Rider put a ding in Burkhart's armor. Eventually Burkhart stopped taking part in the back-and-forth, saying once more that he wanted an attorney and not responding in any form to any question that followed.

Rider and Bosch left the room to discuss their options, which they agreed were minimal. They had thrown a bluff at Burkhart. He had called them on it and they either had to book him and get him his lawyer or kick him loose.

"We don't have it, Harry," Rider said. "We shouldn't kid ourselves. I say we kick him."

Bosch nodded. He knew it was true. They didn't have a case now, and for that matter they might never have one. Mackey, the one direct connection to Verloren they had, was gone. Bosch's own doing had lost him. Now they would have to go back in time and run a full field on Burkhart and search for something that was missed or hidden or ignored seventeen years before. The full depression of their case situation was descending on him like a lead blanket.

He opened his phone and called Marcia once more.

"Anything?"

"Nothing, Harry. No phone, no evidence, nothing."

"Okay. Just so you know, we're going to kick him. He might show up there in a little while."

"Great. He won't like what he finds here."

"Good."

Bosch closed the phone and looked at Rider. Her eyes told the story. Disaster. He knew he had let her down. For the first time he thought maybe Irving had been right — maybe he shouldn't have come back.

"I'll go tell him he's a free man," he said.

After he walked away Rider called after him.

"Harry, I don't blame you."

He looked back at her.

"I went along every step of the way. It was a good plan."

He nodded.

"Thanks, Kiz."

35

Bosch went home to take a shower, get fresh clothes and maybe close his eyes for a while before heading back downtown for the unit meeting. Once again he drove through a city that was just waking for the day. And once more it came up ugly in his eyes, all sharp edges and harsh glare. Everything seemed ugly to him now.

Bosch didn't look forward to the unit meeting. He knew all eyes would be on him. Everybody in Open-Unsolved understood that their actions would now be analyzed and second-guessed following Mackey's death. They also understood that if they were looking for a reason for the potential threat to their careers, they didn't have to look far.

Bosch threw his keys on the kitchen counter and checked the phone. No messages. He looked at his watch and determined that he had at least a couple hours before he needed to head toward the Pacific Dining Car. Checking the time reminded him of the ultimatum he had given Irving during their confrontation in the hallway outside RHD. But Bosch doubted he would hear from Irving or McClellan now. It seemed as though everybody was calling his bluffs.

He knew sleeping for a couple hours wasn't really an option, not with everything that weighed on him. He had carried the murder book and the accumulated files into the house. He decided he would work on them. He knew that when all else went wrong there was always the murder book. He had to keep his eyes on the prize. The case.

He started the coffee brewer, took a five-minute shower and then went to work rereading the murder book while a remastered release of *Kind of Blue* sounded from the CD player.

The feeling that he was missing something right in front of him was grinding on him. He felt that he would be haunted by the case, that he would carry it around with him forever, unless he cracked through and found that missing thing. And he knew that if it was to be found anywhere, it would be in the book.

He decided that this time he would not read through the documents in the order they had been presented to him by the first investigators of the case. He snapped open the rings and took the documents out. He started reading them in random order, taking his time, making sure that he absorbed every name, every word, every photo.

Fifteen minutes later he was staring once again at the crime scene photos of Rebecca Verloren's bedroom when he heard a car door close in front of his house. Curious about who would be parking out there so early he got up and went to the door. Through the peephole he saw a man approaching by himself. It was hard to clearly see him through the convex lens of the peep. Bosch opened the door anyway, before the man had a chance to knock.

It did not surprise the man that his approach had been watched. Bosch could tell by his demeanor that he was a cop.

"McClellan?"

He nodded.

"Lieutenant McClellan. And I assume you are Detective Bosch."

"You could have called."

Bosch stepped back to let him in. Neither man offered to shake hands. Bosch thought it was typical of Irving to send his man to the house. A standard procedure in the old I-know-where-you-live intimidation strategy.

"I thought it better that we talk face to face," McClellan said.

"You thought? Or Chief Irving thought?"

McClellan was a big man with sandy, almost transparent hair and wide, florid cheeks. Bosch thought he could best be described as well fed. His cheeks turned a darker shade at Bosch's question.

"Look, I'm here to cooperate with you, Detective."

"Good. Can I get you something? I have water."

"Water'd be fine."

"Have a seat."

Bosch went into the kitchen and chose the dustiest glass from the cabinet and then filled it with tap water. He flicked off the switch on the coffeemaker and warmer. He wasn't going to let McClellan get cozy.

When he returned to the living room McClellan was looking out through the sliding glass door and across the deck. The air was clear in the pass. But it was still early.

"Nice view," McClellan said.

"I know. I don't see any files in your hand, Lieutenant. I hope this isn't a social call or like one of those visits you made to Robert Verloren seventeen years ago."

McClellan turned to Bosch and accepted the glass of water and the insult with the same blank expression.

"There are no files. If there were, they disappeared a long time ago."

"And what? You're here to try to convince me with your memories?"

"As a matter of fact, I have great recall of that time period. You have to understand something. I was a detective first grade assigned to the PDU. If I was given a job, I did it.

You don't question command in that situation. You do and you're out."

"So you were a good soldier just doing your job. I get it. What about the Chatsworth Eights and the Verloren murder? What about the alibis?"

"There were eight principal players in the Eights. I cleared them all. And don't think I wanted to clear them and so I just did. I was told to see if any of these little pissants could have been involved. And I checked it out, but they all came up clean — on the murder at least."

"Tell me about William Burkhart and Roland Mackey."

McClellan sat down on a chair by the television. He put his glass of water, which he had yet to drink from, down on the coffee table. Bosch turned off Miles Davis in the middle of "Freddie Freeloader" and stood with his hands in his pockets near the sliding doors.

"Well, first of all, Burkhart was easy. We were already watching him that night."

"Explain that."

"He had just gotten out of Wayside a few days before. We had gotten tipped that while he was up there he was re-upping on the racial religion, so it was thought to be prudent to keep an eye on him to see if he was going to try to start things up again."

"Who ordered that?"

McClellan just looked at him.

"Irving, of course," Bosch answered. "Keeping the deal safe. So PDU was watching Burkhart. Who else?"

"Burkhart got out and hooked up with two guys from the old group. A guy named Withers and another named Simmons. It looked like they might've been planning something, but on the night in question they were in a pool hall on Tampa drinking themselves into oblivion. It was solid. Two undercovers were in there with them the whole time. That's what I'm here to tell you. They were all solid, Detective."

"Yeah? Well, tell me about Mackey. The PDU wasn't watching him, was it?"

"No, not Mackey."

"Then how was he so solid?"

"What I remember about Mackey was that on the night the girl was taken he was getting tutored at Chatsworth High. He was going to night school, getting his high school degree."

"Actually, his general education degree. Not exactly the same thing."

"That's right. A judge had ordered it as a condition of probation. Only he had to pass and he wasn't doing too good. But he was getting tutored on the off nights — when there was no school. And the night the girl got grabbed, he was with his tutor. I confirmed it."

Bosch shook his head. McClellan was trying to feed him a line.

"You're telling me Mackey was getting tutored through the middle of the night? Either you're full of shit or you believed a line of bullshit from Mackey and his tutor. Who was the tutor?"

"No, no, they were together earlier in the evening. I don't remember the guy's name now, but they were done by like eleven at the latest and then they went their separate ways. Mackey went home."

Bosch looked astonished.

"That's no alibi, *Lieutenant!* Time of death on the girl was two in the a.m. Didn't you know that?"

"Of course I did. But time of death wasn't the only alibi point. I was given the summaries put together by the guys on the case. There was no forced entry to that house. And the father had gone around and checked all the doors and locks after he got home at ten that night. That meant the killer had to have been inside the house at that point. He was in there hiding, waiting for everybody to go to sleep."

Bosch sat down on the couch and leaned forward, elbows on his knees. He suddenly realized that McClellan was right and that everything was now different. He had seen the same report McClellan had seen seventeen years before but its meaning had not registered. The killer had been inside by the time Robert Verloren came home from work.

This changed a lot, Bosch knew. It changed how he looked not only at the first investigation, but also at his own.

Not registering Bosch's inner turmoil, McClellan continued.

"So Mackey couldn't have gotten into that house because he was with his tutor. He checked out. All those little assholes checked out. So I gave my boss a verbal report and then he told the two guys working the case. And that was the end of it until this DNA thing came up."

Bosch was nodding to what McClellan was saying but he was thinking about other things.

"If Mackey was clean, how do you explain his DNA on the murder weapon?" he asked.

McClellan looked dumbfounded. He shook his head.

"I don't know what to say. I can't explain it. I cleared him of involvement in the actual murder, but he must've . . ."

He didn't finish. Bosch thought that he actually looked wounded by the idea that he might have helped a murderer or at least the person who provided the weapon for a murder to get away with it. He looked as though he knew all at once that he had been corrupted by Irving. He looked crushed.

"Is Irving still planning to tip the media and IAD to all of this?" Bosch asked quietly.

McClellan slowly shook his head.

"No," he said. "He told me to give you a message. He said to tell you an agreement is only an agreement if both sides keep their end of it. That's it."

"One last question," Bosch said. "The evidence box on the Verloren case is gone. You know anything about that?"

McClellan stared at him. Bosch could tell he had badly insulted the man.

"I had to ask," Bosch said.

"All I know is that stuff disappears from the place," McClellan said through a tight jaw. "Anybody could have walked off with it in seventeen years. But it wasn't me."

Bosch nodded. He stood up.

"Well, I have to get back to work on this," he said.

McClellan took the cue and stood. He seemed to swallow his anger over the last question, maybe accepting Bosch's explanation that it had to be asked.

"All right, Detective," he said. "Good luck with this thing. I hope you catch the guy. And I really mean that."

He held his hand out to Bosch. Bosch didn't know McClellan's story. He didn't know all the circumstances of life in the PDU in 1988. But it looked like McClellan was leaving the house with a greater burden than he had come in with. So Bosch decided he could shake his hand.

After McClellan left, Bosch sat down again, thinking about the idea that Rebecca Verloren's killer had been hiding in the house. He got up and went to the dining room table, where the files from the murder book were spread out. The photos from the dead girl's room were at center in the spread. He looked through the reports until he found the SID report on latent fingerprint analysis.

The report was several pages long and contained the analysis of several fingerprints lifted from surfaces in the Verloren household. The main summary concluded that no print lifted from the house was an unknown, therefore it was likely the suspect or suspects wore gloves or simply avoided touching surfaces likely to retain prints.

The summary said that all latent fingerprints lifted from the house were matched to samples from members of the Verloren family or people who had an appropriate reason to have been in the house and touching the surfaces where the prints were found.

This time Bosch read the report differently and in its entirety. This time he was no longer interested in the analysis. He wanted to know where the SID techs had looked for prints.

The report was dated a day after the discovery of Rebecca's body. It detailed a routine search for fingerprints in the household. All topical surfaces were examined. All doorknobs and locks. All windowsills and frames. Every place it was logical to think that the killer/kidnapper might have touched a surface during the crime. While several prints on windowsills and latches were recovered and matched to Robert Verloren, the report stated that no usable prints at all were recovered from doorknobs in the house. It noted that this was not unusual because of the smudging that routinely occurred when knobs were turned.

It was in what was not included in the report that Bosch saw the crack through which a killer might have escaped. The SID team had gone into the house a day after the victim's body was discovered. This would have been after the case had been misread twice, first as a missing-persons case and second as a suicide. Added to this, when a murder investigation was finally mounted the latents team was sent in blind. There was no understanding of the case at that point. The idea that the killer might have hidden in the garage or somewhere else in the house for several hours had not been formulated yet. The search for fingerprints and other evidence, such as hairs and fibers, never went beyond the obvious, beyond the surface.

Bosch knew it was too late now. Too many years had passed. A cat roamed the house and who knows what objects from yard sales had come in and gone out of the house where a killer had hidden and waited.

Then his eyes fell to the spread of photos on the table and he realized something. Rebecca's bedroom was the one place that had not been contaminated over time. It was like a museum with its artwork encased and almost hermetically sealed.

Bosch spread all the crime scene photos of the bedroom in front of him. There had been something gnawing at him about these photos since the first time he had seen them. He still couldn't get to it but now he felt urgent about it. He studied the shots of the bureau and the bed table and then the open closet. Last he studied the bed.

He thought of the photo that had run in the newspaper and took the second copy of the paper out of the file containing all reports and documents accumulated during the reinvestigation of the case. He unfolded the paper and studied Emmy Ward's photo and then compared it to the photographs of seventeen years before.

The room seemed exactly the same, as if untouched by the grief emanating from it like heat from an oven. Then Bosch noticed a small difference. In the *Daily News* shot the bed had been carefully straightened and smoothed by Muriel before the photograph was taken. In the older SID shots the bed was made, but the ruffle fluffed outward along one side of the bed and inward along the foot.

Bosch's eyes moved back and forth from one photo to the other. He felt something breaking loose inside. He felt a little charge drop into his blood. This was what had bothered him. It was the something that was not right.

"In and out," he said to himself.

It was possible, he knew, that the ruffle had been pushed inward at the bottom of the bed by someone crawling underneath it. That would make it likely that the outward fluffing of the ruffle at the side of the bed would have occurred when that same person slid or crawled out.

After everyone was asleep.

Bosch got up and started pacing as he worked it through again. In the photo taken after the abduction and murder, the bed clearly showed the possibility of entrance and exit. Rebecca's killer could have been waiting right below her as she fell asleep.

"In and out," Bosch said again.

He worked it further. He knew that no readable finger-prints had been recovered at the house. But only obvious surfaces had been checked. This did not necessarily mean the killer had worn gloves. It only meant he was smart enough not to touch obvious places with his bare hands, or smudged the prints when he needed to. Even if gloves had been worn during the entry to the house, might not the killer have removed them while waiting — possibly for hours — under the bed?

It was worth a shot. Bosch went to the kitchen and called SID and asked for Raj Patel.

"Raj, what are you doing?"

"I am cataloging the evidence we gathered last night on the freeway."

"I need your best latents man to meet me back up there in Chatsworth."

"Now?"

"Right now, Raj. I might not even have a job later. We have to do this now."

"What is it we are to do?"

"I want to lift a bed and look underneath it. It's important, Raj. If we find something, it will lead us to the killer."

There was a short silence and then Patel replied.

"I am my best latents man, Harry. Give me the address."

"Thanks, Raj."

He gave Patel the address and then hung up the phone. He drummed his fingers on the counter, wondering if he should call Kiz Rider. She had been so distressed and discouraged as they had walked out of Parker Center that she said all she wanted to do was go home to sleep. Should he wake her for the second day in a row? He knew that wasn't really the question. The question was whether he should wait to see if there was anything beneath the bed before telling her and getting her hopes up.

He decided to hold off on the call until there was something solid to tell her. Instead he picked up the phone and woke up Muriel Verloren. He told her he was on his way.

36

Bosch got to the squad meeting at the Pacific Dining Car late because of traffic coming in from the Valley. Everyone was in a private area in the back of the restaurant. Most of them already had plates of food in front of them.

His excitement must have showed. Pratt interrupted a report from Tim Marcia to look at Bosch and say, "You either got lucky during the time you had off or you just don't care about the deep shit we're in here."

"I got lucky," Bosch said as he took the only empty chair and sat down. "But not in the way you mean. Raj Patel just pulled a palm print and two fingers off a wood slat that was beneath Rebecca Verloren's bed."

"That's good," Pratt said dryly. "What's it mean?"

"It means that as soon as Raj runs it through the database we might have our killer."

"How so?" Rider asked.

Bosch had never called her. He could already feel a hostile vibe from her.

"I didn't want to wake you up," Bosch said to her. Then to the others, he said, "I was looking through the original latents report in the murder book. I realized that they went in there for prints the day after the girl's body was found. They never went back after it became a strong possibility that the abductor had come into the house earlier in the day when the garage was left open and hid somewhere until everybody was asleep."

"So why the bed?" Pratt asked.

"The crime scene photos showed the ruffle at the foot of the bed had been pushed in. Like somebody had crawled underneath. They missed it because they weren't looking for it."

"Good work, Harry," Pratt said. "If Raj gets a hit we change directions and move with it. All right, let's get back to our reports. You can check with your partner on what you've missed so far."

Pratt then turned to Robinson and Nord at the other end of the long table and said, "What did you come up with on the call for the tow truck?"

"Not a lot that helps," Nord said. "Because the call was made after we had switched our monitoring to the line at the Burkhart property, we don't have an audio recording of it. But we do have the pen registers and they show that the call came directly to Tampa Towing before being bounced over to the Triple A answering service. The call came from a pay phone outside the Seven-Eleven on Tampa by the freeway entrance. He probably made the call, then drove down the entrance and waited."

"Prints on the phone?" Pratt asked.

"We asked Raj to take a look after he cleared the scene," Robinson said. "The phone had been wiped."

"Figures," Pratt said. "You talked to Triple A?"

"Yes. No help other than to say the caller was a male." He turned to Bosch.

"You have anything to add that your partner didn't already tell us?"

"Probably just more of the same. Burkhart looks like he is clear on last night and he looks like he's clear on Verloren as well. Both nights he happened to be under LAPD surveillance."

Rider gave him her knotted-brow look. He had even

more information she didn't know. He looked away.

"Well, that's just perfect," Pratt said. "So who, what and where does that leave us, people?"

"Well, basically, our newspaper plant backfired," Rider said. "It may have worked in terms of getting Mackey to want to talk about Verloren, but he never got the chance. Somebody else saw the story."

"That somebody being the actual killer," Pratt said.

"Exactly," Rider said. "The person Mackey helped and/or gave the gun to seventeen years ago. That person also saw the story and knew it wasn't his blood on the gun, so that meant it had to be Mackey's. He knew Mackey was the link to him, so Mackey had to go."

"So how did he set it up?" Pratt asked.

"He was either smart enough to figure the story was a plant and we were watching Mackey, or he just figured the best way to get to Mackey was the way he did it. Get him out there alone. Like I said, he was smart. He picked a time and place that would result in Mackey being alone and vulnerable. On that entrance ramp you are up above the freeway. Even with the tow truck's lights on, nobody would see up there."

"It was also a good spot in case Mackey had a tail," Nord added. "The killer knew a tail car would have to just keep moving by, and then he'd have Mackey alone."

"Aren't we giving this guy a little too much credit?" Pratt asked. "How would he know the cops were onto this guy? Just from a newspaper article? Come on."

Neither Bosch nor Rider answered and everyone else silently digested the unspoken suggestion that the killer had a connection to the department or, more specifically, the investigation.

"All right, what's next?" Pratt said. "I think the containment on this is maybe another twenty-four hours tops. After that it's going to be in the papers and upstairs on six, and there's going to be hair on the walls if we don't wrap it up first. What do we do?"

"We'll take the pen registers," Bosch said, speaking for himself and Rider. "And go from there."

Bosch had been thinking about the note to Mackey he had seen on the desk in the service station the day before. A call to verify employment from Visa. As Rider had pointed out when she first heard about it, Mackey wasn't into leaving trails like credit cards. It was something that didn't fit and therefore he wanted to go after it.

"We have all of the printouts right here," Robinson said. "The line that was busiest was the one into the station. All kinds of business calls."

"Okay, Harry, Kiz, you want the registers?" Pratt asked.

Rider looked at Bosch and then at Pratt.

"If that's what Harry wants. He seems to be on a roll today."

As if on cue Bosch's phone began to chirp. He looked at the screen. It was Raj Patel.

"We'll see what kind of a roll right now," he said as he opened the phone.

Patel said he had good and bad news.

"The good news is we still had the exemplar skid from the house in records here. The latents we recovered this morning did not match any of them. You found somebody new, Harry. It could be your killer."

What this meant was that fingerprint examples from the members of the Verloren family and others who had appropriate access to the house were still on file in the SID print lab. None of those examples matched the fingerprints and palm print recovered that morning from beneath Rebecca Verloren's bed. Of course fingerprints could not be dated, and it was possible that the prints discovered that morning had been left by whoever had installed the bed. But it seemed unlikely. The prints were taken off the underside of the wooden slat. Whoever had left them had most likely been under the bed.

"And the bad news?" Bosch asked.

"I just ran them through the California system. No matches."

"What about the FBI?"

"That's next but that won't be so fast. They have to process it. I will send it through with an expedite request but you know how that goes."

"I do, Raj. Let me know when you know, and thanks for the effort."

Bosch closed the phone. He felt a steep letdown and his face showed it. He could already tell the others knew the score before he delivered the news.

"No match on the DOJ database," he said. "He'll try the bureau's base but that will take a while."

"Shit!" said Renner.

"Speaking of Raj Patel," Pratt said, "his brother scheduled the autopsy for two o'clock today. I want one team there. Who wants to take it?"

Renner weakly raised his hand. He and Robleto would take it. It was an easy assignment if you didn't mind the visuals.

The meeting soon broke up after Pratt assigned Robinson and Nord the service station and the interviews of the people Mackey worked with there. Marcia and Jackson would work on pulling reports together and into a murder book. They were still the lead investigators and would coordinate things from room 503.

Pratt looked at the bill, divided it by nine and told everyone to put in ten. This meant Bosch had to throw in a ten even though he hadn't even had a cup of coffee. He didn't protest. It was the price of being late and being the guy who put them on this path.

As everyone stood Bosch caught Rider's eye.

"Did you come directly here or did you ride with somebody?"

"Abel gave me a lift."

"Want to ride back together?"

"Sure."

Outside the restaurant she gave Bosch the silent treatment while they waited for his car from the valet. She stared at the large plastic steer that was atop the restaurant's sign. Under her arm was a file containing the printouts from the pen registers.

Finally the car came and they got in. Before pulling out of the lot Bosch turned and looked at her.

"All right, say it," he said.

"Say what?"

"Whatever it is you want to say so you can feel better."

"You should've called me, Harry, that's all."

"Look, Kiz, I called you yesterday and you chewed me out. I was just working off of recent experience."

"This was different and you know it. You called me yesterday because you were excited about something. Today you were following a lead. I should have been with you. And then to not find out what you came up with until you went in there and told everybody. That was embarrassing, Harry. Thanks for that."

Bosch nodded his contrition.

"You're right about that part. I'm sorry. I should've called you when I was coming in. I just forgot. I knew I was late and I had both hands on the wheel and was just trying to get here."

She didn't say anything, so he finally did.

"Can we get back to solving this case now?"

She shrugged and he finally put the car in drive. On the way to Parker Center he tried to fill her in on all the details he hadn't mentioned during the breakfast meeting.

He told her about McClellan's visit to his house and how that led him to the discovery of the prints under the bed.

Twenty minutes later they were in their alcove in room 503. Bosch finally had a cup of coffee in front of him. They sat across from each other and had the pen register printouts spread between them.

Bosch was concentrating on the reports on the service station phones. The listing was at least a couple hundred entries — calls going in or out on the station's two phones — between 6 a.m., when the surveillance started, and 4 p.m., when Mackey reported for work and Renner and Robleto started live-monitoring the line.

Bosch scanned down the list. Nothing looked immediately familiar. Many of the calls were to or from business listings with some automobile connection clearly apparent in the name. Many others came in from the AAA dispatch center and these were likely tow calls.

There were also several calls that came from personal phones. Bosch looked closely at these names but saw nothing that jumped out at him. No one listed was an already established player in the case.

There were four entries on the list that were attributed to Visa, all the same number. Bosch picked up the phone and called it. He never heard it ring. He just got the loud screeching sound of a computer hookup. It was so loud that even Rider heard it.

"What is that?"

Bosch hung up.

"I'm trying to run down that note I saw on the desk in the station about Visa calling to confirm Mackey's employment. Remember you said it didn't fit?"

"I forgot about that. Was that the number?"

"I don't know. There are four listings for Visa but — wait a minute."

He realized that the Visa calls were outgoing calls.

"Never mind, these were outgoing. It must be the number the machine calls when you use a credit card to pay. That's not it. There is no incoming call listed as Visa."

Bosch picked up the phone again and called Nord's cell phone.

"Are you at the service station yet?"

She laughed.

"We've barely cleared Hollywood. We'll be there in a half hour."

"Ask them about a phone message somebody left for Mackey yesterday. Something about Visa calling to confirm employment on a credit application. Ask them what they remember from the call and more importantly, what time it came in. Try to get the exact time if you can. Ask them about this first thing and then call me back."

"Yes, sir. You want us to pick up your laundry, too?"

Bosch realized it was getting to be a bad morning for stepping on toes.

"Sorry," he said. "We're working under the gun here."

"Aren't we all? I'll call you as soon as we see the guy."

Nord hung up. Bosch put the phone down and looked at Rider. She was looking at the class picture of Rebecca Verloren in the yearbook they had borrowed.

"What are you thinking?" she asked without looking up at Bosch.

"This thing with Visa bothers me."

"I know, so what are you thinking?"

"Well, say you're the killer and you got the gun you did it with from Mackey."

"You're completely giving up on Burkhart? You sure liked him last night."

"Let's just say the facts are persuading me. For now, okay?"

"Okay, go on."

"All right, so you're the killer and you got the gun from Mackey. He's the one person in the world who can put the thing on you. But seventeen years go by and nothing ever happens and you feel safe and maybe you even lose track of Mackey."

"Okay."

"And then yesterday you pick up the paper and you see the picture of Rebecca and you read the story and it says they've got DNA. You know it wasn't your blood, so it was either a big bluff by the cops or it's got to be Mackey's blood. So that's when you know."

"Mackey's gotta go."

"Exactly. The cops are getting close. He's got to go. So how do you find him? Well, Mackey's spent his entire life — when he isn't in jail — driving a tow truck. If you knew that then you'd do exactly what we did. You get out the yellow pages and start calling tow companies."

Rider stood up and went to the bank of file cabinets along the alcove's back wall. The phone books were stacked haphazardly on top. She had to stand on her toes to reach the yellow pages for the Valley. She came back and opened the book to the pages advertising tow services. She ran her finger down a listing until she reached Tampa Towing, where Mackey had worked. She backed up to the previous listing, a company called Tall Order Towing Services. She picked up her phone and dialed the number. Bosch heard only her side of the conversation.

"Yes, who am I speaking with?"

She waited a moment.

"My name is Detective Kizmin Rider with the Los Angeles Police Department. I am investigating a fraud case and wondered if I could ask you a question."

Rider nodded as she apparently got a go-ahead.

"The suspect I am documenting has a history of calling

businesses and identifying himself as someone working for Visa. He then attempts to verify someone else's employment as part of an application for a credit card. Does any of this ring a bell with you? We have information that leads us to believe that this individual was operating in the Valley yesterday. He likes to target automotive businesses."

Rider waited while there was a response to her question. She looked at Bosch but gave no indication of anything.

"Yes, could you put her on the line, please?"

Rider went through the whole thing again with another person and asked the same question. Then she leaned forward and seemed to take a stiffer attitude in her posture. She covered the mouthpiece and looked at Bosch.

"Bingo," she said.

She then went back to the phone call and listened some more.

"Was it a male or female?"

She wrote something down.

"And what time was this?"

She wrote another note and Bosch stood up so he could look across his desk to read it. She had written "male, 1:30 approx" on a scratch pad. While she continued the conversation Bosch consulted the pen register and saw that a call came in on the Tampa Towing line at 1:40 p.m. It was from a personal number. The name on the register was Amanda Sobek. The number's prefix indicated it was a cell phone. Neither the name nor the number meant anything to Bosch. But that didn't matter. He thought they were getting close to something here.

Rider finished her call by asking if the person she was talking to remembered the name the supposed Visa employee had tried to confirm. After she apparently got a negative reply, she asked, "What about the name Roland Mackey?"

She waited.

"Are you sure?" she asked. "Okay, thank you for your time, Karen."

She hung up and looked at Bosch. The excitement in her eyes wiped out everything about being left out of the morning's fingerprints find.

"You were right," she said. "They got a call. Same thing. She even remembered the name Roland Mackey once I gave it to her. Harry, somebody was tracking him down the whole time we were watching him."

"And now we're going to track them down. If they were going down the line in the phone book they would have called Tampa Towing next. The register shows a one-forty call from somebody named Amanda Sobek. I don't recognize it but this might be the call we're looking for."

"Amanda Sobek," Rider said as she opened her laptop. "Let's see what AutoTrack has on her."

While she was tracing the name, Bosch got a call from Robinson, who had arrived with Nord at Tampa Towing.

"Harry, the dayshift guy says that call came in between one-thirty and two o'clock. He knows because he had just come back from lunch and he was sent out on a tow at two o'clock. A Triple A run."

"Was it a male or female caller from Visa?"

"Male."

"Okay, anything else?"

"Yeah, once this guy confirmed that Mackey worked here, the Visa guy asked what hours he worked."

"Okay. Can you ask the day man another question?"

"He's right here."

"Ask if they have a customer named Sobek. Amanda Sobek."

Bosch waited while the question was asked.

"No customer named Sobek," Robinson reported back. "Is that good news, Harry?"

"It'll work."

After closing the phone Bosch got up and walked around the desks so he could look at Rider's computer screen. He told her what Robinson had just reported.

"Anything on Amanda Sobek?" he asked.

"Yeah, this is it. She lives in the West Valley. Farralone Avenue in Chatsworth. But there is not a lot here. No credit cards or mortgage. I think it means it's all in her husband's name. She might be a housewife. I'm running the address to see if I can pull him up."

Bosch opened the yearbook to Rebecca Verloren's class. He started flipping through the pages looking for the name Sobek or Amanda.

"Here he is," Rider said. "Mark Sobek. Everything's basically in his name and it looks like a lot. Four cars, two houses, lots of credit cards."

"There was nobody named Sobek in her class," Bosch said. "But there were two girls named Amanda. Amanda Reynolds and Amanda Riordan. Think she is one of them?"

Rider shook her head.

"I don't think so. The age is off. This says Amanda Sobek is forty-one. That would make her eight years older than Rebecca. Something doesn't fit. Think we should just call her?"

Bosch closed the yearbook with a bang. Rider jumped in her seat.

"No," he said. "Let's just go."

"Where? To see her?"

"Yeah. Time to get off your ass and knock on doors."

He looked down at Rider and could tell she wasn't amused.

"I don't mean your ass specifically. It's a figure of speech. Let's just go."

She started getting up.

"You are awfully flippant for somebody who might not have a job at the end of the day."

"It's the only way to be, Kiz. Darkness waits. But it comes no matter what you do."

He led the way out of the office.

37

The Farralone Avenue address AutoTrack led Bosch and Rider to belonged to a Mediterranean-style mansion that had to have been on the upper side of 6,000 square feet. It had a separate garage with four dark-stained wooden doors and windows from a guest suite above. The detectives had to view all of this through a wrought iron gate while waiting for someone to answer the intercom. Finally a voice came from the small square box on a pole next to Bosch's open window.

"Yes, who is it?"

It was a woman. She sounded young.

"Amanda Sobek?" Bosch asked in reply.

"No, this is her assistant. Who are you two?"

Bosch looked again at the box and saw the camera lens. They were being watched as well as listened to. He pulled out his badge and held it a foot from the lens.

"Police," he said. "We need to talk to Amanda or Mark Sobek."

"About what?"

"About police business. Open the gate, please, ma'am."

They waited and Bosch was just about to punch the call button again when the gate slowly started to automatically open. They drove in and parked in a turnaround circle in front of the two-story portico.

"Looks like the kind of place it might be worth killing a tow truck driver to protect," Bosch said quietly as he cut the engine.

The door was opened before they got there by a woman in her twenties. She was wearing a skirt and a white blouse. The assistant.

"And you are?" Bosch asked.

"Melody Lane. I work for Mrs. Sobek."

"Is she here?" Rider asked.

"Yes, she's getting dressed and will be right down. You can wait in the living room."

They were led into an entrance hallway, where there was a table with several family photos on display. It looked like a husband, wife and two teenaged daughters. They followed Melody into a sumptuous living room with large windows looking out on Santa Susana State Park and Oat Mountain beyond.

Bosch checked his watch. It was almost noon. Melody noticed.

"She wasn't sleeping. She worked out earlier and was taking a shower. She should be down —"

She didn't need to finish. An attractive woman in white slacks and blouse left open over a pink chiffon shirt came hurrying into the room.

"What is it? Is something wrong? Are my girls all right?"

"Are you Amanda Sobek?" Bosch asked.

"Of course I am. What is wrong? Why are you here?"

Bosch pointed to the grouping of couch and chairs in the center of the room.

"Why don't we sit down here, Mrs. Sobek."

"Just tell me if something is wrong."

The panic on her face looked real to Bosch. He started to think they may have made a wrong turn somewhere.

"Nothing is wrong," he said. "This is not about your daughters. Your daughters are fine."

"Is it Mark?"

"No, Mrs. Sobek. As far as we know he is fine, too. Let's sit down over here."

She finally relented and walked quickly to the big chair to the right of the couch. Bosch moved around a glass coffee table and sat on the couch. Rider took one of the remaining chairs. Bosch identified himself and Rider and showed his badge again. He noticed that the glass on the table was spotless.

"We are conducting an investigation that I can't tell you about. I need to ask you some questions about your cell phone."

"My cell phone? You scared me to death over my cell phone?"

"It's actually a very serious investigation, Mrs. Sobek. Do you have your cell phone with you?"

"It's in my purse. Do you need to see it?"

"No, not yet. Can you tell me when you used it yesterday?"

Sobek shook her head like it was an inane question.

"I don't know. In the morning I called Melody from the gym. I can't remember when else. I went to the store and called my daughters to see if they were on their way home after school. I can't remember anything else. I was home almost all day except for the gym. When I'm home I don't use my cell. I use the regular phone."

Bosch's misgivings were multiplying. Somewhere they had made a wrong move.

"Could someone else have used the phone?" Rider asked.

"My daughters have their own. So does Melody. I don't understand this."

Bosch pulled the page from the pen register out of his coat pocket. Out loud he read the number of the phone that had called Tampa Towing.

"Is that your number?" he asked.

"No, it's my daughter's. It's Kaitlyn's."

Bosch leaned forward. This changed things further.

"Your daughter's? Where was she yesterday?"

"I already told you. She was in school. And she didn't use her phone until after, because it's not allowed at school."

"What school does she go to?" Rider asked.

"Hillside Prep. It's over in Porter Ranch."

Bosch leaned back and looked at Rider. Something had just come full circle. He wasn't sure what it was but it felt important.

Amanda Sobek read the looks on their faces.

"What is it?" she asked. "Is something wrong at the school?"

"Not as far as we know, ma'am," Bosch answered. "What grade is your daughter in?"

"She is a sophomore."

"Does she have a teacher named Bailey Sable?" Rider asked.

Sobek nodded.

"She has her for homeroom and English."

"Is there any reason why Mrs. Sable might have borrowed your daughter's phone yesterday?" Rider asked.

Sobek shrugged.

"Not that I can think of. You have to understand how strange this is. All these questions. Was her phone used to make a threat or something? Is this some kind of terrorist thing?"

"No, ma'am," Bosch said. "But it is a serious matter. We are going to have to go to the school now and talk to your daughter. We would appreciate it if you came with us and were there when we spoke to her."

"Does she need a lawyer?"

"I don't think so, ma'am."

Bosch stood up.

"Shall we go?"

"Can Melody come too? I want Melody to go with me."

"Tell you what. Have Melody meet us there. That way she can drive you back if we need to go somewhere else."

38

On the drive over to Hillside Prep the car was silent. Bosch wanted to talk to Rider, to dope out this latest twist, but he didn't want to do it in front of Amanda Sobek. So they were silent until their passenger asked if she could call her husband and Bosch said that was fine. But she couldn't reach him and left a message in a near-hysterical voice telling him to call her as soon as he could.

When they got to the school it was lunchtime. As they walked down the main hallway to the office they could hear the near-riotous collision of voices from the cafeteria.

Mrs. Atkins was behind the counter in the office. She looked a little confused when she saw Amanda Sobek in the company of the detectives. Bosch asked to see Principal Stoddard.

"Mr. Stoddard took lunch off-campus today," Mrs. Atkins said. "Is there something I can help with?"

"Yes, we'd like to see Kaitlyn Sobek. Mrs. Sobek here will be with us when we talk to her."

"Right now?"

"Yes, Mrs. Atkins, right now. I would appreciate it if you or another school employee could go and get her. It might be better if the other kids didn't see her being accompanied by the police."

"I could go get her," Amanda offered.

"No," Bosch said quickly. "We want to see her at the same time as you."

It was a polite way of saying that he didn't want her to ask her daughter about the cell phone before the police did.

"I'll just go to the cafeteria and find her," Mrs. Atkins said. "You can use the principal's meeting room for your . . . uh, talk."

She came around the counter, averted her eyes from Amanda Sobek and headed toward the door that led to the main hallway.

"Thank you, Mrs. Atkins," Bosch said.

It took Mrs. Atkins almost five minutes to locate and return with Kaitlyn Sobek. While they were waiting, Melody Lane arrived and Bosch told Amanda that her assistant would have to wait outside the interview. The girl accompanied Bosch, Rider and her mother into a room off the principal's office that had a round table with six chairs around it.

After everyone sat down, Bosch nodded to Rider and she took over. Bosch thought it would be best for a woman to lead the interview of the girl and Rider understood this without discussion. She explained to Kaitlyn that they were investigating a phone call that was made on her cell phone at 1:40 p.m. the day before. The girl immediately interrupted.

"That's impossible," she said.

"Why is that?" Rider asked. "We had an electronic trap on the line that was called. It showed the call came from your phone."

"I was in school yesterday. We're not allowed to use cell phones during school hours."

The girl appeared nervous. Bosch could tell she was lying but couldn't figure out what the play was. He wondered if she was lying because her mother was in the room.

"Where is your phone right now?" Rider asked.

"In my backpack in my locker. And it's turned off."

"Is that where it was yesterday at one-forty?"

"Uh-huh."

She looked away from Rider as she lied. She was easy to read and Bosch knew Rider was getting the same thing he was getting.

"Kaitlyn, this is a very serious investigation," Rider said in a soothing tone. "If you are lying to us you could find yourself in a lot of trouble."

"Kaitlyn, don't lie!" Amanda Sobek said forcefully.

"Mrs. Sobek, let's stay calm about this," Rider said. "Kaitlyn, these electronic traps I was telling you about are called pen registers. The registers don't lie. Your cell phone was used to make the call. There is no doubt. So is it possible someone got into your locker and used your phone yesterday?"

She shrugged.

"Anything's possible, I guess."

"Okay, who would have done that?"

"I don't know. You were the one who said it."

Bosch cleared his throat, which drew the girl's eyes to his. He stared hard at her and said, "I think maybe we should take a drive downtown. Maybe this is not the right place for an interview."

He started to push back his chair and get up.

"Kaitlyn, what is going on here?" Amanda pleaded. "These people are serious. Who did you call?"

"No one, okay?"

"No, it's not okay."

"I didn't have the phone, all right? It was confiscated."

Bosch sat back down and Rider took over again.

"Who confiscated your phone?" she asked.

"Mrs. Sable," the girl said.

"Why?"

"Because we're not supposed to use them inside school

once the homeroom bell rings. Yesterday my best friend Rita didn't come to school. So I tried to text message her during homeroom to see if she was all right and Mrs. Sable caught me."

"And she took your phone?"

"Yes, she took it."

Bosch's mind was racing, trying to put Bailey Koster Sable into the mold of murderer of Rebecca Verloren. He knew one thing didn't work. A sixteen-year-old Bailey Koster could not have carried her friend's limp body up the hill behind her house.

"Why did you just lie to us about this?" Rider asked Kaitlyn.

"Because I didn't want her to know I was in trouble," the girl said, indicating her mother with her chin.

"Kaitlyn, you never lie to the police," Amanda shot back. "I don't care what —"

"Mrs. Sobek, you can talk to her about this later," Bosch said. "Let us continue."

"When did you get the phone back, Kaitlyn?" Rider asked.

"At the end of the day."

"So Mrs. Sable had your phone all day?"

"Yes. I mean, no. Not all day."

"Well, who had it?"

"I don't know. When they take your phone they tell you that you have to pick it up at the end of the day at the principal's office. That's what I did. Mr. Stoddard gave it back to me."

Gordon Stoddard. Things all at once started to come together. Bosch had tucked into the water tunnel and the case and all its details were swirling around him. He rode the wave of clarity and grace. Everything was clicking. Stoddard clicked. Mackey's last word clicked. Stoddard was Rebecca's teacher. He was close to her. He was her lover and the late night caller. It all clicked into place.

Mr. X.

Bosch stood up and left the room without a word. He walked past Stoddard's office door. It was open and the desk was empty. He went out to the front counter.

"Mrs. Atkins, where is Mr. Stoddard?"

"He was just here but then he stepped out."

"To where?"

"I don't know. Maybe the cafeteria. I told him you and the other detective were here talking to Kaitlyn."

"And then he left?"

"Yes. Oh, I just realized — he might be in the parking lot. He said he got a new car today. Maybe he's showing it to one of the teachers."

"What kind of car? Did he say?"

"A Lexus. He said it had a model number but I forget which one."

"Does he have an assigned parking space?"

"Uh, yes, it is in the first row on the right as you come out of the entrance hall."

Bosch turned from her and went out the door to the hallway. It was crowded with students leaving the cafeteria to start afternoon classes. Bosch started moving through the crowd, dodging students and picking up speed. Soon he was free of them and running. He came into the parking lot and immediately trotted down the parking lane to the right. He found an empty space with Stoddard's name painted on the curb.

He turned to go back in to get Rider. He was pulling his phone off his belt when he saw a silver blur to his right. It was a car coming right at him and it was too late to get out of the way.

39

Bosch was helped up into a sitting position on the asphalt.

"Harry, are you all right?"

He focused and saw that it was Rider. He nodded shakily. He tried to remember what had just happened.

"It was Stoddard," he said. "He was coming right at me."

"In his car?"

Bosch laughed. He had left that part out.

"Yeah, his new car. A silver Lexus."

Bosch started to get up. Rider put a hand on his shoulder to hold him down.

"Just wait a minute. Are you sure you're all right? Does anything hurt?"

"Just my head."

It was coming back to him now.

"I banged it when I landed," he said. "I jumped out of the way. I saw his eyes, you know? The rage, I mean."

"Let me see your eyes."

He looked up at her and she held his chin while she checked his pupils.

"You look all right," she said.

"Okay, then, I'll sit here for a second while you go back in and get Stoddard's home address from Mrs. Atkins."

Rider nodded.

"All right. You wait here."

"Hurry. We have to find him."

She ran back into the school. Bosch reached up and felt the bump on the back of his head. He replayed the clearing memory. He had seen Stoddard's face behind the windshield. It was angry, contorted.

But then he had yanked the wheel to the left as Bosch jumped the other way.

Bosch reached for his phone so he could call in a wanted bulletin for Stoddard. It wasn't on his belt. He looked around and saw the phone on the asphalt near the rear tire of a BMW. He crawled over and grabbed it, then stood up.

Bosch was hit with mild vertigo and had to lean on the car. Suddenly an electronic voice said, "Please step away from the car!"

Bosch pulled his hand away and started walking toward the part of the lot where he had parked his own car. On the way he called central dispatch and put out the wanted bulletin for Stoddard and his silver Lexus.

Bosch closed the phone and hooked it on his belt. He got to his car, started it and pulled up to the entrance so they would be ready to go as soon as Rider came out with the address.

After what seemed like an interminable wait Rider finally emerged and trotted to the car. But she came to his side, opened his door and waved him out.

"It's not far," she announced. "It's a house on Chase off of Winnetka. But you're not driving. I am."

Bosch knew that arguing would waste time. He got out and moved as quickly as his balance allowed around the front of the car and got in on the passenger side. Rider hit the gas and they moved out of the parking lot.

As Rider made her way on surface streets toward Stoddard's home Bosch called for backup from Devonshire Division patrol and then called Abel Pratt to quickly fill him in on the morning's revelations.

"Where do you think he's going?" Pratt asked.

"No idea. We're on the way to his house."

"Is he suicidal?"

"No idea."

Pratt was silent for a moment as he digested this. He then asked a few more questions about minor details and hung up.

"He sounded happy," Bosch told Rider. "Says if we get this guy it'll help turn a lemon into lemonade."

"Good," Rider replied. "We can pull prints from Stoddard's office or home and match them to the print from underneath the bed. Then it's a done deal whether he's in the wind or not."

"Don't worry, we'll get him."

"Harry, what are you thinking, Stoddard and Mackey did this together?"

"I don't know. But I remember that photo of Stoddard from the yearbook. He looked pretty lean. He might have been able to carry her up the hill by himself. We'll never know unless we find him and ask him."

Rider nodded.

"The key question," she then said, "is how Stoddard connected with Mackey."

"The gun."

"I know that. That's obvious. I mean, how did he know Mackey back then? Where is the intersection and how did he know him well enough to get the gun from him?"

"I think it was right there in front of us all along," Bosch said. "And Mackey told me with his last word."

"Chatsworth?"

"Chatsworth High."

"How do you mean?"

"That summer he was getting his GED at Chatsworth High. On the night of the murder Mackey's alibi was his tutor. Maybe it was the other way around. Maybe Mackey was the tutor's alibi."

"Stoddard?"

"He told us that first day that all of the teachers at Hillside had outside jobs. Maybe Stoddard was working as a tutor. Maybe he was Mackey's tutor."

"That's a lot of maybes, Harry."

"That's why we've got to find Stoddard before he does anything to himself."

"You think he's suicidal? You told Abel you didn't know."

"I don't know anything for sure. But back in that parking lot he turned away from me at the last second. It makes me think that he only wants to hurt one person."

"Himself? Maybe he just didn't want to dent his new car."

"Maybe."

Rider turned onto Winnetka, a four-lane street, and started moving faster. They were almost to Stoddard's home. Bosch rode silently, thinking about what might be waiting for them ahead. Rider finally turned west on Chase and there was a black-and-white patrol car with both of its front doors open in the street up ahead. Rider pulled to a quick stop behind it and they jumped out of the car. Bosch took his gun off his belt and carried it at his side. Rider had a point about Stoddard maybe only thinking about his car when he avoided hitting Bosch.

The front door of the small World War II–era house was open. There was no sign of the patrol officers from the car. Bosch looked at Rider and saw that she was unholstered as well. They were ready to go in. At the door, Bosch shouted, "Detectives coming in!"

He stepped into the threshold and got a response from inside.

"It's clear! It's clear!"

Bosch didn't relax or lower his weapon as he entered the living room. He scanned the room and didn't see anyone. He looked down at the coffee table and saw the *Daily News* from the previous day unfolded, the story on Rebecca Verloren on display.

"Patrol coming out!" a voice called from a hallway to the right.

Soon two patrol officers stepped out of the hallway into the living room. They carried their weapons at their sides. Now Bosch relaxed and lowered his own.

"All clear," said the patrolman with the P2 stripes on his uniform. "We found the door open and came in. There's something you ought to see back here in the bedroom."

The patrolmen led the way and Bosch and Rider followed. They went down a short hallway that passed the open doors to a bathroom and a small bedroom that was used as a home office. They entered a bedroom and the P2 pointed to an oblong wooden box that was open on the bed. The box had a foam lining with a cutout in the shape of a long-barreled revolver. The cutout was empty and the gun was gone. There was a small rectangular cutout in the foam for a box of bullets. It was empty, too, but the box was nearby on the bed.

"Is there someone he's going after?" the P2 asked.

Bosch didn't look up from the gun box.

"Probably just himself," he said. "Either of you guys have gloves? Mine are in the car."

"Right here," the P2 said.

He pulled a pair of latex gloves out of a small compartment on his equipment belt. He handed them to Bosch, who snapped them on and then picked up the bullet box. Bosch opened it and slid out a plastic tray in which the bullets were stored. There was only one bullet missing.

Bosch was staring at the space left by the missing bullet and thinking about things when Rider tapped him on the elbow. He looked at her and then followed her gaze to the table on the other side of the bed.

There was a framed photo of Rebecca Verloren. It was a shot of her standing in a green field with the Eiffel Tower behind her. She was wearing a black beret and she was smiling in an unforced way. Bosch thought the look in her eyes was sincere and showed love for the person she was looking at.

"He wasn't in any of the pictures in the yearbook because he was the one behind the camera," Bosch said.

Rider nodded. She, too, was in the water tunnel.

"That's where it started," she said. "That's where she fell in love with him. My true love."

They stared in somber silence for a few moments until the P2 spoke.

"Detectives, can we clear?"

"No," Bosch said. "We need you to stay here and secure the house until SID gets here. And be ready in case he comes back."

"You're leaving?" the P2 asked.

"We're leaving."

40

They moved quickly back to Bosch's car and Rider once again got behind the wheel.

"Where to?" she said as she turned the ignition.

"The Verloren house," Bosch said. "And let's hurry."

"What are you thinking?"

"I've been thinking about the picture they ran in the paper, with Muriel sitting on the bed. It showed how the room was still the same, you know?"

Rider thought for a moment and then nodded.

"Yeah."

Rider understood. The photo showed that Rebecca's room was unchanged since the night she was taken. Seeing it might trigger something in Stoddard. A desire for something lost long ago. The photo was like an oasis, it was a reminder of a perfect place where nothing had gone wrong.

Rider pinned the accelerator and the car lurched forward. Bosch opened his cell, called dispatch and called for another backup unit to meet them at Muriel Verloren's house. He also updated the bulletin on Stoddard, describing him now as armed and dangerous and possibly 5150 — meaning mentally unstable. He knew as he closed the phone that he and Rider were close to the Verloren home and would get there first. His next call was to Muriel Verloren but there was no answer. When the message service picked up he closed his phone.

"No answer."

They turned the corner onto Red Mesa Way five minutes later and Bosch's eyes immediately locked on the silver car parked at a haphazard angle against the curb in front of the Verloren house. It was the Lexus that had come at him in the school parking lot. Rider stopped next to the car and once again they emerged quickly, with weapons ready.

The front door of the house was ajar. Using hand signals they took stances on either side of it. Bosch then pushed the door open and went in first. Rider followed and they immediately moved into the living room.

Muriel Verloren was on the floor. There was a cardboard box and other packing supplies next to her. Brown packing tape had been wrapped several times around her head and face as a gag, and used to bind her hands and ankles. Rider propped her up against the couch and held a finger up to her lips.

"Muriel, is he in the house?" she whispered.

Muriel nodded, her eyes wide and wild.

"Rebecca's room?"

Muriel nodded again.

"Have you heard a gunshot?"

Muriel shook her head no and emitted a muffled sound that would have been a scream if not for the tape across her mouth.

"You have to be quiet," Rider whispered. "If I take off the tape you have to be very quiet."

Muriel nodded intensely and Rider started working on the tape. Bosch huddled in close.

"I'm going up to the room."

"Wait, Harry," Rider ordered, her voice louder than a whisper. "We go up together. Get her ankles."

Bosch started working on the tape binding Muriel's feet together. Rider finally worked the tape loose from Muriel's mouth and pulled it down over her chin. She shooshed her soothingly as she did this.

"It's Becky's teacher," Muriel whispered, her voice intense but not loud. "He's got a gun."

Rider started working on her wrists.

"Okay," she said. "We're going to deal with it."

"What is he doing?" Muriel asked. "Is he the one?"

"Yes, he's the one."

Muriel Verloren let out a long, loud and anguished sigh. Her hands and feet were now loose and they helped her up to her feet.

"We're going up there," Rider told her. "We need you to get out of the house."

They started ushering her toward the entrance hallway.

"I can't leave. He's in her room. I can't —"

"You have to leave, Muriel," Bosch whispered harshly. "It's not safe here. Go to a neighbor's house."

"I don't know my neighbors."

"Muriel, you have to get out," Rider said. "Go down the street. More police are on the way. Wave them down and tell them we're inside already."

They pushed her through the open front door and then closed it behind her.

"Don't let him ruin her room!" they heard her plead from the other side. "It's all I have left!"

Bosch and Rider made their way to the back hallway and went up the stairway as quietly as they could. They took positions on either side of the door to Rebecca's bedroom.

Bosch looked across at Rider. They both knew there was little time. When backup units arrived the situation would change. It was a classic suicide-by-police setup. This was the one chance they might have of getting to Stoddard before he or a SWAT cop put a bullet into his brain.

Rider pointed to the doorknob and Bosch reached out

and tried to silently turn it. He shook his head. The door was locked.

They used hand signals to outline a plan, nodded when they were ready, and then Bosch stepped back into the hallway and prepared to drive his heel into the door next to the knob. He knew he had to do it with one kick. They would lose the advantage of surprise after that.

"Who's out there?"

It was Stoddard, his voice coming through the door. Bosch looked at Rider. So much for the element of surprise. He pointed to her and gave her the silent sign. He would do the talking.

"Mr. Stoddard, it's Detective Bosch. How are you doing?"

"Not too good."

"Yeah, things have sort of gotten out of hand, haven't they?"

Stoddard didn't answer.

"Tell you what," Bosch said. "You really need to think about putting the gun down and coming out. You're lucky I'm here. I just came to check on Mrs. Verloren. But my partner and the SWAT team are going to be here soon. You don't want to tangle with SWAT. Now is the time to come out."

"I just want you to know I loved her, that's all."

Bosch hesitated before speaking. He glanced over at Rider and then back at the door. He could go two ways with Stoddard. He could work on getting a confession right now or he could work on talking him out of the house and saving his life. Both things were possible but maybe not likely.

"So what happened?" he asked.

There was a long silence before Stoddard spoke.

"What happened was she wanted to keep the baby and she didn't understand how that would ruin everything. We had to get rid of it, and then afterward she changed her mind."

"About the baby?"

"About me. About all of it."

Bosch didn't respond. After a few moments Stoddard spoke again.

"I loved her."

"But you killed her."

"I made mistakes."

"Like that night?"

"I don't want to talk about that night. I want to remember all the times before that night."

"I guess I don't blame you."

Bosch looked at Rider and held up three fingers. They were going to go on a three count. Rider nodded. She was ready.

Bosch dropped one finger.

"You know what I don't get, Mr. Stoddard?"

He dropped the second finger.

"What?" Stoddard asked.

Bosch dropped the third finger, then raised his right leg and drove it into the door. It was a hollow-interior door. It gave way easily and swung open with a crash. Bosch's momentum took him into the bedroom right behind it. He raised his gun and turned toward the bed.

Stoddard wasn't there.

Bosch continued his turn, catching a glimpse of Stoddard in the mirror. He was standing in the corner to the other side of the door. He was raising the muzzle of a long-barreled revolver to his mouth.

Bosch heard Rider shout and her body came through the door at full speed as she threw herself into Stoddard.

The crack of a gunshot shook the room as Rider and Stoddard went down to the floor. The revolver fell from Stoddard's hand and clattered onto the floor. Bosch moved quickly to them and dropped his weight onto Stoddard as Rider rolled off him.

"Kiz, you hit?"

There was no answer. Bosch tried to look at her while keeping Stoddard under control. Rider was holding one hand to the left side of her head.

"Kiz?"

"I'm not hit!" she yelled. "I think I'm just deaf in one ear."

Stoddard tried to get up, even with Bosch's weight on top of him.

"Please!" he said.

Bosch used his forearm to knock one of Stoddard's arms out from supporting him. Stoddard's chest hit the floor and Bosch quickly pulled the arm back and cuffed it. After a minor struggle he pulled the other arm back and completed the cuffing. He then leaned down and spoke to Stoddard.

"Please what?"

"Please let me die."

Bosch got up and pulled Stoddard to his feet.

"That would be too easy for you, Stoddard. That would be like letting you get away all over again."

Bosch looked over at Rider, who had gotten to her feet. He could see that some of her hair had been singed by the gun's discharge. It had been that close.

"You going to be okay?"

"As soon as the ringing stops."

Bosch looked up and saw the bullet hole in the ceiling. He could hear sirens coming. He grabbed Stoddard by the elbow and pulled him toward the bedroom's door.

"I'm going to go down and put this guy in a car. We'll book him at Devonshire, hold him there until the arraignment."

Rider nodded but Bosch could tell she was still dealing

with what had just happened. The ringing in her ear was a reminder of how close it had been.

Bosch held Stoddard by the arm as he walked him down the steps. When they got to the living room, Stoddard spoke with a desperation in his voice.

"You could do it now."

"Do what?"

"Shoot me. Say I ran. Take one of the cuffs off and say I got loose. You want to kill me, don't you?"

Bosch stopped and looked at him.

"Yes, I'd want to kill you. But that would be too good for you. You are going to have to pay for what you did to that girl and her family. And just putting you down right here wouldn't even cover the interest on seventeen years."

Bosch roughly pushed him toward the door. They stepped out onto the front lawn just as a patrol car pulled to a stop and cut its siren. Bosch could tell by the streamlined light bar across the roof that it was one of the new cars he had heard about, with state-of-the-art equipment. The department could afford only a few of them in each budget cycle.

The car gave Bosch an idea. He raised his hand and circled his finger in the air, giving the all-clear sign.

As he walked Stoddard toward the car he saw Muriel Verloren walking down the middle of the street to her house. She was staring at Stoddard. Her mouth was wide open as if in a silent scream of horror. She started running toward them.

41

Bosch rode in the backseat of the patrol car with Stoddard on the way to Devonshire Division. Rider was left behind at the Verloren house to calm Muriel and to be checked out herself by paramedics. When they gave her the okay she would drive Bosch's car to the station.

The trip to the division would only take ten minutes. Bosch knew he had to quickly take a shot at getting Stoddard talking. The first thing he did was read the school principal his rights. Stoddard had made some admissions while holed up in Rebecca Verloren's bedroom, but whether they could be used in court was open to question because they had not been recorded and he had not been forewarned about his rights, which included remaining silent.

After reading the Miranda warning off a business card he had borrowed earlier from Rider, Bosch simply asked, "Now, do you want to talk to me?"

Stoddard was leaning forward because his hands were still cuffed behind his back. His chin was almost down to his chest.

"What is there to say?" he asked.

"I don't know. I mean, I don't need you to talk. We've got you. Actions and evidence — we've got all we need. I just thought you might want to explain things, that's all. At a point like this a lot of people just want to explain themselves."

Stoddard didn't respond at first. The car was heading east on Devonshire Boulevard. The station was a couple miles ahead. Earlier, when he had conferred with the two patrolmen outside of the car, Bosch had told the driver to take it slow.

"It's funny," Stoddard finally said.

"What is?"

"I'm a science teacher, you know? I mean, before I was principal I taught science. I was head of the science department."

"Uh-huh."

"And I taught my students about DNA. I always told them that it was the secret of life. Decode DNA and you decode life itself."

"Uh-huh."

"And now . . . now, well, it's used to decode death. By you people. It's the secret of life. It's the secret of death. I don't know. I guess it's not really funny. It's more ironic in my case."

"If you say so."

"A guy who taught DNA gets caught by DNA."

Stoddard started to laugh.

"Hey, that's a good headline," he said. "Make sure you tell them that."

Bosch reached over and used a key to unlock Stoddard's cuffs. He then relocked his wrists in front of his body so that he could sit up.

"Back there at the house, you said you loved her," Bosch said.

Stoddard nodded.

"I did. I still do."

"Funny way of showing it, wasn't it?"

"It wasn't planned. Nothing was planned that night. I had been watching her, that's all. Whenever I could, I watched her. I drove by all the time. I followed her when she got to take the car. I watched her at work, too."

"And all the time you had a gun."

"No, the gun was for me, not her. But . . ."

"You found out it was easier to kill her instead of yourself."

"That night . . . I saw the garage door was open. I went in. I wasn't sure why. I thought I was going to use the gun on myself. On her bed. It would be my way of showing her my devotion."

"But you went under the bed instead of on top of it."

"I had to think."

"Where was Mackey?"

"Mackey? I don't know where he was."

"He wasn't with you? He didn't help you?"

"He gave me the gun. We made a deal. The gun for the grade. I was his teacher. And his tutor. It was my summer job."

"But he wasn't with you that night? You carried her up the hill by yourself?"

Stoddard's eyes were open and staring into the distance even though their focus was only on the back of the front seat.

"I was strong back then," he said in a whisper.

The patrol car pulled through the opening in the concrete block wall that surrounded the back of Devonshire Division. Stoddard looked out the window. Seeing all of the patrol cars and the back of the station must have brought an awakening to him. He realized his situation.

"I don't want to talk anymore," he said.

"That's fine," Bosch said. "We'll put you in a holding room and get you a lawyer if you want."

The car stopped in front of a set of double doors and Bosch got out. He came around and got Stoddard out and then walked him in through the doors. The detective bureau was on the second floor. They took an elevator and were met by the lieutenant in charge of Devonshire detectives. Bosch had called him from the Verloren house. An interview room was waiting for Stoddard. Bosch put him in a seat and cuffed one of his wrists to a metal ring bolted to the center of the table.

"Sit tight," Bosch said. "I'll be back."

At the door, he looked back at Stoddard. He decided to make one last play.

"And for what it's worth, I think your story is bullshit," he said.

Stoddard looked at him, surprise on his face.

"What do you mean? I loved her. I didn't want —"

"You stalked her with one purpose. To kill her. She rejected you and you couldn't take it, so you wanted her dead. And now seventeen years later you're going to try to tell it different, like it's Romeo and Juliet or something. You're a coward, Stoddard. You stalked her and killed her and you should own up to it."

"No, you're wrong. I had the gun for myself."

Bosch came back into the room and leaned down on the table.

"Yeah? What about the stun gun, Stoddard? Was that for yourself, too? You left that out of your story, didn't you? Why'd you need a stun gun if you went in there to kill yourself?"

Stoddard was silent. It was almost as if after seventeen years he had been able to erase the Professional 100 from his memory.

"We got first degree and we got lying in wait," Bosch said. "You're going down for the whole ride, Stoddard. You were never going to kill yourself. Back then, or even today."

"I think I want a lawyer now," Stoddard said.

"Yeah, of course you do."

Bosch left the room and walked down the hallway to an

open door. It was the monitoring room. The lieutenant and one of the patrol officers from the ride in were in the small space. There were two active video screens. On one Bosch saw Stoddard sitting in the interview room. The camera angle was from an upper corner of the room. Stoddard seemed to be staring blankly at the wall.

The image on the other screen was frozen. It showed Bosch and Stoddard in the backseat of the patrol car.

"How's the sound?" Bosch asked.

"Beautiful," the lieutenant said. "We got it all. Taking off the cuffs was a nice touch. Brought his face up into the camera."

The lieutenant hit a switch and the picture started moving. Bosch could hear Stoddard's voice clearly. He nodded. The patrol car had been equipped with a dashboard camera used for filming traffic stops and prisoner transports. For the ride in with Stoddard the car's interior microphone was turned on and the exterior was cut off.

It had worked perfectly. Stoddard's admissions in the backseat would help seal the case. Bosch felt no worries from that direction at all. He thanked the lieutenant and the patrolman and asked if he could borrow a desk to make some calls.

Bosch called Abel Pratt to update him and to assure him that Rider was shaken up but otherwise okay. He told Pratt that he needed to get SID teams to both Stoddard's and Muriel Verloren's homes to process crime scenes. He said a search warrant should be applied for and approved before the SID team entered Stoddard's house. He said that Stoddard was about to be booked and his fingerprints taken. The prints would need to be compared to those found on the slat from beneath Rebecca Verloren's bed. He finished by telling Pratt about the video taken during the ride to the station and the admissions Stoddard had made.

"It's all solid and it's on tape," Bosch said. "It all came after Miranda."

"Good going, Harry," Pratt said. "I don't think we'll have anything to worry about on this."

"Not with the case, at least."

Meaning that Stoddard was going to go down without a problem, but Bosch wasn't sure how he would fare in the review of his handling of the case.

"It's tough to argue with results," Pratt said.

"We'll see."

Bosch started getting a call-waiting signal on his phone. He told Pratt he had to go and clicked over to the new call. It was McKenzie Ward from the *Daily News*.

"My sister was listening to the scanner in the photo shop," she said urgently. "She said a backup unit and an ambulance were sent to the Verloren house. She recognized the address."

"That's right."

"What's going on, Detective? We had a deal, remember?"

"Yeah, I remember. And I was just about to call you."

42

The kitchen at the Metro Shelter was dark. Bosch went to the small lobby of the adjoining hotel and spoke to the man behind the glass window. He asked for Robert Verloren's room number.

"He's gone, man."

Something about the finality in his tone put a hollow into Bosch's chest. It didn't sound like he meant Verloren had gone out for the night.

"What do you mean gone?"

"I mean gone. He did his thing and he's gone. That's it."

Bosch took a step closer to the glass. The man had a paperback novel open on the counter and had not looked up from its yellowed pages.

"Hey, look at me."

The man flipped the book over to not lose his page and looked up. Bosch showed him his badge. He then glanced down and saw the book was called *Ask the Dust.*

"Yes, Officer."

Bosch looked back up at the man's tired eyes.

"What do you mean, *He did his thing,* and what do you mean he's gone?"

The man shrugged.

"He came in drunk and that's the one rule we got around here. No drinking. No drunks."

"He was fired?"

The man nodded.

"What about his room?"

"Room came with the job. Like I said, he's gone."

"Where?"

The man shrugged one more time. He pointed to the door that led to the sidewalk on Fifth Street. He was telling Bosch that Verloren was out there somewhere.

"It happens," the man said.

Bosch looked back at him.

"When did he go?"

"Yesterday. It was you cops who did it to him, you know."

"What do you mean?"

"I heard some cop came in here, told him some shit. I don't know what it was about, but that was right before — know what I'm saying? He got off work and went out and took the taste again. And that was that. All I know is, we need a new chef now 'cause the guy they got fillin' in can't make eggs for shit."

Bosch said nothing else to the man. He stepped away from the window and went to the door. Outside the shelter the street was teeming with people. The night people. The damaged and displaced. People hiding from others and hiding from themselves. People running from the past, from the things they did and the things they didn't do.

Bosch knew the story was going to hit the news in the morning. He had wanted to tell it to Robert Verloren himself.

Bosch decided he would look for Robert Verloren out there. He didn't know what the news he would bring would do for him. He didn't know if it would bring Verloren out or push him further into the hole. Maybe nothing could help him now. But he needed to tell him anyway. The world was full of people who could not get over things. There was no closure and there was no peace. The truth did not set you free. But you could get through things. That's what Bosch would tell him. You could head toward the light and climb and dig and fight your way out of the hole.

Bosch pushed open the door and headed out into the night.

43

The Police Academy parade field was nestled like a green blanket against one of the wooded hills of Elysian Park. It was a beautiful and shaded place and spoke well of the tradition the police chief had wanted Bosch to be reminded of.

At 8 a.m. on the morning following his fruitless night search for Robert Verloren, Bosch presented himself at the graduation check-in table and was escorted to an assigned seat on the platform beneath the VIP tent. There were four rows of chairs in formation behind the lectern from which the speeches would be made. Bosch's seat looked out across the parade grounds where the new cadets would march, then form up and be inspected. As an invited guest of the chief he would be one of the inspectors.

Bosch was in full uniform. It was tradition to fly the colors at the graduation of new officers — to welcome them to the uniform in the uniform. And he was early. He sat by himself and listened to the police band play old standards. As other VIPs were taken to their seats, no one bothered him. They were mostly politicians and dignitaries and a few purple heart winners from Iraq who wore the uniform of the U.S. Marine Corps.

Bosch's skin felt raw under his starched collar and tightly knotted tie. He had spent almost an hour in the shower scrubbing away the ink he'd had put to his skin, hoping that it would take all the ugliness of the case down the drain with it.

He didn't notice the approach of Deputy Chief Irvin Irving until the cadet leading him to the tent said, "Excuse me, sir."

Bosch looked up and saw that Irving was being seated right next to him. He straightened up and grabbed his program off the seat intended for Irving.

"Enjoy yourself, sir," the cadet said before snapping into a turn and heading back for another VIP.

Irving didn't say anything at first. He seemed to be spending a lot of time making himself comfortable and looking around to see who might be watching them. They were in the first row, two of the best seats in the place. Finally he spoke without turning or looking at Bosch.

"What is going on here, Bosch?"

"You tell me, Chief."

Bosch took a turn looking around to see if anyone was watching them. It obviously wasn't happenstance that they were sitting next to each other. Bosch did not believe in coincidences. Not like that.

"The chief said he wanted me to be here," he said. "He invited me on Monday when he gave me back my badge."

"Good for you."

Another five minutes went by before Irving spoke again. The tent was almost full, except for the spot reserved for the chief of police and his wife at the end of the first row. Irving whispered now.

"You've had a hell of a week, Detective. You land in shit and come out stinking like a rose. Congratulations."

Bosch nodded. It was an accurate assessment.

"What about you, Chief? Just another week at the office for you?"

Irving didn't respond. Bosch thought about the places he had looked for Robert Verloren the night before. He thought about Muriel Verloren's face when she had seen her daughter's killer being led to the patrol car. Bosch had had to hurry Stoddard into the backseat to keep her away from him.

"It was all because of you," Bosch said quietly.

Irving glanced at him for the first time.

"What are you talking about?"

"Seventeen years, that's what I'm talking about. You had your man check the alibis on the Eights. He didn't know that Gordon Stoddard was also the girl's teacher. If it had been Green and Garcia running down the alibis — as it should have been — they would have come across Stoddard and easily put the whole thing together. Seventeen years ago. All of that time, that's on you."

Irving turned fully in his seat to face Bosch.

"We had an agreement, Detective. You break it and I will find other ways of getting to you. I hope that's understood."

"Yeah, sure, whatever you say, Chief. But you forget one thing. I'm not the only one who knows about you. What are you going to do, make your little deals with everybody? Every reporter, every cop? Every mother and father who has had to live with a hollowed-out life because of what you did?"

"Keep your voice down," Irving said through his teeth.

Bosch responded in a quiet, calm voice.

"I've said all I want to say to you."

"Well, let me tell you something, I'm not finished talking to you. If I find —"

He dropped the sentence as the chief of police was escorted by with his wife. Irving straightened himself in his seat as the music swelled and the show began. Twenty-four cadets with shining new badges on their uniformed chests marched into the parade grounds and took their positions in front of the VIP tent.

There were too many preliminary speeches. Then the inspection of the new officers took too long. But finally the program reached the main event, the traditional remarks of the chief of police. The man who had taken Bosch back into the department was relaxed and poised at the lectern. He spoke of rebuilding the police department from the inside out and starting with the twenty-four new officers standing before him. He said he was talking about rebuilding both the image and the practice of the department. He said many of the things he had said to Bosch on Monday morning. He urged the new officers never to break the law to enforce the law. To do their job constitutionally and compassionately at all times.

But then he surprised Bosch with his wrap-up.

"I would also like to draw your attention to two officers here as my guests today. One coming, one going. Detective Harry Bosch has returned to the department this week after a few years of retirement. I guess he learned during his extended vacation that you can't teach an old dog new tricks."

There was polite laughter from the crowd on the other side of the parade grounds. This was where the families and friends of the cadets sat. The chief continued.

"So he came back to the LAPD family and already he has performed admirably. He has put himself in harm's way for the good of the community. Yesterday he and his partner cleared a seventeen-year-old murder that had been sticking like a thorn into the side of this community. We welcome Detective Bosch back to the fold."

There was a smattering of applause from the crowd. Bosch felt his face go hot. He looked down at his hands.

"I would also like to thank Deputy Chief Irvin S. Irving for being here today," the chief continued. "Chief Irving has served in this department for nearly forty-five years. There is no current officer who has served longer. His decision to retire today and make this graduation his final action while wearing the badge is a fitting end to his tour of duty. We thank him for such service to this department and this city."

The applause for Irving was much louder and sustained. People started to stand in honor of the man who had served the department and city so long. Bosch turned slightly to his right so that he could see Irving's face and he knew the moment he saw the deputy chief's eyes that he had not seen it coming. He had been sandbagged.

Soon everyone was standing and clapping and Bosch felt compelled to do the same for a man he despised. He knew exactly who had engineered Irving's fall. If Irving protested or tried in some way to recover his position he would face an internal case built by Kizmin Rider. There would be no doubt who would lose that one. No doubt at all.

What Bosch didn't know was when it had been planned. Bosch thought about Rider sitting on the desk in 503, waiting for him with coffee, black just like he liked it. Had she already known then what case the cold hit had come from and where it would lead? He remembered the date on the DOJ report. It was ten days old by the time he had read it. What happened during those ten days? What was planned for his arrival?

Bosch didn't know and he was not sure he even cared. Department politics were played on the sixth floor. Bosch worked out of 503 and that's where he would make his stand. No question.

After the chief finished his remarks he stepped away from the microphone. He gave each cadet, one by one, a certificate of completion of academy training and posed for a photo shaking hands with the recipient. It was all very fast and clean and choreographed perfectly. Three police helicopters flew over the parade grounds in formation and the cadets ended the ceremony by hurling their hats into the air.

Bosch remembered the time more than thirty years before when he had thrown his hat into the air. He smiled at the memory. No one from his class was left. They were dead or retired or washed out. He knew it was up to him to carry the banner and tradition. To fight the good fight.

As the ceremony ended and the crowds rushed to the field to congratulate the new officers, Bosch watched Irving stand up and start walking directly across the parade grounds to the exit area. He stopped for no one, not even those who extended hands of congratulations and thanks to him.

"Detective, you've had a busy week."

Bosch turned. It was the chief of police. He nodded. He didn't know what to say.

"Thank you for being here," the chief said. "How is Detective Rider?"

"She took the day off. She had a close one yesterday."

"So I heard. Will either of you be attending the press conference today?"

"Well, she's off and I was thinking of skipping it, if that's all right."

"We'll handle it. I see you already gave the story to the *Daily News*. Now everyone else is clamoring for it. We have to put on the dog-and-pony show."

"I owed the reporter from the *News* that one."

"Yes, I understand."

"When the dust settles, will I still have a job, Chief?"

"Of course, Detective Bosch. As in any investigation, choices must be made. Tough choices. You made the best decisions you could make. There will be a review but I don't think you will have a problem."

Bosch nodded. He almost said thank you but decided against it. He just looked at the man.

"Is there something else you wanted to ask me, Detective?"

Bosch nodded again.

"I was just sort of wondering," he said.

"About what?"

"The case started with a letter from the DOJ and that letter was old by the time it got to me. I'm wondering why it was held for me. I guess what I'm saying is, I'm wondering about what you knew and when you knew it."

"Does any of that matter now?"

Bosch poked his chin in the direction Irving had taken.

"Maybe," he said. "I don't know. But he won't just walk away. He'll go to the media. Or to the lawyers."

"He knows that if he does it will be a mistake. That there will be consequences for him. He's not a stupid man."

Bosch just nodded. The chief studied him a moment before speaking again.

"You still seem troubled, Detective. Remember what I told you Monday? I told you I carefully reviewed your case and career before deciding whether to welcome you back."

Bosch just looked at him.

"I meant that," the chief said. "I studied you and I think I know something about you. You are on this earth for one thing, Detective Bosch. And you now have the opportunity to do that, to continue to carry out your mission. After that, does anything else matter?"

Bosch held his eyes for a long time before answering.

"I guess what I really wanted to ask is about what you said the other day. When you said all of that about the ripples and the voices, did you mean it? Or were you just winding me up to go after Irving for you?"

Fire quickly spread across the police chief's cheeks. His eyes dropped from Bosch's as he composed his answer.

Then he looked back up at Bosch and it was his eyes that held Bosch's this time.

"I meant every word of it. And don't you forget it. You go back to room five oh three and you close cases, Detective. That's what you are here for. Close them out or I'll find reason to close you out. Do you understand?"

Bosch didn't feel threatened. He liked the chief's answer. It made him feel better. He nodded.

"I understand."

The chief raised his hand and took Bosch by the upper arm.

"Good. Then let's go over here and get a picture taken with some of these young people who have joined our family today. Maybe they can learn something from us. Maybe we can learn something from them."

As they moved into the crowd Bosch looked off in the direction Irving had taken. But he was long gone.

44

Bosch looked for Robert Verloren for three of the next seven nights but didn't find him until it was too late.

One week after the academy graduation, Bosch and Rider were sitting across from each other at their desks while putting the finishing touches on the case against Gordon Stoddard. The accused murderer had been arraigned in San Fernando Municipal Court earlier in the week and had pleaded not guilty. Now the legal dance had begun. Bosch and Rider had to put together a comprehensive charging document that outlined the case against Stoddard. It would be given to the prosecutor and used in negotiations with Stoddard's defense attorney. After meeting with Muriel Verloren as well as Bosch and Rider, the prosecutor set a case strategy. If Stoddard elected to go to trial the state would seek the death penalty under the lying-in-wait statute. The alternative was for Stoddard to avoid risking death and plead guilty to first-degree murder in a plea agreement that would send him to prison for life without the possibility of parole.

Either way, the case summary Bosch and Rider were composing would be of key importance because it would show Stoddard and his lawyer just how strong the evidence was. It would force their hand, make Stoddard choose between the grim alternatives of life in a jail cell or gambling his life on the slim possibility of beating the case with a jury.

It had been a good week until that point. Rider bounced back from her near miss from Stoddard's bullet and showed full command of her skills in putting together the case summary. Bosch had spent all of Monday going over the investigation with an Internal Affairs investigator and was cleared the next day. The "no action taken" verdict from IAD meant he was clear within the department, even though the ongoing stories about the case in the media continued to call into question the department's actions in using Roland Mackey as bait.

Bosch was ready to move on to the next investigation. He had already told Rider he wanted to check into the case of the lady he found tied up and drowned in her bathtub on his first day on the job. They would take it up as soon as they put the paper case on Stoddard to rest.

Abel Pratt came out of his office and stepped into their alcove. He had an ashen look on his face. He nodded toward Rider's computer screen.

"Is that Stoddard you're working on?" he asked.

"Yes," Rider said. "What's up?"

"You can spike it. He's dead."

Nobody said anything for a long moment.

"Dead?" Rider finally asked. "What do you mean, dead?"

"Dead in his cell in Van Nuys jail. Two puncture wounds to the neck."

"He did it himself?" Bosch asked. "I didn't think he had it in him."

"No, somebody did it for him."

Bosch sat up straight.

"Wait a minute," he said. "He was on the high-power floor and on keep-away status. Nobody could've —"

"Somebody did this morning," Pratt said. "And that's the bad part."

Pratt raised a small notebook in his hand. Notes had been scribbled on it. He read from it.

"On Monday night a man was arrested on Van Nuys Boulevard on a drunk and disorderly. He also assaulted one of the cops who hooked him up. He was routinely fingerprinted and booked into Van Nuys jail. He had no ID and gave the name Robert Light. The next day at arraignment he pleaded guilty to all charges and the judge gave him a week in Van Nuys jail. The prints had still not been run through the computer."

Bosch felt a deep tug in his gut. He felt dread. He knew where this was going. Pratt continued, using his notes to construct the story.

"The man who called himself Robert Light was assigned to kitchen duty at the jail because he claimed and also demonstrated that he had restaurant experience. This morning he traded jobs with one of the others in the kitchen and was pushing the wagon that was carrying food trays to the custodies on high power. According to two guards who witnessed it, when Stoddard went to the slide window on his cell door to accept the food tray, Robert Light reached through the bars and grabbed him. He then stabbed him repeatedly with a shiv made from a sharpened spoon. He got two punctures into the neck before the guards subdued him. But the guards were too late. Stoddard's carotid artery was slashed and he bled out in his cell before they could get help to him."

Pratt stopped there but Bosch and Rider asked no questions.

"Coincidentally," Pratt began again, "Robert Light's fingerprints were finally entered into the database at about the same time that he was killing Stoddard. The computer kicked out a bogie — a custody who gave a false name. The real name, as I am sure you have already guessed, was Robert Verloren."

Bosch looked across at Rider but couldn't hold her eyes for long. He looked down at his desk. He felt as though he had been punched. He closed his eyes and rubbed his face with his hands. He felt that it was in some way his fault. Robert Verloren had been his responsibility in the investigation. He should have found him.

"How's that for closure?" Pratt said.

Bosch dropped his hands and stood up. He looked at Pratt.

"Where is he?" he asked.

"Verloren? They still have him there. Van Nuys homicide is handling it."

"I'm going up there."

"What are you going to do?" Rider asked.

"I don't know. Whatever I can."

He walked out of the alcove, leaving Rider and Pratt behind. Out in the hallway he punched the elevator button and waited. The heaviness in his chest wasn't going away. He knew it was the feeling of guilt, the feeling that he had not been ready for this case and that his mistakes had been so costly.

"It's not your fault, Harry. He did what he had waited seventeen years to do."

Bosch turned. Rider had come up behind him.

"I should have found him first."

"He didn't want to be found. He had a plan."

The elevator door opened. It was empty.

"Whatever you're doing," Rider said, "I'm going with you."

He nodded. Being with her would make it easier. He motioned her into the elevator and then followed. On the way down he felt a resolve rise inside him. A resolve to carry on the mission. A resolve never to forget Robert and Muriel and Rebecca Verloren along the way. And a promise always to speak for the dead.

Acknowledgements

The author would like to gratefully acknowledge those who helped with the research and writing of this novel. They include Michael Pietsch, Asya Muchnick, Jane Wood and Peggy Leith Anderson as well as Jane Davis, Linda Connelly, Terrill Lee Lankford, Mary Capps, Judy Couwels, John Houghton, Jerry Hooten and Ken Delavigne. Very special thanks go to detectives Tim Marcia, Rick Jackson and David Lambkin of the Los Angeles Police Department, as well as Sergeant Bob McDonald and Police Chief William Bratton.

All Orion/Phoenix titles are available at your local bookshop or from the following address:

Mail Order Department
Littlehampton Book Services
FREEPOST BR535
Worthing, West Sussex, BN13 3BR
telephone 01903 828503, *facsimile* 01903 828802
e-mail MailOrders@lbsltd.co.uk
(Please ensure that you include full postal address details)

Payment can be made either by credit/debit card (Visa, Mastercard, Access and Switch accepted) or by sending a £ Sterling cheque or postal order made payable to *Littlehampton Book Services*.
DO NOT SEND CASH OR CURRENCY

Please add the following to cover postage and packing

UK and BFPO:
£1.50 for the first book, and 50p for each additional book to a maximum of £3.50

Overseas and Eire:
£2.50 for the first book plus £1.00 for the second book and 50p for each additional book ordered

---

BLOCK CAPITALS PLEASE

name of cardholder _____   *delivery address*
_____   *(if different from cardholder)*
address of cardholder _____   _____
_____   _____
_____   _____
_____   _____
postcode _____   *postcode* _____

☐ I enclose my remittance for £_____

☐ please debit my Mastercard/Visa/Access/Switch (delete as appropriate)

card number ☐☐☐☐ ☐☐☐☐ ☐☐☐☐ ☐☐☐☐

expiry date ☐☐☐☐   Switch issue no. ☐☐

signature _____

prices and availability are subject to change without notice